I0654392

For information, address inquiries to:
Lucien F.A. van Oosten,
421 Ada Ave. Glendora, Ca. 91741
USA

Produced and designed by: Lucien F.A. van Oosten
Illustrated & artwork by: Lucien F.A. van Oosten
Cover Design: Lucien F.A. van Oosten with collaboration from:
Susan Hoskinson

Editorial services given by: Maryann K. Rachford, and Nancy
Gorman for all of their inputs, & Sam Stathopoulos.

Revised Page 15, January 29 2016: Gallery of Characters.

The Rescue - The Irrefutable Saga of K-Bridge Flock

Introduction and Synopsis by: Lucien van Oosten

The second installment of the K-bridge flock continues where the first book, **K-Bridge – A Story about Discovery** leaves off. As many readers have stated, the ending of the first book makes you want to know what happens to the characters. Is Mosaic able to rescue his parents and fellow flock mates?

As the second book unfolds, we have Moth, Mosaic's sister, finding him and telling him that his parents and flock mates are alive and are held captive in a pet and feed store. Mosaic, who has been grappling with how to tell April and Eric that he must leave, now has the ideal and logical excuse as to why he must leave. Therefore, in **The Rescue,** the saga of discovery continues for Mosaic and the birds of K-Bridge.

His best friend Trapper makes the decision he will need to accompany Mosaic on his Rescue mission, which both April and Eric, after some debate, agree to with one condition: Trapper must wear an electronic homing device.

The day that started out with great expectations quickly turn into a struggle to fly as the weather turns again the rescuers, and they have to seek refuge at a grain silo. They easily avoid the weather while spending the night in safety. The following morning, Moth, unbeknownst to her, eats tainted seeds and become very ill, nearly dying. If not for the valiant efforts of her own skills, her companions and the valiant efforts of Ibu, Moth is rescued from certain death.

While all this is happening to the three companions, April and Eric are on their own journey of discovery as they try to figure out the flight line that Mosaic, Trapper and Moth must be taking to attempt the rescue. With the help of their Mother and Father, they figure out the only feasible route the birds must be taking as they head south to the pet and feed store.

Reluctantly Mosaic and Trapper must leave an aligning and recovering Moth, in the capable care of Ibu. They get the valuable route they must follow from Moth. They follow Moths directions to the feed store with little inconvenience. They find the feed store and discover that things have changed since Moth's successful escape. As fore told by Vlinder (Dutch for butterfly), their first attempt at a Rescue fails. This of course creates a very edgy and uneasy relationship between her and Mosaic.

Before they can come up with a second plan, all the birds are bought by Luo's relatives (one of Crafco's allies) and are taken to the game ranch for them to participate in the big event scheduled there; The Passenger Pigeon Derby.

In **The Rescue**, we learn more about the rapscallion of the story, Crafco, his horrible immoral plans for power, and the evil he is willing to unleash upon his kind to get what his heart desires. In this second installment of the story about the K-Bridge flock, we learn what made Crafco and about the alliances he has forged with creatures not of his own kind.

We meet, Joel a crow, whom Crafco saves from an entanglement that would have ended Joel's life, creating a formidable ally and confidant. Joel is one of the first birds outside of Crafco's own species that Crafco truly confides in and through circumstances out of both of their control, Joel helps Crafco get rid of one of his main tormentors.

As we learn more about Crafco's plans to become ultimate leader of all the Railyard flocks. We also learn of the many twists, turns and unlikely allies that fate presents to Crafco that will gain him his ultimate dream.

As Crafco schemes, lays out and works his plans, Mosaic and Trapper discover the truth about the ranch where Mosaic's flock mates and parents have been transported. During their investigation of the ranch and with the reconnaissance they perform, they learn the nature of the ranches existence: it is a game ranch, one specializing in the hunting of birds for sport.

As is so often the case, during their final attempt at the rescue, they succeed in freeing Koffee, Niner and Rambler. The bad thing is that Mosaic is trapped, caught and takes their places. Mosaic, based on Trapper's and his own reconnaissance, does a have a plan, that if followed will give the birds to be released onto the killing fields a very slim chance for survival.

As has been foretold by the sparrows, many do not make it through the shooting galleries. Sky is killed, as are many others, though the most devastating loss for Mosaic is that of his Father. Niner in a heroic effort saves Vlinder from certain death, however he is wounded and succumbs to the injuries he sustained.

The flock and Mosaic are devastated by this turn of events. We leave Mosaic wondering why he did not succeed in the rescue attempts. As the last paragraphs of **The Rescue** concludes this part of the K-Bridge saga, we find Mosaic pondering where and what is happening with **The Quest** group of birds.

Comments from Readers' of,
K-Bridge: A Story about Discovery

I really love it! What blows me away, is how the author gets inside the heads of the characters. We, as readers, become the falcon, frustrated at an embarrassing outcome to her hunt. We become his heroic protagonist, choosing to lead his flock rather than allow his emotions to lead him. Can't say I've ever thought much about pigeons before, much less admired one!
By: Dot Cannon, Over Coffee Pod cast host

I was not sure if I would like the book because I do not know much about pigeons. The book started off slow but as I got further into the book, the story really flowed and I didn't want to put the book down. I read the whole book in 3 days because I wanted to know how the story would end. When I got to those last pages, the ending was good and I was really excited to read the next book. I wanted to know if Mosaic and Trapper would be able to rescue the other birds, and what happened to Whitehead and the others on their quest. I think this book could be turned into a Disney movie because there is a good blend of adventure and intrigue, great scenery, and interesting main characters.
By: Judy Hoskinson

I have read the story, breathless. I was hardly able to put the book down. This is indeed a story of discovery. A story which seems to be about doves but it turned out to be a story of about humans. All these characters, birds, cats and humans, seem to have doubles I know. It seems I have meet them one time or another throughout my life.

The amazing part is that it is indeed a book about birds as well. It is also a book about the world in which we live. The observation of animal behavior and environments are exceptional as well.

There is also a fine humor waved into the story. I humor which makes the reader smile even in dangerous situations. And humor, which also enables us to laugh about ourselves.

Last, not least, there are the Illustrations. The illustrations are small and, except the title, in black and white, but even so the show the skillful hand in the use of various media. The observation of anatomy and art specific features is as exact as the observation of behavior of man and bird.

I can hardly wait to read the sequel The Rescue.
By: Cecilia

Let me first say that this book is amazing! I have known Lucien for a long time and I never knew that he was a writer. I have always been fascinated by the style of his art so when I saw the book and saw that it was illustrated by him I just had to have it. Once I got into the story, I absolutely could not put it down. He gets you involved with the characters, he takes you into their thoughts and feelings so that you identify with them and you forget that they are pigeons, not humans. Sometimes you even feel that their thought process is more organized than a human. When I turned to the last page I thought, wait a minute are there some pages missing, what happens next? Since then I have learned that he is writing a sequel. In this book, he did a great job of leaving the reader with two different cliffhangers where you want to know what happens to the characters in the story, the ones that departed on the quest, their positive interaction with humans and what happens to Mosaic and Trapper in their rescue attempt of Mosaic's flock mates. I am looking forward to reading about the pigeons continuing adventures. As in any good story, there are always "bad guys" and that is also true in this one!
By: Sylvia Chapman

The Rescue -

The Irrefutable Saga of K-Bridge Flock

This book is dedicated to:

My Family
and
all those that have supported me in getting this
sequel completed.

Gallery Of Characters

Mosaic

Trapper

Cole and Colors, front: Rambler & back Pepper

Shadow   Sky   Millet

Kott

Crier

Whitehead

Pepper

Dufus

CRAFCO

DONKEY

REAPER

MOTH

Chapter 1

The three flew against the wind with the energy that should have had them zooming along at a break neck speed of forty-five miles an hour. However, because of the head winds of thirty-five miles an hour, they were actually only traveling at a forward speed of ten miles an hour. Mosaic thought back on the events of the day before and all the desires and needs that had dictated, actually demanded of them to start on this new course of action. His mind took him back to the previous day's fine morning.

Mosaic had watched the sun come up over the trees. He had been excited as April had carried him out into the yard and he had taken that first breath of great-smelling morning air. It had felt great to fill his nostrils with that first breath of clean crisp air as it went down into his lungs. All the way down the air yelled at every cell of his body, get up it is time to get excited about the day. "Get up; it is time to get excited about the day! Get up all you sleepy heads; it is time for a good fly!"

Mosaic stirred, stretched his wings, shook his muscles, and then walked over to the water dish attached to the cage and had a long drink of water. "Aah; he thought:" "that really tastes good."

"Good morning and how are we feeling today?" April asked, as she placed clean grain into the feeding dish.

"I don't know about how we are feeling, but I'm feeling fine," was Mosaic's tongue and cheek response. "I'm ready to be let out. I want to fly." He said with impatience in his voice. "Can you let me out?"

April gave a little laugh. "Very funny. Maybe I'll just let you stay where you are." she teased back. "You should eat before you go flying," she continued as she watched him pace back and forth in front of the cage door.

He did not want to eat and he could not have said why. Maybe it was the same bad dream he'd had three days in a row now. The dream he hadn't mentioned to anyone; the dream that showed him living out his life in the cage, never to be allowed to fly again, never to be free again, always dependent on April, or Eric, or other humans he didn't even know.

"Aren't you going to eat?" April asked him again with impatience in her voice.

"No, I'm really not hungry. I've drank already. I really want out. I really want to fly," he said to her question, with a little impatience in his voice

Without another word, she smiled. April had opened his cage door as he was speaking and out he had rushed. True, most birds are morning creatures, but with this type of a glorious day all creatures should have been birds, so they could fully appreciate this unbelievable day, he thought as he flew into the air.

"Meet me at the loft," she shouted after him.

As he flew one circle around the house, he then headed to the lofts landing board. "There are certain things that just make a pigeon's day, such as a good, clean source of water and easy access to it," he thought. April met him there and opened the yearling section of the loft, and out spilled the A.E. flock.

He, Trapper and the rest of the A.E. flock had taken to the air the minute they were out of the loft and had started flying and tripping away from the loft, getting their exercise and enjoying the fresh, clean-smelling sun-filled morning. The air had been crisp and cool, more like a late fall day than an early morning summer's day. "Great flying weather," he thought. "The type of day made for a pigeon that loves to fly and soar."

April and Eric were great as far as humans were concerned. However, Mosaic did not like the cage, and always having to wait until one of them came and let him out to fly was a little disturbing to him. It was against his nature; he had been born wild and free to do as he pleased. Well, at least in regards to when he could and could not fly. He had not missed the responsibilities of being the flock leader, but he had missed the K-bridge flock, nevertheless. "Why isn't anything easy," he thought. He liked April and Eric and their manners and the way they had cared for him. However, he had not liked waiting for them to appear and let him out so he could go flying. Even though he had liked them and loved the clean water and dry fresh food brought to him daily, he did not like being in the cage. He knew that the loft would not be any better. Either place made him dependent on them and he had always been his own boss, caring for his own needs and wants, and as of late, the needs of the K-bridge flock. However, even with that responsibility, he had been the boss of himself.

So, like so many mornings since he had escorted Trapper home and had the run-in with the screech hunter, he had waited impatiently for either April or Eric to let him out. He could not have said why; all he knew was that he had wanted out. Well, maybe the dream had given him the creeps. Having the same dream three nights in a row did not seem natural to him. He guessed it was the ominous bad feelings that the dream had given him that made him jumpy. "Enough," he told himself. "You are flying with friends, so just enjoy it." However, he had made up his mind about one thing: He would tell April that he would be leaving the next morning. He had made up his mind. He was going to go home and the next day would be the day.

Trapper had watched his friend flying, knowing that there was something bothering him. In fact, Trapper had been concerned about Mosaic for several days now. There was something bothering his friend, but what that was he did not know. Every time he had tried to bring it up it seemed that Mosaic had changed the subject. Almost as if he knew the questions that Trapper wanted to ask and not wanting to answer them, for to answer them meant they might come true.

Today Mosaic again seemed deep in thought as he flew. Trapper had made up his mind that today he was not going to let his friend avoid the questions. Therefore, he flew closer to Mosaic so they could talk. But before he had the opportunity to ask, Mosaic said, "Tomorrow I'm going to go home."

"I figured as much," was Trappers response. "Have you told them yet?" He pointed to April and Eric standing next to the loft, and watching them from below.

"No, not yet. I'll tell them tonight when we get back from our flying," he said. "You're not going to talk me out of it?" he asked Trapper.

Trapper responded by saying, "No! I thought you would have left long ago. You have been ready for the last week. I knew you were staying for other reasons, I just wasn't sure what they were."

"Me either," was Mosaic's response. "Why had he stayed," he thought,. "Because he had wanted to learn more about humans? No! And yes!" he thought, "It had been because he hadn't wanted to hurt April's feelings." However, he also realized that no time would have been right, and anytime would have left April feeling bad. "I guess I was trying to spare April's hurt feelings."

"No," replied Trapper. "You were trying to avoid those feelings for yourself."

With that Mosaic had shaken his head yes. "True," he thought, "He hadn't been doing it for April, or Eric, or even Trapper." He had been doing it for himself as much as for anyone, and now it was time to leave. "Raptors!" He though. "This isn't going to be easy."

Then a wonderful thing happened. Moth had appeared out of nowhere, and with her, his reason for going and rescuing his family and fellow flock mates. Once she had arrived and they had talked, his reason was solid, and now none could complain, or give him a really big argument on why he should not go. The great creator, or maybe fate, was looking out for him after all.

April stood mesmerized as she watched the birds flying overhead. She loved to stand and watch the birds flying. She often stood there and wondered what it would be like to be that free. She relished the early morning air. Its coolness and crispness always made her happy. She was a morning person. The sunrises were always beautiful to her. No two were ever quite the same. Each one as it rose into the sky always seemed to say to her, "Here I am again, the sun, your friend, and it's going to be a new amazing day."

To her it was a another day filled with promise. A day filled with possibilities for new adventures, for new truths to be discovered and old truths to be re-enforced. Another day to do what was good and right, another day to reinvent yourself, to re-define who you are, to re-enforce your beliefs. At the age of thirteen all was right with the world. She was doing well in school, she had a loving Father and Mother, and a pretty good older Brother who she loved and adored. Even though she would never tell him that, because sometimes he was a royal pain in the neck, or another part of the body girls were not supposed to comment on.

Overall, today was great day. It had started out just as she liked, with a beautiful sunrise. She had started her day with her favorite breakfast of chocolate chip pancakes and a tall glass of chocolate Ovaltine milk, after which she had begun doing her very favorite things watching her birds flying and daydreaming about what it would be like to be able to fly like them.

She stood and imagined having wings and unfolding those wings, and with great shoulder muscles jumping into the air, out-stretching those wings and catching the air with powerful downward strokes and then feeling herself be lifted. "Wow!" She thought. "This is really great." In her mind's eye, she saw the ground disappearing underneath herself. She felt the morning air in her face, and she felt alive and free. Just as she was really getting into the experience, Eric walked up and asked, "What ya doing? Pretending to be flying again?"

"Yah! Want to join me?" was her response.

"No, not right now, we have to come down to earth my little chickadee, we have to clean the yearling loft while they are enjoying themselves," was Eric's answer to her, as he pointed to their flock flying overhead.

"You know, Eric, you are such a wet blanket some times," She said with a tinge of disgust in her voice.

"Yep, that's me," he responded, "and I have my feet in reality as well. Pigeon dung reality, if you know what I mean. So let's get it over and done with." Neither one really liked the loft cleaning duties but it was all part of being a pigeon flyer.

"Eric, have you noticed anything strange about Mosaic lately?" She asked him with concern in her voice as she took the shovel from him and opened the door to the loft.

"No, not really. Well maybe, he seems more restless the last few days." He said, deep in thought. "He seems more on edge. Every time I see him in his cage, he is pacing. Like he needs to get out right away. At least over the last couple of days he has been acting that way, and it is not as if we do not let him out every day. Has he said anything to you about it?" He finished his thoughts and comments with a question to April, knowing pigeons and humans could not really talk to one another, but April had this strange ability to know what the birds were up to – or so it seemed.

"No, he hasn't. But I've noticed the same behavior and I'm a little worried about him," was her response to her brother's remarks.

"Do you think he's thinking of going home, and he doesn't know how to let us know?" Eric blurted out, as if he were afraid saying it would make it so and blurting it out would not!

April stopped and looked at him, "Do you really think that's it?" She asked. It was the one thing she had not really wanted to admit could be the issue. Now that Eric had brought it out into the light of day, she could not deny that leaving was probably the reason.

She did not wait for Eric to answer her rhetorical question, but answered it herself.

"You know Eric, you are probably right. And I'll ask him about it later today when he comes in from flying," she responded, as she continued to clean the loft.

Eric responded by saying, "I want to be there when you do. Okay?" April just shook her head yes to his request. They continued there cleaning of the loft without another word to each other. Both involved in their own thoughts about when Mosaic would be leaving. Each one had independently concluded that, that is what would happen. Just when was the unanswered question.

The day had gone by rather slowly and with apprehension, compared to how it had started. Mosaic had come back, he had brought his sister, and he had explained what was going on and that he would be leaving the next morning. This was at April and Eric's insistence that it was better to start first thing in the morning with a fresh new day in front of you and a full crop of good food and clean water inside of you.

———————   ———————

So here they were, battling the winds. It had started out as a clear and calm day but as they had left April and Eric's and had made it to the farmlands, the wind that had started out as a breeze had picked up to become a fierce obstacle to their progress. It was hampering their ability to fly easily and make any reasonable headway.

The head wind pushed against Mosaic and he felt he was not making any forward progress. For all the energy he had been expending he should have been moving forward at a great speed. The reality was that they were barely moving, and it had only gotten worse over time.

Mosaic looked at his companions, Moth and Trapper who were struggling as much as he was and in them, he saw his own fatigue.

They were working very hard just to stay in the air and even harder at trying to make a little forward motion. At this pace and with the effort it would take them all day to reach the foot of the mountain pass and they would be exhausted once there and not have the energy to make the climb to get through the pass.

Trapper looked at Mosaic as if reading his mind and said, "Let's go to the grain station and wait out the wind there. At least it will provide us shelter and also food and water before we go on."

Mosaic nodded yes. He then pointed to Moth to follow Trapper, and they diverted themselves from their present course and headed for the grain silos. This course of action was a little easier, but still required a lot of work in combating the strong winds from pushing them off course. What would have taken only thirty minutes on a calm day took hours, and they arrived at the silos just as the sun was setting in the west. They were bone tired and glad to be out of the weather and in a comfortable place to sleep. They had settled into the top of one of the buildings along its rafters and slept peacefully as the wind howled and gusted all night long.

His companions slept as bone tired beings do, but Mosaic was hampered by the dream and of the day's events, of telling April and Eric, he had to go. As seen in many dark dreams, there was an unknown shadow hovering over him. The shadow was total darkness – an all – encompassing void. As his dream progressed, it sucked all the light out of his world, so that in the end he was flying, blindly. He could not see where he was going. The darkness also seemed to have taken away all of his other senses ability to function as well, because in the end he couldn't, see, smell or feel, He felt nothing, just emptiness.

Interesting Pigeon Fact

Pigeons are considered to be one of the most intelligent birds on the planet and able to undertake tasks previously thought to be the sole preserve of humans and primates.

http://www.pigeoncontrolresourcecentre.org/html/amazing-pigeon-facts.html#how_old

Chapter 2

It had been late yesterday that Mosaic had come back with a dark cream-colored hen, Moth, whom he had introduced to April and Eric as his older sister. He had also announced that he would be leaving to go home. He had explained to them that Moth had brought news about his family, that they were still alive, being held captive, and that he had to go and attempt to rescue them.

April had told him that she understood his reasons for having to go but was saddened by the fact the day had come that she had prayed would never come. Yet come it had, and she had dealt with it rather well considering that not only had Mosaic announced his leaving, but also that Trapper had stated he was going with Mosaic as well.

April had voiced her objections, as had Eric, but Trapper had given her a very convincing argument as to why he should go. Mosaic was his friend and still recovering from his injuries and would need his support in helping him find and rescue his family and fellow flock members. Trapper had reasoned and used the argument that if April and Eric could have flown they would have gone without hesitation. Even though they could not fly, if there had been any away to help they would have; they would have come too. Both Eric and April knew that Trapper had been dead-on the mark in his assessment of their feelings and desires.

April had convinced them to at least wait until morning, and at that time they would let Trapper know if he could go. All agreed to wait until the following day. Eric and April had discussed it with their parents that evening over dinner, and to Eric's surprise, April had convinced her parents that Trapper should go. Still, she wished there was a way of knowing where they were and that she could help Mosaic as well.

Their Father said he had an idea: why don't they put an electronic signal sender on Trapper? That way they could monitor where the pigeons were. Maybe he offered, they could go and follow the pigeons on the weekend and help if at all possible. April thought it was a great idea. Eric thought so too, but he stated his misgivings about actually being able to do it. He had stated all kinds of things that could go wrong, but mostly that the device would malfunction.

The next morning had come, and they had gotten into a very detailed discussion with Trapper, Mosaic and Moth. First, they had told Trapper he could go, but only if he wore the electrical sending device on his leg. He had agreed, and they had put a small metal band with a disk attached to it onto his leg, which made a very low beeping sound. "What's that noise?" Trapper and the others had asked.

"Oh, that is the signal. Is it bothering you?" April asked.

"Well, no, not really. I guess it will be okay. As long as it's no louder than that, we can live with it." was his guarded response. The other thought that came to him was that he was now a belled cat.

Next, they got a detailed description of the type of terrain Moth had flown over to get to where their loft was. Eric took detailed notes as April asked all kinds of comprehensive in-depth questions. Following that they said their goodbyes and watched the three birds fly off into the clear blue cloudless sky.

The day had started out with clear calm skies, only to change several hours after they had departed into a strange eerie fog, which had rolled in and had made it difficult to see more than 100 yards. The fog had lasted until noon, at which time a strong southerly wind had come up and blown it all away. The wind had increased throughout the afternoon. It had blown in gusts so severe that they had blown over trees and power lines all over the area where April and Eric lived.

April had been sitting at the window watching the small maple tree in the neighbor's front yard swaying and bending under the force of the winds when Eric came into the room.

"You are really worried aren't you?" he asked her. Before April could respond he added, "Me too! Especially with the wind and all."

April responded with a shrug, saying, "Yea, I suppose I am. I'm worried because of the strange weather we had this morning... one minute blue skies, then that strange fog, and now these winds. It's like bad omens, birds and fog don't mix. You don't think they got hurt, do you? Flying through the fog and all this mess with the winds worries me."

Eric looked at his little sister and decided to be honest and not try to cheer her up, so he articulated his concerns as well. "Yea, I'm worried a little as well, but Trapper told me a smart bird knows when to land. And Trapper's a smart bird so they should be fine." Eric looked at his sister's response, which was a raised eyebrow, which caused him to quantify his remark. "He told me he'd never get caught out in a wind storm again, especially after his last experience."

Again, April said nothing but just raised her eyebrows in mock surprise as she gave Eric a little 'what did I just hear you say smile' and then asked, "How did you know what Trapper wanted anyway?"

"What!" was Eric's response to his sister's look. Feeling somewhat defensive, he said, "He told me! And... and he also told me he was going and that you had said he could." April continued with that 'what did I hear you say' self-satisfied smile.

"I thought you said pigeons and humans couldn't talk." April said looking at him with that 'I got you' expression on her face.

"Well, you know: live and learn," was his somewhat quiet, 'I have no defense', lame response. "And why didn't you tell me you had already said he could go before we even talked?"

She said, "I'm sorry, it just seemed like the right thing to say at the time." That was her only reasoning, and April chose to not pursue it any further; she agreed she should have said something to him first. She said she understood why he should be upset and said she was sorry she had not talked to him before she had brought it up at dinner.

Eric, who also did not want to pursue it and get into an argument, said he sort of understood and suggested they do something together, like play checkers or Chess. April nodded, "Sure!" was her halfhearted reply, still looking out the window.

"Which game? You know they are smart enough to know to come out of the storm. They're not dummies you know," he asked and stated, as he went to the desk drawer and opened it.

"Checkers, I guess. It's easier to play. Yea, you're right, they are smart aren't they? After all, they did find their way home and Moth was able to track them down as well," she said with a little smile on her face and a little contentment in her voice.

With that said they set up the game at the dining room table and started playing the game by rote, with one winning and then the other. Both seemed bored and while they were playing, both were thinking of the birds. They did not have their minds on the game at all. April finally said, "I wish we could have helped and gone," ending the sentence with a sigh.

"I know, April, but what could we have done? We can't drive or fly, and that really limits our capabilities to follow... to do anything. I wish I was older and had my license," was his reply as he shrugged his shoulders. "Do you want to play another game?" Eric asked. "We can't go outside and there's nothing on the television. We can't follow their movements until Dad brings home the receiver tonight. So what do we want to do? I'm a little bored with checkers and I really don't want to play any other game. What do you want to do? Come on, April, you always have ideas. "

April listened to his several questions and remarks and then came up with an idea. "I know, but I feel so helpless. I feel so useless, as if I should be doing something. Let's invent a game then, like..." She paused as if deep in thought. "Want to figure out where they went?" She asked him with a little excitement in her voice. "Moth did give us a lot of information, and with what Trapper and Mosaic have told us over the past several weeks we should be able to figure it out."

Their Mother had been listening from the kitchen doorway, where she had been standing with a plate of chocolate chip cookies and milk in her hands. As she stepped into the dining room, she placed the cookies and milk onto the table and said, "You two are really worried about the birds aren't you?"

Both shook their heads 'yes' and April said, "I wouldn't be so worried if it weren't for the bad weather – especially the winds."

"Yes, I know," replied their Mother. "I heard you two talking and I think it's a great idea to try and plot their course. April, why don't you tell us what the birds told you and Eric will write it down. Then Eric will tell us what he remembers. You will write that down and maybe we can ascertain where they are going. What do you two think?" She asked as she finished explaining her plan to them. "Maybe we can make a week-end trip of exploration out of it once we figure out where we think they are going."

"Really, Mom? Do you think we could?" was Eric's response.

April smiled for the first time that day. "Gee, Mom that would be great and fun to boot. Like a treasure hunt!"

Eric interjected, "You mean more like a scavenger hunt road race, don't you? Like in the movie 'It's a Mad Mad Mad Mad World'. This should be fun. Lets get the maps and get started. This is going to be fun." He said with excitement, "We can figure out where they are going easily. Mosaic and Trapper both have explained and described their journey to get here many times. I'm sure we can piece it together. Let's get the map." Eric went to the desk and got out pencils and paper and an old map of the area.

"Eric, don't be silly," April said. "They didn't tell us in map terms, using freeway and street names."

"I know, but this is like solving a puzzle with clues they gave us thrown in," he said, "And what else is there to do? Sit here and wait and mope and feel sorry for ourselves? At least this way we are trying something. April, you start, and I'll write, he finished as he picked up a pencil and placed the writing pad in front of him.

"Mom!" April started, but her Mother supported Eric's views and gave her encouragement by offering, "If you do this I will drive you myself, if your Dad happens to be busy. We'll make it a family trip – an adventure."

April smiled at the prospect. "Okay! I like playing detective. I'll give this a try", she said with misgiving in her voice. "Maybe we can figure it out – where they came from and all, and where they might be going. It won't be easy, but it should be a fun challenge."

"That's the spirit," her Mother encouraged. "You have nothing to lose is correct, and it beats sitting here and pining the afternoon away."

"Okay, April, start remembering and talking," was Eric's impatient response to them getting started.

So off they went, with April talking and Eric writing everything April said. They stopped frequently, with Eric reading back what April had said, then April elaborating on this point or that description. It was slow work, and some of what April said made no sense, but they had decided to put it down on paper and then review it and see what came out of it. Once April had finished Eric and her switched places, with Eric talking and April writing. By the time they were done they had eaten all the cookies, had drank all the milk, and had twenty pages of notes between them. They had looked at the old map several times, and had realized it was not new enough or detailed enough to be much good for what they needed. They had mentioned this to their Mother, as she had looked in on them several times to see how it was going. She had called their father who had said he would stop by the library on his way home and pick up additional maps and reference materials.

She had come back in to tell them, "I called your Father and he'll stop at the library and get whatever maps and books he can on the areas south of here. Why don't you two just try and decipher what you have written, and once your Dad gets home and we've had dinner we'll all work on the project together."

Both looked at their Mom and said "thanks" and it that would be great if they could help them with the difficult and complicated task of figuring out what was what.

So April and Eric decided to do what was easy first: look for descriptions and words that were in both of their recollections of what they had heard being said. "You know all three of them talked about human rivers of black and gray," Eric said

"I think I know what those are," April offered. "I think those are roadways and freeways."

Eric agreed, especially when he remembered how they said humans use them to travel about in their many colored boxes. Now they had one good piece of information that they both agreed to as being correct and accurate. It had gone that way all the rest of that afternoon. They solved one piece of the puzzle after another as the wind blew and howled all the rest of the day like a wild animal trying to break in.

The orb – like the color of a sun rising with funny marking: on it turned out to be a 76 service station sign, and the four legged creature – man used for pulling with wings, turned out to be the Mobil flying horse logo. Their Mother had figured that one out. And so it went: with a little bit of this meaning that and something else meaning this. They figured out the description the birds had given them of what they had seen on their journey home.

They puzzled over the Trapper and Mosaic comments about neatly manicured landscapes, which the pigeons had called man-made and natural.

"Well, what would be man-made and natural and manicured all at the same time?" April asked. She continued, "Well, it could be a park, or a ball park, but they are too small for the expanses they were describing. Or..."

"Farmlands!" Eric shouted as he interrupted April's thinking aloud.

"Yes, that makes good sense" April said giving Eric that 'don't do that again' look and added, "Now their description of man's flying machines makes sense… and the mist of death coming from them…" before April could finish, "Would be crop dusting!" Eric again interjected, cutting April off. With that 'I got it' jubilation in his voice.

"Yes, that works," April said, raising her hand to stop Eric, who was about to once again cut her off. She continued, "There is a lot of farmland in the valley south of here." April finished her original thought and continued with a new one, "And there are several passes through the mountains all along the valley as well."

"Sorry!" Eric said. "I just got a little excited with what we have discovered. We're on a roll." April did not respond to Eric's apology; she just waited, knowing he had more to say.

"Yep," Eric continued, "There are several man-made gray rivers running north and south through the farmlands and many cutting across the mountains as well. Makes sense, and now we need to find a large body of water or a lake close to one of the freeways. Let's look at the map and see if we can figure it out. This should be easy," he said, as he opened the old map out onto the table. Of course it wasn't; it took them better than a half hour to find all the freeways and roads that crossed the mountains from the farmland valley. They eliminated most of the roads, and of what was left; four did not have any lakes near them. Eric looked puzzled, "I don't understand. We should have found the lake easily," he said to April. "Maybe we got it wrong; maybe we didn't hear them correctly," he finished, still studying the map.

April had been looking as hard as Eric had at studying the map and had not seen any lake either. "How old is this map anyway?" she asked. She then proceeded to turn the map over to see if she could find a date on it. "No wonder," she said. "This map is ten years old."

"So what!" Eric exclaimed. "Lakes just don't disappear, no matter how old the map is," was his response to April's inquisitive 'I do not believe you're for real' look. April again looked out the window and got a worried, pained look on her face. "It's really still blowing out there. It hasn't quit; I wonder if they got caught in it or if they were forced to land and take shelter in a safe place?"

"They are smart birds." Eric said. "If nothing else, Trapper would know better than to try and fly in this weather. Especially after his last experience in this type of wind." Eric stopped, looked at April, and felt that they had already had this discussion. Just as he was going to make a point of it, their Mother came into the dining room from the kitchen and said "Why don't you two stop and take your minds off this for a little while and help me with dinner. Eric, you peel the potatoes, and April, you clean and break the ends off of the green beans for me while I work on the meat loaf."

"But, Mom, we need to work on this some more; we aren't getting anywhere, and if we stop now…" April started to protest.

With a firm kindness in her voice, her Mother cut her off, "I know dear, but I think this break will help you," she said, and with that she ushered them out of the dining room and into the kitchen. "I need the help, and you two need a change of scenery. It will not take you long and then you can get back to this. Believe me, by taking your minds off of it for a little while, it will help you to concentrate and when you get back to it, you'll see." With their Mother's insistence, they went into the kitchen and helped with dinner.

As is so often the case, when the mind is working on a task that requires no real thought such that it can perform by rote and is relaxed, things come to it. Sometimes solutions to problems it has been working on for hours, tidbit of information that had been missed or forgotten during times of strenuous concentration and focus, become clear and well-defined.

This type of thought came to Eric as they were working side by side to get all the ingredients ready for dinner. "You know," he said, "I bet that lake is – new maybe man-made – one of those new get away vacation communities or maybe a new reservoir. What do you think April? Mom?"

"Maybe," was April's reply. "Do you want to add garlic to the potatoes?" she asked her Mom. "It does sound like a real possibility," April continued in response to Eric's comments.

"Okay with me," said their Mom "Peel four to five cloves and add them to the water with the potatoes, and we'll let them all boil together. When your dad gets home with the newer maps we'll see if what you suggested appears on the map along the roads you believe they took through the mountains," she finished.

"I'll do it," Eric said. "I'm peeling the potatoes and I want to smash them after they get done cooking. Yes, we'll have to see if they show up on any of the maps Dad brings home."

"You mean pulverize them, don't you?" April teased.

"Yep, pulverize, destroy, and crush," Eric added, as he slammed his fist into the palm of his left hand. He smiled from ear to ear as he did a mashing motion of his fist into the palm of his hand to over-emphasize the pulverizing of the spuds he intended to do once they were cooked.

"Okay! He-man," April teased. "I think Mom and I get the picture."

"Finish peeling the potatoes, Eric," his mother directed him as she put the meat loaf into the oven and set the timer. April had been breaking the ends off of the green beans, breaking them in half, and then placing them into a pot of water. "You know what?" She continued, "They said as they came through the mountain pass, they diverted from the route in order to get a drink of water. That should tell us what pass they took."

"And I remember them talking about staying at man-made cylindrical buildings that stored grain. That is where they stayed the night and got both food and water on their way here," Eric chimed in. He continued his thoughts out loud, "What could the cylindrical buildings that stored grain be?" He stopped peeling and brought his hand to rub his chin. "Humm, I know! Grain silos! I bet that's what they were talking about," he exclaimed excitedly.

"Well the lake should have shown up on the map, and it didn't; would the silos be there on any map?" April wondered aloud.

"Well, let's go and look," Eric and April almost said in unison as they started towards the dining room door.

"Wait a minute you two. Finish with what you are doing," their Mother said, stopping them in their tracks.

"Aw, Mom, please!" April said. Eric had already stopped and was heading back to finish the potatoes, but he stopped and waited to see what his Mother's response was going to be to April's plea. "No, we'll have plenty of time once everything starts cooking. You two finish and then we'll all go look the map over and see what we can find," was her response to April's plea and Eric's hesitation. "I'll help you both," she said with a smile. Picking up a knife, she smashed and peeled the garlic for Eric and helped April clean and break beans. They were done in no time with her help.

About this time, their Father had arrived home from the library with a handful of books and several fold out maps. He yelled, "Hello, where is everyone?" He walked through the kitchen door from the dining room, where he had left the items he had checked out from the library.

He kissed his wife hello and hugged each one of his children, and all asked him the same question differently. "I thought you were stopping at the library?" his wife asked. "Where is the stuff from the library?" Eric asked. "Dad, you didn't forget to go to the library, did you?" April wanted to know.

"Well, that's a fine hello," he teased. "Since when has the library been so important? I thought you'd be glad to see your hard working Dad just home from the mines." By the looks on their faces, they were not in the mood for teasing, so he said, "It's all on the dining room table."

With that, they all went from the kitchen into the dining room, and April and Eric were amazed at all the books, magazines and maps laying there for them to look at and use.

"Wow, look at all this stuff! If we can't figure it out after we go through all this stuff, it can't be figured out." Eric said to April. "Let's get started," he finished. Only where to start was the question. "The books, the magazines, the maps... maybe there is too much information," he thought. April, seeing the overwhelmed look on Eric's face, suggested they each take a group of items and start looking through them using their written lists as a guide for what to look for.

"Dad, where is the receiver for the sending device we placed on Trapper?" Eric asked.

"Mr. Franz is bringing it by on his way home from work later this evening – probably after dinner," was his Dad's response to Eric's question and April's concerned look.

So with that they each took an item – April the magazines, Eric the maps, while their Mother and Father divided up the books. Most of the magazines were either travel or the farmer's almanacs. The maps were in both book and fold-out variety. Eric started with the one they had and then put the rest in chronological order. Some were earlier versions of what he had and some were later, all the way up to a year before the date they were currently working from to determine the way the birds were flying to get to the feed store. Their parents took the assortment of seven coffee table – type picture books and just stacked them and started looking through them, one by one. It went that way until their Mother got up and went into the kitchen to finish dinner. "You may leave the mess as it is. We will eat in the kitchen at the breakfast table tonight," she announced as she left the dining room.

"Thanks Mom," April said. "Let me help you set the table." April's eyes were getting tired and she was a little disappointed that so far nothing had come of their research efforts. Eric got up and headed for the kitchen as well, with a look of dejection on his face. "I'll help too," he said.

They finished their assigned tasks and headed back to the dining room and the maps. Eric had told April that he had narrowed it down to three passes. Each one had a lake next to the roadway and he had asked April to look at the latest map he had found which showed these lakes. As they looked at the map, April said, "Eric, even the fourth pass has a lake right here. How could you have missed it?"

"I saw it, but it's too far away from the main thoroughfare,." Eric responded to April's notification of his missing an obvious possibility.

"Well maybe for us, but not for the birds," April exclaimed with a little exasperation in her voice. "You can't overlook the obvious or we'll never figure this out!" She said accusatorily as if Eric were purposely trying to not do a good job and really didn't want to find the right flight path the birds had taken. "Eric, you have to pay attention…," she had started, but their Dad, realizing they were both tired and hungry, stepped in and said, "You two go get ready for dinner, wash your hands. We'll all work on this after dinner; when we can put a new perspective on this."

With that said, April and Eric scowled at each other and left the dining room and got ready for dinner. It was true they were tired and dissatisfied with what little headway they had made for all their labors. The wind was still blowing which did not help with their concerns for the birds' well-being. Both were upset with themselves for not having been able to solve the mystery of what path the birds had taken to get home. Both had desperately wanted to be the one to solve the riddle yet neither had. Over dinner they had talked about how they were feeling, and their disappointments. When each had heard the others frustration, they had laughed and then started kidding each other. By the time dinner was done, both felt that the answers were closer than they thought and, with their parent's help, they would figure it out. They finished dinner and cleaned up as a family, after which they went back into the dining room and reviewed April and Eric's notes. They compiled a list of important landmarks as the birds had described them, and then all looked at the latest map Eric had found. Their dad had gotten out a bright yellow marker, and they had marked their house on the map and then the roads that lead from where they lived to the farmlands. All had agreed that was a safe thing to do because the birds were definitely traveling south. Next, they worked on the silos, or collection stations based on what they read in the farmer almanacs. This narrowed it down to two possible passes through the mountains. Then by deduction of what the birds had said, they realized that the lake could not have been right by the roadway, so that eliminated one of the two passes. Amazingly, once that had been done several of the landmarks they had described just appeared to be there. They had been there all along, but now they were where they should have been, and things fell into place all the way down to finding the rail yards.

By the time Mr. Franz stopped by with the receiver, they had a map with over a dozen bright yellow marks on it. Their Mom had offered Mr. Franz coffee, which he accepted. Mr. Franz drank his coffee while giving them a demonstration on how the receiver worked, and when he pointed it southward they were able to pick up a soft little pinging sound. "That would be the signal," he said. April and Eric were delighted beyond words as they heard the sound emitting from the receiver. Mr. Franz smiled, finished his coffee, and got up to leave, saying, "Good luck and have fun with it." With that, he said his goodbyes to them and left to go home.

After he had gone, April explained, that they were half done, and now they had to try and figure out what Moth had described. However, their Mother had said, "This is enough for one day's work tomorrow; is another day, and we'll finish it then. You two get ready for bed."

So April and Eric, with some grumbling and slight protesting, got up and got ready for bed. April asked if she could keep the receiver in her room. She fell asleep to the soft pinging sound of the receiver in her ear.

Interesting Pigeon Fact

The pigeon has also been found to pass the 'mirror test' (being able to recognise its reflection in a mirror) and is one of only six species, and the only non-mammal, that has this ability.

Chapter 3

There is an old question that has been asked since time began for man and all creatures ... are creatures born good or evil? More exactly, are they imprinted towards one type of behavior or another? Rest assured that all creatures are born with the will to live, to survive and to grow. From the simplest one celled creature to the largest and most complex, they all have the desire to continue to exist.

Is it their environment that determines whether they turn out good or bad? Is it by what they are taught, or is it how they learn from that environment? Or more importantly, is it determined by the decisions they make during the process of growing and developing, or how others treat and respond to their existence?

So if there is no creature born good or bad ... then why does it appear so? Always remember evil is born through despair, feelings of hopelessness, of jealousy, of greed and through ignorance. So choose your words wisely, when you describe the two! Furthermore, in how you treat others around you.

Crafco's life started as most of his species starts: at the smooth birth stage. After that, fate, or his environment, or nature, or all those things combined dictated how he turned out. His smooth birth was not an exceptionally unusual event, except that in this particular nest of his parents', there were three smooth births, and Crafco's was the last of those births. Normally in the pigeons world there are only two smooth births per nest. It is said, that having three was a sign. Some believed it to be a good sign, while others saw it as a sign of bad things to come.

Those that say it is a good sign say it speaks of prosperity within the flock, especially to the birds that have the triplet smooth births. Others say it is a bad sign of gluttony, and gluttony is evil and causes all kinds of problems; from sweet blood, to wounds that would not heal, to corpulence-all bad things for all involved.

His father walked around as if he owned the world and was all caught up in the pride of having brought this good luck to the flock. He totally ignored any negative talk and rumors associated with the triple smooth births. Among the majority of the pigeons of the Northeast flock none could recall it ever having happened before; the few that could were not happy about it. Most saw it as a good sign, yet many had forgotten the possible negative implications that this type of birth could mean.

His mother on the other hand had an uneasy feeling about the whole affair. It started with the fact of how difficult the births had been-not just the third, but all of them. She was only two seasons old and had only had three nests prior to this one, her last having gone full term. Those two had died mysteriously. They had gone for a training flight and had never returned, and they had just disappeared from the face of the earth. Their other two attempts at raising a family had ended with the eggs and the sun-stage ones being taken from the nest. All those things had taken their toll on her emotionally and physically.

Her mate had been so self-absorbed that he had not taken notice of her diminished condition, of how much these three smooth births had taken out of her. However, others had, and their concerns were fed by his lack of concern for his mate. "It wasn't natural," they would be heard saying. "A hens body isn't made to be a squab factory." And so it went; the comments about his father's inappropriateness to be a good mate.

The depletion of her mineral reserves and other bodily stores of fat and energy had been devastating to her health. At first, she thought she would recover with time but that had not happened at the rate she had wanted. She was tired all the time and some days had great difficulty getting herself to the food and water supplies. There were days she did not really feel like eating and where she was just thirsty. Then, just days before the coming out party, she had finally started to feel good and the first egg had hatched. In addition, the first-born was demanding food minutes after its birth. Within a day after that, the second one hatched and from that point on her health was permanently on a downward spiral. When the third egg hatched two days after the first, she knew she was going to have a real battle on her hands. Feeding three dependent mouths and herself would really be difficult in her condition and would eventually be devastating to her well-being.

By this time, her mate had come down to earth and had taken on the majority of the feeding tasks, but even he felt overwhelmed. She knew it was only a matter of time before her health would totally fail. It was very difficult on her physically and emotionally, especially since she feared their third birth would probably not survive into the second week. It was in the end of the first week of his life that tragedy had struck, as most would have told it, but for Crafco it was the true beginning of his life.

As Moth was flying north searching for Mosaic and the route he had taken, Crafco watched the occupants of the K-Bridge and thought back on how lucky he had been: how that the rats' raid had occurred at the beginning of his second week of life, and that he had survived it. Yes indeed, it had been a great day, the day the rat had made its appearance. It had taught him several valuable life lessons. The most important was that birth order wasn't all it was cracked up to be, and secondly, that fate was always there to disrupt the game of life-or, more accurately, the plans you made for your life.

The rat had shown up minutes after his Mother had left the nest and twenty minutes before his Father made it back from his early morning food and water flight. If his father had been on time, things would have been quite different. While getting his drink, he had chosen to brag about these three youngsters and how lucky he was and the good fortune this was bringing onto the flock. However, from that day forward, with the death of his older sibling, Crafco thought to himself that nothing but misfortune had befallen his immediate family and the flock.

The large scruffy brown rat, the size of a bantam chicken, had crept out from between a crack in the boards and out of the shadows where it had been patiently waiting for the opportunity to strike. The rat had stopped, had sniffed, looked him over with its dark brown eyes, and had smiled. "You aren't enough for a good snack," the rat said between sharp gleaming teeth and his halitosis breath that smelled like rotted garbage. Then, it looked at Lingo, the biggest and with a broader smile of total satisfaction said, "You, on the other hand, my little fat chubby one are a real meal, fit for a rat of my distinction."

"Don't, eat me; take him instead… please!" And with that, Crafco's older brother Lingo, had pushed 4-2, Tin, towards the rat.

"Don't! Get away from me! You're the oldest; you're supposed to protect us," said Tin, as Lingo pushed him towards the rat. "Please, don't…." were the last words spoken by Tin as the rat grabbed and bit Tin in the neck behind the head crushing his vertebra and windpipe, killing him instantly. Just like that, a life was over, and with it all its promise gone.

The rat smiled at Lingo, "Thank you, and now it's your turn." As the rat was talking, Lingo had been moving in a circular motion and away from the rat. They were lined up so that it was the rat, Lingo and Crafco. The rat lunged, but Lingo was too quick, and what the rat caught was a piece of Crafco's little wing instead. Which the rat spit out instantly. "Why you little! …" the rat exclaimed with a snarl, as he turned and then jumped at Lingo again. This time Lingo was not fast enough and the rat had him by the leg. Lingo was struggling as the rat was pulling him and dragging him from the corner towards the direction from whence he had originally come. Not letting go of Lingo's leg, the rat picked up his dead sibling as he passed him. Their Father arrived just in time to rescue Lingo.

With a pair of sharp slaps of his right wing, their father had hit the rat in the face. The first slap had hit the rat above the eye and the second whack hit it right between the eyes, causing the rat to let Lingo go. The rat, realizing that he could not stay the fight, or have both his victim and intended victim, took the one unable to struggle, ran into the darkness, and disappeared.

Their Father rushed to examine Lingo. "Are you all right?" He asked. Then he turned to Crafco, "How about you, are you okay? Are you hurt?" Crafco could not find his voice. He just sat there in the corner cowering, shaking in total shock. 'How could Lingo have done it,' he thought, as his Father examined him carefully and discovered he was fine. His father admonished him, "You're fine, snap out of it, because this is a part of life!" He then turned his attention to Lingo, "Why my boy, you are hurt," he said. As he examined his leg, he praised Lingo, because being hurt to their Father meant that Lingo had fought and tried to protect his siblings. "You're such a brave lad. Trying to save your brothers like that and all."

Crafco learned two very important lessons that day. One, that things are not always what they seem when you stumble upon them, and the other do not draw conclusions that are not substantiated. He alone had the knowledge of what was the truth about what had happened. That he alone knew what was true. He thought, knowing the truth was a good thing. In this case, a powerful tool, or so he originally thought.

With the death of his brother Tin, he got more food, thanks to his mother who from that day forward fed him first, because she felt guilty about what had happened. Lingo, who had always complained in the past when this had occurred, was conspicuously silent. Now, never asking for food first, but always letting it be known he was not hungry. If his mother went to feed him first, he stepped away from her and Crafco always would step up to be fed. Lingo had said it, only once, that he did this because of the traumatic experience that poor little Crafco had gone through, in seeing the rat kill Tin. However, in truth, he had made a pact with Crafco: for Crafco's silence about what had really happened, he would insist that Crafco be fed first. Because of this behavior, Lingo became the pride of his parents, and this endeared him to all that heard the story. He became everyone's fair-feathered pigeon and the corn kernel of this parent's eye and that of the flock.

Crafco on the other hand did not care at first. He was getting more food than he had ever gotten before. He was in heaven, in a state of bliss because of always being full, of always being first. However, after a while he started to resent being first. When he had first become aware of it, he had told himself, "Who cares that Lingo is getting all the praise." As is often the case, as Lingo was given praise, Crafco was getting the "poor little one" from his Mother and "okay small fry" resentment from his Father. All the kudos were always being directed toward Lingo. Crafco constantly heard, "Wasn't he wonderful"… "So kind and considerate of his little brother"… "No wonder he acted so brave against the rat." The more his parents and visitors to the nest did this, the more Crafco resented not having told the truth. In addition, no matter how good he told himself he had it, a small part of his mind started to resent Lingo, Crafco now found himself to be in an unbearable situation. Crafco had become just the other child, the little brother, the lucky one, the poor little brother. The more he heard this, the more he wanted to bring his older brother down, the more he wanted to tell the truth, to tell all what had really happened that fateful day, the day of the rat.

On one of those days when his mother and father were praising his older brother again for insisting that Crafco be fed first and how unselfish he was being and had been the day of the rat, the truth came out. Crafco had just been fed, as had Lingo, when their parents went into their 'automatic praise mode' as Crafco had called it. He could not stand it any longer. The truth, like a hot burning liquid in his mouth, came spitting out. As is so often the case when the truth has been distorted by half-truths, lies and pride, his parents did not believe him. Even worse, his parents did not only not believe him, but instead they accused him of being ungrateful, of being selfish, of thinking only of himself, despite all that his older brother had done for him. His Father had been so incensed by all that Crafco had said that he slapped Crafco with his wing and told him never to speak of it again or he would be disowned and abandoned.

Crafco mouthed back that he already felt abandoned, that they only paid attention to Lingo. It was always, "Lingo this" and "Lingo that" and that they did not love him. He understood he was only a burden, had been a burden, and they wished he had died instead of Tin.

Both his parents were flabbergasted by his accusations and denied his allegations. From that day forward, only his mother fed him and paid any attention to him. His father never again acknowledged him, re-enforcing what Crafco had known all along. To his father, Crafco no longer existed. What Crafco had hoped to happen most by his telling of the truth had turned out the exact opposite of what he had intended and wanted. His intention for telling the truth was not for the sake of the truth but for personal gain. He was not telling the truth to clear his conscience or relieve his burden of a lie but to try to bring his brother down and win the affections of his mother and father. He had done it out of spite, out of a need to be the one that everyone liked, that everyone respected, that everyone loved. It had backfired on him, as that train of reasoning usually did.

Lingo, on the other hand, saw the reaction and was at first angry, wanting to lash out. However, he recognized his parent's reaction and knew if he became defensive, he too would lose. He understood pigeon nature, and psyche better than most and played it cool and correctly. He insisted that his parents be understanding and that Crafco had gone through a traumatic experience, and that they should forgive Crafco because of his age. Yet he made sure they retained their feeling of shock towards Crafco. In addition, in their father's case, he re-enforced his total rejection of Crafco from that day forward. The news of the accusations that Crafco had made against Lingo traveled through the flock like wildfire. The story was helped by his father's disgust of Crafco's behavior, and in his desire to protect Lingo, he told the story himself. He did not want this story to become rumor and then be accepted as fact. Therefore, he figured that if he told the story himself, he could keep Lingo's reputation from being tarnished.

Lingo, for his part, insisted that his parents and the flock not hold a grudge against Crafco and that they forgive Crafco because the trauma and horror of that day, the day of the rat, was still adversely affecting Crafco greatly, and he may never get over it without understanding and compassion. In doing so, Lingo became the hero once again, and felt that he now had the upper hand. The truth had set him free and had rescued him from a life of fear and of servitude to that fear, in the sense that he no longer felt he had to acquiesce to Crafco in any way.

Crafco realized he had miscalculated several things. The first was that in not telling the truth right away it had lost its value. The second was that blurting out what he truly felt about how his parents were treating him was a mistake; he should have done it in a more subtle way. His biggest mistake was underestimating how

Lingo would react. He had thought Lingo would go on the defensive, but instead he had turned gracious in his actions and demeanor, at least in public and around their parents.

Privately, when he and Lingo were alone, Lingo treated him like dirt. Lingo called him all types of derogatory names and was always threatening him with bodily harm if he ever betrayed him again in anything. Crafco's dislike for his brother and father simmered, as does a pot constantly being fueled. They fed his anger by constantly insulting him, ignoring his existence, treating him as a second-class bird. He lost all feelings for them. The only emotions that were left were the raw bones of distain, loathing, and hatred. He knew that someday he would get even; he would have to do something or bust. The feeling of contempt for them increased after his mother died of malnutrition and grief. The two had been heard telling others that Crafco was responsible for her early passing. When Crafco tired of hearing the rumors, he had confronted his father and brother with it one day; both denied it to his face. However, Crafco had overheard his father saying to Lingo one day, "If she hadn't been so obsessed with keeping Crafco alive; if only she had not believed his story, if only she had let nature take its course, she would still be alive. She was soft and pathetic in her emotional belief in what Crafco had said; I told her if she ever spoke of her beliefs out in public, she would be sorry, and look what happened to her. Oh well, it is just us now. We don't need her or her weakling!" He had finished telling Lingo.

Crafco had always known that his mother had loved him but he never knew how much she had loved him. He never had wanted to believe that his father hated him. Crafco had known that his father disliked him, but his mother had said he was wrong. However, she had been wrong which had angered him, not towards her but towards them. True, she had given him false hope. She had always shown him love and understanding, and she had been wrong. Her kindness and sweetness had blinded her to the truth of her mates and the oldest sibling's true personalities. He had heard it from his father's own lips; even though he had always believed it so, it was still a devastating reality, a shocking thing to have heard and to face never the less.

Crafco, from that day forward, knew where he stood with both his father and his brother. The following day his Father had thrown him out of the nest and made it a point to ignore him no matter where they accidentally met. At first, it affected Crafco. He would either get depressed or would fume and rage inside at the treatment, but even that subsided after he replaced it with hate and plans of revenge. He would get even with both of them one day, he promised himself.

He watched the K-Bridge flock going through its paces. He had watched them support one another in their daily activities. 'What twits,' he thought, 'Family had no value. The flock is only useful if it does your bidding'... he hesitated and then continued 'All things you do,' he thought 'must benefit you first, and if it helps others, then fine. If not, tough!' he thought. He had learned that lesson after his father had thrown him out.

Crafco could barely fly when his Father had tossed him out on his wing. If it had not been for a kindly old bird named Storyfeld who had taken him under his wing, he possibly would have starved to death. Storyfeld had two sides. One side was a vagabond, a traveler, a mooch and the best flimflam bird ever. The other was a Good Samaritan, a humanitarian, and the gentlest bird the Great Creature ever put on this earth. The one side complimented the other perfectly; he knew how to get what he wanted, so that he could do what he wanted, to live by his own standard of good heartiness. His appetite for doing good had no bounds.

Yes, that kindly old bird named Storyfeld had taken him in. Storyfeld had rescued him from certain death, for a young bird unable to fend for himself would never make it. Storyfeld was a believer in helping the down and out, the abandoned bird, the sickly, the weak, downtrodden, and the orphaned. Storyfeld believed that there was good in all things and events. He believed that kindness overcame cruelty and neglect. So long as you did what he said and wanted, he would help you and teach you how to survive.

He gave Crafco the one thing no one else had given him to date, which was respect. Even his Mother, who had loved him, had not shown him the same kind of respect that Storyfeld had shown him. Storyfeld really cared about him and genuinely believed in who he was and that he could succeed and really become a productive member of the flock. Unlike his dad, who had felt Crafco was a canker that brought truly bad events on those that he met. Storyfeld had given Crafco respect, and in doing so, Crafco had started to feel better about himself. This look of self-confidence that Crafco started to feel inwardly started to show outwardly, in how he carried himself. Unbeknownst to Crafco this scared Lingo to distraction. Lingo's greatest fear was that Crafco would gain respect and then be believed if he ever told the truth about the incident with the rat again; and if he was believed, that would affect Lingo's first-class status within the flock, something Lingo feared losing most. Because of that fear, Lingo would eventually, once again causing Crafco great pain. Lingo would have others be leery of Crafco by spreading untrue stories about his brother. That he had a mental condition; this caused them to stay away from Crafco, which had the desired effect, which kept him isolated without friends.

Many feared Storyfeld, because he turned no one away who needed a helping wing. They feared that this trait would eventually bring a major disease or some other unknown evil into the flock and then all would pay for his careless soft heartedness. The majority agreed that being kind was good, but only to a point. The flock leader and his council had tried to put bounds and limits onto what Storyfeld did, but as is so often the case with intangibles, everyone had their own idea about what was acceptable. Doing all he did was okay for immediate flock members. For those within the rail yard, it depended on whom you asked; some thought this was a good thing, and others did not. Most thought taking outsiders from other than the immediate flock should not be tolerated, and yet there were those that thought it was a good thing. But, not so for helping the outsider, especially those that came from outside of the rail yards, most of the birds thought that was folly. This confusion amongst the flock and especially between its leaders turned out great for Storyfeld and his charges, because he wound up regulating himself to his standards, which meant he helped anyone that showed up on his doorstep.

As fate would have it, a sick bird did show up and asked for help. Storyfeld, as was customary for him, took the bird in and tried to nurse it back to health, but the bird died. Within days of the bird's death, others, seemingly healthy birds, in the flock became ill as well. Several were brought to Storyfeld for treatment. Rumors ran wild that the bird that Storyfeld had treated was the cause of this sudden and unexplainable illness that had befallen the flock.

Crafco's father became sick with this mysterious illness as well and was brought to Storyfeld for treatment. Crafco had not wanted to take him in, but Storyfeld would not hear of it. Crafco tried to explain to Storyfeld that it was a mistake to do so, but Storyfeld stayed true to his convictions and did everything he could to safe Crafco's father. However, it would not be so; Crafco's father died within a day after having been brought in for care. All the others that had come down with the same symptoms also were dead within days after showing signs of being sick. The strange thing was that as quickly as the mysterious illness had arrived and taken some, the stealthy sickness had left.

Crafco had tried to figure it out by doing an investigation of sorts, but seeing how all the involved birds were dead it was nearly impossible to find out what had happened. He had heard his dad talking out of his head as Storyfeld was treating him. Most of what he had said made no sense. As Crafco talked to others that had treated some of the other birds, a pattern did develop. All the birds had been together days before they became ill, yet none that had been exposed to the sick bird that Storyfeld had treated became ill. The fact was, none that had actually been in contact with the sick bird had become ill, and none had died. Crafco had deduced that the sick bird was not the cause of the twelve that had died. Nevertheless, the angry crowd that had confronted Storyfeld at his nest had not listened. To be more accurate, their instigator, his brother Lingo, had not listened. Lingo had kept the mob from listening to the logic of Crafco's arguments on how the sick bird could not have been the cause of the rest getting ill and dying.

Lingo blamed Storyfeld for his father's death and that of the others and went on a campaign to get him ousted from the flock. Not all the sick birds had died when Lingo started his negative, angry crusade, blaming Storyfeld for the deaths and wanting him thrown out of the flock. However, as each inflicted bird with the mysterious illness died, Lingo's words carried more and more weight and eventually even the reasonably clear-headed thinkers doubted Storyfeld and his philosophy of doing good. Crafco, who was not as elegant a speaker as Lingo, tried to defend his mentor but failed. An angry, ugly mob bodily ousted Storyfeld and destroyed his nest and all his belongings.

Lingo had done it for purely selfish reasons. He had wanted his parents nest site, and he feared Crafco and the knowledge he possessed about the day of the rat. He resented that Crafco was doing well. He resented that anyone was actually helping Crafco. He had hoped that when their dad had thrown Crafco out that Crafco would die, eliminating him as a future threat. Then, that goody two-feet, Storyfeld, had taken Crafco in, and every time Lingo saw Crafco now he looked better and better. Lingo had been trying to figure out a way to eliminate Crafco as that threat ever since he perceived Crafco to be a threat. Therefore, he had figured out that he must eliminate the benefactor of Crafco's newfound belief in himself. He had been plotting for a month, spreading un-substantiated rumors about Storyfeld, and then the sick birds, and his father's sickness had solidified the plan, and the rest had been easy. 'The majority of the flock's population are sheep,' he had thought. 'Easily lead by exaggerating truths or lies and playing on their fears.'

Of course, none of those that had taken care of the birds had asked the question of how they had gotten ill, or how they thought they had gotten ill. They had only asked the questions of what their symptoms were and how they were feeling. However, if they had asked the correct question at the correct time, they would have discovered that the group had all flown to the park several days before they became ill. They had eaten grass seeds that had a strange color to them, and all had a strange taste in their mouths after eating them. In addition, all had come down with the symptoms of having a burning sensation in their throats and crops after having drunk water. What none had known was that the seeds had been treated with two chemicals, one to make them grow and the other to prevent them from being eaten by bugs. These two things were harmless individually but together created a chemical reaction when water was applied that formed a deadly poison.

Crafco was devastated by the events and his inability to do anything to prevent them. When he found out that Storyfeld had been found dead, he blamed Lingo and swore revenge on his older brother. He had learned a lot from Storyfeld including the most important lesson of all: to always let those you help know that it was not free; a debt had been incurred and would someday need to be repaid. Crafco claimed Storyfeld's destroyed nest area as his own, which none objected to, he started to clean it up, and that is how Crafco found a home to call his own.

Crafco smiled to himself; 'Yes, Storyfelt had given him a lot...,' he thought as he looked at the K-Bridge. Nevertheless, he, Crafco, had really done the rest. He had created good alliances and had used every event that had presented itself to his advantage. 'Where are those two dunderheads? They should have been back already,' he thought. Crafco thought how easy it had all really been... after he had rescued Joel that is, after providence had given him the opportunity. He thought back on that day, how it had been a normal early summer morning...

The sun was shining brightly in a cloudless sky. The temperature at 9 AM was 85 degrees Fahrenheit in the shade. Crafco had gotten up slightly depressed and had nothing to do, so he had cleaned up the mess that the mob had made of Storyfeld's nest. He was alone, and he wanted to do something, but had no one to do it with; he had no friends, no allies. He needed to be alone, away from the flock, so he decided to go to the stream and take a dip to cool off and bathe at the same time. He had flown to the northern end of the stream and had followed it south for approximately two hundred yards when he had come upon a sandy area with several shallow pools of standing clear water along its length. 'The ideal spot.' he thought. 'There is plenty of clear area around it so that no one or thing could sneak up on me as I bathed.' At the east side, about three yards from the pools there was a stand of trees whose branches projected out over the sandy bank. 'A good place to dry off and preen myself after my bath,' he thought.

He made several additional passes along the banks of the stream and noticed nothing threatening. He landed on the sand, which felt hot on the bottoms of his feet causing him to rush to the first pool of water. At first, the water had felt cold to him and it had made him shiver, but within minutes it felt warm and comfortable, ideal for bathing. 'A bath,' he thought, 'A good way to clear the mind, to get relaxed.' He stepped into the water and started to splash and slosh around in the shallow pool of water until he was good and wet. It was then that he heard the low appeal for help coming from the low-lying bushes randomly dispersed on the far shore from across the stream's flowing water. At first, he thought it was the breeze rustling through the leaves. However, the second time he heard it he knew it was a voice asking for help. Not a shouting or excited voice, but a low, hoarse whimpering, whispering voice.

"Can you hear me? I am over here. Please help me," It said. "Whoever you are, help me, I'm over here. I will make it worth your while. Please help me!"

Crafco did not answer; he did not move. He was scared to do either. He was afraid to breathe, to even take his next breath. He had to be careful; he was soaking wet and in his current condition he would have a difficult time escaping from anyone or anything. He had heard that the slithering ones used this type of ploy to get unsuspecting birds close enough so they could strike and get them into their coils of death. Instead of responding right away, he shook out most of the water from his feathers. As he was doing so, the pleading voice once again could be heard.

"Whoever you are, please; I'll make it worth your while. I will be in your debt forever. I'll do anything you ask, just help get me out of this, please!" This time the voice sounded exhausted, as if the owner was on its last legs and done for.

Crafco got his courage up; he could not have exactly told you why. Maybe, because the voice had sounded so desperate, so depleted of energy, or maybe, maybe because he had mostly dried off. On the other hand, maybe it was the promise to do anything its rescuer asked, so Crafco responded, "Where are you?"

"Here, here…" The voice was even more depleted as it said, "over here."

"You'll have to wait a minute, I can't see you anywhere. Where are you?" Crafco asked, as he kept removing water from his feathers and replacing it with oil using his beak between questions.

"Over here," said the disembodied voice. "I'm here in the bushes by the rocks at the base of the trees."

"Okay, I see where to go," Crafco responded, as he saw the bushes shaking unnaturally over across the stream to his left. "I'm coming; keep talking to help me zero in on where you are."

"Hurry!" the voice directed. "I'm in the bushes! You are a saint!"

Crafco chuckled to himself at that. 'We will see,' he thought, as he flew across the stream and carefully started looking in the bushes. There, all tangled up in netting and twine, lay a crow. Crafco moved slowly towards the crow. As he approached the crow turned and gave him a child-like innocent smile.

"Please help me," said the crow, in the same hoarse whisper of a voice that Crafco had heard earlier pleading for help.

"It looks pretty bad," said Crafco "I'm not sure what to do, or where to start, or how to do it. What's your name?" he asked the crow.

"Joel, owner of the bush," was the crow's reply.

Crafco laughed at that. "Joel, owner of the bush," he repeated. "I'd say, you are more, Joel conquered by the net, would be more accurate."

Joel responded with a hoarse, gravelly laugh, "Yes, I must look pathetic. Help me get out of this, will you? You'll never regret it. I promise on my Mother's grave, if she were dead. I'll be your comrade... forever."

"Forever!" Crafco repeated. Crafco had heard these types of promises before and had never seen them fulfilled. He had no bases to go from because no one had ever made him that type of promise. However, never the less, he had heard other similar promises. In addition, the bird making it had always had a reason to renege on their promise. Still, what did he have to lose? "I'll help you and then we'll see how good you are to your word." As he worked on untangling the netting and twine, he talked about how he did not know why he was doing what he was doing. or the what or why for of it. He had enough problems of his own without getting involved with Joel's problems.

Joel responded to Crafco's grousing, "Well, you can count on me; just untie me, will you, and tell me what's eating at you."

So Crafco did start to tell Joel what his troubles were, and as he was doing so and freeing Joel, a plan had started to formulate itself in his mind of how the crow could help him get rid of his older brother. After an hour of hard work, Joel was free, and the minute he was, he jumped up and headed for the stream.

"Hey, where are you going?" Crafco yelled after a running Joel, afraid that he was taking off and leaving him holding air. Crafco followed Joel, who did not respond, as he jumped into a shallow pool of water at the streams edge. Where he, drank, and drank for what seemed like twenty minutes. Two minutes later, he finally stopped and taking a mouth full of water, he gargled and then he spit it out. He did this several times. "Sorry," he said, "but I haven't had a drink in a day and a half. My throat and mouth were really dry and had an awful taste in it…" He stopped as he looked at Crafco. "And I forgot how good water tastes," he finished lamely, "Know what I mean?"

Not waiting for a response from Crafco, he continued, "So my little pigeon friend, what's your name? And how can I help you?"

Joel asked. "Want me to visit your tormentor and break his wing or his leg for you," he said in an Edward G. Robinson type soft gravelly voice.

"My name's Crafco. No!" he said, responding with his name and the no more forcefully than he had intended. "You don't need to do that. I'll deal with him somehow," Crafco said. Why had he said that, he thought? Maybe it was that Joel had hit the nail on the head. That Joel had looked at him and listened to him and had seen what his heart wanted most, and no one had ever done that before, except maybe Storyfelt. It was freaky and scary to realize that this crow had so easily put together what Crafco really wanted.

"Okay, have it your way, but by the way you were talking I'd say you really have a major problem there," Joel replied, with a raised eyebrow. "A problem I could help you with and none would ever know. I could make it look like an accident. No one would know you were involved in any way. Wouldn't it be easier on you if he were a little indisposed, you know... limited in what he could do for a while?"
Something in Crafco's body language, in the look in his eyes, the expression on his face, told Joel that if he did what he had just offered, Crafco's life would be easier. Seeing that in Crafco's expression; Joel made the offer that if Crafco ever wanted him for anything, "just leave a bent feather in the tree, there", he said pointing to the tree above where he had been trapped. With that, Joel handed Crafco one of his feathers.

Crafco said he would; if he really needed Joel's help he would leave the feather. With that, Joel left, saying he was hungry and needed to eat. But before he left he hugged Crafco goodbye. Crafco stiffened at this, but Joel seemed not to notice as he thanked Crafco once again, let him go, and then flew away saying, "Remember, I'm here if you need me, just ask."

Crafco smiled to himself, in spite of himself as Joel flew away; he had a friend, or better, an ally. An ally that could help him with Lingo; but how he was not quite sure yet. He would have to work on it, he thought: how to use Joel's offer to his advantage.

Therefore, for the next week, Crafco had come to the stream, the pools, and the tree to bathe and take in the sun, with the hope that Joel would be there. The first day he had gone Joel was not there, but on the second, he was. Joel was taking a bath in the shallows, and Crafco had landed and asked if he could join Joel in the shallows. Joel had said "sure" and had asked him how it was going with him. So Crafco and Joel had made small talk, while taking their baths and while sun bathing.

Crafco and Joel met like this for the rest of the week. They had made small talk. However, their conversation always came back around to two things. One was Crafco's rescue of Joel, how Joel owed him, and the other was Crafco's problems with the flock and Lingo. Crafco, who was not sure why, had told Joel about Storyfeld and what had happened. Joel had told him he needed to get rid of the chip on his shoulder; he needed to enjoy life and the day.

"Life is too short, my friend, to keep worrying about it. Worries are like un-kept wounds, if you do not deal with them, clean them up and let them heal, they will kill you. In your case, getting rid of Lingo would go a long way to healing that wound you are carrying around with you," Joel told him very matter of factually one day. As Joel continued with his advice and philosophy about undealt-with problems, Crafco's mind had wandered and strolled along the paths of his past.

Lingo, he thought, had been furious with him ever since the day Crafco had tried to set the record straight with his parents about the rat incident. Crafco had done it for two reasons: one to set his mind at rest, but mostly to try to bring that high and mighty Lingo down. Of course it had all backfired; his father had abandoned him at that point, and Lingo had snarled at him and from that day forward had pestered and bullied Crafco every chance he got regardless of where they were or what the situation had been. At first with little jabs and digs about Crafco's intelligence, and then his looks and, his actions; every negative thing Crafco did Lingo pointed out and made it worse. At first, it was not with Crafco around, but after a while, it was anytime Crafco was within hearing distance and eventually it escalated to constant harassment. Usually this was done with an attempt to be funny, as a joke, but those seemed to be the cruelest and most hurtful. His Dad and older brother seemed to have signed a pact between them to make his life miserable. As this continued Crafco had drawn into himself, and eventually had lashed out, been kicked out and had landed in the care of Storyfeld. Even that little bit of joy his father and brother had taken from him. He was bitter and resentful. "Why should I care what happens to Lingo," he thought. "What good has he ever done me?"

"Hey! Are you listening to me?" Joel stopped and asked Crafco.

"Oh! Sorry, I was thinking about…" Crafco started to reply when Joel cut him off. "Well, if it's that important that it takes you away from my brilliant philosophy of life, then you had better tell me."

Crafco shrugged his shoulder, "Sorry, yeah… sure, I'll tell you if you really want to be bored." Crafco had told Joel a lot about his personal life but never the story about the rat: never about his parents, the significance of his birth order, and why Lingo and he did not get along.

"Bore me," Joel replied and then waited for Crafco to start. Crafco started from the beginning. He explained about the three births in one nest, what some believed about it being a good omen and others thinking it was a bad omen. He told him all about the rat and the death of his middle brother, about Lingo's part in it, his parents, and the flock's reaction to it. About how he had tried to tell the truth about what had happened and the reactions of all to it, about his mother's death, his father's reactions, rejection, and being thrown out; about, Storyfeld, and what had happened there. Through Crafco's entire story, Joel had listened very carefully and attentively and then said, "Why don't you just stand up to him? Just tell him where to get off and be done with him, you will feel better for having done it. It appears to me that a part of you still wants to be family with him. But the bottom line is you really don't need that type around, family or not." Joel could see by Crafco's reaction to what he had said that Crafco's dealings with his brother was, by rout, a learned response brought about by what Crafco was, a pigeon. 'No wonder their kind always are the victims, the prey, the food,' Joel thought. 'how sad!'

"I guess you're right. But he's my brother, and he's family," Crafco said meekly. "He's older, and I need to show respect…"

"Respect!" Shouted Joel as he shook his head. "You got to be kidding me, why?"

"Because…" Crafco started to reply. Joel broke in and cut him off, "Because that's the pigeon way. Because that is the way of the flock and how it is supposed to be. No wonder your kind is always prey. Sorry!" Joel said as he saw Crafco recoil physically from Joel's last comment.

"But it sounds as if you're saying that because it's the right thing to say," Joel continued, "You are supposed to respect him because he's your older brother, or it's because that's what your parents taught you, or what the flock expects." Joel paused to see if he was even close to being accurate and by Crafco's lack of denial he thought he was and finished with, "Sometimes that's just wrong. Sometimes family is not family at all, sometimes family treats you worse than a stranger. Sometimes those that you pick as friends treat you with more love, respect, and understanding than family. Is that the way it is supposed to be? No, but it seems that is what you have, my friend. Yes, it's a shame, but that's what you have indeed," Joel finished, shaking his head in that slow 'it is a shame' way.

Joel had given voice to Crafco's beliefs. Yes, that is the way it was supposed to be, and yes, that is the way it really was for Crafco. Strangers had treated him more like family than his family had, all except for his mother. She had loved him, but she had also been wrong and blinded by the propaganda of the flock and the belief in family. She had told him that both his father and Lingo really did care about him and loved him. She had told him that repeatedly. He had been ashamed, for he did not feel that way towards Lingo; with his father the feelings had been more confusing. He had wanted to believe his mother about his father, but over time, his father had disproved his mother's words as well through his actions. Crafco thought he had just been thinking these thoughts, but when Joel responded with, "Life's really a messy, unfair thing. Isn't it?" Crafco realized he had been speaking his thoughts for him quite accurately.

Crafco and Joel continued to talk. As Crafco talked to Joel, and Joel with Crafco, he knew Joel was expressing the feelings he had as well. As Joel said, "A good pigeon understands his birth order, his responsibilities to the family and to the flock."

In Crafco's case, however there-in lay the problem. Other birds were either born first or second; he had been born third in the same nest, an event that occurred every twenty years or so. Very few understood what a pigeon born in that spot needed to do. So some expected him to act as the first-born, taking on leadership rolls and duties, while others expected him to be the follower, the one being told what to do. The uniqueness of his position, was if he had thought it through, he would understand both sets of feelings. The curse of too much knowledge and not knowing what to do with it or how to deal with it was Crafco's plight. Of course, Lingo's behavior and treatment of him had not helped. The truth was, that Lingo was a bully, a coward, not very confident in who he was and on top of that a very mean spirited bird, especially towards Crafco.

Therefore, Joel surmised from Crafco's inputs that Lingo was scared, and also scarred by the rat incident and as he continued to talk Crafco realized that Lingo was the problem, and that all his mixed feelings towards his older brother were justified. In coming up with that conclusion and the right rationale, it was also justified for to him to take action, concerning Lingo.

He told Joel about what his Mother had told him about being third born. That they seldom made it, that the last two had died before they reached their second week of life; that the wisest of Seers, Oodoo, had told her to treat him like all the rest, to treat him no different, and that Crafco would find his own path. His mother had done her best, from all Crafco could tell, to try to follow that advice, but once she had died all semblance of normalcy had left his life. It seemed as he looked back, that his Father and Lingo had done everything to disrupt it, as he saw it, and because of that, his feelings towards them were anything but affection. Those feelings had also caused him great confusion until today. It seemed that giving them voice had helped justify them and the actions that they dictated he take against Lingo.

The nice thing was that he now had a friend, a bird he could discuss things with; Joel treated him as an equal. Over time, it seemed they could discuss anything. In addition, Joel understood his feelings towards Lingo and even approved of them, saying, "Birds get treated as they treat, and the actions that treatment warranted and whatever happens they bring upon themselves."

'Yes,' Crafco thought, 'I am not responsible for how they treated me, and they created the feelings I am having by their actions towards me. It is entirely their fault that I am feeling this way,' and with that germ of a thought, a plan, started to formulate. When he had first helped Joel out of his predicament, he had not thought of this, now, after having told Joel his story, his feeling of isolation was a full-blown plan of revenge, of eliminating Lingo from his life. As he spoke it aloud to Joel for the first time, Joel nodded his head approvingly, "There you go; let's get rid of that pain. I'll help you." In addition, as they talked, it became more Joel's plan than Crafco's plan. Joel took it over and told Crafco not to worry; he would handle it.

Joel had gone and talked with several of his buddies who loved to harass pigeons or any other birds that flew. "So here is the plan," he told Ajax, Rover, his cousin Jerald and brother Jeremiah. "We chase the light blue check, who will be flying in the air space between the park and the rail yards. You all have met Crafco; he'll be racing along in the same air space. We leave him alone but we harass the one he is racing."

"Can I hurt him a little?" Rover wanted to know with a devilish look in his eye.

"Your idea of hurting something a little comes close to months of hospitalization and rehabilitation," was Jeremiah's response to Rovers request.

To Rover's request Joel responded, ignoring Jeremiah response; "You all can do whatever you want, short of killing him. Remember leave Crafco alone." Rover nodded with a devilish smile on his face as he told Joel he understood. Crafco would be spared, but Lingo was free to be played with as much as he liked.

With that, all agreed, and the plan was in place. Crafco would challenge Lingo to a grudge road race from the park to the rail yards five miles away. It would be just the two of them, Crafco against Lingo. Flying against one another any route they individually chose to fly. The first one back at the Northeast flocks' hall would be the winner. The prize would be their individual nesting sites; the winner would get the loser's nest site. The loser would leave and never return to the Northeast flock ever again.

The plan was a simple one, and Lingo was an easy mark. Crafco had baited him and Lingo had bitten and accepted the challenge. Crafco was surprised at how easy it had been to get Lingo to accept the conditions of the race. Lingo for his part saw it as a done deal. He could out-fly Crafco blindfolded, and just in case, his two best buddies would follow and delay Crafco, assuring Lingo the win and getting Crafco out of his life forever. Yes, Lingo had thought it was all too simple. In one foul swoop, he would be rid of the thorn in his side and become richer with one more nesting site in the process. He waited impatiently for race day, and never thought as to why Crafco had challenged him.

Crafco for his part was a little nervous, and when he told Joel of his uneasiness, Joel had said for Crafco to start flying the race and never to look back. Whatever happened he did not want to be anywhere near to where Lingo was. They had figured Lingo would take the shortest route, and Crafco was to take the second shortest route. Crafco understood and told Joel once the race started he would not look back, only ahead. That became his credo from that day forward, "never look back."

The day of the race arrived. Tin and Tag followed Crafco from the race starting point and about ten minutes into the race started to crisscross Crafco's flight line as a means to slow him down. They did not say much except to yell unkind insensitive comments at him, calling him a slow poke, a loser, SAYING he would never win, and why didn't he just quite, encouraging him to just give up.

The Crows for their part were doing similar things to Lingo. Lingo, however, did not like what the crows were saying and instead of ignoring them started to make derogatory comments in reply to theirs. As is so often the case, Rover, who was spoiling for a reason to attack, was given one in between his eyes when Lingo made a very negative comment about his mother. With that, Rover actually hit Lingo, and when Lingo retaliated, several of the other crows attacked Lingo as well. Before Lingo knew it he was hurt, and then badly hurt. Hurt to the point where he could no longer fly because they had broken his wing. As he had started to fall, they had hit him so hard in the head he was knocked unconscious, from which he never woke as he fell onto the ground and broke his neck.

Crafco fared better than Lingo had; he made it home without bodily injury. When Lingo had not returned at the end of the day, everyone was worried, but it was too dark to go looking for him. The next morning, Crafco and several of Lingo's friends and the flock's outflyers went looking for him. It was not long before several of the outflyers had found Lingo's broken body under the power lines, and had brought it back to the flock's common room.

Crafco was as shocked as all the rest at Lingo's death. This was not what the plan had been; he had wanted Lingo humiliated, to live a life dealing with the shame of having lost. He wanted to see Lingo broken, not dead. Joel had assured him Lingo would not be killed, only hurt. Something had gone terribly wrong. However, as Crafco looked at Lingo's broken body, he realized he did not care. Lingo, the pain in his side, now was forevermore gone, and a part of him relaxed and felt at ease and peace with the whole thing.

As he looked back on it all, he realized meeting Joel had changed his whole life. From that day forward, he gained confidence and it allowed him to come to the realization that he was destined for greater things.

'Where are those two,' he thought, 'they sure have been gone a long time.' When he had arrived over an hour ago, they had almost physically attacked him for being late. They had verbally been on him the minute he had landed, and now an hour later they still were not back. When he had arrived, both stated as one "Where have you been. Thank heaven you're here; we need a drink and food." And with that both were ready to take off.

Crafco asked, "Before you two leave, anything happen over the night while I was gone?"

"No!" Reaper responded. "Several came and several left again, nothing out of the ordinary. Just normal flock-like business," Donkey added to Reaper's "No" response.

"Can we go?" Donkey continued. "We're thirsty and hungry. We've been here all night and you're late. What kept you, where have you been?"

"That, my friend, is none of your business. Go get your nourishment and then come right back," was Crafco's reply. With that, his two cronies took off and he took over the surveillance of the K-Bridge. 'The things you have to put up with as a leader,' he thought, as he watched them flying away. As is so often the case when the mind is doing a mundane task, his mind started to wander and it continued with the thoughts of how he had come to where he was today.

'Yes,' he thought, 'rescuing Joel has indeed changed my life.' It had been the first step towards establishing his current self: the self that was confident and proud, the self that knew what he wanted, the self, which would do whatever it took to for him to fulfill his dreams, his desires. Joel had been Fate's instrument. Joel had been the key to unlocking his potential. Many would say he was evil, but the reality of it was he knew what he wanted and that nothing would stand in his way of achieving his dream. He knew what the majority thought; he had heard the whispers as he walked by, behind his back. "Evil has a name, and it's Crafco." He would chuckle under his breath whenever he heard that. It simply was not true of course; he just knew what he wanted and that was that. Those that had tried to stop him had not succeeded; simply put, fate had not allowed anyone to stop him.

He had been weak, but his alliances with Joel, Talon and Luo had made him virtually unstoppable. The one alliance that scared him the most was his alliance with Ignoble Vile, loyal servant of Oother. Oother was the shadow of pure evil, and Crafco had signed up with him because Vile had promised him the one thing he most desired to become, Ruler of all the rail yard flocks. Of all the alliances large and small, Joel was the start of him finding himself, and because of that distinction, Joel was his favorite.

Thinking back on it, if Joel had not stepped in and taken action against Lingo and taken him out of the picture, he would still be the ineffectual, whimpering, self-doubting bird without a path forward. It had not been easy, for Lingo's friends were suspicious of him and had hounded him day in and day out, following him around and trying to connect him to Lingo's death. At first, he had been scared they would find out his involvement in Lingo's accident and death. He hadn't asked Joel to do it, but never the less he hadn't discouraged Joel from his original plan of slowing down Lingo and bringing him down. He was not sure where the plan had gone wrong, but the end result was that Lingo had died.

Tag and Tin had been Lingo's best friends. They had watched him mercilessly from the day of the race onward, and they had kept him under surveillance because of their suspicions. They had kept him under surveillance like a pair of spies, keeping him isolated from the majority of the flock by spreading rumors and through innuendo that he was somehow involved with Lingo's death. And even though many knew that the two of them had followed Crafco on race day, it did not seem to deter many from believing them, that somehow Crafco was involved because he had the most to gain.

Tag and Tin were identical twins in color, body type and disposition. They were a rare occurrence in the pigeon worlds;

identical twin were almost as unusual an incident as were three eggs to a nest. Because of their rareness they were often listened to where others would not have been; they had a mystic quality about them that caused many to believe them at their word. After a morning of relentless harassing by them, Crafco had flow to the stream in the hopes of meeting Joel. The sky was gray and overcast, reflecting his mood of discontent and unhappiness with being hounded by the brothers.

He had arrived at the stream to find no Joel. He landed and got a drink of water and had started picking at small grains of rock and minerals when he heard a rustling amongst the leaves and reeds on the far shore. It was in the same area along the streams shore where he had rescued the trapped Joel several months earlier. Thinking it might be Joel trying to sneak up on him he headed towards the noise. "Joel, is that you?" No response, "Joel come on out. I need to talk to you," he said as he approached the noise.

He jumped up on the rocks overlooking the weeded area between the rocks and the vertical banks. 'Nothing,' he thought, 'how strange.' He could have sworn he had heard noise coming from there. He saw something shiny lying on the ground in an area where the weeds had been trampled and packed flat. The shiny spot pequed his curiosity and he jumped down from his vantage point and headed to examine the shiny spot, to discover it was a spot of blood. The little bit of sunlight had caught it just right and sent its silvery reflection up to his eye. Upon further investigation, there were several more blood spots close by the first. Someone or something had been laying here and that someone had been hurt. 'I better be careful; maybe I should leave,' he thought. And just as he was having this thought, he heard a noise behind him, and he turned and there sitting on the rock where he had been standing moments before stood a Screech Hunter. "Well, well," it said, "The Great Creator does provide," with a slight smile on its face.

"Hello, my survival, my strength, my energy. What's your name?" it asked.

Crafco was scared, and his legs were starting to shake involuntarily. 'What to do,' he thought.

"Come, my little plump pigeon, at least do me the honor of allowing one to know your name so I can do you proper homage and give proper thanks to the Great Creator for bringing you my way." With that, the Screech Hunter moved slightly to realign his balance and when it did, Crafco noticed the grimace of pain that crossed its face. It was hurt, the blood on the ground was its own. 'A hurt Screech Hunter,' Crafco thought. 'So that was the cause for the blood and the trampled weeds.'

The Screech Hunter gave Crafco a leeringly cool smile, as if he knew Crafco's thoughts, "Even hurt, you are no match for me. I am still faster than you could ever imagine in your wildest dreams. So, just tell me your name or I'll just have to kill you without knowing."

Crafco thought, 'think, what Joel would do?' Be resourceful, he would have said; you're never dead until you stop breathing.' "Look," Crafco spoke out loud, buying time to think, "you don't want to kill me. I'd only feed you for a day or two and in your condition, you would still need to heal, have sufficient food, or you would die." The more Crafco talked and saw the look of that reality appear on the screech hunter's face, the more confidence he gained. "It would be weeks until you could hunt and without being able to hunt you would die. You'd starve to death as it were." Crafco stated putting emphasis on the word death.

"Maybe there is some truth in what you say, my little meal. But, at least I'd have three days of food that you could provide, and anything can happen in three days," was its calculated response to Crafco's comments about its well-being. "I do appreciate your concerns about my survival, but as I said earlier, three day of food is better than none. And who knows, maybe I could have you last me four days, if I sucked the marrow out of your bones!" It said with a certain amount of glee.

"Look!" said Crafco, with a great deal of concern in his voice, "I can bring you food on a regular basis, like several times a week," he paused, waited a second then continued, "until you get better."

"Really, several times a week? How do you intend to do that? I do not eat grains, I eat meat. You are a grain eater. How do you plan to supply me with what I need?"

As the Screech Hunter was talking, a rough plan had started to formulate in the darkest recesses of Crafco's mind. Now only if he could articulate that whiff of a thought well enough to get the Screech Hunter to accept it or even consider it. "I can bring you meat," Crafco said with bravado and confidence he did not really feel but still brought forth in his voice.

The Screech Hunter lifted his right eyebrow and shook his head, "no" and gave Crafco a sly smile. "Do I look like I was born yesterday? I let you go and you will never return, and then where am I? I'm really dead, that's where I am," he responded to his own question.

"No, let me explain," said Crafco "I have several enemies, and I'll bring you a pigeon later today that you can kill and eat. You would be helping me make my life easier, and I'd be helping you by bringing you fresh meat, as it were," he finished, as a shiver ran down his spine at the thought, the image, his voice created in his mind.

The Screech Hunter did not seem to comprehend what had been said at first, for he showed no reaction; he just stared at Crafco, as if he were looking right through him; or maybe a better description would be to say, as if he were trying to look into Crafco's soul. The look was one of piercing dissection. Then he quietly said, as if adding emphases to his words, "Really, a very interesting proposition. You'd bring me a fresh bird?" Pausing as if thinking through his next comment, he then continued, "A bird a day? A question for you to ponder, what would prevent you from ever returning, once I allowed you to leave? You know I'm hurt and I couldn't follow you and hunt you down."

"Yes, I guess you'd have to trust me a little. By the way, it would not be every day, but every fourth day or so. I could arrange it and you could help me get rid of some thorns in my side. And I could help you get better in the process," Crafco responded, with more confidence than he had felt when the Screech Hunter had first confronted him. The fact that the hawk had even listened meant that Crafco had won in part. As Joel had so often said, "if anyone stops long enough to listen, you have gained some ground. You had in essence given yourself the opportunity to win."

"Interesting, very interesting," the hawk said, as it rubbed its chin directly under its sharp hook like beak. "But how do I know you'd keep your word?" Of course that was both of their dilemmas, the Screech Hunter's and Crafco's; how did he know that Crafco would keep his word and how did Crafco know the hawk would not turn on him now or at a later date or time.

Crafco had the answer; it was the truth, one of those times in his life when telling the whole truth would save his life. With passion and a little edge of angry emotion in his voice, he said, "Because I have several tormentors and I'm sick and tired of them, and I don't have the means to make them stop. However, with your help, your talents, and skills I do. Because I don't want to die when there is so much I still want to do, don't you see?"

Again, the Screech Hunter raised an eyebrow, which Crafco later learned was a sign that it was thinking and digesting the information it had just been given, especially on major decisions of importance.

"Okay! My name is Talon. Seeing how we are going to become partners in this you should know my name," Talon said.

Crafco gave a sigh of relief and said, "Great, I'll be going then."

"Wait just a minute, my impatient new friend. What's your name? And what is your plan?" Talon said with a little surprise in his voice as he had moved to block Crafco's path for leaving.

"Sorry, forgot, little nervous you know," Crafco said shyly. "My Name is Crafco, and my plan is simple. I'll bring the birds with me here and that is the one you are to take. I'll bring them into this clearing area and then you jump them from ambush. You can't fly, can you?"

Talon responded, "No, I can't fly at present. Still, from ambush that seems so dishonorable. It feels like I would be a thief. I think I should just confront them and then take their life so they know what's about to happen."

"Look," Crafco said, "You aren't able to do this in your condition unless you attack from cover. At least the first one or two; once you have your strength back, you can do it your way. And besides, when you attack in the air, you attack from cover; you use the clouds and the sun, don't you?" He did not wait for a response and continued; he felt he was on a roll. "Of course you do, why? Because it gives you the advantage, it assures you a greater chance for success. Well this is no different, but because of your debilitated condition, it makes it ten times more important that you succeed with your first strike. Because if you miss and they get away my life would really be over, especially if anyone found out how I was involved. So I cannot afford for you to miss, to fail. Understand?" Crafco said with more force then he had intended.

Talon looked at Crafco, if he had had any doubts about Crafco's commitment they were washed away by Crafco's little speech of why he had to do it a certain way. "Okay, let's discuss the particulars of your plan a little further." With that said, the two discussed the plan and then choreographed the entire attack scenario. They walked-through the attack sequence more than once and with each walk through, they refined who would do what until both felt that there could be no other outcome but success. When Crafco finally left to lure in the first victim they had what was to happen down pat, each knew what the other was to do and both were confident that the only outcome would be Talon's triumph over the victim. Once they had talked about the plan to the minutest of detail Crafco left.

He knew what he wanted to do and whom he wanted to do it to, just 'how' was the question. He would get rid of his main problem birds, Tag and Tin. As he flew to the Northeast flock's rousting and nesting areas, he hoped the first bird he would meet would be Tag. He disliked Tag more than Tin, and Tag was the smarter of the two and so in Crafco's mind the more dangerous. If he could get Tag to bite on his story he knew he could easily get the rest of Lingo's old crowd to fall for his story as well. As he formulated the story, he also realized the Screech hunter was week from his injuries and Tag was young and strong. He would need to have the first kill by Talon be a bird of lesser strength, of lesser youth; he would need to pick one of the flock that was older. It seemed the fates must have been smiling down on him that day because the first bird he encountered as he landed was Tag. Maybe his plan would have to change, because fate demanded it.

"Tag! Tag!" Crafco shouted in an excited, enthusiastic voice when he saw him, "I need to talk to you." As he approached Tag, he said in a quieter and calm voice, "I've found evidence as to what happened to Lingo. I need you to help me with it. I need you to hear what a crow saw."

"Why should I, Crafco? You know I believe it's all your doing what happened to Lingo." was Tag's cold and nonchalant response.

"I know what you believe, and that's why I need you to come with me so you can hear it for yourself and know that I had nothing to do with Lingo's death. I've found a crow that saw it all and he's willing to talk to just one other bird of the Northeast and tell his story," was Crafco's response.

"Why me, Crafco?" was Tag's cautious question. "Why not one of the major flock leaders?"

"Because if you believe him, being Lingo's number one best friend, you can tell the others and then you can all leave me alone, that's why. And then maybe I can have some peace and get on with my life," was Crafco's pleading in an almost whiny voice. "Please!"

"Okay!" he said, "Wait here, I'll be right back." With that instruction, Tag left Crafco standing and wondering where he was going and for what purpose, Crafco did not have to wait long for an answer, a few minutes later Tag returned with Tin in tow. Tin gave Crafco a sheepish but at the same time an arrogant look.

"Let's go!" Tag said in a very demanding voice. "Let's go meet this crow you supposedly found."

The three took off, with Tag and Tin following closely behind Crafco. Crafco's mind was racing. 'This is not good,' he thought, 'an unhurt Screech Hunter could have handled both Tag and Tin, but a hurt one, and the way Talon had looked when he had left him…' "Hey, are you listening to us at all?" Tin yelled, getting Crafco's attention, "Where are we going?" he finished.

"To an area by the stream, follow me." Crafco responded, and with that he picked up his speed. His mind went back to the earlier problem it had been occupied with. 'In Talons condition he'd be lucky to take out one healthy young pigeon, let alone a pair,' he thought. 'Oh well, all I can hope for is that he will see what is happening and not respond. And then I'll have to go back later with an alternate victim… what's a pigeon to do, with the best laid plan as it were… even they get diverted and altered. If this goes wrong …' and his mind raced and reeled at all the possible scenarios of what the consequences would be for him, and he was scared all over again. If this failed, he would be forever harassed and disbelieved. He would be an outcast; he would be hated and mistrusted. He saw nothing but disaster and his own demise if what he had planned to do with Talon failed. As seemed to be so often the case in his life events were overtaking his plans and all he felt was dread and anxiety about what he was doing and in what he perceived could happen. He said a little prayer to the Great Creator as the threesome flew to the stream, and to one of their deaths. However, the die had been cast and there was no turning back now. To say it was a little joke or mistake would have been worse than finishing and not having the plan be fulfilled.

Crafco led and the other two followed. When they got to the spot in the stream where they were supposed to land, Crafco made several circles and pointed out the sandy bank along the stream where they should land. The others followed his lead as he made a circular flight pattern and then landed.

Upon landing with a distrustful look in his eyes, Tag asked, "So where's this crow?"

Crafco ignored the look and the sarcastic tone to Tag's voice and yelled, "James, where are you?" all the while thinking, "Do not respond, don't respond.' It seemed like an hour, but in reality was only about ten seconds when a response came from the opposite bank.

"I'm here behind the rocks. You know I cannot talk to you out there, in the open. And who are those two with you? We agreed there would only be one. I have a reputation to maintain, you know."

Crafco started to respond, but Tin took over instead, "Look buddy, we didn't fly out here to play games. We know crows and pigeons do not normally talk. We are no more interested or in favor of this than you are, but we want to know what happened to our friend Lingo. Crafco here says you saw what happened to him on the day he died. Is that true?"

"Yep, I believe I did," said the disembodied voice, "I'm not going to shout out my story, nor am I going to tell you out in the open for all to see or stumble upon us. I have a reputation to maintain. So you had better come over here." There was no response from the three pigeons. The two looked at each other and when they looked at Crafco, he just shrugged his shoulders. "Well?" asked the voice after a minute of silence.

Tin looked at Tag. "I don't like this, it doesn't feel right." Both leered at Crafco, who responded to their inquisitive, irritated looks, with "Let's just go and get out of here, it's not that important."

However, the bait had been thrown out, the line was being tugged, and like a hungry fish, Tag took the bait. "You stay here and I'll go. Watch my back then," he said to Tin. "Come on Crafco, you come with me. You lead the way." 'If anything bad comes out of this,' Tag thought, 'you'll be in the lead,' as he motioned to Crafco to go, 'and if there are any surprises they will happen to you first.'

Crafco led the way; he jumped and flew across the stream and landed on the far bank with Tag right behind him. Then he walked over to the rocks and jumped up onto them, looked around, and then jumped down into the grasses in the little clearing beyond the rocks. Tag mimicked Crafcos moves and stayed on his heels the whole time. Once they were in the clearing, they noticed the black feathers strewn about and the blood.

"What is this?" Tag asked with fear in his voice. Crafco too was scared and the look on his face caused Tag to realize that Crafco also was totally surprised by what they saw. This heightened his fear even further, but before Tag could respond to Crafco's look and his own fear and flight response there was a flurry of motion behind Crafco. Before Tag comprehended or could react to what was happening, he saw Crafco being shoved out of the way and he saw the Screech Hunter's sharp beak and meat hook like claws coming towards him. "No!" escaped his lips in a loud last gasp. Before he could react, he felt the claws digging into the flesh of his chest and then the pain and the disbelief registered in his mind. 'I'm dead,' he thought for only a split second, as the Screech Hunters beak severed the vertebrae that held his head to his neck.

Tin, who had concerns, a nagging 'feather at the nape of the neck' feeling that this was not right, had started to follow Tag and Crafco. Just as he had taken a half a dozen steps, Tin had heard his brother cry out, had heard the fear in his brother's voice but not the exact words, and he had reacted and flown over to the rocks. He touch landed there for only a few seconds as his mind had registered what his eyes were seeing: Crafco being attacked and shoved and his brother being knocked over by a Screech Hunter. He saw the beak and the claws and the flurry of motion, heard the scream, and saw the blood shoot out from Tag's chest and saw the head being severed and then the body of his brother fall limply to ground at the killer's feet. He saw all that in seconds, then his instincts took over and he fled.

Crafco, had been shoved, knocked down and rolled head over heels to the opposite end of the little grassy clearing. He had hit his head and was a little woozy and completely surprised at what had happened. He had heard and not seen any of Tags demise, but he had seen Tin. He had not seen him land on the rocks, but he had seen his shock and his blurred, flurried rise to escape.

Crafco didn't think either; he reacted, and his instincts took over as he also took to the air. Flying a little erraticly, he flew a short distance to the other side of the stream and ran as he hit the ground and hid under a bush. He had not expected to see what he had seen; the blood, the look of terror on Tag's face just seconds before he was decapitated lingered in his mind. He realized he was shaking uncontrollably. His forehead hurt and as he felt it with his wing, he noticed a bump and that he had a small cut, because when he brought his wing down he saw a little blood on it. 'Damn!' he thought. 'Why had Talon been so rough on him and why had he attacked from behind Crafco, rather than from behind Tag? It had not worked the way they had planned it and choreographed it. 'So now what,' he thought. 'Slow down', he told himself, 'let your head clear,' He waited a few minutes, trying not to think about any of it. And as he waited to gain some semblance of control, Tin flew over to where he was hiding under the bush and in a very excited voice directed Crafco, "Crafco, come on, get out from under there. We need to get out of here." Tin, who normally was a very arrogant, in-control pigeon was anything but. "We need to get out of here before it comes after us. Come on, will you?" Therefore, Crafco accommodated Tin's urgent plea, and they took off together.

As was common amongst most herd animals of all types, once the hunter had made its kill, they ran to find safety. The Great Creator had determined the routine and train of thoughts; be thankful it wasn't you, find safety, and pray for the victim and then go on with life. Count yourself lucky and muorn the dead, but go on with life.

Tin and Crafco were flying as fast as they could in an attempt to escape the images in their minds almost as much as their fear that the killer would pursue them and do to them what he had done to Tag. Crafco, flying more at Tin's insistence rather than out of fear for his life, was now back in control and knew it had actually gone better than they had planned. When they got to the Northeast flock's meeting area they reported what had happened to Shamus, their new flock leader. Shamus sent for Oonal and the rest of the council so they could all hear what had happened. Once they all arrived, Tin retold his story of what had happened. They all listened intently to his story and at the end, they snorted in disbelief.

Shamus looked at Crafco and asked him if he had anything to add. Crafco started to tremble a little as he thought of what had happened, at how quickly Talon had attacked and killed Tag. Even hurt, the Screech Hunter had been agile and quicker than Crafco would have ever expected. Just to thinking of how close he had been to meeting that same fate had started him trembling. All believed that his physical reaction was based on the shock of it all, but in reality, it was all instinct and an involuntary reaction to what he had done. Had seen and how much better it had turned out. They took his shaking as a sign of fear and shock, instead it was a reaction of his joy at how well it had gone. It was his reaction in not trying to smile or even laugh aloud at his triumph over Tag. "No, I have nothing to add." Crafco said with a quivering voice.

"Of course he can't. He was knocked down and almost unconscious when I arrived. If I hadn't yelled at him to get up, he'd be the second victim of that Screech Hunter's deadly attack," Tin interjected before Crafco could respond further. Crafco looked at Shamus and then at Oonal. "No, he's right. I was rolling along the ground and nearly knocked unconscious by the attacker."

With that, Shamus and Oonal let them go and thanked them for reporting what had happened. The news of the attack spread throughout the rest of the flock like a wild fire, as did the restrictions placed on anyone going to that section of the stream until it could be determined where the Screech Hunter was or whether it had moved on or was it making that area of the stream its nesting site.

Crafco had left Tin at the public meeting place and gone to his nesting area to get some rest. Until he was in the seclusion of his private place, he did not smile, but once there he could not help but chuckle to himself and be very pleased with what had happened and how well it had all really gone. It had gone perfectly, even better than he had thought it could go in his wildest dreams. Tin telling the story of what had happened had sold it and he did not even have to explain why they had gone. In Tin's excitement, he had left that out, and none had asked. It had gone perfectly, just perfectly. He was not suspected of anything and he was rid of one of the main tormentors in his life.

However, where had the black feathers and blood come from? Had Joel accidentally walked into the trap? He was worried about that possibility, but he knew he could not do anything about it now. He would have to wait until the day after tomorrow before he could go to that section of the stream again.

The rest of that day and the next went by mostly uneventfully, except for the whispering. It had not decreased but instead it had increased every time he walked by any group. Everywhere he went he heard the whispering and it was driving him crazy because he did not know what they were saying. Then on the second day, a black check came up and introduced himself to Crafco.

"Hi! My name is Donkey. You really fought off a Screech Hunter trying to save Tag?" Donkey asked.

"Where did you hear that nonsense?" Crafco asked

"It's what everyone is saying. It's true isn't it?" Was Donkey's response. Crafco did not respond and Donkey took that to mean yes. He then asked, to Crafco's surprise, "Can I hang out with you, can I be your friend?"

Crafco was taken aback by the question. No one had ever wanted to be associated with him, let alone be considered his friend. Never having been in this situation before, he shook his head yes and gained a shadow named Donkey. At first, he was faltered, but as the day turned to night, his shadow was still there and when he got up the next morning, there was Donkey waiting for him, which caused him some concern at first, but over time, Crafco liked having a servant. For the next day, Donkey hung out with Crafco, trying to anticipate Crafco's needs and wants and then trying to fulfill them before Crafco could even ask or know he had the need. Anything Crafco asked, Donkey did. In addition, when he went to his roost, Donkey went and stayed outside in the main hall all night. On the morning of the fourth day there he was. "Donkey, you been here all night?" Crafco asked him.

Donkey shook his head 'yes' in response to Crafco's question. "Why?" Crafco asked.

"Because you're lucky and I want to be your friend and hopefully some of your luck will rub off onto me."

"You're crazy," was Crafco's response, "But okay, Donkey." Crafco continued, "You stay here and watch my nest sight and roosting spots. I will be back after a while. Is that alright with you?"

"Sure, Boss! I'll stay and guard your stuff. I'll stay," was Donkey's reply to Crafco's request, and so from that day forward Donkey became Crafco's lackey.

As it had happened, from one day to the next, Crafco went from being a nobody to being a pigeon that had a loyal admirer, and from all appearances and actions a devoted one at that. Crafco left to go to the stream, and he needed to go alone. He was not ready to share his secrets with Donkey or anyone, a wise decision that would pay off in triplicate later on in Crafco's life.

As he flew to the stream he was wondering what he would find there. Would it be a field of blood and guts and feathers and bits of uneaten flesh? He was trying to steel his mind to what he might possibly find. The one thing he did not want to do in front of Talon was act shocked and weak. All sorts of pictures of what he thought he might find at the grassy clearing between the rocks ran through his mind. He had not really wanted to go. He had promised Talon he would be there today, and he felt that Talon could be a valued ally in the future. A resource that he could not squander and would need access to and could use and exploit for his own benefit in the future.

When he got there, he landed at the pools by the sandy bank of the stream, stopped and got a good drink of water. He then flew to the rocks that overlooked the grassy area, and to his amazement the area was relatively clean. The grass was trampled flat, but there was only a few dark spots here and there where the blood had dried. Other than that, the area looked clean and natural; there were no real signs of the death that had occurred there four days before. He hopped down from the rocks and found nothing; no bones, no feathers, no remains. He found none of the things he had imagined he'd find. 'Amazing,' he thought, 'how different than what I had envisioned,' As he was absorbed in his private thoughts, a noise from behind him brought him back into the present. As he turned, there behind him stood Talon, looking better than he had the last time Crafco had seen him.

"Hello Talon, how are you?" Crafco said with a little surprise in his voice.

"Well!" Talon said, "Fine! Surprised at how clean I look?"

"How did you know that's what I was thinking?" Crafco asked.

"It's easy; by your actions, of course, and your facial expression of shock and wonder. It always surprises me how herd creatures always seem so surprised when the hunter can predict their actions. That is what makes us the hunters. We survive by being able to read what our prey is about to do. We learn to look for the subtle signs of weakness, slowness, confusion or anything that will give us the advantage. It is how we must be or we would die. Well, how did it go? Did they blame you in any way or did they believe you that it was a random act? A 'wrong place at the wrong time' type of situation for Tag? Well?" Talon queried.

"Yes, they believed us. Tin gave his account of what he saw and I did not really have to confirm or deny it. How did you set it up that way, with the crow feathers and all? You didn't kill a crow did you?"

"Are you kidding me? In the condition I'm in, I was lucky to have been able to take down that pigeon friend of yours," Talon said sarcastically. "If it hadn't been for the fact I caught him by total surprise it could have turned out quite differently," Talon stated matter of factually, and then continued, "But it worked out remarkably well for all concerned I'd say. Well, maybe not for all," Talon said as he pulled a flight feather that had belonged to Tag out from under his wing. One out of six," He said to Crafco.

"If you pull it off I'd be in your debt for a long time, I'd be your loyal servant, or is that 'ally', as it were."

They talked and made plans, and Crafco wanted to know where Talon had gotten the black feathers from; Talon explained that he had laid a trap and had caught a black bird, who had been so kind as to have donated its feathers to his cause.

So it had gone; Tag's girlfriend and Tin's girlfriend and then some of Lingo's other buddies had all contributed to the cause and with their generous donations, Talon had gained his strength back. Crafco had gotten rid of his main opposition and tormentors at that time, and he had gained prominence within the flock. Talon had gotten his strength back and had told Crafco if he ever needed a favor all he had to do was give the sign. Talon gave Crafco one of his feathers and told him to place it at the top of the smoke stack and then Talon would know he needed him, and he would then meet him here at the grassy clearing.

Yes, Talon had been a great recourse and ally over the years. They had become friends of sorts, cautious friends, but whenever Crafco needed his help Talon had obliged. He had helped dispose of several of Crafco's major concerns and foes. Talon had always been there and had served him without question.

His mind wandered back to what he was doing. 'Well, well,' he thought, 'no Mosaic for over a day now, as reported by Donkey and Reaper, and so far this morning no sign of him either.' Interestingly enough no pepper colored grizzle as well. The lingering question, the question he wanted answered, where was that young upstart Mosaic; could this mean that Mosaic was gone or dead or hurt or what? He would have Reaper and Donkey stake out the bridge for at least another week before he made his move, but so far, it looked as if it was going to be easier than he had thought. He had it planned and the only rough spot he had envisioned was how to deal with Mosaic.

Donkey and Reaper finally returned. Crafco then asked them several additional questions. "When was the last time you saw either the one called Mosaic? Or the pepper-colored grizzle?" he asked.

Both looked at each other, as if the other would have a better idea. They acted as if neither had been spying on the bridge for two weeks now. They shrugged at each other, and then had a semi-private conversation as if Crafco was not there. After a short debate between them, they came to an agreement that it had been at least two weeks since they could remember seeing the grizzle. "And when was the last time you saw Mosaic?" Crafco asked again.

This time they looked at each other, and again conferred, "A couple of days ago at the pools," replied Donkey. "We asked Rambler how Mosaic was, and he said he was fine, and that we had just missed him and pointed to a pigeon flying high in the sky heading this way."

"Could you recognize him?" Crafco asked.

Donkey and Reaper answered in unison, "Well, no, not really. We could not see clearly that it was him. He was pretty far away, but Rambler had said it was him and had pointed him out." Without hesitation, they said, "and why would Rambler lie?"

Crafco asked very patiently as an adult would talk to a young child, "I know. But when was the last time either one of you saw him with your own eyes so you could recognize him, like with you own eyes?" he asked in a slow even l keeled voice.

"Now that you ask it that way, at least two maybe three weeks ago. I think it was the last time we actually saw the pepper colored grizzle as well, now that I think about," Reaper replied to Crafco's latest question. Donkey shook his head yes the whole time Reaper had been responding to the question.

Crafco smiled. 'Yes,' he thought, 'my plan will work quite well. In a couple of more days I'll be flock leader of the K-Bridge and with one swoop of Luo's raid, I'll be rid of all current residents of the bridge and several other possible adversaries as well.' Crafco gave instruction as to what he wanted Donkey and Reaper to do, which was nothing but watch the bridge, and said he would be back tomorrow. With that instruction given, he flew off into the afternoon sky.

'Yes,' he thought as he flew along, 'life is going to get a lot better for me really soon.' All he had to do was work the plan and make sure that all the participants, both willing and unwilling, were where they were supposed to be and all would work out in his favor. Crafco flew along and alone, very content with himself and life. He was finally going to get what he deserved, his own flock to lead, and area to manipulate and control.

Interesting Pigeon Fact

The pigeon can also recognise all 26 letters of the English language as well as being able to conceptualise.

http://www.pigeoncontrolresourcecentre.org/html/amazing-pigeon-facts.html#how_old

Chapter 4

The three companions had found refuge from the severe windstorm at the grain storage silos and had spent the night listening to the wind howl like a hungry wolf trying to find a meal. At first light Moth was the first one up, she had been the first one to fall asleep the night before. She got up to a ravenous appetite. Therefore, she had gone looking for something to eat and had found a large pile of uneaten maize. She had also found a tube of cool water, flown to its edge, and taken a long drink. After this, she returned to the roasting area just as Mosaic, Trapper and several of the locals were waking and getting up.

"Morning you two." Moth said, "Time to get up. Get yourselves something to eat and then we can be off. Time it is a wasting."

"Did you find food? And, some cool water to drink?" Trapper asked as he stretched his legs and then wings over his legs; first his left-wing and then, his right one and he yawned as he did this, saying "Because I'm hungry and I could use a good drink of water as well."

"Yes, I did. There is a whole pile of uneaten maize at the back of the silos. Plenty for everyone and then some, I'd say." Moth said in response to Trappers questions.

"You don't mean the pile of white corn, do you?" a blue check, local asked with concern in his voice.

"Well, yea! I suppose some of it was white corn, why?" Was Moth's response to the blue check that had asked the question.

"Several birds that have eaten that seed have gotten sick. As a matter of fact, none have been seen since they have eaten the corn. I suggest you make yourself throw up, purge yourself of those seeds, and get a good drink of water and go find a good healer and hope you don't get ill."

"Are you saying those birds died?" Mosaic interjected.

"Could be." Said the blue check, as he shrugged his shoulder in a gesture of who knows.

"Yep, some have never been seen again," restated the blue bar white flight sitting next to him.

"Better safe than sorry I always say," finished the blue check as a closing comment to his earlier statement, with a concerned look on his face.

With that, warning Moth flew to the ground, stuck her left flight feather down her throat, and proceeded to throw up all the food she had eaten less than fifteen minutes earlier. Then she flew over to the water tube and drank, then flew back to the ground and proceeded to doing the sticking of her flight feather down her throat. She did this again and again retched up the water she had just drunk. She repeated this revolting cycle several more times. She then, flew back up to where Trapper and Mosaic were sitting and watching. Both had gotten queasy stomachs as they watched her retching up her food and water.

"Watching someone throwing up isn't my idea of starting my day off on the right foot. But that doesn't deter my hunger and thirst," Trapper said looking at Moth with concern and with a little gleam of mischief in his eye, "And nothing is going to keep me from taking the time to eat and get a good drink of water. Want to join me?" he offered to both Moth and Mosaic as he flew down to the field adjacent to the silos.

Mosaic and Moth followed Trapper; they flew down to the ground near to where Trapper was eating grass and weed seeds. After they had eaten their fill, with Moth looking for the small pebbles of minerals that could help settle her stomach. When all three were full, the three flew over to the water tube's edge and got a long drink of water before heading out on their journey once again.

"How are you feeling?" Trapper asked Moth after they had finished getting their drink. "Do you think we should ask where we can find a local healer?" he asked

"I feel fine." Was her response to Trapper's questions, "My crop is a little queasy, but nothing to worry about" she said with confidence to dispel Mosaic's look of angst.

"Looking at you two, one would think I was dead already. By the looks on your faces, I would say you do not believe me. Let's go!" She said as she ascended into the clear light blue sky and made one circular pass over their heads. "What are you two waiting on, a better invitation?"

They looked at each other, shrugged their shoulders, "I guess she should know how she is feeling," was Trapper's response to Mosaics continued look of concern.

"Okay! Let's go then." Mosaic said to Trapper as they both took off to join Moth in the sky above the silos. Nevertheless, Mosaic did not feel the confidence that he used as he spoke the words and joined his sister. The three made one final pass over the silos and then headed south again on their journey to try to rescue the rest of Mosaic's and Moth's family and flock.

They had been flying for about an hour and a half and were well within the mountains when Moth said, "I feel bad, that she needed to land." As they landed, she got sick again, and threw up until she was having the dry heaves. She said she needed water. Mosaic and Trapper looked at each other; there was only one place; either of them knew about, but it was fifteen minutes from where they were currently located. They explained to Moth about the lake and asked her could she hold out and make it until they could get there. She said she could, "What choice do I have?" she asked

None; was the unspoken response from her two companions, so the three of them took of heading for the lake. What under normal conditions would have taken only fifteen minutes, took them more than thirty minutes in Moth's current condition. Upon landing at the lake, she threw up and what she regurgitated did not look normal. It was a strange sage green-yellow color thick pasty like substance and it smelled like dead decaying flesh.

They both looked at her with great alarm. She looked bad; her eyes were not clear and bright anymore. Her Cere at her beak was normally a bright white, but was now a sickly gray in appearance and her nostril had a pinkish glow to it. In addition, her eye ring, which was also normally white, was an even sicklier looking greenish gray in appearance. She definitely looked really bad.

They watched her stumble over to the water's edge, where she took a long drink of water, smiled, and instantly, turned and threw it all up. Again, what she regurgitated was not just liquid, but the same pasty substance. She made these drinking attempts several times with the same results, after the twelfth time she was very emaciated, and she just lay there unable to move.

Trapper and Mosaic felt helpless, what were they to do? Here was their companion, their friend, his sister, who appeared to be dying and they were helpless. Each asked the other what they could do; nether knew anything about healing, about herbs, tonics or potions. Moth finally moved and in a parched hoarse voice said, "I can't seem to keep any water down."

"What can we do?" Trapper asked in response to her statement. Mosaic asked, "Moth, what can we do to help you? You know a little bit about healing is there anything we can do?" Moth did not seem to have heard either of them. Mosaic who was frantic walked over to where Moth was lying, and gently shook her. "Moth, you've got to help us; you know some healing stuff, what can we do to help you? Moth, please, don't die, Moth help us! You have to try. So many are depending on us, you just can't give up on me or them." Referring to the birds needing to be rescued or maybe, it was the tone in Mosaic's voice or the fact that so many were depending on them and her; that she found the strength to direct them, she said, "Find me some moss and bring it to me. Please!" Moth said in a barely audible voice. With these instructions, Mosaic flew to a cluster of rocks, with Trapper in tow. "What's moss?" he asked Mosaic

"It's this green slimy stuff that's growing on the rocks at the water line and just below it." Mosaic explained as he started gathering it. Trapper followed suit and started gathering the dry moss from the rocks and boulder further up the shoreline. They each gathered a mouthful and flew back to where Moth was, "I'll need at least ten times that much," she said as she placed it into the water next to her. She asked for more, with that they left her to go gather more moss. They made six more trips each before Moth told them she had enough.

They then sat back and watched her place all the moss into the lakes water and then when it was good and wet and slimy they watched her eat it all. She gulped it down in pieces that you would have thought would have choked her but to their amazement it didn't. She also did not throw any of it up, and in a short span of time, maybe twenty minutes she was on her feet and looked energized. "Let's go," she said, "this will only last so long." With that said she took to the air and started heading south at a remarkable speed for a bird that had looked emaciated such a short time earlier. Mosaic and Trapper were hard pressed at first to keep up with her pace. It was as if she had the devil on her tail and was trying to out fly it. Mosaic and Trapper both tried to get her to slow down a little and conserve her energy, but her response had been that while she had it she should cover as much air space as possible. However, within twenty minutes Moth's pace had slowed considerably, her body was shaking just a little, and within another twenty minutes, she was throwing up green slime as they flew.

The shaking got worse as they flew south, and every time she was done going through the shakes, she would throw up more of the green slimy mossy solution. It was not long before they exited the mountain pass and were heading south along the same path that Mosaic and Trapper had taken weeks before. Moth was not doing so well in her attempt to fly and keep up a decent pace; in fact, Trapper and Mosaic had slowed the pace way down, and had started circling Moth as they flew along. They had slowed down to the point where they were not making any real progress southward.

It soon became apparent that she would have to land or fall from the sky from fatigue. She definitely could not go on anymore and she pointed to the ground. She then descended and landed and stumbling along the ground in a vacant lot adjacent to the main concert man-made river.

Mosaic and Trapper landed next to her and with great concern in Trapper voice asked, "How are you doing? You really look bad. Can you go on? At least make it to the shade tree." He finished.

Moth shook her head yes, but her actions said no. She tried to walk forward and take off to fly again and she stumbled and fell over. There she lay on her side, in the hot sun unable to move, looking very exhausted. Panting for every breath and saying, "I need a drink of water. I need something cool to drink. I need my mother." She said in a small child like voice. After which she closed her eyes and just lay there very still, panting, laboring for every breath of air and then her panting stopped and her breathing became very shallow and slight, so slight you could barely see her chest moving.

Mosaic thought, 'she has died.' Trapper thought, 'she has passed out.' Each asked the other what should we do? They answered each other by agreeing that moving her into the shade would be a good thing to do. They tried to move her into the shade of a nearby tree; they tried, but could not lift her. However, they could support her if they could persuade her to help. With much persuasion and with her help they supported her, and she half walked and they half carried her, half dragged her into the shade. All three collapsed in the shade of the tree. As they had been struggling to get Moth into the shade, several pigeons had flown overhead, all heading south.

Trapper and Mosaic sat down next to Moth, exhausted and they rested watching Moth's shallow breathing, each deep in his own thoughts.

"She doesn't look good at all, Trapper thought. I hope she doesn't die, if she does I hope Mosaic can deal with it and that we can continue with our rescue trip. However, he thought, it would be really difficult without her directing them; did they have enough information to continue? She had given them a lot of good information and directions, but not in enough detail in his mind for them to find the pet store without her. He sighed inwardly, guessing the entire rescue is in jeopardy. 'Well,' he thought, I guess we need to pray, and with that Trapper started to plead, in a silently prayer to the Great Creator to spare Moths life.

Mosaic was thinking almost the same thoughts as Trapper, except he was trying to think of what he could do to ensure that Moth did not die. 'What to do,' he thought. Looking at her lying there, she did not look good. Her breathing had evened out and she seemed to have stopped perspiring, but he knew she would need liquid soon. The question was where to get it and how to get it to her, and those were the two problems he felt he needed to solve immediately. He knew she could not get to water in her current condition. He also knew he didn't know where there was any water close by, and the more he thought about it the more hopeless it seemed. Every approach required him to leave to search and find a water source, and then a means to get it to her. 'Yes,' he thought, 'if I found the source, I do not have the means to get it to her.' These thoughts went around and around in his mind and all he was doing was sitting there in the shade of the tree, feeling useless, helpless, and a little angry.

As they, both sat there thinking their bleak, defeatist, and depressing thoughts they did not notice a group of five pigeons had started to circle their location. They would fly really close to the location of the tree, then swing away, and then back again in an oblong pattern rather than a circular pattern. On their third pass by the tree one of them yelled, "Do you need help?" At first neither Trapper nor Mosaic responded, both still lost deep in the recesses of their individual minds contemplating the situation and what options they had. Again, on the next pass, several of the circling birds yelled the question, which brought Trapper out of himself and in doing so; he looked up, saw them and yelled back, "Yes! We do! Can you help?"

His yelling brought Mosaic back, to the here and now as well, as he heard the lead pigeon's response to Trappers just asked question. He also recognized the pigeon asking the questions, to his surprise, it was Maggie.

"Help is on the way, hang in there." Maggie told them, "Ibu said she'd be here soon and to stay calm, and to keep the sick bird calm and in a cool place. You two aren't sick are you?"

"No, we are okay. How long before she gets here?" Mosaic shouted back, "How did you find use?"

"I'll explain later. Soon, maybe ten minutes or less," came the responses to his questions.

Mosaic looked at Trapper and then down at Moth, who stirred a little and opened her eyes and in a barely audible voice asked for a drink of water. "What did she say?" he asked no one in particular as he bent down to hear what she had said. In a soft and gentle voice he asked, "Moth I'm sorry I didn't hear what you said. Did you just ask for water?"

Moth barley nodded her head yes and with what seemed like a great effort and in a very low soft voice she said, "Yes, please."

Mosaic looked at his sister, helpless, What to do, how to get her water, how to get a container? His mind raced to try to answer his own questions. Then, it hit him he could use his mouth. He yelled up to the circling birds, "Can you take me to water?"

"Yes!" Replied one of the circling birds, "Follow me," it said as it broke from the rest of the small flock flying overhead. With that, response Mosaic took off telling; Trapper he had an idea and to stay with Moth and that he would be right back.

The red check led him several blocks north of the field to a shopping mall that had a fountain at its main entrance. Mosaic landed on the edge and took a long drink of the water. 'Boy this sure tastes good,' he thought. He then took a large mouthful of the water, did not swallow it and took off back to the vacant field. By the time, he reached the shady spot under the tree he thought his cheeks would pop. Trapper turned Moth's head and Mosaic carefully let the water from his mouth trickle into Moth's mouth. Moth choked and then, spit out half of the precious liquid, but did manage to swallow some of it, and all she could say was, "More."

Mosaic looked at Trapper, "your turn," he said, and with that, Trapper took off to be escorted to the fountain. He and Trapper performed this routine five more times and just as Mosaic was getting ready to take off for the sixth trip to the water source, to their surprise, Maggie arrived.

Maggie had seen Trapper giving Moth the water mouth to mouth and as she arrived under the tree, she said, "Let's try this," as she removed a small metal flask from around her neck. She asked Mosaic for help in positioning Moth's head so she could get some of the amber liquid from the flask into Moth's mouth. Mosaic knew the routine and carefully moved Moth's head into a good position so she could drink. Moth helped, for, she had gained some awareness as they had gotten more of the water into her, but she was far from being able to move without help.

"This will give you strength, my dear, until Ibu arrives." Maggie reassured Moth. Looking at Mosaic and then Trapper she said, "I'll tell you two more as soon as she is better hydrated." With that said all her attention went to Moth and making sure Moth drank all the amber liquid from the flask. Maggie told Mosaic she had the situation under control. With the way, she said it; Mosaic stepped back and sat down, and relaxed a little and watched as Maggie attended to Moth. Maggie gave Moth sip after sip of the amber liquid until it was all gone. "Now we wait and see." She said, "Ibu should be here soon. In the meantime let me explain." in response to Mosaic and Trapper's confused looks.

However, before she could continue she looked down at Moth. With an expression of surprise and concern she said, "Oh my!" with that she laid down next to Moth and covered her with one of her wings, at the same time she directed Trapper to lie on the opposite side of Moth and to place his wing over her as well.

To Trappers amazement, Moth felt very cold. "I know." was Maggie's response to the look on Trappers face, "Just stay close to her, share your body heat and it should elevate her body temperature back to normal, so she won't freeze to death while we wait for Ibu." Trapper just shook his head yes and with a chattering beak said, "I'll do it for as long as I can." Within five minutes, Mosaic relieved him and Mosaic too was shocked at how cold she felt. Mosaic and Trapper had moved her into the shade about thirty minutes ago because they were afraid that she would boil to death and now he was afraid that she would become a frozen brick of flesh. Looking at Maggie and with his beak chattering he said, "This thing that has her, it's really bad, isn't it Maggie?"

"Yes my boy, it's beyond me to do more than I've already done. I have been a healer for seven years now and I've never seen anything like this, ever. I hope I was in time and that Ibu gets here soon, if anyone can get this out of her system she can." with that Maggie shivered a little and moved closer to Moth to be able to share her body heat.

"What's wrong with her? I thought it was a little food poisoning. It is just something she ate; she just ate something that was bad, right?" Mosaic said this as a means to reassure himself that Moth would be okay, why Moth was ill. However, by the look on Maggie's face he knew it was more and he knew that he did not want to really know the answers to the questions he had just asked based on her facial expression and body language. Still, a part of him really did want to know what had a hold of his sister and yet another part did not.

"Oh my dear boy, if that were all it was that would be enough; she has been attacked by something much more serious and deadly then food poisoning. She has been attacked by an ally of a very sinister character." Maggie said with a little fear in her voice, "A very unpleasant character indeed." She added with emphases on the badness of the individual who had orchestrated this illness.

Mosaic looked at her puzzled, and almost as if he was talking to himself, said, "Who would want to attack my sister, especially with the intent of killing her? She has no enemies." He stated to no one in particular.

"I'm not sure it was her that they were after." was Maggie's response, "I believe they were really after someone else instead." She hesitated and then went on; "it's not my place to say more, especially on something I have very little knowledge of. I've said enough already, Ibu can explain it better and knows more of the history than I do." She finished with a look of apprehension on her face. However, Mosaic felt she knew more about the asked questions and those not asked then, she was willing to say. That she had only barely answered the questions that had been asked, and guardedly at that; what was it about this that had Maggie looking at Moth with such a worried expression on her face. She stopped talking and started to sing a lullaby to Moth, "Hush little baby don't you cry…" she sang in a very low comforting voice, which seemed to cause Moth's body to relax.

Before Maggie got a chance to finish her song, Major, Ibu, her Son and several other pigeons arrived. Ibu and her Son arrived in a 57 Chevrolet convertible and the birds arrived on the wing. As the car pulled up to the curb and before it had come to a complete stop, Ibu had opened the door and stepped out and was walking to where the pigeons were attending to the ill Moth under the tree. In her hand, she carried a black doctor's type of valise that she placed on the ground next to Moth, as she knelt down to be better able to examine her. She was asking Maggie several short, concise questions, "How is she? What have you given her? What was her reaction to what you gave her? Does she have trouble breathing? What is her body temperature?"

Maggie responded with short concise answers as she moved away giving Ibu access to Moth "Not good. I have given her the nectar you told me to give her and she drank it all with coaxing and our help. No trouble breathing, but she went from being very hot and feverish to being very cold, once she had drank the nectar."

"I see! Normal reaction to the nectar, which means she has been poisoned," was all Ibu said as she hurriedly opened the bag and started pulling out all kinds of little bottles and other equipment. Things that Mosaic had never seen before nor had any idea as to their use. The majority of the instruments that he saw come out of the bag he did not like the looks of because of their shape, sharp edges or points which gave them an ominous unsavory appearance. Maggie noticed the look of concern on his face as the various pieces of unknown hardware came out of Ibu's bag to be laid out on display, "Don't worry, if anyone can help Moth it will be Ibu. Just have faith and pray she got here in time."

Ibu was not paying any attention to what was being said, instead was working at a fast feverish pace. She had laid out a white dishtowel, had very carefully moved Moth onto it, was now putting the index finger of her left hand under Moth's wing, and had started counting under her breath. As she was counting, she was also giving instruction to her Son who had just come up holding a strange plant with long sharp shaped leaves. "Break off one piece of the leaves and squeeze the sap out of it onto the plate that was lying on the ground next to her. Then, add some distilled holy blessed water in it, equal amounts, mix it up until it has an even consistency and color." Her son followed her instructions as she continued to pull additional bottles of different ingredients from the bag. "Now add a drop of the Eucalyptus and a drop of the witch-hazel and one drop of the fennel seed oil and mix it thoroughly. Then, place it into the syringe and add the plastic plunger to the end of the syringe, be sure the air has been evacuated out once all the ingredients are in the barrel."

She then carefully rolled Moth on her side and opened her beak slightly while her son inserted the plastic tube down Moths throat, and then Ibu squeezed the contents of the syringe down into Moth's Crop. Seconds later Moth started to cough and choke and the gray white-green vile, revolting smelling paste like substance came shooting out of her beak and onto the ground. "Oh my!" Ibu said with great surprise, "That shouldn't have happened this is more serious than I thought!"

Mosaic, not knowing what to do or say was in shock at what had just been done to his sister. Ibu asked what type of seeds she had eaten. He offered additional information on what types of seeds she had eaten and what the local birds at the silos had told them about them. "It's just the bad seeds she ate, right?" Mosaic asked after he had given Ibu the information.

"Oh no, my boy it's more than that unfortunately." Ibu said, "It's a lot worse than having eaten some bad seeds. It is a dark and evil power that has entered her body. However, we will discuss that later, please let me work. Maggie, Major, take Mosaic and Trapper over there so I can work uninterrupted, and tell him all you two know." With that, Ibu returned to her task of giving instructions to her Son. "Now remix the previous solution and add in some of the dry powdered lake moss, we need to draw this poisonous evil out of her."

With that Maggie and Major ushered Mosaic and Trapper away from the shade of the tree. Trapper looked at Major and then Maggie, "Okay, what's going on with Moth? It's just something she ate, she'll be fine right?" Neither Major nor Maggie responded to the questions, at least not as quickly as Mosaic had wanted. He reiterated Trapper's questions, "Well, she's going to be all right, isn't she?" but by their hesitation he knew it was not an easy a question for either one of them to answer.

Major held up his wing as if to say, slow down, give me a minute and then he said, "Where to start?" He paused, and for approximately a minute, there was not a word spoken as Major collected his thoughts. Maggie was starting to show signs of impatience, in her fidgeting from one foot to the other. Major then took a breath and started his narrative, "Do you know the story of the Great Creator and the story of creation." He then looked at Mosaic and Trapper for a response. Both nodded their heads yes. "Sort of," Trapper said, "Doesn't everyone?"

Major did not respond to Trapper answer; nor to Mosaics slight dip of his head to indicate a cautious yes, "I bet you never heard the story of how pigeons once saved the world from Damien and his evil disciple Oother."

"Who are Damien and Oother?" Mosaic asked, with a look of confusion on his face. Trapper looked at him with disbelief on his face, "You got to be kidding me, you've never heard of Damien?" Mosaic shook his head no, to Trapper's question, and tapping him with his wing saying, "Have you heard of them then? Why don't you tell me about them, then?"

Knowing of a little shove could get out of hand, and before it went any farther, Major cleared his throat, "Now yearlings." he said with authority, getting ready to step in, as if he were afraid a fight might break out, and realizing it wouldn't; continued, "Well then let me start from the beginning. The Great creator created some beings like himself, so he would not be so lonely and would have company and someone to talk to and not feel so alone. He also created the Universe, the Earth, and some say other places away from the Earth, but a lot like the Earth. He also created the Universe, which took him quite some time. Many hundreds of years as we count time, but in how he counts time it took only days. Well, he created it and put many things in it. Those mostly have disappeared; well actually, they were destroyed when he and his fellow creatures, his creations, got into this terrible fight."

Major stopped long enough to see if there were any questions, and when there was none he continued, "Some of his followers were jealous of him and his powers. They had the free reign of the heavens, but they wanted more. Actually, as the story goes, they wanted to become rulers of the different parts of the Universe. They wanted to divide it up and each wanted a section to control, and they wanted to become Creators. The Great Creator saw they were not interested, or good, in taking care of what they wanted. They only wanted the power, to rule and control. However, being the Great Creator, he did give each one of them a planet and specific instruction on what to do; and if they did what was asked of them, he would grant them the powers they desired. Of course, taking care of a planet unto itself was a great responsibility; especially the great responsibility of taking care of all that lived on that planet made the task even more difficult." Again, Major paused to take a breath, paused and looked at them to see if they had any questions before he once again started talking. They had puzzled looks on their faces, but by their lack of verbal response, he assumed they did not want to voice their questions, so he continued.

"After a short time, all the planets under the control of these 'would be' Creators, were in disarray, and headed for complete decimation and ruin. One of the planets he had retained for his own was the Earth. He let the events of their lack of care take its course and all came back to him to ask for help, but he answered them that they must learn how to do it themselves, for he had given them all the knowledge required to save their charges. However, none could and most came back asking for his forgiveness and asking, would he take them back and teach them more and that they would never ask for anything and wait until he said they were ready to rule on their own. Those that had come back did not blame him for their shortcomings. However, not all felt that way. One in particular named Damien blamed it all on the Great Creator, and accused him of not really having given them all the powers they needed to succeed. Damien saw what the great Creator had kept for himself and wanted it, accusing the Great Creator of not having played fair. That he wanted to be an equal and rule jointly by his side. The Great Creator didn't think it would be a good idea nor in the best interest of what he had created, and said "No!" So those that were demanding this equality became angry with him. All those who had not realized their ineptness started to plot to overthrow him and were going to take it by force, and so the heavenly hosts were divided. And, eventually the two factions had a major fight, a war, as it were, and many on both sides were destroyed."

Trapper looked puzzled and asked, "If they were all so powerful and if the Great Creator was the most powerful of all and knows everything, as Deacon claimed, how could his followers have been able to do that? I would have thought he would have never allowed it to begin. I would have taken total control." As he finished with his last thought stated matter-of-factly, he looked at Mosaic for confirmation.

Mosaic's response was more mature for his years and yet naive, "Maybe he wanted friends that would like him, for who he was and not for what he could give. If he were all that powerful, where he had created it all, even them, maybe they were afraid he would take it all back and leave them with nothing, not even their lives. Still, from all I have heard, the Great Creator created all things to please himself. I think because he loves to create, is why he created; that is why he made them and why he gave them so much, because he loved them all. They just didn't understand him and his feelings about it all." Mosaic stopped, feeling that he was starting to sound lame and that he was rambling, he turned to Major, "So how are pigeons involved, and who is this Oother you mentioned?" he finished in hopes to get the answers that would straighten out his inner confusion and redirect the conversation away from what he considered rambling.

"Yes, Mosaic. To continue," Major cleared his throat, "you are correct about him. He loved to create, but hated what was happening. During these fights several of his creations, some planets were caught in the areas where great battles occurred and all life on them was wiped out, decimated into large balls of stone and dust leaving nothing there for anyone to rule. The Earth and its solar system were caught up in one of these fierce and vicious battles between Damien's forces and those of the Great Creator's. During that, mayhem the planet, Mars was turned into what it is today. The Earth as it is today is different than it was then, because during that same battle a large great big boulder hit it and a created a gigantic dust cloud that blocked the sun's life giving rays of energy and the majority of life from that time on our planet died."

"The Great Creator was very saddened and angered by this and proclaimed he'd had enough of this bickering and fighting. You see the Earth and this part of the universe was one of his favorite places to visit, and relax and watch his creations go about their lives."

"Damien had been his favorite overall; the one he had taught had the most potential. He was one of the best and brightest and also the most ambitious of the entire heavenly host and he was the one that wanted to be the Creator's equal, which of course history shows, he really wasn't. He wanted to be totally equal with the Great Creator. Unfortunately he was basically young and arrogant." Major finished and then looked at them to see if Mosaic or Trapper had any questions about what he had told them so far.

Trapper shrugged his shoulder and shook his head yes, and asked, "If the Great Creator can do anything and knows all possible events and outcomes, then how did he miss what some of his closest followers were up to? And, why didn't he just put the kibosh on them and their plans?"

Major looked at Trapper and then at Mosaic who was shaking his head yes, as if to say, "Yeah! How come?" Before Major could reply Maggie responded, "Well I've heard it said that he wanted to create creatures that did have the capabilities to talk and be free thinking. Not all the creatures he had created up to that time had those capabilities. It is said he became lonely and wanted to share what he knew, the ideas he had. Therefore, he fashioned creature that could do that, he created his companions to be freethinking and he gave them access to all that he had and knew. While some were very satisfied with this arrangement, many were not and one in particular, Damien, wanted to be equal to the Great Creator. Damien didn't like the idea of being subservient and no matter how the Great Creator appeased him he wasn't satisfied." Maggie stopped with a look that said, 'I am rethinking my next thoughts before I speak them.'

"So Damien started to plot and scheme as to how he could replace the Great Creator. Damien wanted to become the Great Creator. He knew he could not do it alone he had to find allies. As the story goes there were others who were not satisfied with the status quo either. He found others, and with them to bolster his ego and confidence, he started a war with the Great Creator." Maggie stopped again, with a sad look on her face, and she let out a sigh, then she took a deep breath and continued, "They say Damien figured that, even if he lost, the Great Creator wouldn't cease his existence. He knew that the Great Creator loved all his creations unconditionally, and had never eliminated or disassembled anything he had ever created. As the war continued, the Great Creator had always taken prisoners and had always exiled them to the far reaches of the Universe and allowed them to live in solitude, never allowing them to become involved in anything again. However, Damien did not have the same reverence for life as the Great Creator had. During the many battles of the war, many of his creations had been killed, destroyed or annihilated by Damien and his followers. This saddened the Great Creator greatly, because he knew that it would take an enormous effort to recreate what had been taken away. What saddened him even more was the fact that at that moment in time, during the entire war, he would not have the time to recreate what had been destroyed. Even though he had the power, at that moment in time he had no time." Maggie again stopped as if collecting her thoughts and, then continued with her narrative, "And so it went. The fights, the victories, and yes the defeats." She stopped, seeing the looks on their faces.

"How is it possible?" Mosaic asked.

"He's the Great Creator, he knows all, and he can do all. Can do anything?" Trapper interjected.

"Yes! It is said he knows all." Maggie continued, "But knowing all and wanting to control all is quite a different issue. At one time, I believe, or it is believed that he tried to control all. Instead of control, within these creations, he wanted companions and he felt that he needed to allow them free will, so he would know they were in fact his friends. He gave them that capability, but he did not give them all his knowledge and that is why Damien was jealous and felt slighted and wanted more, he wanted it all. Many of his creations changed during this terrible time, some changed slowly over time, many were destroyed in some cases to extinction, like the Dinosaurs, in others only those loyal to him were exterminated; or he had to change them so they could survive."

"Like what creatures would that be?" Trapper interrupted Maggie, with an inquisitive look on his face. "I thought all creatures were created as they currently are?"

"Many creatures were divided in their loyalties, many species weren't. Amongst those that weren't, there were members of their species that wanted to stay loyal and there were those that didn't, they wanted to follow Damien and those that did were changed forever, such as the good mosquitoes, they were destroyed. Those that followed and were changed to this day still battle their species decisions of long ago, like the rat."

"Wait a minute!" Mosaic interrupted Maggie once again, "mosquitoes are pests that carry diseases and death. Are you telling me that at one time they were good? And, even rats were good?" shaking his head, "well they're just plain disgusting!"

"Oh, yes, it is known that at one time they were good. As a matter of fact all creatures were born good and it was the choices they made then that still affect each of their kind today. Mosquitoes were special messengers of the Great Creator, their size allowed them to go places where others could not go. Damien turned some of their species, mostly the female, and they followed him and defeated the good mosquitoes that followed the Creator. Their alliance with Damien turned them into pests, and Damien changed them so they could live off of anything, even blood, and once they drank the blood of their fellow creatures they were changed forever. Only the females suck blood, the males still live off the nectar of the flowers, for as it happened the males that followed Damien were all destroyed, the females that followed the creator were all destroyed, and the only way that they could remain in existence was as they now are. The fact that they live off of different foods caused them never to be able to dine together, and this was done by the Creator at the behest of the males that had remained loyal to him"

Trapper again interrupted Maggie, "If Damien can do the same things as the Great Creator how is any of us ever to know who expects what, who directs, who's to follow, who is directing us? Trapper finished his question with a puzzled look on his face, "Damien or Great Creator?"

"Yes, that is a difficult question, all right." Was Maggie's response, "I suppose the key is that the Great Creator would never ask us to do anything that would possibly hurt another…" Before she could finish her thought Mosaic interrupted, "How can you say that? We are always being hunted and harassed and killed by other creatures. We are hunted by the Falcon, the rat, and man has hunted some of our kind to extinction." He finished with an edge of disbelief in his voice.

"Yes, you are correct. However, that was not what was originally intended. However, the evil that Damien released has run rampant and out of control and the Great Creator has played heck trying to bring it back into control." Was her response, and then she hesitated, looked a little confused and then continued with the second part of her thought, "I think all creatures have come to the realization that once something has been released it is really hard." She paused, "If not impossible to bring it back into containment and get back to the original norm…" Maggie again paused, hesitated and stopped as if she was not sure how to proceed with her intended message.

Major however seemed to know where Maggie had been trying to go. He had more to add and took over the narrative by saying, "I think what Maggie is trying to say is, evil had been released and it had become its own entity, and how and why can't really be understood by us; or why the Great Creator allowed it is beyond me as well. Maybe he, like all things born out of his creation, he cannot just destroy them. Maybe it fascinates him and maybe, like our Asian brothers belief, there is a Ying and a Yang for everything, everything has a balance. Without evil maybe, there would be no means to truly measure good? I do know this; we have to fight it, the evil, with all our might, strength and being," he paused, "is all I know for a fact. One of the major evils that Damien helped create was Oother." He finished.

"Who is Oother?" Mosaic shook his head in a side-to-side motion agreeing with what he had heard as he spoke his question aloud. He had been listening intently and with great interest and had decided that there were evils in the world that he did not understand. They had been released during all battles of the war between the Creator and Damien and their followers. Also, based on what he had heard that had been resolved with Damien's defeat. In addition, he guessed what was happening in the Universe now; Damien and his sparse band of followers had initiated a type of hide and run and hit and then do it again and again type of warfare. Another question that had come to mind as he had been listening, which he asked was, "Which side had his species chosen to help and be loyal to?"

They listened with great interest, the conversation continued, Major explained and told the story of how pigeons had been tempted and that at first they had resisted Damien. Damien had gone after them as a species almost from the start because the Creator had made pigeons to be the messengers for and of peace. During the worst battles of the war, pigeons had not wavered from their role. Damian went after our kind. This was after the Great Creator, had expelled Damian, and cast into the pit that several of our kind had been turned. "A dark day for all of pigeon kind," Major had said lowering and shaking his head in disbelieve, "Yes, a dark day in the entire Universe for all the Creator's creations. The day that some of his most trusted followers had been turned."

Maggie looked at Major, "Yes, Dear, a dark and sad day indeed for all of pigeon kind. But we must not linger on the negatives of it and we must finish the story and then explain why we think these three are involved." As she patted him on the shoulder, which seemed to give him the strength and the support he needed to go on.

"The story of Oother," he said with a sigh. "Oother was a pigeon born a long time ago, when man was relatively new to the Universe and the Earth. As we have told you, the wars were over, Damien had been expelled from the heavens and thrown into the pit, where he became the ruler of the darkness. Many of his followers were cast into the pit with him, where they could serve him, and are the examples to show all what happens to those that follow Damien or take the wrong path. Even though all those that had served Damien during the war had been cast into the pit, there were others who over time became dissatisfied with their lot in life and with those disheartened souls Damien found a means to raise havoc and has done so ever since. Most of the time he creates little irritations that cause great pain and suffering. Every now and again, he finds a soul that has a natural power that he can exploit and really causes great pain and suffering and destruction to the masses. He does this not because he hates the common creatures, but because he wants to hurt the Great Creator. "

"Okay, we get the picture already, so who is this Oother?" Trapper said a little impatiently.

This caused Major to pause and Maggie to give Trapper, the Motherly 'be respectful' look before Major continued. "You see Damien, has been on the prowl from that day forward, constantly on the lookout for those that desire power and wish to obtain it at any cost. Oother was one of our kind that wanted power at any price. He was a healer and a seer, he had been given a brilliant mind and with it, he had a great drive and was very ambitious. However, he had not been given the gift of patience and because of this lack of patience; he used all means available to advance himself. He wanted to be greater than what was considered normal, and what could be gained by time and experience. He was the type of ripe fruit that Damien thrived on, plump, juicy and ready for

Damien's manipulations and lies." Major shook his head in disgust and then spat out, "Yep, ripe for the picking"

Major shook his head in slight disgust as he continued to tell the story of Oother, of how one of Damien's followers, a bird named Ignoble Vile, had found him and had promised him all that he desired. With Ignoble Vile guiding Oother, over time he became another weapon that Damien used to attack the Great Creator and his followers. Ignoble Vile, with Damien's help, gave Oother the education, knowledge and means to become all that Oother wanted. With this power given to him, Oother became an evil power that almost destroyed all the pigeons of the world that would not follow him. His plan was to control the world and all its creatures as Ignoble Vile's, or ultimately Damien's lieutenant on this planet. His plan was to use the pigeons as he had used the rat, to spread death and diseases throughout the world and with this army in place, he would rule the world as one of Damien's right hand men. However, not all pigeons of the world were power hungry nor did they want to serve Oother and ultimately Damien. The Passenger Pigeon was their greatest opponent and had the largest numbers, and Oother realized and convinced Ignoble that as long as they had the numbers they did Oother would never be able to conquer and rule the planet in Damien's name. For you see every battle that Oother had waged up to that point he had lost because of them, for you see they were loyal to the Great creator down to the last bird. So Damien planted the seed in man and man went on a vicious campaign of hunting the Passenger Pigeon, all the way to extinction." Major and Maggie with a very cheerless expression on their faces shook their heads and Maggie said, "May the Great Creator bless and keep them in his warm embrace for all time because of all they sacrificed."

"Yes!" Major agreed reverently and then he continued, "There were lots of little skirmishes between the followers of the Great Creator and Oother and Damien's during that time. Of course the two saddest were the complete extinction of the passenger pigeons and that of the Giant Dodo's. Their kind will never be seen again. The Great Creator realized he had to step in and take control. He did so by giving the birds of the yards, some special emblems, which were really weapons that would allow them to regain control and would allow them to neutralize Oother and his followers and at the same time foil Damien's plans for total conquest of our planet. The emblems he gave to the four flocks of the yards were the blue feather, the crystal gem pin, the everlasting seed and the purest of waters. Over time, the yards became the rail yards and the four flocks took on the names of the four directions. The flocks there became the keepers of the power that would forever keep Oother at bay and locked away." As Major stopped to pause and take a breath before continuing with the story, or to answer questions he noticed out of the corner of his eye Ibu was moving Moth. As she was doing so she was telling all that Moth was stable and could be moved now, but that she still didn't look as good as Ibu had hoped and that she would know better in the morning. "It was out of my hands now," she said, "only the Great Creator knew what her fate would be."

She also informed all she would be taking Moth to her house, where it was warm and safe and she had all the finery and special ingredients to try and further treat Moth's poisoning. She also addressed the unasked questions that were on all their minds that once there she would explain what she knew and what she believed had happened. In addition, what she still could do to help bring Moth back from the brink of death.

As she had been talking she had been walking to the car and had gotten into it and with the words "Follow us." the car and its three passengers had sped away from the curb and towards Ibu's house. Major, Maggie, Trapper, Mosaic and the rest of those that were there had taken to the air and were following overhead. None saying a word to the other, each caught up in the labyrinth of thoughts and questions, moving through the many pathways of their individual minds, trying to get to a reasonable conclusion, trying to find that exit that made sense and would bring them out into the uncluttered truth.

Interesting Pigeon Fact

There are many theories about how pigeons manage to return 'home' when released 100s of miles from their loft. A champion racing pigeon can be released 400-600 miles away from its home and still return within the day. This amazing feat does not just apply to 'racing' or 'homing' pigeons; all pigeons have the ability to return to their roost.

A 10-year study carried out by Oxford University concluded that pigeons use roads and motorways to navigate, in some cases even changing direction at motorway junctions.

Other theories include navigation by use of the earth's magnetic field, visual clues such as landmarks, the sun and even infrasounds (low frequency seismic waves). Whatever the truth, this unique ability makes the pigeon a very special bird.

http://www.pigeoncontrolresourcecentre.org/html/amazing-pigeon-facts.html#how_old

Chapter 5

*While Moth had been on her journey to find Mosaic to tell him
that some of their family and flock members were alive and held
captive at Vande Ber Pet & Feed store. Crafco was plotting,
scheming, and watching K-Bridge in order to try to take it away
from the few remaining members of the K-bridge flock. The bird
named Naught Vlinder was contemplating her situation and was
admonishing herself on how she had wound up where she was.*

The black check white flight hen looked at her surroundings and
sighed. Ever since she had arrived three days ago, correction, she
thought, had been sold to Vande Ber Pet & Feed, the bird they
called Niner had gotten progressively sicker. To her he had been
different somehow, and yet he was no different from the majority
of the other pigeons confined in the cramped little loft at the back
far corner of the cinder block walled courtyard area of the feed
store. The loft had been built and located with all the correct
thoughts in mind for the well-being of its future occupants;
however, with the passing of time the courtyard had been filled
with other cages stacked head high with all types of other birds and
mammals. The area was not designed for the number of cages and
different types of creatures it now housed. The disposal of sewage
wasn't antiquated and the hired help was not amiable to taking
proper care of its disposal, sometimes it would be days before the
feces and urine combination of waste was properly disposed of.
The originally designed, open to the sky, airy courtyard now was
covered two thirds with a tarp that held the air in until it became a
stagnate pool of acid bad smells, of pet dander and urine. Over
time, she thought even a bird with Herculean strength and health
would be overcome by it all and fall ill and eventually die. Even if
the airflow had been improved, she thought the food and water
would eventually kill you. Yes, she had come from the Taj Mahal
to this tar-paper shack of lofts and she found her surroundings
were very depressing indeed.

If she had been rancorous towards those from her own loft that had wound up with her in this living hell, she would have taken delight in their disbelief in being there with her. Instead, she felt sorry for them, for they truly had not been able to do anything about having wound up here she thought. The others from her loft were the two blue bar sisters, Little Blue and Champion Hen, not bad birds, but they were indeed prima-donnas. Besides them, there was another blue bar their cousin, Darling Girl, who Vlinder liked because she was more down to earth. Then, there was her best friend, Mona, a red check grizzle, which rounded out the birds that were healthy. All were underachievers, except for Mona who had done rather well during the young bird race season, but had stopped performing when her future mate, a young up and coming red check, named Mystic had been culled. After that had happened Mona had given up, being lackadaisical about her appearance and her performance. Funny, Vlinder thought back on how she had admonished Mona for giving up on life and then two weeks later, she, Vlinder had basically done the same thing. She had tried to explain it away and justify it by saying it wasn't the same, because what had happened to her had been so much different, but in the end she had done exactly what Mona had done, she had quit on life.

The reason the five of them were so healthy was that the weeks before they had been sold to the pet store their previous owner had taken them through the medication and vitamin regime to prepare them for racing season. That was another reason why they were all in shock at having been sold to the pet store, for birds were seldom sold after that costly preparation for racing season. As she watched the hen Koffee, she was amazed at the hen's energy. In all this filth, the hen seemed healthy and bright in spirit, and she realized that every time the hen approached her mate he seemed to brighten up as well, as if her health and attitude were infectious. She then shrugged her shoulders and thought what a waste of time and energy, her mate was a walking dead pigeon unless she could get him out of this death trap of a loft, and looking at their situation realistically that would be impossible. She looked at her surroundings and shook her head "yes" in response to her own thoughts at how impossible the situation really was.

As she looked at her surroundings, she wondered how had it all come to this? Less than three months ago, she was one of the top flyers in her loft. She had believed she was invincible, she had the genes, and she was the right body type to be a winner. She had the desire, once and the brains to be a top flyer, not only in her loft but also in the combine. In the combine, she thought, Tate would have said that was either arrogance or confidence. To say you could be the best out of several thousand birds was arrogance, but she had done it as a young bird, and so to say it at the beginning of the yearling race season, was confidence, backed by past performance.

She'd had a really great young bird-flying season. She had won two races overall beating out a thousand on each race day. On the first race at a distance of one hundred and fifty miles as a bird flies, she had beaten everyone by one and a half minutes. The following week at one hundred and seventy-five miles as the bird flies, she had beaten the entire combine of a thousand birds by forty-five seconds. Then, in the third week, from two hundred miles, she had been fifth overall and again at two hundred and fifty miles, having been beaten by her brothers from her own loft, and her first cousins from her owner's father's loft. In each case, she had only lost by sixty seconds. After which, her owner had pulled her from competing in the next two races. He had sent her on the training flights, but had rested her on the actual race days. She had not understood why, because she had felt that she could have competed at both those distances, three hundred and three hundred and fifty were not that far. However, her owner had not sent her. "Humans were such fickle creatures," she thought. They are always talking about getting a bird in condition by sending them on training flights and then holding them back on race day made no sense to her at all. Didn't they understand that race day was just another means to continue with the conditioning? Shaking her head to her own inner speak as if she were talking with another bird in a normal conversation. Movement caught the corner of her eye and brought her back to the current place and time.

All the birds in the little loft had moved to the farthest corner of the loft away from the door. A heavy set human was opening the door with one hand as he held a scoop full of food in the other. He did not clean the feed dish; he just poured the new grain into the dirty feeding dish. He then turned over the watering dish onto the floor of the loft. He then poured in new water spilling it onto the loft floor as well, creating a wet messy paste of water and pigeon manure. He then turned, not bothering to clean it up or put sand down to absorb the wetness as he closed the door and walked away. All creatures knew that constant wetness on the feet caused colds and respiratory problems. These humans, she thought, were so unclean, so ignorant about other life forms.

What a mess, she thought, no wonder all the birds in the loft were ill. She watched as the pet store birds and her old loft mates all made a mad dash for the new food all except the hen named Koffee and her mate. They flew down from the upper perches and walked over very dignified and as they approached the birds already feeding made way for them so they could eat. She then realized after having seen this behavior several times now that they were important and had a special power over the others in this small loft. So what, she thought, what did it matter, they were all doomed if the rumors were true and she continued her thoughts of how she had come to this.

After having been held out for two races her owner had flown her once again. Starting with the One hundred and fifty and then the two hundred mile race, where she had taken second and third place respectively again having been beaten only by her brothers. Young bird race season had been over before it had even started; she thought. Not a whole lot of time for a bird to prove their worth. It had been the first proving grounds to establish if you were good enough to keep and train for the adult racing season and not have to go through the culling jury.

Culling was a process by which humans selected the racing pigeons they would keep. It was their way of picking the best racers and breeders to be retained for their individual lofts. The problem with the process, as Vlinder saw it was that there were no set standards, or an all-knowing standard to follow. Therefore, loft pigeons were subjected to their individual fancier' selection processes and rules for being kept or weeded out birds. Of course, to make it even more madding, there were different rules applied by each fancier and each used different culling methods. All very confusing!

For example, some fanciers believed that in order to improve the breed you killed all those birds that did not meet the requirements. To those fanciers the culled birds became part of the mulch pile. Yet, others killed the culled birds and sent them to stew pot. While others, as her owner, sold unwanted birds only to pet stores, and others only to new fanciers just starting out in the sport, or just wanting to find a recreational pigeon. Yes, she thought being a racing pigeon on the ropes was a difficult and stressful thing to be. Of course, you did not wind up there unless you did not perform. Racing pigeons like her, unlike some breeds, where looks or color or the kind of plumage you had determined your fate during the judging, hers had all been on performance.

The standards with fanciers applied, for her particular breed, the racing homer, were all over the place, all depending on the level of the owner. Some fanciers wanted birds that raced well or that could breed winners, the means by which they selected or the criteria used, varied greatly, even with the most knowledgeable fanciers to select the best in either of these two categories. As she had learned in the crates, on race day from other birds from other lofts, the standards were all over the map. Some fanciers picked birds they would keep on body type, wing conformation, family history, eye sign color and racing results per individual bird. Yet, others used any combination of the previously mentioned criteria and still others used what they felt or believed to be good or had potential. Yes she thought, life for her kind was hard, what was a bird to do, with so many different expectations to have to meet? You did your best she thought. What else was a bird to do? She believed it was all in the hands of fate, luck as it were, if you had it on your side you were fine. If not you were doomed.

It was hard for a pigeon to know what to do sometimes. Stories abounded where a bird had done really well only to discover that its parents or siblings were gone because its owner hadn't been patient enough. All racing pigeons faced that dilemma. Like all creatures, they had their good days and their bad days, but with pigeons fanciers they were only allowed to have good days. There were plenty of fanciers that didn't understand that simple fact of life and many a great pigeon was disposed of before its time. There was a lot of pressure to perform because if you didn't, not only, your life could be forfeited but the lives of all your living relatives as well. There were plenty of fanciers that believed that a good flier did not make a good breeder. With most, the minute the bird's performance dropped below a certain percentage of wins they were axed, both figuratively and literally. Of course, it also worked in reverse sometimes a bad flyer could produce great flyers; genetics were funny that way. So it went give and take and always wondering if your next race would be your last because some younger, stronger bird would beat you out. Some days she wondered if it had been worth it. Today was one of those days as she looked at her deplorable surroundings and watched the pet store birds fighting and scrabbling for the food given in filthy conditions.

Yes, being a loft pigeon presented its difficulties and sometimes it was hard to know where you stood and what to do, but it did have its benefits. Fresh water, good food given daily and a clean airy place to live, she had always believed would be hers for life. She had believed in the goodness of her owner and it appeared that by where she was now she had been wrong. Well maybe she was better off than those that had been killed outright. On the other hand, was she really better off than they were, she thought once again surveying her surroundings. They had no more worries, while she had to rethink her entire existence, her entire belief system. Once again she looked around at her deplorable surrounding, was she really better off?

The pet store loft she was in was more a large cage, than a loft. It was not clean by her standards; as a matter of fact, it was downright filthy compared to her old home. True, they did feed them every day, but the food trays were not cleaned, as they should have been and the water troughs were soiled within an hour after fresh water had been poured in them, sometimes within minutes because their caretaker did not bother cleaning them before adding the new water. Between the overcrowding, the bad feeding and watering conditions it was no wonder so many were at different stages of illness. Even worse, for those that were sick weren't isolated and put into quarantine, but remained with the regular population increasing the chances that all the birds in the small loft would become infected as well. It would take only days under these conditions for all of them to get sick as well. She knew she was healthy and strong, but under these conditions she too would be overcome by the deplorable conditions of this little loft and become ill herself.

"Oh my," she thought, "how had it all come down to this"? Less than a year ago, she was at the top of her game, one of the best in her loft; as a matter of fact three weeks ago she had still held that distinguished position. Now look at her, here she was, sold to a hole in the wall pet and feed store, sitting way in the back in a cramped grimy, grubby little loft with everyday common street pigeons.

She had gotten here because of several unfortunate events during her yearling-racing season. It had been one bad thing after another and her owner's naiveté about what was going on. Her training and exercise flights had gone without incident and on the first race day, she was ready. She was in shape, in good spirits, both in body and mind; both she and her owner had known it.

They had gone to the clubhouse on Saturday afternoon where she had been counter marked and placed into the race crate with others, most not from her loft. Some she recognized many she did not, they were birds of all ages. She was starting her life as a full-fledged racing homer. She had passed her young bird season with excellent results and now she was in the big boys competition. They had been taken from the clubhouse, to the transport truck, their crate had been slid into place and locked down as had all the others crates from her club and all the crates from all the other competing clubs. Promptly at 3 a.m., Sunday morning the truck headed out for the release sight one hundred and twenty miles away as a bird flies to point "A" From point 'A" the distance to each loft was figured. Most birds flew between one hundred and forty to one hundred and seventy-five miles. The ride up was pleasant, the cool morning air came in through the air vents and three hours later, the truck had reached its destination.

They had been offered fresh water as they had watched the sun come up over the horizon. They had taken a long drink and they knew that within thirty minutes of having been offered the water all, the doors to all the crates would be opened and all the occupants would make a mad dash for freedom. In the pandemonium of a thousand birds being released through a space that normally allowed only hundreds to pass at any one time, it had happened.

She was at the lower level of the stack of crates where normally in the past, she had been on the top, and so she was not prepared for what was about to happen. As the birds were released and as she stepped out of the crate to fly, the birds from above pushed her down and she had been hit and pushed down towards ground, and she had actually hit the ground. She had not hit the ground hard, but hard enough to bruise her breastbone, ruffle and cause here to lose a few of her a feathers.

The hit had also been hard enough to knock the wind out of her for a few precious seconds and it had taken her several minutes to regain her breath. The place where she had hit the ground was sore and a bump had formed there. Every time she took any deep breaths, it had hurt and had caused her to slow down. The pain made it difficult for her to fly at any level of efficiency, or at any pace that would allow her to be competitive. It had gone badly, with all her efforts and concentration, trying to cope with the pain and because of it; she had been six hundredth out of a thousand birds, way below her performances as a young bird.

Her owner at first had been really upset and disappointed, but once he had examined her and had discovered her injury, he had told her he understood why she had been so late. He had kept her grounded for two weeks. After the end of that time, her bump had gone down, but the pain had not subsided. It had been a deep bone bruise, which had stayed sore for the whole two weeks and still caused her some discomfort every time she took a deep breathe. Her owner had started her training flight regime again, but it was still painful to fly, especially before her muscles were warmed up. The pain definitely was hampering her flying. Even after two additional weeks of training the pain was still there. After the third week of training was done, the skin was healed and the bump was gone, as was the sharp cutting pain. However, the dull throbbing discomfort, like an itch that could not be scratched, remained, and which really worried her because in all other respects she felt fine.

Based on her appearance her owner said she was ready for the second series of short distance races. Next week they were flying the second one hundred and fifty mile race of the season. Many of the yearlings that had not done so well so far were anxiously waiting for their second chance to prove themselves, and all the birds in the loft knew that if you wanted to stay as a racer in this loft they needed to be able to compete and more importantly win. She had stayed mostly to herself during her rehabilitation, and now another week had passed and she felt she was ready. The only birds that had visited with her were her brothers and her best friend Mona. This was the best she had felt since the accident and she knew she could handle the race distance. She would be fine, she thought maybe not finish first, but she would be within the first five birds to her loft. She was as sure of that as sure as she was about her own name.

Unfortunately, as fate would have it, once again her crate was not placed at the top level of the transport truck; however, the good thing was she was not at the bottom either. She was one level down from the top. The bad thing was that in her crate there was an overbearing bully of a bird that had told all in the crate that he was to be the first one out. When she had said "no way," he had attacked her, if slapping her once could be called an attack. The bad thing was that the slap had been at her breastbone, exactly where the old bruise had been and it had taken her breath away.

It had taken her several minutes to catch her breath back and there was a nasty little pain coming from where she had been slapped. She blew the feather apart where the pain was, which was at the exact same spot she had been previously hurt, and there was a red welt. It did not look as bad as it felt and so she decided she would be fine and she settled in for the night and the truck ride to the release spot. The next morning at first light, as she awoke, she felt stiffness across her breast where she had been hit. She stretched and rubbed the spot where it felt tight and to her surprise, it was very tender to her touch.

In this first light of day, she re-examined the area that hurt and to her surprise, she found that the red welt had turned into a black and blue bruise with an outer edge of yellow brown. It looked nasty and hurt slightly at the touch. She took a deep breath and that too caused her a little pain as well. It seemed, however, not to hurt as bad if she sucked the air in slowly between her puckered beak all the way down towards her intestines. So, she did this breathing exercise while the sun was breaking the horizon, the fresh air revived her from her sleepiness and woke every muscle in her body. She was ready she thought, let the race begin! Water was served and all the birds took a good drink, and the compartment was abuzz with excitement as all its occupants awaited the opening of the door, which would be the signal that the race had begun.

The front compartment door opened and as she was moving towards the opening when the bully pushed her aside, "Where do you think you're going?" he said as he exited through the opening, followed by the balance of the birds. She was the last one out and took to the air in a relatively clear release site. She did not circle, but headed straight for her loft. She had decided what landmarks to use; she was not going to spend precious time doing her circling orientation routine so often used by her kind to get going in the right direction. She had seen the lead birds and where they had headed, and in doing so knew what direction to take and was flying within the birds of the first kit of racers within minutes. Within this group where three of her brothers, Tate, Vlig and Norm, all three greeted her warmly as she joined them, but it did not take her long to realize she could not keep up. Once again, she was having trouble breathing and had to slow her pace. To her amazement, her three brothers slowed down to keep her company.

"What are you three doing?" she asked.

"Keeping you company." Tate said in response to her quarry.

"You shouldn't. Are You crazy! We will all wind up in the culling pile. So please get going don't worry about me." She said in a pleading whinny voice, "Please Tate, get going will you?"

"No. Vlig wants to know what is wrong with you. Are you sick, or what? You looked perfectly ready last night, what's wrong, what's going on with you? You tired, or sick or what?" was Tate's reply.

"I'm fine, really," she said. But Tate wasn't the oldest and best racer in the loft for no reason; he was smart and could read a bird's voice inflections and body language really well. "No, I think there is something wrong alright, so give, what is it?" With that question asked and not answered, they all flew without saying another word, just waiting for her to mull it over and then come out with it.

"Okay!" she said, "If I tell you, will you then get on with racing and not playing nursemaid to me?"

Tate's response was, "We'll see, once you tell us, then we can decide." Once again, there was silence as she realized they would not leave her unless she told and even with her telling them, they might still decide to stay with her. She hoped once they knew she was all right and only had a small bruise, they would leave her and get back into the race. She told them what had happened and instead of leaving they became enraged, and talked about slowing down even more and waiting on the bully and doing him some harm. She talked them out of that plan, but they also had decided to fly home as a group and nothing she could say or do, caused them to change their minds. Instead, as they flew home they came up with all types of schemes and elaborate plans of dealing with the bully if they ever were so lucky as to be shipped with him. They all laughed and kidded about it and it took the stress out of the race and out of finishing first. As a matter of fact, she found it relaxing and easier to fly and they made reasonably good time.

They still finished in good standing within their own loft; of the twenty birds sent, they had come in seventh through tenth. Their owner was not happy about how they had placed, but he had surmised something had gone terribly wrong for his four best flyers to come in so late. He defiantly was not happy, but he also was not going to cull any of them over one bad result. Instead, they trained that next week and she felt better with each passing day and then it was Saturday again, and they were once again being crated and being prepared for yet another race. This one would be easy for it was only for a distance of two hundred miles. "Nothing but a cakewalk," Tate had said, "Yes sir, easy Sunday, Nothing but a cakewalk."

Yes she thought, 'her brothers and her were always the front-runners or flyers as it were on short little hops as this race would be.' Her Older brother Tate had won several races during his young bird season and again was doing really well in this his yearling season. Where she had all bad luck, it appeared Tate had all the good luck. Of the three nests that her parents had bred that year, there had been six healthy youngsters. Tate was 9-1 son, his nest mate Wings had been lost during young bird season as had Norm's nest mate Speed. Both Wings and Speed had been great flyers but never returned from the three hundred miler. They were lost and none knew why or what had happened. They had all grieved their loss, but they had gone on with the task of living, flying and winning.

After two bad incidents, it seemed her luck had changed. The bruise had not gone away, but at the same time, it had not hurt her the entire week of training flights, so she felt confident that she had turned the corner on her bad luck. On race day, she felt elated. She had been placed in the crate at the clubhouse with her three brothers, Tate, Norm, and Vlig her nest mate. Their Crate had been placed on the top level of the transport truck. She was happier then she had been in weeks the top level, with her three brothers and a distance of two hundred miles, yep! Tate had called it correctly; this would definitely be a cakewalk, a distance they all could excel at and win.

On top of all that, the three had told her that she wasn't going to have any problems this time, they would make sure of that and as a foursome they would fly together as a group. With this plan they would finish the race one, two, three, and four; of course who would fill which position was a constant debate and kidding session between them almost all night long. At midnight, they all fell asleep and finished the long ride to the release site without incident.

At first light, the sunrise woke them, it caught them relaxed and yet in an excited mood. They were given their normal early morning water. Then, the doors of the compartments were opened and her brothers made sure she was not bumped or shoved, and that she left cleanly. They all met over the transport truck at the release site. They made one circular orientation pass and then as a kit of four, they headed south towards home. They were one of the first groups to break for home and within minutes, they had passed all the other small groups of birds that had already headed south.

They flew at a good even pace, each switching position from head to rear of their small "V" flying formation. They flew along laughing, kidding, and thoroughly enjoying themselves. Maybe that is why it had happened, they were being too cocky, too playful and not paying close attention to their surroundings, or maybe they were being too impish, or … who knows, but it had happened and it had devastated her, and it had cost her. She had come in two days late to the loft because of it.

They had been flying along when Tate had broken away and had flown two hundred yards ahead of them, egging them on and laughing at their slowness. When out of nowhere a screech hunter in a stooped dive, had plucked Tate out of the air. She had watched in total horror as the killer had hit Tate squarely in the back, which had broken him from his flight and had sent him plummeting towards the ground as lifeless as a falling rock. However, before Tate had hit the ground the screech hunter, had made a twisting maneuver, had grabbed him in his claws and with two passes of his sharp beak had nearly severed Tate's head from his Body.

As all this was happening, her mind had screamed… No! Her other two brothers had yelled scatter and as is normal in this circumstance for her kind, they scattered. They diverted their flight from normal forward flight, to erratic flight and had all three gone in different directions.

She had flown downward for cover and had made it. From her hiding place, she had watched the screech hunter carrying Tate's limp broken body away. As she watched, she started to shake all over and she had started to cry. She cried until there were no more tears left. She also found she had no energy or desire to continue with the race. She watched kit after kit of pigeons flying by and she had not moved. Her grief had paralyzed her. The images of Tate's death played over and over again in her mind. 'She should have been more careful, more alert, she should have… she should have known better… she this, she that, and in every scenario she

blamed herself for not being more watchful, more careful, more…
more what?' she thought. And, so it went in her mind until her
mind had shut down in the need for self-preservation.

She had stayed there in hiding until she became thirsty and even
then, she had not moved at first. She had finally tried to fly, only to
discover she could not get her wings to function, to work properly.
Every time she tried to fly, she flew only a few yards and then she
would get the shakes so bad she could not stay in the air and she
would have to land again.

She continued this process of trying to fly and not going very far
for several hours, and with each passing minute her need for water
increased, her anxiety increased as well. Finally, her mind's
survival instincts won out over her grief: "Look little miss dizzy, if
you don't let me take control you're going to die of thirst," and a
part of her conscious mind gave way to her unconscious mind and
she took to the air. She flew in a very erratic pattern, not in a
straight line, but in an unpatterned zig zagging southerly direction
towards home. After an hour of this type of flying, she spied water
and flew to it. It was not as good as most water, but it was wet and
she had not realized how dehydrated she really was. She stayed by
the water for over an hour she did not stay out in the open, but hid
in the bushes nearby, coming out at regular intervals to get a drink,
until she was thoroughly hydrated. The other amazing affect the
water seemed to have on her, it got rid of her shakes and it calmed
her down.

After having consumed all the water she could drink, she seemed
to be able to think more clearly. She decided to take a bath, she
had felt the need to get wet, and cleanse herself of all her grief. She
felt cooler and this seemed to help her come to her senses. It was
late and she would need a place to roost and rest for the night. So
she decided, to stay as close to the water as possible. She would
get a good night sleep and in the morning get a good drink of water
and then find something to eat, and then head home.

Near the water supply were several large trees. Some had
branches over hanging the water. She took off, flew to one of
them, and found an acceptable branch. Where it intersected, the
trunk is where she chose to settle in for a good nights rest. She

made herself comfortable and watched the sun go down in all its vibrant colors and shades of oranges and reds. As she watched it go down, she wondered if Norm and Vlig were all right, had they made it home or where they out here somewhere as she was? Were they as upset and confused and saddened by it all or were they at the loft safe and sound living by the herd animal's credo, "Life happens, death happens, life goes on, for those that lived." With those thoughts in her head, she fell into a restless sleep.

The night was uneventful; except for the fact, she had a constant running nightmare of Tate being killed. She never really woke up, but had a very disturbed, restless sleep that really was not restful or refreshing at all. Tate had been her guardian, her protector, and her best friend in a lot of ways. He had been her security blanket, he had taught her how to fly and win, he had always told her to be alert, because danger had been everywhere. In her dream those words were being spoken to her by Tate every time, just before the attack had happened. The sadness she felt in her dream was palatable as were the words, and both caused her to gag, and in her dream the tears would flow again, and they would build into a pool that would eventually engulfed her and she would be drowning in them. Then, the scene would shift and she would be gasping for air, flying along with Tate, and it would start all over again. This time with the last cycle of drowning, she woke up with a start, as the sun's first light had cast an eerie light across her eyes like the claws of a screech hunter just before they plunged into unsuspecting flesh. Once awake she realized it was only the first light of the sun peeking between the branches and leaves of the tree she had been sleeping in that had caused the ominous shadows. She gave a sigh of relief at her discovery and she yawned and stretched asking herself where the night had gone, and gave another sigh of relief at it being over. It was only a nightmare, she reassured herself, as she yawned a second time and stretched some more to get the stiffness out of her joints. 'She felt unrested, was that even a word,' she asked herself? As she rubbed the sleep from her eyes, she remembered the dream had been a real event, that Tate was dead. She really did not want to do a thing, she wanted to do nothing, or anything, except to just stay here in this tree and absorb the sun's warming rays of energy and mourn.

After having sat on the branch for quite a while, time did not matter, she sat absorbing the warmth she decided she was thirsty and just as she was about to fly down to the water, movement caught her peripheral vision. It was only a shadow, but its shape caused her to stop and re-hide herself. She had done this by instinct, without conscious thought and it was a good thing because two screech hunters floated down from the skies to the water to get a drink. They drank slowly and as they drank, they talked about their great hunt and good fortune of the day before. Each had plucked a pigeon from the sky and had a scrumptious feast, fit for a king.

From where she sat, Vlinder had heard everything they were saying. She wondered if either one of them had been responsible for Tate's death. Before they were done, she was sure that the larger of the two had been the killer. The sadness she felt, and the thought of not being able to seek revenge or restitution caused her to become week and dizzy with the ineptness she felt. Once again, the depression of the events from the day before engulfed her and she did not move nor take a breath until the screech hunters had finished their drinking and had flown away. She was sweating, as a droplet of perspiration ran into her eyes and it stinging her, is when she realized she had been holding her breath. She forced herself to take a slow outward and then inward breath, but she did not move as other's came and went, partaking from the pool's cool water.

She watched deer and ground squirrels and all types of small mammals come and go. She watched all types of wild creatures drink and leave during the morning hours. While so occupied with apprehension the morning had passed. Her staying in hiding, which seemed logical, as she watched others drink as she became progressively more parched, yet fearing to come out and get a drink for herself. What if they return was all she could think, and with her in the open, she would be an easy target. Because of that fear, she kept herself hidden, and watched and waited, for what she was not sure, all she knew was, she had to wait.

Just before noon, a small flock of mourning doves descended onto the water's edge and started to drink. After several minutes of drinking, they started to take baths in the shallows at the water's edge.

She could not have told you why, but she felt it was safe and so she flew down and joined the doves. It felt good to take a long drink from the cool water. Not until then she had not realized how thirsty she had been, she drank her fill. While doing so she had a brief discussion with the doves, who invited her to join them in their bath, which she did. As she bathed all the tension left her body and as it did, she was overcome by exhaustion. She had planned to head home after her drink but now she was not ready to go. Instead of leaving, she was hungry and wanted something to eat. When she mentioned to the doves that she was hungry, they invited her to join them, for after their bath they were going to a nearby field where it was believed the grass seeds had ripened. She decided to join them, the rumor had been correct, and by the time they were done foraging it was almost dusk again. She decided to return to the trees at the water's edge, get a drink and again spend the night there, so she said her goodbyes, and headed for her roosting place from the night before.

She decided to get a good nights sleep, and then, she would get up early the next morning, hydrate herself and then head straight home. The night passed with her having the same nightmare about Tate's death, her feelings of inadequacy, and this time Vlig and Norm were in it as well, only instead of them having gotten away they too were plucked from the sky. Instead of them being dead, they were being carried off alive, screaming in agony at her, "Why! Why Vlinder did you allow this to happen?" With that scene fresh in her mind, she woke with a start. Sweat was pouring down her face and into her eyes; it was the salt in her perspiration that had stung her eyes causing her to waken. It took her a second to get her bearings and remember where she was. That she was safe in a tree and only Tate had been taken, she told herself. Vlig and Norm would be at the loft when she got home, she reassured herself they had made it home. However, the dream had exposed her deepest fears, what if they had not made it? What if the pigeon the other screech hunter had taken, as a meal had been one of them? She admonished herself, for Tate had always said, "Stay in control, don't let your imagination feed your fears; the greatest paralyzer is allowing your fears to control your thoughts". She could not go back to sleep after the vivid dreams she had just experienced and so she stayed awake and every little noise made her jump. Her fear was fully in control as she waited for sunrise, and it was not until the light of day broke the horizon that she gave a big sigh of relief and actually felt the tension leaving her body. She did several deep breathing exercises, which helped as well; re-oxygenating her blood woke her up and allowed her conscious self to regain control over her fears.

She looked around cautiously, saw that the coast was clear and flew down to the watering hole. She hydrated herself by taking several long drinks of water, which also seemed to help perk her up. She looked all around again and scanned the skies, which were clear, and cloudless, and a pretty soft morning blue. The air was crisp and it felt good to inhale deep breaths of the clean air. She smiled to herself in spite of all the sadness she felt, and said, "It's a beautiful morning to go flying." With those words fresh on her breath, she took to the sky and headed home.

Her journey home should have taken no more than two hours, but because of her state of mind and her inability to control her grief it took her most of that day to get home. She would be flying along just fine and then, her mind would replay the events of the day Tate had died and she would have to land and gain control again before she could continue. Twice she had seen a shadow out of the corner of her eye and she dove for the turf, only to discover it had been a dove or sparrow that was flying by. Once she had spied a screech hunter a mile south of her flight line and she had landed and gone into hiding, carefully searching the skies to be sure, it was gone before she would once again taken to the air. She would tell herself this was stupid and then the next time she would just keep going, but with anything unusual she slowed down, landed or diverted from her course.

If it had been any other pigeon, she would not be reacting like this, she told herself. However, it had not been any other pigeon it had been Tate. Tate and she had a very special relationship; they had been very close they had been kindred spirits. They had always watched out for each other; they had been best friends, more than brother and sister, but each other's confidant. They had both been the best at flying, they had loved competing, they had loved race day. All within their flock had realized that with these two on the race team, their loft would never lose and all would benefit. When one succeeded the whole flock succeeded, and all with sadness shared the accolades they received and all that was gone now. To her all that had been good and fun about flying and racing was gone now. Therefore, her thoughts went from, all was gone at two years into her life, all the fun had departed and life looked really bleak to her.

She arrived at the loft late that day, much to the delight of the race team, who had given her up for lost, especially Vlig and Norm. Both realized she was not the same sister that had flow with them two days before. She was listless and looked dull, and worn out. She had seemed genuinely happy to have seen them both alive, but it was obvious to them both that Tate's death had sapped some of the life out of her. They had tried to cheer her up over the first two days after her return, but all attempts had met with failure.

Their owner had looked at her, and had blamed her late arrival on the bruise he finally noticed from the previous week. He had asked several of his fellow fanciers to come over and look at her as well. Their comments were not encouraging, "Mud on her feet, not a good sign..." You're taking a risk... hurt twice... they never seem to be the same..." I strongly suggest..." and so the advice had gone, with the final suggestion being to cull her, "No I couldn't..." and with that and after all of them had handled her, and given their opinions, they returned her to the loft and walked away.

Her overall appearance did not improve over that following week. She looked like a very ill bird. Her owner had put her on medication, herbs and vitamins, which she took as a good sign. After that week, he had called over his fellow fliers for one more set of examinations. They looked at all the birds and made their recommendation, "Yep a keeper... maybe a keeper... and then nope... get rid of it." Then they came to her again, "I wouldn't keep this one..." "Doesn't look healthy..." "This little hen from a week ago... never seem the same..." and so the conversation had gone on her second evaluation round.

She had not been interested in their comments or opinions and assessments. 'Maybe she should have been more interested in what was being said," was her thought. But, her conclusion was, 'it would have changed nothing! What happened would have still happened.' Then, two days later, she was sold to the pet and feed store, with the rest of the unwanted, unimportant, underachievers from her loft. Here, she sat with a bunch of unkept, unhealthy, common street pigeons. She felt desperately alone, and a little scared. She admonished herself, 'What's there to be scared of? You're alive; you could have wound up on the mulch pile,' she thought. Yes, she was lucky; her former owner had felt he owed her a second chance. She was lucky she decided. She was alive, at least and had been given a second chance. At what, or for what, she did not know. However, she would at least make the best of it. Tate would have wanted that, and for his sake and in his name she decided she would survive, and if ever given another chance to race she would do her best, she would be the best. She came from a long line of winners, of champions, and they weren't quitters. She had made up her mind, as she watched the birds around her struggling to stay alive. She would stop feeling sorry for herself and she would succeed, live, and once again prosper.

   The difficulty of that promise would be sorely tested over the next weeks, as life happens to do when thrown into unusual circumstances.

Interesting Pigeon facts

In scientific tests, pigeons have been found to be able to differentiate between photographs and even differentiate between two different human beings in a photograph when rewarded with food for doing so.

http://www.pigeoncontrolresourcecentre.org/html/amazing-pigeon-facts.html#how_old

Chapter 6

As Mosaic and his companions were battling high winds on their journey south to rescue his parents and flock mates, others were plotting out dastardly deeds. As April, Eric and their mom were making dinner and trying to puzzle out what route the birds were taking to get to their final destination, others were planning discord. Crafco, in the meantime, was scheming as to what his next move would need to be in order for him to reach his goal of becoming K-bridge's new flock leader. Up to this point, all his carefully laid plans to be able to control and occupy K-bridge had met without reaching his desired goal. Crafco and his cronies, Donkey and Reaper sat hidden behind the leaves of the young Jacaranda tree, and from this vantage point, they watched the goings on at K-Bridge.

Donkey and Reaper had been spying on the remnants of the K-Bridge flock for several weeks now, ever since the big race that had occurred between the young K-bridge flock leader and a loft pigeon the K-bridge flock had rescued. During this entire time, they had not been able to answer Crafco's number one question, which was, "Is the young flock leader there or not?" Neither Donkey nor Reaper had been able to answer him. One day Donkey had a brilliant idea, well, at least for him it was a brilliant idea. The idea was to go down and ask outright, where was Mosaic, which he had done. He had gone down and asked and had gotten an answer that made sense, to him anyway, but was not supported by any proof or by anything they had witnessed. One of the flock birds, the one named Rambler had said, "He was off on an errand and wouldn't be back for at least a couple of days." An answer that Donkey had found acceptable, but when he had stated it to Reaper, Reaper wasn't sure. Donkey, with puzzled look on his face had asked him, why would he be lied too? There was no reason, so Reaper had concurred it made sense, and both had accepted it, forgotten it and had not given it another thought.

However, since they were given the answer that Mosaic was running an errand and would be back within two days, and yet Donkey and Reaper had been watching K-Bridge for days and had not seen him. Of course, they had not been there every minute of every day. Despite Crafco's specific instructions to always have one of them watching the activities of the birds at the bridge, they had become hungry and thirsty, and it was no fun eating alone, so they had taken short breaks together during the day to do both.

One day Crafco had showed up unannounced; he had found the watch post abandoned and to say he was not happy, would have been an understatement. When the two spies, watchers, returned and he had found out this had been a regular routine on their part, he was furious with them.

They had tried to explain to him that they would get hungry and thirsty and this seemed to happen to them both at the same time, so they had gone together to get sustenance. They said this going together did not happen all the time, but rather every now and again. They did not want to eat alone so they had gone together. They explained that today they had lost track of time and they were sorry. Besides, he should know that it was not good for a pigeon's digestion to hurry too much or to always eat alone; after all, it was their nature to be social, he should have known pigeons were social creatures. After, they had explained their philosophy to Crafco he became incensed and had ranted and raved at them, calling them incompetent and non-thinking, and even worse, dunces. As Crafco admonished them for their lack of thought, they were both cowering at his rage, but not sure why it was directed at them. They could not be held responsible that Mosaic came and went unnoticed, now could they?

But Crafco wouldn't listen to their logic or their excuses, "How was he ever going to make life better for them and the rest of his followers if his two most trusted advisors and comrades weren't reliable?" he asked them.

Crafco had learned how far to take his berating of these two, and then he switched to making them feel badly about what they had done by appealing to their sense of responsibility to their fellow flock mates, he appealed to their nature, their social side. He was a craftsman at it; belittle one minute and then skillfully appealed to the berated individuals' sense of duty. He knew how to manipulate those loyal to him, so that he got what he wanted, at least most of the time. After the tongue-lashing they had received, they felt remorse about having let down the entire flock and Crafco. Both felt badly and assured Crafco they would not let it happen again, and that he could trust them to do things right and as he wanted. Crafco had given then very specific instruction on how they should rotate the watch so that there was always someone there to watch what was going on, at all times, at the bridge. He also assured them that there would be times where he would come take over the watch so they could go eat together. "But only if they followed his new instructions to the letter." Crafco stated emphatically

However, he had not told them how long to wait before they left for the night and returned to start their watch. Crafco had left it up to their discretion and best judgment, and yet, again their leaving and arriving was stomach driven. If they were hungry or thirsty, they left earlier than when they were not driven for the need for sustenance, as it normally did at their arrival in the mornings to start, their surveillance of the K-Bridge occupants. Their surveillance of the K-bridge flock was always at the mercy of their love of food or their need to eat. They had never left more than forty-five minutes before the sun had gone down, or arrived earlier than forty-five minutes after the sun had risen. As a matter of fact, anyone who was aware of them being there could have set the time of day by the routine these two followed. It was a good thing Crafco did not know that aspect of their surveillance schedule, or he would have been angry at their reliability.

Crafco, upon arriving late one evening, found the surveillance spot at the tree abandoned, and so he had waited, and as the sun was going down his two accomplices hadn't returned, so he spent the night. The next morning, lucky for them they arrived about ten minutes after sunrise to a very unhappy and ill-tempered Crafco. Crafco had wanted to know why they had left early. Their response had been it was not early; that they had left plenty of times at that time of day. Not a good thing to have said because with that added bit of information Crafco went off like a Roman candle. He once again ranted, raved, and showed his displeasure with their lack of understanding of how critical the situation really was. How was he ever going to be able to determine what was really going on at the bridge and where the young flock leader really was, if they could not follow his simple directions?

"Boss," Donkey spoke up, "We have been tracking the goings and comings of every bird that has arrived and left the bridge for many weeks now, and I'm of the opinion he hasn't been around."

"You are of the opinion, are you? How many times do I have to tell you two that I need to know? Not a guess, or we think, but I need to know! Who comes and who goes from that bridge. I need to know how many spend the night and when." Crafco spat this out with a tinge of disgust in his voice. His plan required that he know, he thought in frustration, and these two dunderheads wanted to give him their opinion! 'Calm down', he told himself, 'they have been doing a wonderful job. Who else do you know that would have sat here day in and day out? The truth was no one, but these two'. Instead of continuing to show his displeasure, he took a deep breath and asked them to report what they had seen.

They gave a detailed report of all the comings and goings as best as each could remember. From what they had told him almost every day was pretty much the same, birds came and went in a hodgepodge, irregular order. Sometimes there was no one at the bridge at all. However, they reported, every evening there was a minimum of ten to twelve birds that spent the night at the bridge that much they said was clockwork, an undeniable fact. Crafco carefully interrogated them on the numbers of birds that spent the night at the bridge, and it appeared there was a pattern. Some nights, like Wednesdays and Thursdays, there always seemed to be twenty-five birds that spent the night at the bridge. "Why?" Crafco asked aloud as he was thinking it. Reaper responded, "That because on Thursdays and Fridays they have like training sessions and they go to specific areas of the rail yard and fly through all kinds of obstacles".

"Really," Crafco responded, "and how would you know that, if the two of you are always supposed to be here watching the bridge?"

"Because we were curious," Was Reaper's response. "So on several occasions we split up and one stayed here and the other followed the group that left. We thought that maybe they met Mosaic there, and we wanted to know what they were doing." Of course the real reason was that they wanted to know what they were doing because it seemed every time a group returned they were always laughing and happy and kidding each other. However, Reaper was not going to tell Crafco that, he was not as stupid as Crafco thought he was.

Crafco was not as gullible as Reaper thought he was either, for he realized that they had done it probably out of curiosity and not out of any real plan to see if Mosaic was there or not. Either way Crafco did not care, for this was the type of information he needed so that he could plan his next move accordingly. He wanted to know the comings and goings of all the birds at K-Bridge, so they told him day by day what they could remember. As they were giving Crafco the accounts of each day, Reaper kept trying to look sideways nonchalantly, but his attempt to go unnoticed as he looked to the side got so sadly obvious that Crafco finally asked what he was doing. His response was, "Uuh, Nothing." Reaper said blankly. Crafco, with irritation in his voice said, "Do I look like I was born yesterday, do I look stupid? Why do you keep looking away, instead of at me as we are talking? Are you hiding something? "

With nervous response Reaper said, "No, I ain't hiding nothing… honest, I'm not." He stopped to see what Crafco's response would be, and when Crafco didn't say a word, but just kept looking at him, Reaper finally said, "I was looking at my day sticks and number counting stems."

"You're what?" Crafco asked with genuine interest in what Reaper had said. He gave an encouraging smile at Reaper and asked him to explain. With Crafco using his most pleasant voice of encouragement, Reaper explained that it was really difficult to remember what birds had come on what days and what the number had wound up staying the night. Because of that difficulty, he and Donkey had come up with day sticks and number stems. He showed Crafco a stick stripped entirely of bark and that would be day one, and then a sick with two areas stripped was day two, and so on for each day of the week, and for every week the day sticks would start over again. Then, they used grass stems to represent the birds, one for each of the birds that spent the night. When Crafco looked at the area where the sticks and stems where he smiled. "So this would be yesterday and last night before you left. Fourteen birds stayed the night at the bridge, right?" asked Crafco. Reaper studied the pile Crafco was pointing to; he was moving his beak as he was counting the stems, and then counted them again, "Yes." Reaper finally replied with hesitation in his voice.

"Very clever," Crafco said, as a compliment to their ingenuity. Yes, very clever indeed. With that accolade they looked at the piles of stems and after looking at two weeks of counters, it appeared that the average number of birds that had spent the night had gone up. He had told them that for the next week or so they too would have to stay the night, for he needed to know exactly how many birds were staying at the bridge. With that instruction given, he decided to stay and spend the night along with Donkey and Reaper. Because he had arrived early, he decided to watch the new method they had invented, he wanted to see them using their counting stems, and to his surprise they had the count correct. At about ten minutes before the sun finally set two, more birds joined those already at the bridge. Crafco, Donkey and Reaper spent a very easy calm and uneventful night watching the bridge and its occupants. At first light, they watched the K-Bridge birds wake up and start milling around and then the entire group sixteen birds took to the air and left the bridge unattended. Crafco mentally counted the number of bird and took notice of those he recognized. He did not recognize six birds as K-bridge flock. However, which he identified as birds from the north flock. Four of them were Shamus's sons and two were his daughters, and the balance he did not recognize at all. "How often is that group here?" Crafco asked pointing to Shamus' offspring out to Donkey as they flew by.

Donkey shrugged his shoulders in an uninterested I do not know manner. "I'd say some of them at least every night." Reaper replied, before Crafco could reprimand Donkey for being a slacker. "Some every night... hum." Crafco repeated more to himself rather than to either of his two companions. Crafco smiled to himself, and he stretched and yawned. He then told his two underlings he had an important appointment he could not miss and that he wanted at least one of them to stay on watch all the time. If they needed food or water they would have to take turns, or they would have to wait until he returned. However, under no circumstances were they to leave their post unattended. One of them must be there watching the bridge at all times, and he did not care if there were any birds there or not. They understood just how serious Crafco was when he said, "I'd hate to have to suspend you two because I've grown very fond of you and I trust you two will do the right thing, and not cause me to have to reduce your function and bring in additional help. That is a very difficult decision I do not want to make. Understand?" he finished more forcefully then he had initially intended. However, by the looks on their faces, the intent of his message had made it home to their small brains, and both said in unison, "Don't worry Boss, we won't let you down!"

They both took the words "reduced function" and "bring in additional help" as statements meaning, "To be replaced." Both knew Crafco well enough to know he did not reduce functions; he seldom gave second chances, they felt lucky. Birds that displeased or crossed Crafco were never seen again because they disappeared or were found dead or dying. So both shook their heads yes, they would not let him down, and they would both do exactly as he had directed. Both said they understood his instructions and they both assured him they could be trusted and they would wait until he returned before they would go for food and water.

Crafco said, "Good, I know you two won't let me down, again." He smiled as he pulled both of them in close to him and he once again restated that he knew they would not let him down. With that direction reinforced, Crafco released them, telling them he'd be back in a couple of hours, and took to the air leaving them to ponder his words.

Even though he had scared them, he knew that they only had a certain attention span; to say it was short was an understatement. If nature called and the urge became too great they would do what was required. He only hoped that they would do it one at a time. He realized it did not matter how much he threatened them, at a certain point in time they would acquiesce and then tend to their own needs, all creatures did. In his own way Crafco liked them, well, he liked the control he had over them, he liked the control, but as is so often the case one brain cannot control three bodies, but in this case, Crafco believed that's exactly what was needed, if he were to get the required results and information to get his plan to work. He had to admit they had come up with a good way to keep track of the number of birds at the bridge on any given night. Overall, they were not very bright and he had to do most of the thinking for them. He had made a veiled threat and they had responded for their body language had told him so. For now, they would do exactly as he had commanded and he felt confident that they would be there when he returned from his visit to Luo.

Crafco flew the seven miles from K-Bridge to the east end of the rail yard's outer perimeter and across the four lanes of the busy highway to the rail yards main, eight-story office building in fifteen minutes. It was an old building. Built in the early forties, and still looked as imposing as it had when it was first built. The historic society had claimed it as their own, and they and the railroad had spent money on it over the years to keep it in pristine condition. It still housed all the offices of the railroad, and rail yard workers and executives, and was one of the most beautiful buildings for at least fifty miles in any direction.

As he approached it, he diverted his flight path and headed directly to the eighth-window sill in from the corner, which was Lou's office. The window had been left open and as he landed, he walked onto the inner ledge of the window to find himself standing in Lou's office. There sitting on the inner ledge of the window were two small clean bowls, one with pigeon food and the other with clean fresh water. Sitting in a chair two feet from the ledge sat Lou, a middle-aged Chinese man. Lou always wore a suit, and tie, as far back as Crafco could remember, regardless of the weather; he always had a jacket on as well.

Lou smiled at seeing Crafco, and welcomed him saying, "Hello my friend, welcome to my humble office. Please come in, you are right on time, as always and at this early hour you must be hungry and thirsty. Please eat; drink, and then we will talk."

Crafco responded to Lou's greeting, "Hello Lou, how are you this fine morning?" Lou smiled back at Crafco and once again insisted that Crafco eat before they started to talk about anything, "A full stomach will not disturb the brain, because an empty one always does." He said.

Crafco started to eat. He really did not like or dislike Lou, but he definitely liked Lou's manners and that every time he visited there was always food and water offered. To Crafco Lou was a human, a means to an end, another resource for him to exploit. While on the other hand Lou saw Crafco as a good luck charm, a good omen, and the reason for all his good fortune. Lou thought back... The fates had brought them together five, no six years ago, and they had developed a cordial and co beneficial type of relationship, one built on trust and friendship.

Lou watched Crafco eat and thought back on the first day they had met. It had been a stormy, miserable cold and rainy day the first time Crafco had appeared, all wet and water logged on Lou's windowsill. Lou, who had been depressed and at his wits end that day had been contemplating all that had gone wrong in his life, and what to do about it including ending it all. Suddenly he was diverted from his thoughts when he heard a tapping on the window. The tapping had taken his attention from himself and had redirected it to the window. Lou had seen Crafco sitting there at the window, all wet and disheveled, and he had walked to the window, opened it and had invited Crafco in from the cold and wet.

For Lou, the minute he had let Crafco in on that miserable night his luck had started to change. It had started with a small mental change, and a little light had gone off in his head. He remembered what he had once been told by a fortuneteller; that a bird would enter his life, when least expected and that would be a sign that his luck and kismet would be reversed. A few minutes before Crafco had arrived Luo would not have believed that a bird of any kind would have entered his life that it would have been impossible, even though he really believed in fortunetellers. The fortuneteller he had seen this five days earlier, had foreseen this moment, had said it would happen, she had predicted a bird would enter his life and that would be the reversal of all his bad luck.

Well, he sure had needed it; for his boss had just informed him he would not be getting the promotion, which Jim Shea would be getting it instead. This was bad news seeing that he and his brothers had just bought a two hundred acre ranch, they had figured on the extra money from the new position would be the means to make the payments. He could not back out of it now, all the papers had been signed and the families had all moved onto the property. He was the oldest and he was to be the supplier of the cash to get things going and to keep things going. With the news, of not getting the promotion, he had gotten this morning all the plans they had all made looked like they were in jeopardy. He had stayed late at work and had been going through the numbers, his income and the bills that needed to be paid every month. Things had not looked good to him, no matter how he figured it. They had miscalculated, and had counted on those "birds in the bush", as their own. Yes, he had admonished himself for not having been more careful, he should not have counted what he did not have, and now all was in jeopardy for his family

Now it was not; here was the bird. The bird the fortuneteller had said would change his life had come. How, he did not know, as he looked at the water soaked pigeon. Still he knew it would, it all made sense somehow oddly enough it felt right. As he watched Crafco eating, he thought to himself, he was not superstitious, but his lucky number was eight and it was the eighth day of the eighth month that this pigeon... his lucky bird had showed up. Looking back on it, from that moment on everything had changed, it had not even seemed odd to him that this pigeon and he had been able to talk, and it had all seemed natural. Crafco and Lou had talked for hours that first day as if they were kindred spirits. Both were ambitious and had desires to be great and powerful. As they talked both realized, they needed help getting there.

Crafco listened to Lou's explanation of his dilemma, his needs and his desires. While listening, Crafco to the realization he could help, but did not tell Lou how. He wanted Lou in his debt; and he figured there was definitely a benefit in having a human ally. The fact that Lou and his family had wanted to start a hunting ranch was what had sparked the idea in Crafco's mind and if Lou bought into his idea, then Lou could help Crafco with his plans to eventually become a flock leader.

Crafco was debating with himself should he tell Lou about his plan, or should he try to make him an unknowing ally. Crafco had caught on almost instantly that he was a special sign to Lou. Crafco was not sure how he realized this but he knew that if he could help Lou, Lou would do as he asked. Therefore, Crafco had listened, had listened with great intent, and as he listened, his mind was racing, putting all he heard in perspective. While he had been feigning interest, he had developed, a plotted, a plan that would resolve Lou's short-term problems, and him with his long-term problems, and eventually help Crafco with his ambitions and long-term goals and aspirations as well.

The actions he was contemplating unbeknownst to Lou would forever bind them together, and from that day forward their fates were intertwined and inseparable. Crafco had been smarter than his human counterpart, or at least that night he was. Crafco the bird was the brilliant one that night. Crafco saw Lou as an instrument to be played, so that he Crafco, could win his ultimate prize, to become flock leader, to rule an area of the rail yard and all those that lived there.

Crafco was eating heartily from the food bowl, and he then stopped and took a long draw from the watering bowl, "Ah!" he said, "That sure feels good. I just love this water that you make with the Jasmine in it." As he looked and smiled at Lou, "Mind if I eat a little more?" he asked Lou.

Lou smiled back at Crafco, "No, my friend. Eat ... eat until you are full. After which, we'll talk and make our final plans." With that said Lou got up and went to the pot sitting on the counter, and took out a tea bag and made himself a cup of green jasmine tea. Lou returned to his chair, he sat down and let his mind once again wandered back in time to how Crafco had helped change his fortune.

On that first day, Crafco had explained to Lou that he needed a chance to run things, and that he Crafco, would arrange for that to happen. When Lou had asked how, Crafco had told him not to ask, but to just be ready to take charge. Crafco had spent the night in Lou's office and at first light of the next morning; he had flown away, still not telling Lou his exact plan.

The first thing Crafco had done was feed Lou's superstitions and he had done this by arranging and causing an accident to Mr. Shea, Lou's only obstacle to his promotion. Crafco had done a flying aerial attack on Shea as he was descending a flight of stairs at one of the warehouses in the rail yard. Shea had fallen down two flights of stairs, broken his right leg in several places, his right arm, and had been knocked unconscious and had been in a coma for two weeks. During that time, and during Shea's convalescence, Lou had been given the job. Only temporarily at first, but as time went by, and Shea could not return, Lou was given the job permanently.

Crafco had visited Lou almost daily during those first early weeks, to develop the relationship and to be sure Lou knew that his luck and new found success was due to Crafco's appearance in his life. Of course, Lou would have believed that even if Crafco had only come to visit once a week. Crafco had made a point of getting information for Lou. Crafco and his cronies had made a point of gathering tidbits of information about the rail yard activities that he had passed on to Lou. This had made Lou seem really knowledgeable and insightful and the upper echelons of management took notice of this. Lou appeared to be on top of things and was very much in step with what was happening at all areas of the rail yards.

One of the biggest concerns at the rail yards had been on how to control the pigeon population. Not all the efforts taken to date had worked. Even all the time spent on the pigeon roosting sites by the rail yard employees had never resulted in getting very many pigeons, maybe a dozen per raid.

Lou however, changed all that with Crafco's help. It was really quite simple, for Crafco knew more about pigeons than anyone did, and he helped Lou invent new equipment and plans on how to perform a raid and get the best results. Lou would tell Crafco that he was a Godsend, and one of the best friends Lou had. Crafco had not done it out of friendship, or even because he liked Lou, rather because it had opened up space. Empty now of occupants and several of the areas of the rail yard would now be open space that Crafco now could claim, as his own. This was all a part of his elaborate plan to eventually become flock leader. It even was Crafco that had suggested that the pigeons could be used at the Game Ranch, as part of the birds the hunters could hunt. He and Lou had discussed it right after Lou and his family had made the first successful raid at the building near one of the switch relays, this first raid had netted them thirty birds. Lou was trying to figure out what to do with thirty unwanted pigeons. To kill them out right and dispose of the bodies seemed a waste and the animal rights group's would be all over him. He did not even want to take a chance on negative publicity; he was too new in the job and wanted nothing to jeopardize him keeping it.

It was Crafco who had suggested keeping the birds at the ranch and then, having a pigeon hunt. Luo and his family took it from there, and even Crafco would not have expected his meager idea of a pigeon shoot to have turned into an annual event where several thousand birds were needed to make it a success. Luo and his family had done two shooting hunts a year, the annual spring and winter "Passenger Pigeon Derby". At first, it had been a one and a half day event, twice a year, they charged several hundred dollars per hunter and they would prepare the birds that were shot. They also raised squab birds and each hunter, at the end of the hunt, would get two squabs to take home. The pigeons that were shot were birds bought at pet stores and those captured at the rail yards, and any place else, owners of private property wanted them removed. Luo's family would charge to remove the pigeons, and then would charge hunters to shoot them for sport, and they would prepare them as well for a great feast on the nights' meal after the hunt. It worked out so well the first year that they decided to do two big events every year for hunters to shoot pigeons. In the meantime they also added other shooting events monthly for other game birds; pheasants, quail, prairie chickens, doves in season, turkeys and then the twice yearly the big Pigeon Derby shoot. Which now was a two and a half day event, with a waiting list.

As Luo's fortune changed and improved, Crafco's plans seemed to always end up the same. It seemed that no matter how well

Crafco planned, how cleverly he schemed his plans to become a bona fide flock leader they always fell short. Every time he failed, he would think the world was against him, that the fates despised him. He in turn would feel like giving in, but then the rebellious part of him would take control and not let him acquiesce. Yet, there was a part of him, the part that was at the core of his being, his basic energy, that would take hold and take control and he would once again start planning. When this happened, his resolve to succeed would find new life. He would explode into a new flurry of thoughts and plans and actions to take him to the top.

So here, they were six years later Luo was doing great and Crafco was still trying to obtain his dream. So as Crafco finished his breakfast and took his last drink of morning water Luo asked him, "Crafco, my friend, how are you this fine lovely morning? You look fit, but as if you have something on your mind." Luo finished very politely and with a warm smile on his face.

"Luo, I'm here because I have given more thought to your problem of being short on birds for the annual event. I came to tell you, I believe I can help you fill in part of your shortages. You will probably have to have some people ready in short notice, probably within a day or two at the most. I believe I can have about twenty birds available for you to snatch from their perches." Crafco said in a very businesslike fashion to Luo's salutation.

At hearing that Luo smiled even broader, "Crafco, not even a hello for your old friend? Is it always business with you? There is more to life than business and getting ahead. You need to stop and take the time to appreciate life, before it totally passes you by."

At that, Crafco did stop, and he smiled back at Luo, "Easy for you to say. You're at the top of the world; you have gotten everything you want." Then shaking his head he said, "While I still have to slave and scrimp to make it. For a pigeon in the real world, it is tough. We have many obstacles to overcome just to get a decent meal and clean water. Luo if you only knew how difficult it can be some days."

Luo looked at Crafco realizing that Crafco had not obtained what he most desired and feeling sorry for him, nodded his head and said, "Crafco, okay then, as you wish, back to business. How and where can I expect this delivery?"

Crafco shook his head and laughed at the way Luo stated things, "Deliver!" he smiled, "You mean capture don't you? They will be at the K-bridge, same as thy were the last time."

Luo looked with surprise at Crafco and said, "The K-Bridge! I was under the impression we took all the birds that were there the last time. They could not have re-populated the bridge that quickly! Based on our past history with the pigeons it takes months for them to re-settle any place we've raided in the past."

"Yes, normally that is correct. However, not this time my friend. There were ten that slipped through your nets from your last raid on the bridge and they still occupy the bridge. As long as they do, I can't claim it as open space, nor can I take control of it until it is."

"Crafco, I need more than ten birds, I'm short fifty birds and I'm working with pet stores and private breeders to make up my shortfall. It just isn't worth my time and effort for just ten birds." Luo said as he rubbed his chin, which was a thing Luo always did when he did not want to insult the person, or in this case, Crafco, a bird he owed a lot to, basically his success and families good fortune.

"I understand, what if I told you I could guarantee that a minimum of thirty birds will be there two nights from now? Could you get enough of your associates together, would that be worth your while?" Crafco asked, knowing by Luo's body language that Luo had already made up his mind that he would do it.

Luo laughed, "Sure, for that quantity. If you guarantee the quantity, I'll arrange it." Luo really did not care if Crafco did or did not, he needed all the birds he could get his hands-on. By any means, he would have been there to take them, but he wanted to get as much out of the raid as he could. He knew Crafco well enough to know that Crafco knew he needed more; and if at all possible, Crafco would get him more than the measly ten birds.

Luo would get his three brothers and their four oldest children to help him this time. On the last raid on the bridge, he had hired several non-family members and they had kept the birds they had caught and sold them elsewhere, this time he would only use family. His brothers may complain a little about taking the kids out of school, but the kids would love it, a reason to stay out all night and then a day off from school on top it all. "Sure!" He repeated, "You make sure they're there and I'll take care of the rest."

Crafco nodded his head yes, "Very good." He said, "I'll have the birds there and I'll call late on the day of the raid, so I can tell you exactly where they will be roosting, so you don't miss a one this time. Missing those ten the last time cost me the ability to claim the bridge for my own. This time I want no mistakes!" Crafco said the latter a little more forcefully than he had intended. He did not or had not wanted to offend Luo, based on Luo's facial expressions he had not.

Luo responded to Crafco's concerns by saying, "Crafco, my friend, you worry too much. If you give me, their locations all the birds will be removed from the bridge this time, I assure you. The only reason we missed a few the last time, was because of the sheer numbers that were there. This time we will not leave until we have them all. I promise you we will get them all this time. I need you in charge as much as you want to be in charge." He finished his comments to reassure Crafco of his commitment to him and his desires.

"I know." Crafco said in response, "It is really a good working relationship, we have here. You can help me keep those that are against me totally out of the picture. Yes, you are indeed a good and trusted ally." Well, one of four Crafco thought.

Luo had assured Crafco that nothing would go wrong. They spent about thirty minutes discussing the plan and all the particulars of the plan. Crafco assured Luo he would supply him with the exact number of birds that would be at the bridge. After which Crafco left, and as he flew back to his two spies on watch at the bridge, he reflected back on his other three allies, Talon, Joel and Ignoble Vile. Yes, he smiled to himself, he had it all worked out if one ally failed him he had the others that could help him meet his aspirations for greatness.

Interesting Pigeon Fact

Pigeons are highly sociable animals.

They will often be seen in flocks of 20-30 birds.

<a href="http://www.softschools.com/facts/animals/pigeon_facts/589/">Pigeon Facts</a>

Crafco had given his two cronies very specific instructions after his meeting with Luo to be sure they took special notice of where the K-bridge flock and their guests roosted. He had also told them he wanted to know their movements and all activities at the bridge. They had informed him yesterday after having been given the new instruction for only a day that they knew that pretty much already and that they had spent the day making sure. Crafco had wanted to be sure about this and had spent the whole day confirming their information. The one thing he had noticed was that there were more birds than he had thought there should have been. He had drawn up a crude map using a scrap of paper and some mud, which he would take with him the next time he visited Luo, so he would be sure Luo did not miss a bird the night of the raid. He had stopped by again this morning to be sure Donkey and Reaper where still there watching, and it appeared that all was as it should be at the bridge. The only thing he had found unusual was the number of additional birds at the bridge that morning. However, Donkey had assured him it was not at all unusual, that regularly large numbers of birds showed up some mornings. He explained with confidence those were the days they held special training sessions, and competitions through the courses K-Bridge flock values so highly. Crafco knew about the different flying courses that the K-Bridge flock liked to fly and always thought it a waste of time and energy, but each to their own he thought, soon it wouldn't matter how well they flew because they'd ultimately be eliminated, gone from the bridge and his life forever.

Now to finalize step two of his plan, to rid himself of the K-Bridge flock remnants and the troublesome birds at Southeast flock of the rail yard all in one fell swoop he thought. He indirectly controlled the flock on the northern perimeter of the rail yard through his ally Oos. Once that both parts of his plan were completed he would claim both of the areas, one through the puppet leader he had put in place; he would have uncontested power over the entire Southeast section. In addition, the other he would control K-Bridge as well, not bad he thought. He would then directly be in command of the largest section of the rail yard and over time, he would rule it all. He was getting excited about the possibility and his heart had started to race at the thought of being in charge; patience he would tell himself, one-step at a time. He had been so close before and always something had happened, things had gone wrong and he would have to start all over again. Now it finally appeared that fate unequivocally was on his side and all his careful planning was coming to fruition.

Crafco looked at Donkey and Reaper, and said, "Remember, one of you needs to be here at all times. Do not leave the watch unattended, understood!" He stated rather, then asked.

"Sure," they said in unison, "We understand! We know what to do. We will not let you down Boss, and we will keep tabs on where every one of them stays here at the bridge. Go ahead and take care of whatever you got to do, we'll be here." Donkey reassured him.

With their reassurances fresh in his mind, Crafco had departed to meet with Kimber, the brother of his puppet flock leader of the Southeast flock Trent. Crafco had always thought of Kimber as being arrogant, impatient and a bore. Crafco didn't like him at all and so what he was about to do to Kimber and his small group of followers didn't bother him one bit. The way Crafco saw it Trent was jealous of Kimber and Kimber was jealous of Trent's status as flock leader, and so Crafco had played one against the other. Kimber was smarter than Trent was and posed the greatest danger to Crafco's plans and so he had to be neutralized, the same way Niner had been a threat and needed neutralization. Kimber had a small, but very loyal and militant following. Getting Kimber out of the way by conventional methods had not been an option. Kimber had been overly confident and he had told Crafco that if anything happened to him, his followers would come looking for Crafco. The implication of the words and how they were spoken had left nothing to the imagination as to what Kimber meant. If anything happened to him, his band would take their revenge out on Crafco. This, in Crafco's mind, had sealed their fates along with Kimber's.

Of course, as was so often the case with Crafco, he had misread almost all of Kimber's reasoning for wanting his own space.

Kimber really was not jealous of Trent; he just did not like the fact that Trent seemed to be under Crafco's control. That Trent had no mind of his own. It seemed every time Crafco had visited with Trent that Trent would start with his innuendos and sarcastic remarks, saying; that he wanted him to leave that he needed his group's spaces, and that he was taking care of Kimber.

Crafco had lain out a plan and by manipulating Trent and keeping a constant dialog with Kimber. He had convinced Kimber that he had come up with a way for him to get his own area to be flock leader over. It was to homestead the unoccupied area of K-Bridge. Crafco had found a loophole in the pigeon laws that would allow Kimber and his group to homestead the areas of K-Bridge that the current flock did not have birds for that could occupy the bridge adequately. What made it even better Kimber had told Crafco that he had heard a rumor that the young flock leader hadn't been at the bridge for weeks. This delighted Crafco, for it meant that those that were there were leaderless and would do as protocol dictated. Pigeon edict would not allow them to refuse Kimber's group at least an overnight stay, as long as they arrived one hour before sunset, and as long as they could convince the birds at the K-Bridge, they were on a journey. If it all worked out as planned he'd be rid of two loose end in one fell swoop, both problems gone.

Therefore, the plan had been hatched; conveniently fitting into all the other things going on in Crafco's scheming mind and unscrupulous world, and today it would be set into motion. In addition, tonight, he thought, it would see fruition and all my worries will be over. Well for now anyway. He would have the K-Bridge flock out of the way, be rid of Kimber and his followers, yes he thought, part one of his plan would be completed. Tomorrow he would move his own group of followers from the Northeast flock to the bridge and set himself up as flock leader. Yes, Crafco, said to himself, patting himself mentally on the back, you will have it all tomorrow.

As Crafco approached the Southeast section of the rail yard, the outflyers had met him, recognized him and flown with him and had escorting him to their meeting hall. With his escorts in close proximity to him, he had landed and walked into the hall. There, waiting for him, was Trent, Kimber and several of the other flock dignitaries.

Trent stepped forward and greeted Crafco warmly and with genuine joy at seeing him. As he hugged him he asked, "How are you doing today, Sir?"

"I'm fine, just fine and you Trent?" was Crafco's response, as he turned to greet Kimber who had not moved from where he had been standing. "And how are you Kimber? Ready for an exciting day?" Not waiting for an answer Crafco proceeded to greet all the rest of those that were waiting.

Kimber was not quite sure how to respond. Should he say he was apprehensive of the whole thing? Or that he really did not trust Crafco. That he believed that Crafco must have had ulterior motives. That he did not want to go through with it, and that he had major reservations about the whole plan. Kimber felt there was more to the plan then what he had been told, and that what he didn't know... what that was, but he felt very uneasy, and apprehensive, but instead he said in a low voice as Crafco moved away from the rest, "Yes, we are all in for a very interesting day of major changes. How do you think those left at the K-bridge will respond?" A stupid question Kimber thought after he had asked it.

Crafco shot Kimber a mocking wry smile and in the similar low voice, "According to protocol, I'm sure." was Crafco's narcissistic response to the questions. Crafco continued still smiling, "They will allow you to stay, to spend the night. They will more than likely be a little hostile, I am sure, to you staying beyond the evening. However, if I am correct about the young flock leader not being there, they will eventually acquiesce to you because etiquette and custom dictates they do. If I am wrong, then you may have a fight on your hands, or they may accept your group and welcome you into their flock. Either way you will be accepted as either new flock members and leader, or have to fight to become the leader. Neither action is out of the norm, so quit worrying. You look hesitant... having second thoughts?" Crafco finished with a raise eye crest.

Kimber had thought he looked perfectly normal. How had Crafco picked up on his feeling of uneasiness? Was he that easy to read, or had Crafco just been lucky in his assessment of the situation? Of course, what Kimber did not know was that Trent had told Crafco of their many conversations dealing with the plan and his trepidation's about it being the right thing to do.

Crafco did not wait for an answer to his question and continued, by restating his question, "You're not having second thoughts are you? Because you're the one that wanted to have a flock area of your own, you wanted to be a flock leader." Crafco hesitated for effect and then continued, "Here is your opportunity. I'm giving it to you on a silver platter." After having said that Crafco waited for a response.

As they had been talking all the rest of those that had been in attendance to greet Crafco had left. Trent, Kimber and Crafco had retreated to a private area to get into and finish their in-depth conversation. The conversation was mostly between Kimber and Crafco, with Trent just listening and occasionally nodding in agreement with Crafco or Kimber as the situation demanded, not wanting to seem aligned to either's position.

Kimber looked at Crafco and said, "Yes, I wanted the opportunity…" To an audible sigh of relief from Trent and a good, but cautious, I'm glad to hear that node from Crafco. However, what Kimber did not say was, "I'm not Trent and if you think I'm going to be another one of your puppet leaders, you're mistaken. What is in all this for you, Crafco? Why this sudden interest in my well-being and me?" He wanted this opportunity all right, but for good reason he had never spoken those words to Crafco. He knew Crafco, and Crafco, gave nothing without wanting something in return. He thought this and instead of being forceful, he decided to be bold, by calmly almost as an afterthought, saying, "And, Crafco what's in this for you?"

"Well, as you know I have helped Trent gain the position of flock leader of the Southeast flock. All I asked of him was to be his advisor and to be allowed to help whenever possible. Which Trent kindly agreed to…" as he looked at Trent who sheepishly nodded, yes, while Crafco finished his comment "and so Kimber I ask that you consider that as well"?

Yes, Kimber thought, Trent had agreed. In addition, ever since that day, from that point forward, as Kimber saw it, Trent became Crafco's puppet, doing almost nothing without Crafco's blessing, or what Crafco wanted.

"Yes, Crafco," Kimber responded, "I definitely want the opportunity to be a flock leader and to be able to help those that need my guidance. Yes of course," he responded with a slight pause, "when needed, I will seek out advice and I will definitely keep your kind offer in mind." Kimber hoped Crafco had gotten the message, and fully understood his meaning. He glanced to see what Trent's reaction was and Trent had a slight look of shock and anger on his face, but he said nothing, just nodded.

Crafco just smiled and shook his head as if in approval, "Good, I'm glad that you haven't changed your mind." he said. "Just stay with the plan and all will work out for the best." I will be rid of you and your interfering ways soon, enough he thought. Even with your cautious and careful attitude, you are transparent to me. You act so high and mighty, always trying to whip up trouble between Trent and me. Nevertheless, just stay with my plan, my "little Lingo" and I will be rid of you soon enough. Crafco called anyone he wanted to get rid of a "little Lingo", for it reminded him of his overbearing brother and what he had done to get rid of him, and all the pain he had endured before Lingo had met with a very unfortunate accident.

Smiling inwardly "Good, very good!" Crafco said, "Let's go over the time table of the plan once again." Crafco seemed so concerned Kimber thought. There is nothing to the plan, you go late, you get invited to stay and then you do not leave ... Kimber, daydreaming, had missed some of what Crafco had said but acted as if he had heard it all. "I'll come by and visit you tomorrow afternoon with several pairs from the Northeast flock that need nesting space. They will ask you because they will believe you are flock leader. You will give permission as if you are the flock leader, which will seal you being the flock leader." Crafco finished looking at Kimber as if waiting for an answer. Kimber apparently had not responded quickly enough to Crafco's liking, which caused him to discuss the plan and the timetable one more time, which Kimber found absurd, but politely listened. Soon after re-explaining the plan one more time and with Crafco satisfied all was comprehended, Crafco left with Trent in tow.

Kimber had watched them go, and gave a sigh of relief, then his mate, a blue bar white flight hen named, Smalt stepped from the shadows and hugged him saying, " There is more to this than meets the eye, you know?"

"Yes." He said in response to her question, "I believe there is, but I haven't been able to figure out what his angle is. I can't imagine him doing this out of the kindness of his heart." Kimber said with a weary expression on his face. "What is his angle? Him doing something good, or right seems against his character from all I have been able to ascertain, and there is something here we're missing, but what?"

"But we've checked out all the angles, and looked at it from all the different perspectives we could think of and it's all within pigeon laws, customs and propriety to do what we are planning." She responded to his concerns. "I even, created a "for instance" scenario which I talked to Oonal about. And he and my younger sister Flights looked it all up in the leaves, and all that we are planning is legal based on the precedence already set by previous actions, taken by other flocks in the past."

"Yes, I know, and that's what worries me even more. I cannot guess Crafco doing something within the normal requirements of good manners. His reputation realistically does not fit his behavior or actions on this." Kimber said with suspicion in his voice. "By the way, what did Oonal and Flights say when you told them? I thought they would both have objected."

"I didn't tell them what we were actually planning on doing; I told them it had to do with Trent." She said with a smile. "About Crafco, Yes, dear I know. But what can we do?" She stopped and waited for his response. When it did not come she continued, "We'll follow the plan and keep our eyes wide open. You have told the Outflyers and Watchers to be vigilant so when we travel we will all be on high alert. There's nothing else to do, except not go." She finished.

"No," He said, "That's no longer an alternative. Trent expects us to go, so he can reassign our nesting and perch areas. He told me yesterday he has a waiting list and needs the room. If we stay, there will be trouble. I believe he has already promised our spots and has pairs waiting, chomping at the bit to move in."

"That twit! I thought we had until today to change our minds?" she replied with disgust in her voice.

"Technically we did, but he talked to me yesterday and told me what he had done and I promised him we hadn't changed our minds. I told him we were still going forward with the plan. I told him how disappointed I was with him, because even if we had changed our minds, I couldn't have stayed without there being big trouble for all." Kimber stated in a tired voice with a ting of animosity towards his brother.

"Some brother! He is always doing these types of things to you. Why doesn't he think?" Smalt said in disgust with a tinge of loathing in her voice to her own rhetorical question. She really did not had not liked Trent, from the first time she had met him. She thought, 'he was too self-centered and in her opinion, he was always taking advantage of Kimber's good-natured gentleness and easygoing disposition.' She felt that Trent was a bore and that he was not as smart as Kimber and was always using Kimber for his own gain.

'With the brothers, so it had gone,' she thought. The smarter one, the one with the common sense always supporting the one with the lesser intelligence that was until she had come along. She had suggested and maneuvered Kimber so he could also become a flock leader. What it really amounted to was giving him confidence so that he felt he could actually do the job that he already was doing by how he was always getting Trent out of scrapes. She had made him aware that he was the one that was always helping Trent and getting him out of difficult situations.

With her helping him see the truth of the situation, Kimber had finally seen his own abilities. She helped him see he could do the job as well if not better than Trent could. What had made it easier was that there were others who saw it too, that they were disenchanted with Trent and they were willing to follow Kimber. He had become a sub-leader with a loyal following within the Southeast flock. This had both been a good and a bad thing. It had shown him that he was a natural leader, and it had given him confidence, yet it had put him at odds with Trent, and of course with Crafco. The tension between the three had been mounting, palatable in its discord and had been heading towards a crescendo that hadn't looked favorable for any, and then by a sheer stroke of luck the K-Bridge business and its availability had popped up and had been presented.

Trent had suggested to Kimber that he and his small band leave and make any unoccupied section of the K-bridge their new home, that they could homestead it and that it was all perfectly legal. Kimber, always on the alert and being careful, had researched it and had found it all within the rules of pigeon society and laws, but did that make it right was his concern. There were several ways he could do it. One through outright conquest, through fighting for the position, or he could become an alternate flock leader and eventually the flock leader of K-bridge if the current flock leader did not return, which was his preference. The latter was the simplest and least painful for all. Therefore, they had decided they would homestead a section of the K-bridge not in use and then as time went by, he would slowly take over. He would bring his own following and when it came to a vote to see who would be flock leader, he would win easily, cleanly, with no trouble, just the way he liked it, orderly and with acceptance by all.

Hence, that was the plan. At first, it had been difficult to accept that Trent had come up with it and had found the loopholes in the laws. However, it became apparent over time that his puppet master Crafco had actually come up with the information, which was some cause for concern. Kimber did not like or trust Crafco. Kimber had told her that Crafco was not the good type that he could not imagine Crafco doing anything for anyone without there being some ulterior motive.

With her sharing the same concerns, she had gone to Crafco and had asked him directly what was in it for him? She had been amazed at Crafco's response and candidness, which at first she thought was somewhat brutal at the time, but as she had thought about it, it seemed quite accurate. It was simple he had said, Kimber and his followers occupy a lot of Southeast's prime areas that he... a slip of the tongue that Crafco ignored and corrected, he met Trent needed. Kimber was a leader with no place to go and no area to lead. Given that, Trent was flock leader and that he Crafco, was not about to allow anyone to replace; it was the only logical thing for Kimber to do. If Kimber did this, then all would be satisfied and no battles or fights would be required. There would be no disruption to the Southeast flock's every day routine, and that was always a good thing for any flock.

Crafco had also explained how prime an area K-bridge was for families and bringing up youngsters. Even though what had happened there had been a tragedy, life must go on. There was plenty of room there and the current flock leader was very young and inexperienced. That Kimber should not have any problems deposing him, especially with his following. A simple vote and it would be done. Crafco had made it all sound so simple, so forgone in its conclusion, only a fool would have said no. And, that was why Kimber had so many second thoughts she thought, it did all seem too simple, too good to be true and in cases where this was the under lying concern, normally true.

Trent had seen it as a positive as well. What else would she have expected from Trent? In addition, once Crafco had suggested it, Trent had pushed it on Kimber to make a commitment and to do it. She knew that Trent had been frustrated with Kimber's stonewalling and delays, as much as she had. However, she knew her mate; he had to be sure it was legal and all above board. He had researched it, had talked to others, and had Smalt research it as well and she had found it all proper; it was a legal thing that could be done. With the knowledge, it was legal, Kimber had talked to his followers about what had been proposed and all had agreed they would all go and that was what had settled it. All ten pairs and the five singles had all committed themselves to the plan. There were also three other pairs that had said they would join him once he became the established flock leader.

The day had come and today they would go south, they would enact the first step of the plan and get invited to stay.

———————————   ———————————

At K-bridge things had started out quite normal for a flock without their flock leader and with the knowledge, they were under constant surveillance. The sky was gray and the sun, which was out, was having a hard time breaking through the gloom. There was a fine mist in the air and the morning was wet and damp. At the K-bridge, the feelings were as gloomy as the weather. Millet stood at the edge of the shelter that the bridge supplied and watched those watching him. He saw movement out of the corner of his eye as Shadow approached Millet; he turned slightly to acknowledge Shadows arrival.

"Are they still there?" was Shadow's question to Millet as he approached.

"Oh yes, they are still there. I sure wish we knew exactly who they are, and what they want. Every time we get near they seem to disappear." Millet said a little frustrated.

"I think it is Crafco's two associates, based on what Flick said about them being two dark Checks," Shadow replied as a response to Millet's question.

"I think them being dark checks is an interesting thing, but that they are Crafco's cronies is just Flicks own blindness of what he wants to believe and his dislike of Crafco. There are a lot of dark checks in this world you know? And, as rumor has it, Crafco isn't the only one interested in the Bridge." Millet stated matter of facially.

"You're right Millet. But I'm not just basing my beliefs on what Flick said, but on what happened at the pools two days ago, between Colors and Donkey and again with Rambler." Shadow said with suspicion in his voice.

"You don't mean that innocent encounter between them and his natural question about Mosaic and how he was doing, do you?" Millet said in response to Shadow's comments.

"Well, yes, it's not just because of the questions, but more as to where he was and what he was doing. That is what I am talking about. I found that interesting, you know, with it all coming out of the blue and all. Donkey has never ever taken an interest in us before. I just find it strange, and the rumor is that he really is associated with Crafco." Shadow hesitated, "And that's what worries me." He finished.

While they had been talking, Colors had awoken and she had meandered over to where they were standing. She stretched herself as she asked them, "What are you two talking about so intently?"

Both turned and greeted her, "Morning" they said as one, and then Millet continued, "Just talking about our two friends out there." Pointing to the Jacaranda tree off in the distance, some two hundred yards out, as they all could see a slight movement among its branches.

"I think they've got company, from the looks of things." Colors replied, "Changing of the guard, I think."

"Could be, I sure would like to know who they are and what they're up to? Must be important to have caused them to stay all night in this kind of damp unfriendly weather." Said Flick, who had walked over to the three, unbeknownst to them, for they had been so intent on trying to see who was out there. None responded to his comments so he went on with, "I'm telling you its Crafco and as sure as I'm standing here whatever he's up to isn't good."
All of them shook their heads in agreement; if it was Crafco, it probably was not a good thing. They all stood there several more minutes engaged in speculation as to all the possibilities and watched their watchers. If it was or wasn't Crafco, they all agreed it wasn't a good thing and that they would all have to be and stay

especially alert, and be on the lookout for the unexpected. By this time, Rambler had joined them as well. Rambler, who had taken over temporally as flock leader in Mosaic's absence, looked at his companions and said, "We have a busy day ahead of us, and we should go and get some nourishment and exercise. I'm stiff and need to loosen up my muscles, before our guests arrive."

They had invited Flicks six brothers, and several birds they had met at the pools, to come over and participate in the track and obstacle course training day. Flick had been bragging to his brothers ever since he had been doing it with Mosaic and Trapper, that he could beat any one of them with one wing tied behind his back, and so they had finally accepted his invitation to come, practice, and see what it was like. In addition, several of the younger birds at the pools who had witnessed the race between Mosaic and Trapper had wanted to come over and had wanted to learn the courses and participate. They had finally gotten up the nerve to ask them the other day if they could learn the courses, and of course, Rambler had said yes.

"One thing." Colors said and asked, "what about leaving the Bridge unattended? Do you think it's a good idea, seeing as we have a constant pair of admirers out there watching our every move?"

"I see no reason not to go on with our daily lives and routine. We know they are there and have been for some time now. We know we are close to breaking the laws of occupancy and flock ownership, but what's a bird to do? We can only hope and pray that Mosaic and the quest group are all right and will be returning to us soon, safe and sound. Until then, we go on with our lives." Shadow said matter-of-factly as he shrugged his shoulders to emphasize what is a bird to do.

Sky had joined the group as these discussions were taking place and she spoke up, "Shadow's right, we need to act as we always have, any major change in our behavior and we'll only raise suspicions on what's really going on here. And that would cause us more grief and unwanted inquiries then I want to deal with."

Yes, they all agreed that what Sky had said made the most sense. "So let's get everyone up and go eat," Flick stated matter-of-factly and finished with an enthusiastically, "I'm really hungry!" as his crop growled to emphasize his need to eat.

"You are always, hungry." Colors said laughingly, "I believe you have a hollow wing." She teased him.

"Yea, a hollow wing," mimicked Shadow, "the only one I ever saw that could eat more than you, is Trapper. I wonder how they are." He finished by taking a deep breath and then releasing it slowly as if he were freeing all his pent up tension as he exhaled. He then looked at the group sheepishly "I wonder if Moth found them?" he said letting out another deep breath and then he continued, "I was really glad to hear that some of the flock is still alive especially Niner."

"I think we should have gone and rescued them," replied Rambler, "We could have you know, and then we'd have had a real leader again." he said indicating he did not like his role as temporary flock leader. In addition, unlike Mosaic did not have natural tendency towards leading. "No disrespect to Mosaic" he finished.

"I know you're not comfortable with your role as temporary flock leader, but you're doing a fantastic job." Shadow said smiling at Rambler with encouragement. "Besides we discussed it in great detail," he continued, "and it was decided we couldn't leave the bridge without a flock leader for that long a time, especially with our friends out there spying on us every day. You my friend were elected, so just accept it and …. Well you're doing a great job." Shadow finished still smiling.

In an attempt to change the subject, "Moth should have allowed me to have accompanied her," Colors chimed in.

"Well she didn't, and we voted on that too." Was Sky's response as they all spent ten more minutes discussing and restated their opinions on that decision.

"We discussed this at the time and we agreed on the course of action taken" Rambler responded to their grousing, "What's done is done," he finished, "and I'm hungry, too. So let's go eat!"

Of course, they were not done and they all stood there for another half an hour discussing where Trapper and Mosaic could possibly be. Had Trapper made it home okay? Where was Mosaic if Trapper had made it home, why wasn't he back? Had Moth found them? The speculations as to the answers to that question were mind numbing especially for the small group of survivors from the last raid the humans had made on the bridge. Colors finally said, "We'll have to pray for the best and hope they are all okay. What do you say to a morning prayer?" All agreed and they should and they said a little prayer, which they normally did not do. After which they all rose from the K-bridge and headed for the square for breakfast.

Back at the Southeast flock everything had gone pretty much as normal for a day where moving was the big issue for just about everyone, both the ones leaving and the ones staying seemed to be engaged in the event. The hens spent the day cleaning their nesting areas, so that whoever moved in would not have to. You did not want anyone to think you were a slob and not a good housekeeper. In the meantime, the cocks cleaned up the areas around the outside of the nesting and roosting areas because the hens wanted it done. After which they prepared themselves, finished packed any small momentous they had and were ready for the short flight to K-Bridge.

All of Trent's followers were occupied by their different tasks and the day had passed without incident. The only irritant was Trent's constant visits to see how it was going. After the eighth visit within four hours, Kimber finally told him to stop, with his persistence and impatience. Which of course Trent denied he was doing. Kimber told him, to either help, or to stop and stay away. Kimber told him in a humorous way that he was acting like a bird with a gas buildup that could not flagellate to get rid of the pressure.

Trent had not thought it was funny, and had reacted to the comments by saying, "How rude and uncalled for…" but Kimber thought his comment clever and funny and did not care, for it had the desired effect. Trent had not returned the rest of the day. Everything had seemed to go more smoothly from that point on, with everyone doing things in a more relaxed, but hurried fashion, if that were possible, apparently it was by the way, things were progressing. Now an hour and a half before dusk they were ready to go.

Kimber had sent one of his group's outflyers, named Dixson, to let Trent know that all was in order for others to move in and that they were ready to leave. The Dixson had returned in short order and told Kimber, that Trent was pleased, but very busy and thanks, he would talk to him later. Kimber was not pleased with his brother's lack of propriety. He looked at his mate and shrugged his shoulders and then at his small group of twenty-five followers. "Okay!" he said, "No, point in prolonging this, let's go." With that, he and Smelt took to the air followed by the outflyers and the rest of the flock. They circled the Southeast flock's nesting and roosting areas twice, and many waved and shouted their good byes. The flock responded, with waves and shouts back and then they were off on their short trip and their anxiously anticipated new lives.

———— ————

For the K-Bridge flock and their guests the day had gone well and they had been busy and had a lot of fun. Their day had started by going to the square to eat, then to the pools to drink and bathe both in the water and in the sun. There they had met up with Flicks six brothers, who were all excited about the plans for the day. All six seemed to be speaking at once, saying they could not wait to learn and compete at the courses they had heard so much about from Flick.

At the pools, they were also joined by four birds from the flock that occupied the outer perimeter rim of palm trees nesting sites just north of the rail yard's Northeast flock. In addition, there were six birds that lived around the square that also joined them and wanted to become skilled at, and compete in the courses they had heard so much about.

Flick was pleased with himself; he had recruited a total of sixteen birds willing to spend the time to be trained on the courses. Yes he thought, the next time they held a competition there would be the possibility of having plenty of challengers. When Mosaic returns we are really going to have an event he could be proud of, and so the day had started and the group had flown over to the rail yards and had practiced all day long, and, before anyone realized it, dusk was upon them. Rambler had asked them all to stay and spend the night. All had accepted his invitation and they had gotten to the bridge about ten minutes before a group of birds not expected had circled the bridge and asked permission to land and spend the night.

They explained they were on a journey, needed a place to rest and spend the night. Every pigeon raised properly knew it was bad manners to refuse such a request. It was so because basically, if you were ever in a similar situation you would want to be allowed to spend the night, rest and recuperate. "What goes around comes around", was one of a pigeon's favorite saying, and so they always allowed wayward travelers permission to spend the night. Thus, the first part of Crafco's plan was accomplished successfully; Kimber's group were being allowed to spend the night at the bridge without incident or suspicion.

Crafco sat with Donkey and Reaper watching the activities at the K-bridge and he was pleased. By the looks of things, all was going according to plan. He was delighted at what there seemed to be many extra birds at the bridge this evening. The more birds the merrier he thought. By all counts there were twenty-seven total in Kimber's group. Then he had counted six, and six more and four which equaled sixteen and then there were seven more, the total number of all the birds there was fifty-four. He had Donkey and Reaper count them separately and it took several tries but in the end, they all had come up with Fifty-four. Oh yes he thought, Luo will be pleased, "You two stay here and keep an eye on what happens, stay the night, I'll be back in the morning. Have a good night." He said with enthusiasm and a tinge of joy in his voice. With that said he left them and flew over to Lou's office

Lou was happy to see him as usual. He and Lou had discussed their good luck at the plethora of birds at the K-bridge and Crafco had explained where they were roosting. To say Lou was pleased would have been an understatement; he was elated at the news of the quantity of birds waiting for the picking. He kept reassuring Crafco, how great it was and that he was not to worry, for he would catch them all and in the morning, the bridge would be cleared of all birds.

With those reassurances fresh on his mind Crafco left Lou's office and flew home to the Northeast flocks roosting and nesting areas. He wanted to be sure that he was seen there, so no one could connect him with the events that were about to occur.

————————   ————————

The sun had set on a wonderful day as all the residents and guests settled in for the night at the K-bridge. Kimber, who had been apprehensive, finally relaxed and felt all the tensions melt away out of his body by the ease of having him and his group be allowed to stay. The birds that normally occupied the K-bridge had been friendly, cordial and had been genuinely glad to have them stay. They shared the K-bridge with their guests, giving them an entire section unto themselves, where they could rest, relax and feel at home. His entire group and the other guests had settled in for a nice peaceful night of rest and relaxation. When at around midnight or so, Kimber was awakened by a strange noise, it sounded like something scrapping against the concrete sides of the retaining walls of the bridge. He also thought he heard voices, very low and whispering voices.

However, as he listened more intently he heard nothing but silence. The silence was deafening, which did not register in his mind at first that something was wrong. What was wrong was the silence, the lack of insects making their nightly noises. In addition, by the lack of hearing, the other birds relaxed breathing; he knew that several others had been awakened by the eerie silence as well. It suddenly it dawned on him, as he was waking up his mate, Smalt, it happened, pandemonium broke out; the silence was what was wrong, but that realization of that being wrong came too late.

Bright lights came on everywhere and blinded him, he heard shuffling noises, and fighting noises and shouts of let me go! He was grabbed around the middle, lifted from the shelf he was sitting on and unceremoniously and roughly placed into a wooden cloth crate. The top of the crate had slates that allowed him to see out and he watched unable to do anything, as others were being grabbed as well, and were meeting the same fate as he was. It was then to his horror began. Within, only for a few seconds, he saw a hand grabbing, and groping at Smalt; then it had her around the head and neck and she was fighting it and pulling away… and the next thing before his view was blocked, he saw her body flopping around on the shelf as the hand still had her by the head. He was then pushed back into a corner of the crate as additional birds were being shoved into the container.

He did not realize it, but he had screamed out, "No!" and he had collapsed, almost as much as he had been pushed into the corner. One of his outflyers, a hen name Trouble, put her wings around him and hugged him and consoled him, she had witnessed what had occurred to Smalt as well.

It took the humans fifteen minutes to confiscate all the birds at the bridge and thirty more to verify that they had not missed a one. They then lit a small fire and had plucked clean the three birds that had been accidentally killed during the capturing maneuver. Within fifteen minutes of having started the fire, the three birds were roasting over the flames. The smells of cooking pigeon flesh assailed the nostrils of those in the crates and all were wondering who would be next. However, as time passed they came to the realization that they were not to be eaten, at least not on this night.

At first light, the crates they were in had been roughly transported into the bed of an old fifty-seven Chevy pick-up truck sitting on a service road alongside of the bridge. The humans that had captured them were having a small conversation with a human that had come up from the service road. From the tidbit of the conversation, they could overhear it sounded as if they were going on a trip, which would take them too many places where additional birds would be added to the crates that sat in the bed empty. The next thing they knew they were being offered water, which they drank with relish and then they were off.

Kimber had watched all this still in total shock and disbelief. "Where is Smalt?" he had finally asked, and had gotten the answer he didn't want to hear. The answer came from a bird, one of his outflyers named Trouble, "Dead Kimber." She paused as if searching for words, and with hesitation said, "I'm sorry Kimber, but I believe she is dead."

He shook his head no in total disbelief, and asked, "Are you sure?" He asked in a barely audible whisper." In his mind's eye, all he saw was her face, her smile... and with a faraway look in his eyes, he asked once again, "Are you sure?" not wanting to accept what they had told him.

"Yes, almost certain, we did a head count and all the birds at the bridge, except for four have been accounted for. The bird called Rambler said he watched the humans cook and eat the bird's last night, about an hour and half after the raid. But he wasn't sure who they were."

"She's gone then?" He asked again in disbelief.

"Yes, I think so." She responded to his question once again. He gave her a slight painful smile of disbelief and understanding. He then turned and moved to the rear of the crate and with unseeing eyes he looked away and out at the passing scenery. All was just a blur of colors and shapes, his life was over he thought, and there is nothing left, just space and endless time.

Interesting Pigeon Fact

Pigeons have excellent hearing abilities. They can detect sounds at far lower frequencies than humans are able to, and can thus hear distant storms and volcanoes

<a href="http://www.softschools.com/facts/animals/pigeon_facts/589/">Pigeon Facts</a>

Chapter 8

Mosaic, Trapper, Maggie, Major and the rest of the birds from the stadium that had come to help them, were all flying overhead as the car carrying Moth went through the stop and go approach humans used to travel from one point to another. Mosaic though how frustrating for humans having to go all those different directions they have to take to make it to their final destinations. How confusing he thought. We have it so much easier, you find out where you wanted to go and then you do it in a straight line, from point "a" to point "b", the shortest distance between two points. By the time, they had made it to Ibu's house twenty-five minutes had passed. "What a waste of time and energy!" Mosaic said to Trapper. "We could have done it in seven minutes; worst-case, know what I mean!" He finished.

"Yes!" Trapper responded by saying, "Human's travel is so slow, they travel slower than snails. They go about it in such a confusing manner, they are so time wasteful."

"It sure explains why they are so rude and irritable. Having to travel in their antiquated manner would irritate the most saintly of beings." Was Mosaic's response to Trapper's comments, who just shook his head yes.

Maggie interjected, "Not all humans are stressed out by their mode of travel. As a matter of fact, Ibu loves it and enjoys going slow and seeing everything along the way. She calls it sightseeing and says it's fun and relaxing."

"Maybe, but I can't see it." Said Mosaic, "Most of them seem not to enjoy it, based on the expressions on their faces, and the hostility in their voices as they shout to each other and give each other all types of hand signals." Maggie decided not to get into a disagreement with Mosaic and just shook her head yes, as if saying you have a point, but I still thinking there is more to it than you are willing to acknowledge.

They all made the customary circular pass around Ibu's house. Maggie, Major, Trapper and Mosaic had landed on the garage roof. The rest of the birds had landed on the telephone pole and wires that were at the rear perimeter of the property. There they relaxed and started to preen themselves and settle in for the night. The four companions sitting on the garage roof watched Ibu exit the car carrying Moth as she shuttled, in a shuffled manner down the driveway, as she headed for the back of the house. When she reached the back door, while opening it, she turned and instructed Maggie, "Go to the Medicine room window." With that said, she disappeared through the back door and from sight.

Maggie said, "Let's go! Follow me to the Medicine room window." and with that she took off from the garage roof for the far side of the house. There she landed on a protruding wooden planks attached to a large window, which acted as a landing board. The window was divided into two parts on the lower half, is where the shelf was attached for their convenience. The window was propped open by a four-by-four piece of wood, which allowed access to the room. As Mosaic turned the corner of the house behind Major and Trapper, he saw Maggie disappear from sight through the opening at the bottom of a large window. He followed Major and Trapper as they landed on the board protruding from the ledge of the window, which also extended into the room allowing him to walk into the room as well. The board that he had landed on gave him visual and physical access to the fourteen by twenty foot, medium size room, Maggie had called the medicine room.

The room looked very utilitarian in its décor and layout. On the opposite wall from the window sat several cages on white linen cloth that covered a metal table. Above the table, there was a shelf attached to the wall and on it, there were stacks of neatly folded towels and cloths of various sizes. On each side of the table stood a tall cabinet with five shelves whose front was covered by glass doors. Behind the glass door of the cabinet starting, on the bottom shelves, both across and from front to back, stood neatly arranged bottles going from large too small. On the next shelf up, arranged in the same manner were more the bottles, there also were boxes of various shapes and size arranged in the same manner. On the Middle shelf, there were numerous containers of gauze bandages of all types and tape. Then, on the fourth shelf there were all kinds of things, items of various shapes and equipment that Mosaic had never seen before, nor had any idea what they could be used for. Looking at them, made him queasy, he hoped he never got ill. On the top shelf, there were more stacks of towels and linens and the like. In the cabinet to the left there seemed to be a duplication of the items that were in the right side cabinet.

However, of course, the left side cabinet was not the same, but to the untrained eye of a pigeon, they both looked the same. The Cabinet of the left contained the holistic types of medications and treatments. While the right cabinet contained the conventional medicines and treatments, because Ibu believed that both were required to properly, treat a patient in today's world.

There were three overhead lamps one that illuminated the table's work area and then two more, one for each cabinet. There were also two floor lamps one standing next to a window and one next to the rocking chair on the wall to the left of the window, and next to the door that gave access to the rest of the house. On the opposite wall, there stood an old roll-away desk and swivel chair, and next to it stood the other floor lamp. In addition to the desk, there also stood two shelved metal carts on rollers.

Attached to the wall on each side of the window they had used to enter the room through were two shelves as well. One contained all sizes and types of books on the treatment of illnesses, held up by two eagle-head bookends. On the other shelf, there were also a few books and half a dozen figurines of various birds. The more he looked around the more he realized there were all types of pictures and photos tacked to the walls of all types of creatures, from birds to cats, from domestic to wildlife.

Intermixed with all these nick knacks were clear class containers, bowls, and jars of various potpourris. The room had many smells that assailed the nose. There was the strong smell of alcohol, along with tings of formaldehyde that shocked his lungs and awoke every cell in his body. After that particular odor, which seemed to have cleared his lungs, and made him more aware of the other subtle smells that permeated the air of the room. There was a small fan sitting on a small side table next to the door and depending on which direction it was moving and how the air was flowing, there came the faint smell of cinnamon and apple to him from the direction of the small table it was sitting on. From the desk came the smells of sage and from the bookshelves there came the smell of either eucalyptus or lavender. There was also the faint scent of witch hazel in the air. With each smell, his mind and body reacted differently; and most of the smells seemed to relax him and they brought peace to his being. Even with the strain of all that had happened, he smiled and knew all would be all right. 'Yes', he thought, 'this place brings peace, contentment and the feeling that all would be okay that there is hope'. He had lost some of his apprehension, and he felt he could let his guard down just a little because he knew was among friends. 'Because, they would help him make things right. Whatever that meant', he thought. He did not know why he had that feeling, but never the less he felt secure. After what they had been through that is what counted. "Maybe that was the intent of all the fragrances mixing, that filled the air, they were there to relax them," he had surmised

Lying on the table, on the kitchen towel she had been wrapped in, lie Moth. At first Mosaic thought, she was not breathing and his anxiety levels shot through the roof for only a second because as he looked closer he could see her shallow breathing. He could see her breast moving ever so slightly up and down, or was it the fan moving her feathers as it made its orbital pass, as it moved air across the room. No, he thought, he could actually see it moving up and down. He gave an inward sigh of relief, 'good,' he told himself, 'she is alive.'

Ibu, also known as Sojourn to her friends had been moving about the room doing this and doing that, opening the right cabinet and then the left cabinet, removing all types of jars, tools and equipment. She now was taking from the cabinet a metal bedpan, a long piece of tubing and a syringe, and a large plastic squeeze bottle that also had a tube attached to it she placed all of that on one of the metal carts her son had brought over to her. Then, she went back into the cabinet and removed several bottles, a small mortar and pestle, which she placed onto the cart alongside of all the other things sitting there, patiently, waiting their turn to be used. At least it seemed so, to Mosaic, as he attentively watched the old women as she worked in what seemed to be a maddeningly slow pace.

Her son who had left reentered the room carrying a plastic bottle of distilled water. "Good!" she said, "I thought you'd gotten lost" she finished, "put the bottle down here," as she pointed to the metal cart she had just pulled over to the table, "and get the small pump from the closet, please." As she was giving him instructions, she had shuffled over to the desk had taken a key hanging on a gold chain from around her neck and had unlocked the drawers of the desk. As she was doing this, she was still giving instructions. Her son following her instructions, had walked over to what appeared to be a blank wall, pressed a button that looked like a nail which then allowed a small ring latch handle to pop out. He pulled it and the wall section slid out of the way revealing the closet it had concealed. "Once you have the pump, please grind up four eucalyptus leaves and six tablespoons full of aloe Vera sap, to that add three level teaspoons of witch hazel. Once that has been smashed and mixed into a paste, grind three leaves of mint into it. Let me know once that has been done" she finished.

She continued opening the drawer and removed a beautiful, very ornately decorated red brown box. The box was about five inches long by four inches wide by approximately four inches high. The sides of the box was covered with carvings of Ivy, intertwined with flowers that looked like jasmine buds and the top had the same border of Ivy and flowers, in the center of the border, was a scene of two birds flying over a river and through a clouded sky.

"There you are." She said to the box in a very loving and gentle voice, "It's time to see your contents once again. I hope that all I have heard and know is enough for it to work again." She said this aloud as if she were talking to the rest of the occupants in the room, but at the same time saying it to the box as well, as if it could understand her words. She then took her index finger and the middle finger of her left hand and made a "V" with them, which she placed into the two recesses in the front of the box. She then pressed inward and a small flower piece of the carving slid out of the way revealing a key-way. Keeping her finger in place, she then took the key she had been holding in her right hand, inserted it into the key-way and made a half turn with it. She then continued to press her finger into the beveled recesses, which allowed her to continue to turn the key, and then the lid sprang open.

As she did this, and as the box's lid opened, Mosaic could have sworn he saw a sparkle of blue-green light emerged from the box, as did a strong overwhelming smell of jasmine flowers in bloom. As the contents of the box became exposed to, the light of the room and the inside, the view seemed to be rather plain, considering all the elaborateness and ornateness of the box and its opening sequence. Exposed to the light for the first time in who knows how long, were six pink-red-brown earthenware little pots, with a black cork in each pot's neck. As she looked inside she said, "Lord, thank you. I hope it's enough Lord, and that they still have your blessings and the powers to heal."

"Mom!" her son said interrupting her praising of the Lord, "What do you want done next, I think this is mixed thoroughly and completely as you instructed?"

"Lord! Oh my Lord, where has the time gone!" she said in response to his query, "take it and mix it all up in the water, the gallon bottle and then we'll do the pumping of the stomach." In reality, only two minutes had passed since she had given him the directions on what to mix and in what quantity. Ibu, having said that, took out all six of the little clay pots and set them on the desktop. She then walked over, took the mortar and pestle to the closet and washed them out in the sink that was hidden from view. She then came back out carrying the two items she had just cleaned; and a small butcher's block, which she set out on top of the metal cart. Again, she gave her son instructions, "While, I mix the energy paste, you'll need to pump her crop. Can you do it without, help?" she finished.

"Yes, Mom" he said, "you do what you need to do and I'll do this. It shouldn't take long to evacuate the toxicants out of her at least as much as we can, then it will be up to her." As she went back to the little pots, he took a small tube and placed it into Moth's beak and he then took another smaller tube and placed it into her nostril. He then took the larger tube and attached it to the pump's outlet side. Then, he took another tube from the pump's inlet side and stuck it into the jar with the cleansing mixture he had created. Mosaic wanted to watch both of the humans as they were working, but as he saw the tubes going and coming from Moth he decided to watch Ibu instead. What she was doing looked less painful.

Ibu had taken and opened one of the bottles, taken out two seeds and placed them into the mortar and started to grind them up into a powder. As she, was doing this Mosaic heard the pump start and its soft whirring noise caused him to look at what was going on with Moth? He noticed Moth had been moved, she was now lying on her left side and he witnessed the liquid being drawn from the jar, and down the tube stuck into Moth's mouth. He saw it disappear and then he saw the green slimy liquid coming from her open beak, pouring out into the bedpan. He gagged and almost threw up himself at what he saw and quickly had to look away. He felt pale and he knew he was light headed, and close to fainting, so Maggie put her wing around him for support and said, "They know what they are doing. Are you going to be okay? Maybe you'd better sit down."

"I'll be… fine, thanks." He said as he refocused on Ibu and what she was doing. After the two seeds she had placed in the mortar bowl, had been mashed and pulverized, she had added a little liquid to it and turned it into a thick yellow creamy paste, to which she was adding an amber liquid from one of the other, little clay pots. She only added two drops and then worked the liquid into the seed paste. Mosaic thought, 'it looked like the golden rays of the sun, a liquid sunshine." He thought, "how stunning.' The ingredients in the mortar had a shine to it as if rays of light were coming from it; it shone with a dazzling aura of golden yellowish-orange light. Ibu, kept working, mixing and then stopping only long enough to open another pot and from it, she poured a clear liquid into the mortar, thinning out the paste but not the light's brilliance. "It's ready!" she said.

"Good, because I'm done as well, I think I have evacuated all that can be evacuated," her son said, "Her crop is clear. I'll get the syringe." he picked up a sealed plastic package, ripped it open in one motion removing a cylindrical tube like object from the bag and then the plunger, and inserted it into the tube. While he was doing this, Ibu walked over to him with the mortar and its contents. He then took the tip of the metal needle-like tube, protruding from the cylindrical tube, and placed it into the honey like consistency ingredients sitting in the bowl of the mortar and pulled back on the plunger drawing the liquid into the cylindrical tube. Ibu then attached a clear plastic tube to the end of the needle like tube and they carried it over to where Moth was laying. She then cautiously opened Moth's beak and inserted the tube as her son gingerly and ever so gently, with great care applied even pressure to the plungers and emptied its contents into Moth's crop.

Ibu giving a sigh of relief and said, "We've done all that can be done. Now we wait and pray the Lord is with us, and her." Her son smiled at her, "Mom you are amazing. Can I get you anything? A cup of tea?"

"Yes." She replied, "With honey and a cinnamon stick in it would suit me just fine."

With that, he left the room saying, with a smile, "As the doctor ordered."

All four of the birds had watched everything without a word having been spoken. Mosaic and Trapper were amazed at all the different gadgets and smells that had assailed their eyes and noses. The smell of sage and that of citrus from the hidden closet, the witch hazel and all the other ingredients used in the treatment of Moth was unbelievable to their senses. It amazed Mosaic how quickly these smells had driven out the acid, toxic smell that had come from the bile they had pumped from Moth's crop. He hadn't noticed it, but Ibu had dropped several leaves of mint and Basil into the bedpan, and the combination of these two herbs had neutralized the toxic smell exuding from the liquid.

Mosaic wanted to ask a question earlier, but he had been afraid that he would have interrupted Ibu as she was working, but now he felt more at ease and decide to ask, "What is wrong with my sister, can you tell me? Do you know what caused all this? Is she going to be all right? Is she going to die?"

"Don't know yet. I know you are concerned about her, about your family, your friends and where they are. However, you will just have to wait, and be a little patient. I'm working on getting you the information you need so you can continue your journey; so you can save and rescue them, but you'll have to give me a little more time and I will see how I can get you the information you need to know where to go. Just give me a little time." She said this almost more to herself than to Mosaic and the others.

Mosaic stood there, mouth agape, and gave Trapper a how did she know that is what I was going to ask next look on his face. Trapper in response just looked a little dumbfounded; as if he were saying; don't ask me, how should I know.

Ibu giggled to herself and with a serious expression on her face said, "The good Lord has blessed and cursed me with this gift to know things." She said this so matter-of- factly that there was no explanation or reason needed; neither would one be given as to what the gift was or why not to believe her. By the look on her face, the birds realized that was all of an elucidation they were going to get, because by her body language and the way she had spoken the words said she did not know the answer either.

Therefore, the rest of the day had moved from early afternoon into late afternoon before they realized it. Ibu had gotten her cup of hot tea, and had explained what she thought had happened; that Moth had eaten some seeds that had been laced with some pesticides or worse, the seed had been set up purposely to try and catch them off guard and kill them all. That Moth, having thrown up the majority of what she had eaten almost right after she had eaten them, had saved her life, as well as eating the lake moss and throwing it up. Of course, the final thing that had saved her life, or at least Ibu hoped so was getting herself involved. And, so the conversation had gone with some speculation as to who would have set such a trap, and why. Time had passed rather quickly and the realization of how much time had passed hit them when they heard small rumbling, growling sounds coming from their crops. Trapper who seemed to have the loudest of these rumblings, said after an exceptionally loud rolling sound, "Sorry! Just a little hungry." He said lamely and a little embarrassed.

In between taking care of Moth, Ibu had been explaining the effects of poisons on the body and how getting rid of the substance early was so important. She restated several times that Moth having thrown up right away had probably saved her life, or at least given her a fighting chance. The thing that worried Ibu was that they had flown for so long afterwards and that what really should have been done was Moth getting rest and treatment sooner. "But what's done, is done." She said, "You all must be starved. How rude of me not to have been more attentive to your needs." Having said that she got up and in her shuffling slow walk, she went to the closet, opened a small trash can like container sitting on the floor in the corner, opened the lid, took the coffee can sitting there and filled it with grain. She then came back to the shelf where they had been sitting from where they had been watching all the activities as Ibu and her son had been doing while attending to Moth. She reached up to the bookshelf and took down a metal ice cube tray, set it down and poured it full of grain from the coffee can. As she was doing this, she said, "Eat, eat, please forgive my rudeness."

As Mosaic walked over to the food tray, he passed the front of the windowpane and looked at himself in the reflection of the glass and was shocked at how disheveled he looked. First thing, eat and drink he thought, and then take a warm bath, before turning in for the night was his comment to himself as he started to eat the clean, great looking food before him.

——————————— ———————————

Moth found herself flying with Mosaic and Trapper on a perfectly beautiful day. The Sun was out and hanging like a great yellow ball in the heavens; the sky was a brilliant light blue with wisps of little white puffy clouds strewn about. The air smelled clean and fresh, for the windstorm of the day before had blown away all that was impure and nasty. Everything to her smelled and looked clean as it did just after a good rain had fallen. She could not remember how she had gotten into this beautiful landscape and day, but she did not care, it was wonderful and she was happy and at peace with the world.

She also could not remember when it had changed, but it seemed within minutes of her feeling at peace with the world and all her surroundings, and then she suddenly found herself fighting for her life. In the wink of an eye, the dark shadows that came from nowhere, were making swooping, diving attacks on them, no! She realized the attacks were on her. One of the assailants had lost apiece of itself during one spectacular harassing dive and she had inhaled it. In that instant she had become deathly ill, and she knew she was in for the fight of her life.

The sickness that overcame her instantly affected her sight, because she no longer could see either Mosaic or Trapper, when she knew they had been flying alongside only moments before. Nevertheless, she reasoned they were still there because, she could hear somethings, a slight flap of wings breaking air and that they were only hidden by the darkness that had consumed all the light. The darkness had also dampened all noises because, she realized some of the sounds she could hear was them calling to her as if they were shouting to her down a very long tunnel. She could hear them, only as whispering echo barely audible, but at the same time, she could hear them quite clearly. It was freaky and surrealistic, they were there yet they were not visible to her, and they were there but barely audible to her.

To her benefit, she did not panic, and she told herself you are flying through a really dense cloud and any second now, they will reappear. However, of course, they did not and the next thing she knew she was flying through a blizzard as cold as ice. The icy wind was cutting her clean to the bone, and the next minute she was flying through an arid, barren, baked dry environment. Yet, keeping constant surveillance over her, the dark shadows were always there, hovering, gliding just out of reach and sight, yet she knew they were there, for she could not see them, but she sensed them.

It got so hot that all the moisture in her mouth evaporated. She could feel every ridge in her tongue as if they were great cavers that caused it to feel so abrasive; all she wanted to do was pluck it out of her beak. All of her feathers were on fire and she wanted to pluck them out, to try to get some relief from the burning pain. She became so hot that she felt all the liquids had been slowly cooked out of her. She felt herself no longer flying, and then she saw them, Mosaic and Trapper, standing over her. The shadows were gone. How she had come to be lying on the ground, she wondered. All she knew was she was exhausted, hot and dehydrated. Every joint, muscle, organ and feather in her small body ached all the way down to their individual cells. I still have feathers she thought, I thought I plucked them all out long ago. Where was she; she wondered, her thoughts were like wisps of smoke, solid one minute and then nothing, zilch, just that wanting of water, moister consumed her. The thoughts raced through her mind, at such speed they were unclear, and yet there as clear as day. However, the answers to her unasked questions did not come.

It was agony to move. If it was not hot it was cold and she was stiff and if she was not stiff, she just hurt all over, she ached. She knew she was lying near water, for she could hear the waves lapping against the shore, and she could smell the moisture. Then, it appeared to her as a beautiful blue-green lake, spread out before her, and she moved with great pain and effort, and took a drink of clean sweet water. However, all she tasted was a harsh liquid that mixed with her bodies chemicals and salts, which recoiled against her stomach and then it all came back up as if a gusher had shot from her mouth. As it came up it tasted sweet and then came the aftertaste of stomach acids, digestive juices, repulsive and sour. She quickly drank more water and used it to rinse her mouth and then she spit it out, she did this several times. She then tried to drink again, with the same unpleasant results. This ordeal went on for several more attempts in a row and with each expulsion of the liquid; a little bit more of her strength left her as well.

She realized she was losing the battle. She knew she needed to win; she knew she needed help, but who and how the help would come, she was not sure. Then, she saw them again, Mosaic and Trapper looking at her with great pained expressions on their collective faces, looks that said, what can we do, how can we help?

All she could remember, and the how and why of it was lost to her, was she asked them to get her green lake moss. They complied with her request and they supplied her with the moss, and she sucked it in and it made her feel better. She asked for more and she ate ravenously, all that they brought. She ate it as an animal possessed, she inhaled the greenery and as she did so she felt her sluggishness going away, her vision was clearing and her breathing was becoming easier and more regular.

As she looked up, there standing over her, were two of the shadow creatures. No, she thought not again, not now. The aberrations became Trapper and Mosaic, as her vision brought them in to clear focus. Their faces were like pictures framed with expressions of apprehension and fear, but she ignored that and said, "Let's get out of here; we have a rescue to perform." Both wanted to know if she was all right, but instead of answering their individual questions about her well-being, she answered by taking off into the air and saying, "Let's go, time it is a wasting! And I'm not getting any younger!"

With that having been said, or at least what she thought she had said, she had taken to the air and started south once again resuming their journey. Mosaic and Trapper flew alongside of her with ease, but within a short time from having restarted their trip, she started to feel sick again. It started with her stomach recoiling to the liquidated moss she had eaten. It felt as if there were small creatures running, and jumping around in her crop and then they started to run up and down her throat. Upwards it came, and she threw up large glob of green slime, and as the slime fell towards the ground it turned into the dark dreaded foreboding shadowy shapes that had tormented her earlier that day. To her amazement, the slime had taken to the air as well as it did, it formed itself into the darkness, into black gliding shapes that never hit the ground.

The sky, which had been bright blue, turned a shade grayer. With each retching, the slime turned into yet an additional shadow creatures and the sky turned progressively darker as it filled with their presence. After the fourth time of this occurrence, the shadows started to dive at her again, and this time they seemed to have gained a voice. With each dive, there came an eerie noise as that of fingernail scrapping on a blackboard, and barely audible words of, "You're finished this time." With every pass, that murkiness feeling that the black shadows exuded made she felt weaker. She once again lost track of Trapper and Mosaic as she tried to avoid the constant wretched behavior of shadow creatures that now seemed to number hundreds.

She could hear Trapper and Mosaic asking if she was all right, could she go on. Why didn't they see the shadows she thought, was she going crazy or were they? Wasn't it obvious why she was having trouble flying? So it went, her avoiding the shadows that swooping and diving at her and by doing so, it was slowing her down. She was doing some crazy erratic flight maneuvers and at every turn, no matter what she did, there they were. Diving at her, blocking her flight path, blocking her progress, harassing her, impeding here progress and zapping her strength.

Then it hit her, these had to be the dreaded Shadows of Death that her mom had always told her existed that she had thought were only imaginary; fabricated by parents to make their youngsters behave. Now she knew better and a brand new terror gripped her heart for if they were the Shadows of Death of so many stories, they would never quit until they got their prey and devoured it. They would not give up until they devoured not only the flesh but also the soul of whatever they were hunting. While she was occupied with her own unbelievable fears it happened, she didn't dodge fast enough and one of the shadows hither ever so slightly on the wing, which went unbelievably cold the instant it was touched. The muscles froze and she lost control, and went plummeting down towards the ground. She took her good wing and adjusted herself and in doing so, she hit the ground softer than expected and harder than she wanted, which knocked the wind out of her.

There she lay in the field, semi-conscious, with the sun beating down on her and the shadows still making menacing swoops over her head. She looked up and could not see the sun, but she knew it was shining, draining her of moisture. She looked up and could see in the distance an oasis, where not far away there was shade, but she could not get her body to respond to her brain. She knew she could not reach it, she had no strength left... okay she thought if she could only have one wish before she died, it would be to lie in the shade of the tree at the oasis on the cool ground and die. Then, as if her mind had control of the elements, of nature itself, she felt herself being lifted ever so gently and the next thing she knew she was laying under the shade of the tree.

Having succeeded with that, she had slipped in and out of consciousness, for what seemed like hours and had awakened with a parched throat and had wished for water and there, as it if by some strange magic, water was being poured down her throat, and then she fainted. What awoke her next was the bitter cold she felt all the way down to the marrow of her bones. Once again she wished for the heat of the sun to drive away the chill and "Wallah" she started to feel warm and comfortable. With the heat came the overwhelming need to sleep and rest, for she was so tired. This cycle went for her slipping in and out of consciousness. A part of her knew things were being done to her, but she didn't care; so long as they didn't wake her up; let them do what they wished.

She then had a sweet taste in her mouth and then she heard a voice asking her questions. It came from nowhere and then she realized it really wasn't just questions but also giving instructions. It was a combination of both and she knew she would have to respond because the voice was not going away, and by its tone, she knew it would not until it got what it wanted. How rude, there is nobody home she thought, go away.

However, the voice knew her name and talked to her as if they had been old friends for a long time. "Moth, we need to know something. I know it's hard for you right now," the voice said.

You aren't kidding Moth thought. What do you want she thought, let me rest... can't you see I am tired?

"I know," the voice said. "I need directions to the feed store and then you can rest. We need the information so we can rescue the others. Mosaic and Trapper are here; they need your help. They need directions."

"Yes, the rescue, the feed store…?" confused at first and then, a portion of her mind seemed to understand. Nevertheless, the Shadow Death was still out there, lurking, waiting, and if she moved, even to speak, it would pounce and it would be over, she'd be devoured, gone forever.

"Moth you need to think of something really pleasant and beautiful. Moth if you do the shadows cannot get you, I promise, it has to be what you know to be true. Moth, please help me help them and you. You need to trust me and believe." Then, the voice changed into the voice of her mate, Razor. "Razor is that you?" she asked. She had not thought or talked about him on purpose, for what if she failed? Then she would have lost him forever and now here he was asking for her help, asking her to remember.

"Yes Moth." The voice responded, "Remember the plan, and to get help. Moth we need you to succeed in this, give them the information. Moth remember the rose, the dew drops, the gentle fragrance of the flower, you remember, the nice subtle sweetness of the aroma?"

Yes, she thought, the rose, that beautiful single rose, and as she thought of it, it appeared out of the blackness, one beautifully formed single red rose. A piece of the Creator's perfection, it was lovely, and so fragile. The clearer the rose became the more the darkness that surrounded it disappeared, from black to gray to clear. She was lying on the ground unable to move, she was bound by unseen restraints, next to a precipice. The precipice's depth was indeterminable; she could not gage it because you could not see its bottom. Across its opening, standing on the other edge there was bird, a pigeon, which she recognized as her brother.

"Mosaic!" she yelled, "Don't move, and don't try to cross over the opening, you'll be killed!" How she knew this she did not know, but as sure as the sunrises in the east she knew it to be true. He stayed where he was and just shook his head yes, and she shouted out the directions to the pet store. She gave him every detail and landmark she could remember. When she finished he waved and then disappeared as quickly as he had appeared. She then heard the voice of Razor saying, "Good Girl, I love you, take care… all will be all right." She felt warmth overtake her entire being and then she fainted from mere exhaustion.

——————————— ———————————

"Is she going to be all right?" Mosaic asked as he watched Moth's body go limp again.

"Yes, I believe so. We have gotten the poisons out of her system, now it's all up to her." Ibu said, "But she still needs a lot of rest and good clean food and water. We will feed her by the tube until she wakes and gets stronger. I will nurse her back to health, but you had better finish eating and drinking something yourself, you two need to be off by first light. Something tells me you have very little time. Your adventure is just beginning, and you have a long way to go."

Mosaic looked at the Ibu and then at his sister and realized he could do nothing that he already hadn't done. He knew nothing about healing. Staying there he would only be in the way and all the sacrifices Moth had already made would be for not if he did not rescue the birds from the pet and feed store. With reluctance, he did as Ibu asked, he ate and drank and got some rest for who knew what tomorrow would bring.

Interesting Pigeon Fact

They are amazingly resourceful creatures, able to survive in the midst of predatory humanity.

http://www.animalaid.org.uk/h/n/CAMPAIGNS/wildlife/ALL/346/

Chapter 9

They had been flying for about an hour now, and Mosaic was contemplating if they had made any wrong turns. The directions that he had obtained from Moth with the help of Sojourn, that is what Ibu had asked them to call her. The direction given had been easy enough to follow, but never the less he couldn't help but wonder if he had misinterpreted anything. He was sure they had not missed the first two landmarks. How could you miss the stadium and then the man made riverbed that ran adjacent to it? Moth had said follow it to where the river ran into the big water. Sojourn had called the ocean, the big water. Then turn left and follow the shoreline south until you came to another river that ran into it. At that point head mostly east, or ten degrees south of east and it would cause you to fly to the town where the pet and feed store was located. As a matter of fact that direction would cause you to fly right over the pet and feed store, one could not miss it had been Moth's last words to him.

As they flew they discussed all the strange things that had befallen them since they had decided to head south with Moth and rescue their flock members and family. They talked about the oddity that Moth had eaten the bad food, seeing how she was a Taster and birds of that persuasion and training rarely ate bad food, at least the good ones didn't, and Moth was considered one of the best. It was also strange to Mosaic that she had known what to do once she had eaten something bad; or was that part of the training? Must have been, if it was he had not known it and as a flock leader, he should have known.

Trapper told him not to be so hard on himself, as far as he knew most flock leaders went into training themselves, and he was sure if Mosaic had been given some formal training, he'd have been taught that and many more things that flock leaders needed to do and know. Of course, this had the opposite effect on Mosaic then Trapper had intended it made him even more aware of his youth and his own insecurity in his infancy at being thrown into the position he was in, a flock leader.

Mosaic knew that Trapper was only trying to cheer him up. Still Mosaic could not help it, he felt depressed by what he was told. He should have known, he thought and said so, and of course his friend asked him, "How should you have known, by osmosis? You aren't psychic you know!" Trapper gave him a come-on really look, continued, "Look you may be good and knowledgeable, but as my dad always said, the old ones can teach you a lot of things, but experience is the best teacher. Doing is learning, so long as you learn from your mistakes. So my friend let's face it, let's be real here, you didn't have a choice"

"I guess you're right, but…" Mosaic started, but Trapper cut him off, "Anyway you look at it, what has happened to us so far would never have been taught in any class by any instructor or by any mentor. Now would it! " he finished.

They stopped talking, with each caught up in their own thoughts, about what had been said and if they were going the right way. Just as he was thinking, this is the wrong way that they had turned the wrong direction, the big water came in to view. "There it is!" He said to Trapper as he pointed to where it lay. With excitement in his voice of wow, we made it!

"Good," said Trapper, "Let's find a place to get a drink and maybe a bite to eat."

Mosaic smiled and nodded his head, for it was good to see that Trapper had not lost his appetite. At least none of the craziness of the last two days had affected his friend's stomach and his love of food. It was somehow reassuring that Trapper was hungry, it meant that maybe the world wasn't coming to an end, as all that had happened to Moth would have indicated.

As they approached the ocean, they spied the beach and log wooden roadway that protruded out into it. There was a large sign over the entranceway that read, "Pier Number One, Gateway to the Pacific Ocean". On the pier, there were several restaurants and smaller eateries. There were also several small flocks of birds milling about. Which meant there was food served and given out there on a regular basis. At the beginning of the roadway that took you onto the pier there was a large tiered fountain, and protruding from its center was a large metal post and attached to the top was a flock of metal carved pelicans in all types of flight positions that indicated they were about to land.

Their first stop was at the fountain to get a drink of water. One of what they thought was a local pigeons was there as well, relieving its thirst. Trapper said, "Hello, we're not from around here. Do you know where there is a good place to get a hand out?" he asked between drinks.

"Don't know," was the response, "I'm just passing through myself, on a training race, you know? Just need a wee bit of water as it were, and then I'm off." With that said the bird took to the sky and headed north without another word or how-do-you-do.

Trapper gave Mosaic a look of, "okay now what?" Mosaic who had not heard the loft pigeon's response, asked, "Are all you loft birds that dedicated, where you can't even stay a second and answer a simple question."

Trapper smiled, "How did you know? He didn't know anyway, he was a foreigner."

"Oh! Pointing to Trappers leg, the metal owners band, gives you away every time," said Mosaic, "Now what?"

"We go there." Trapper said pointing to the pier and the several large buildings sitting on it. "I'm sure there is food there, at least my nose says so."

"That's good enough for me; I'll trust your nose anytime when it comes to food and eating. Let's go." Because over time Mosaic had come to know Trapper and had placed him in the pigeon occupation of Taster; and sure enough there were people there eating and sharing their food with the local birds. There were pigeons, blackbirds and seagulls all partaking of tidbits being thrown at them, so Trapper and Mosaic joined in and ate their fill. Once done eating they flew back to the fountain got a drink and were off again, flying down the shoreline continuing their journey southward. Happy and content to be full, they flew at an easy pace and within an hour, they reached the next landmark described by Moth. There they turned and headed east, by ten degrees south.

As they were flying, they had been talking about this and that, and then as conversations often do, they came back to Mosaic's feelings about his lack of knowledge, "Do you remember what we were talking about earlier? I guess you're right, but I still feel so inept with all the stuff that happened to Moth. Good thing Maggie, Major, Levon, Ibu and all the rest came along."

"Yes my friend the fates were looking out for Moth, and us, that's for sure! If we'd all eaten that seed I shudder to think…" and shudder he did, it was not voluntary and he went into an erratic dive.

"Trapper, will you stop!" Mosaic yelled after him, "that's not funny."

"Sorry," Trapper said as he rejoined Mosaic, "Like I was saying, if it had been all three of us we'd all three be dead, lying by the lake. Levon did a nice job, but that Sojourn, what a healer she turned out to be. Amazing all those tools, herbs, and medicines she used. I bet she could heal anything. I wouldn't have thought that from the first time we came through there when Maggie and Major took us there to eat" Trapper finished. It was obvious that he was really impressed with her healing skills, as was Mosaic.

With appreciation and admiration in their voices the conversation had gone. With both of them commenting on Levon's performance and that of Ibu Sojourn, and of course the information they had been given, that neither wanted to believe. It was hard for them to imagine, that they, pigeons were all on the verge of a great battle and a possible war, a war between good and evil. Trapper had believed everything Sojourn had said until she started to talk about war and battles and how they would be pivotal in it all. Mosaic agreed with Trapper, it was hard to believe that all that had happened had been planned, and that the outcome of the plan had been to prevent them from interfering with the ultimate plan, of total war between good and evil. They looked at each other with neither knowing what to say except, no, it was not possible, and they each flew on not saying another word, totally engrossed in their own thoughts.

They flew over cultivated lands, row upon row of neatly placed tomato plants all ripe with fruit. There were also green fields of alfalfa and hay. As they climbed a slight grade of rolling foothills they flew over orchards of fruit trees, citrus, apple and the smell of avocados filled the air. Then, they flew down into another valley of a sea of green fields. As they started their glide from their downward motion along the backside of the foothills they had just climbed they reached more farmlands. Then, at the bottom of foothills they had just ascended, Mosaic pointed down to a large house and stable surrounded by neatly white fenced pastures. Held within the pastures were horses of all types of colors, just as Moth had described it, he thought to himself, they were going in the correct direction. Now we should continue and fly over that other range of foothills in the distance. If he remembered her directions, correctly there in that valley there would be the town. In that town is where the pet and feed store was located. The pet and feed store that contained his Mom, Dad and fellow flock-mates.

His stomach tightened with anticipation as they climbed the last set of foothills. As they approached their crest, his mouth felt dry and he felt apprehensive, once over the top, he let out the breath that he did not realize he was holding. There in the distance stood the town. Almost there he thought, so close and yet still so far. As they flew along the valley, they passed the many landmarks Moth had described; they passed the junkyard of rusted out cars of all types of vintages and years.

Then they came upon the large sign of the drive-in dairy that had a large replication of a Holstein cow rotating on a vertical post stuck into its underside. Once they passed the cow, per Moth's directions, they would fly another three hundred yards and then they would reach a large white wooden church. On the side of the church where the wooden cross stood, place in the center on the lawn, was the street they were to follow for four and a half miles. Mosaic and Trapper flew along the tree-shaded street in a relaxed, but at the same time anxious manner. Both were wondering what they would do once they arrived at the pet and feed store. That seemed to be the million-dollar question neither one could answer because neither one had verbalized their concerns on what to do once they reached their final destination, other than rescue the flock.

They had flown along and talked about everything but what they would do once they reached the pet and feed store. Trapper had not asked because he felt that it was Mosaic's responsibility to tell him what the plan of action should or would be. Mosaic, for his part, was hoping that Trapper would volunteer a plan of action. Trapper looked at his friend as they flew down the street and asked, "Given any thought on what we should do once we get there?"

Mosaic gave him a sheepish, childish smile. "No, I guess I figured we'd wait and see what the lay of the land was before we decide what we could do."

Trapper chuckled to himself and shook his head as he said, "Makes sense, I should have figured you'd have given it some thought, but I am surprised that you do not have a plan. Nevertheless, you are right. We really don't know much about the place or even where they are keeping your family. So waiting makes good sense."

Mosaic just smiled back at Trapper and nodded his head yes, as if he were saying that is the only plan, none plan that is logical at this moment in time.

They had flown the four miles down the street under the canopy of the trees, they reached an intersection where they changed course. They climbed up and were now flying just above the trees. After a half-mile off on their left stood Vande Ber Pet and Feed just as Moth had said it would be. It was an old building constructed in the shape of an old wooden western livery stable. The front had a set of large double doors and on each side of the doors was a large window divided into four equal, square sections. The wooden boards that created the walls ran vertically up to a pecked bell shaped roofline. The entire building looked classic in its red rust brown, trimmed in white, look very rustic, countrified and stood out from its surroundings.

As they passed it they made a circular sweep around the store, and on the left side of the building was a parking lot. They flew over the parking lot and over a vacant lot, which was cultivated with all types of small plots of vegetables, flowers and fruits. At the rear of the store was a parking lot and beyond that stood a large wooden ranch style house. On the right stood a building that had a large boot with a silver spur and sign attached that read, "Silver Spur Veterinary Hospital and Boarding House." All around that building there was also a parking lot, so that the pet and feed store stood like an island within all that asphalt.

The pet and feed store building had a cinder block wall that fenced off a rear patio area that was covered by a large canvas tent like structure. At the top of the block wall was a mesh fencing, about a foot and a half high, all the way around that intersected the canvas roof, except where an eight-foot long roll-away gate broke the wall and created an opening so that when it was rolled back, trucks had easy access to the patio area. The roll-away gate went from the ground to just one foot below the canvas roof. That space was occupied with a two loops of coiled barbed wire, one going in each direction. The area was definitely designed with the intent to keep those not wanted out.

Mosaic and Trapper made two additional circular passes around the store and then they landed on the telephone pole on the left side of the store. They were on the side with the gate in the wall, but they could not see through it cleanly or clearly because woven between the chain links were slats of wood that prevented seeing in or out through it.

"Well, we really can't see much from here." Mosaic said to Trapper, "I guess we'll need to get closer in order to see anything."

"Yep, we have come too far, so let's go down and see if it was worth all our efforts, and sacrifices." Trapper said in response to Mosaic's comments. With that, both jumped off the pole and floated down to the top edge of the wall between the top of the wall and the bottom of the canvas, on the side where the gate was. What they had thought they had seen from the air was confirmed when they landed on the top of the wall. The area between the two was covered with a wire mesh that prevented access to the patio area. They started walking along the length of the wall to see if there was an opening. They stopped and looked through the mesh to the courtyard area below.

Within the courtyard stood cages of all sizes and shapes containing all types of birds and small mammals. Standing there in the far corner stood a small pigeon loft. The back wall of the building formed the back wall of the small loft. Protruding from the wall were two four-foot walls of wood and chicken wire mesh. The four-foot sidewalls were covered with a one-foot wood plank that ran up the sides and across the top to create a small shelter and shade for its occupants from the elements. The entire front was also wire mesh, with a six by five foot door framed in it. The small loft was seven feet high, by six feet across and four feet deep. Also, in the front wall was a shelf where a watering dish was placed. There were vertical straight wires spaced one and half inches apart, which allowed the birds inside access to the watering dish, but not to the outside world. All the wood of the little loft was painted an off white.

As Mosaic looked in at the loft, sitting on the watering tray shelf, sat his mother. Mosaic was beside himself with joy at seeing her, "Mom!" he yelled. She was looking around to see who was shouting at her. "Over here Mom, I'm up here, up here! Can you see me?"

She was looking all around, confused, like she was disoriented, but then she looked directly at where he was standing, and he knew she had seen him by the shocked look on her face. Then she smiled, "Mosaic, is that you? Niner, its Mosaic!" She turned to her left as she yelled that part of her comment to someone behind her, she then she turned back around. "Mosaic how did you get here?" she yelled excitedly.

"Mom, calm down," He yelled. In her elation, she had started to jump up and down with excitement. "We'll be down as soon as we figure a way in, and then we can talk." In the meantime, Niner, his dad, had joined his Mother and she pointed to where Mosaic and Trapper were standing. "Boy is that you, and is that Pepper with you?" Niner asked loudly.

"It's me alright, no, just me. We have come to get you out dad. Just stay in there, I mean hang in there, and we'll figure out how to get in and how to get you out!" He shouted, in between keeping down tears of joy.

One of the humans came out the back door of the store to see what all the commotion and noise was about; she looked all around and at first did not see anything. She walked over and checked each one of the cages to be sure they were all locked. As she did this, a large orange tabby cat dashed out from underneath the last one, she checked in the corner by the gate. "Okay," she said under her breath, to no one in particular, "He's gone, everything will be all right." as she finished looking around. After having looked everywhere and finding nothing out of order, she shrugged her shoulders again she spoke to herself saying, "That's what caused all this commotion? One little cat," annoyed she went back into the store to finish her duties.

When the human had come out Mosaic and Trapper had ducked down and made themselves as small as possible. They had stayed hidden as best they could during the whole affair as the human went through her examination of all the cages in the patio area. They stayed still and did not move, even when the cat was flushed out and escaped through the opening between the wall and the gate. Once the human had left, and it appeared to be safe, they moved and started to look for a way in.

Trapper looked at Mosaic with a wide smile on his face. "What?" Mosaic asked him. "Stay where you are?" Trapper said and then he started to laugh. Mosaic at first felt annoyed and then he saw the humor in it as well and he too started to laugh. The laughing seemed to break the tension and knots he felt in his stomach, as he felt more relaxed and in control after he had a laughing fit for about a minute. "What are you two doing up there?" Niner asked, "Are you two all right?"

Trapper responded because Mosaic could not, he was wiping the tears from his eyes, "Yes, sir we are fine, we just need to figure out a way in. Give us a minute, just stay there!" he said with a little chuckle, shaking his head in an attempt at imitating Grouch Marx's voice.

Mosaic, shrugged, gave Trapper a quick jab with his wing, and walked over to the section of the wall adjacent to the loft, that way he could talk with his mom and dad without having to shout and attract unwanted attention. Niner and Koffee had not moved from the watering shelf the whole time that the human had done her searching and investigation of the patio area. They had just stood there, watched, and waited until she finished and had left. Niner had stayed there just in case Mosaic and his friend needed help. They had also not spoken at first as Mosaic and Trapper had started their walk around the wall and before they had broken out into their laughing fit. Niner had not said anything else to them and had waited until Mosaic was on the top of the wall adjacent to the small loft. Niner then asked in rapid succession, "What are you doing here? It is not safe. How did you find us? Where is your sister? Why isn't she with you? Is she alright?"

Mosaic said," Dad slow down. I will explain everything, but just how do I get in? So we can talk in a normal voice and not have to shout or talk so loud."

"Okay, son, Moth got out through a small opening by the wall, the cover and the gates post, over there." Niner said and pointed to the spot where the three things came together. Mosaic and Trapper saw where he was pointing and flew over to the area Niner had pointed out to them. Sure enough, the fencing was pulled away from the top of the wall outward leaving just enough room for a pigeon or any small animal to squeeze underneath without difficulty.

Trapper and Mosaic looked at one another, "Should we both go in?" Trapper asked, "Or should one of us stay here and keep watch? Before we go in, shouldn't we talk about a plan on how to get them and us out?" "All valid questions,' Mosaic thought. However, he really did not have a plan for any of them.

"I don't know, but let's go in and get a better idea of the lay of the land, and what is being used to keep them in the loft? For instance, how the door closes? Maybe we can come up with a plan once we get a better look at it, and maybe they can help us formulate that plan. After all, they have been here longer than we have and should have an idea of what to do. We will both go in, you keep guard and look out for the humans, and I will investigate and ask them what they think we can do. Okay?" was Mosaic response.

Trapper agreed to the plan such as it was, but really wasn't confident they'd be able to do much, at least from what he had seen so far, but he wasn't going to say that to Mosaic. It was definitely worth a closer look. Without doing the looking and closer investigation, they would never know. Therefore, with one doing the investigating and the other keeping watch it seemed like a safe enough plan, so long as they remembered where the escape hole was in the fence. "Okay, but keep track of where this hole is, so if we need to get out quick, we can." He said.

With that decided, they both slipped through the hole and looked at the wall from the inside out. What a different perspective this is, Mosaic thought, and right away, he had a feeling of foreboding, even though it looked the same it felt different. 'Be careful!' he said to himself. This really is giving me a feeling of claustrophobia, somehow even worse than when I was in the medical cage recovering. The canvas gave the place an eerie gray dank feeling and look. "Stay alert!" he said to Trapper.

"Got it Boss." Trapper replied, "Let's go and find out what we need to know and get out of here. Now that I'm in here, I don't like it much, the place look like a prison" which it did with its block wall and the barb wire.

They flew over to the ground by the loft and as they did, Niner and Koffee flew down to the ground inside the loft as well. All three had smiles on their faces and were genuinely happy to see each other.

"Okay," Niner said, "We do not have a whole lot of time, so tell us where is Moth? How did you find us? How is the rest of the flock, how many escaped that night? How are you doing and feeling? You look tired."

"Dad, slow down, and I'll explain everything and answer all your questions." Mosaic said and then explained everything that had happened at the K-bridge after they had been taken away. How some had become a part of the quest group, having to go to find the emblems that the ones left at the bridge had to survive with less in the group. How he had met Trapper and how he had helped him get home. How he had escaped death thanks to Trapper. He then explained about Moth's arrival, her illness, or more accurately, her poisoning, her battle with it, and Ibu's roll in her getting better. He told then of their journey and how they had found the pet and feed store, and their intent to try to rescue them, to get them out of there.

As he had been talking a silver red bar, grizzle cock had flown down and joined Niner and Koffee as had several other birds, including a dark check white flight hen. The silver and red bar grizzle cock said, "Hello Buddy, how's your sister? I could not help but overhear you talking about her. So she's all right, or will be all right?" Mosaic looked at Razor. He did not like being called buddy and the fact that Razor had done it from the first time they had met had not exactly endeared him to Mosaic, and that he had kept it up after being asked to quit irritated him to no end. His father had told him it was Razors' way of trying to get Mosaic to feel he belonged, or that Razor belonged. Either way Mosaic still did not like it. Other than that little irritating habit, Razor was good bird, loved his sister and had always been good to her, been a loyal mate. Even though the greeting had once again put his beak on edge, Mosaic decided to be civil and answer Razors' questions.

He explained what had happened and that earlier this morning Moth was resting well and was expected to recover. He left out the part about how Ibu was not sure how much of the original Moth would be there when she finally awoke. No need having him and his parents worrying about something they could not do anything about was Mosaic's feelings.

Razor had listened intently to every word and a part of him realized that Mosaic was not telling all he knew. Instead of pressing for more information, he thanked him, stepped back, and just listened. Mosaic was surprised, but pleased that Razor, nor his parents, were not pressing him for more information, because whatever else he told them would have been speculation, and would have caused his Mom, Dad and Razor unnecessary worry. Instead of giving any more details on Moths condition, he changed the subject, "How can I get you out of there? How did Moth escape? With all that went on she only said she slipped out the door when the human who was feeding you wasn't looking."

"Yes, that is true." His mom said, "But she hasn't made that same mistake since Moth escaped."

"So you don't think I could distract the human next time she opens the door and while she is preoccupied with me, you could get out?" he questioned.

Niner shook his head, "No, don't think so, but it is worth a try. Never know, maybe a few of us could get out." Niner, did not look as convinced as he was trying to sound, "I guess anything is worth a try, at least it's better than just sitting in here waiting." he finished.

"Probably wouldn't work. Humans may seem stupid, but they're not." Said the dark check white flight hen that had been listening to their conversation.

"Who's this naysayer?" Mosaic asked, a little disgustedly and with an edge of challenge in his voice almost as if he were saying to her, okay then, you come up with a better plan.

"Oh dear!" said his mother, "Sorry, my dear, excuse me. But this is Vlinder and she is really smart and knows a lot about loft etiquette and how to survive under human rules." She ushered Vlinder forward and introduced her to Mosaic. "Dear this is my son Mosaic, Mosaic this is Vlinder." Both nodded to each other, acknowledging each other's existence and in a low, almost inaudible voice said, "Glad to meet you", which was not displayed by their tone or mannerisms.

Mosaic dismissed her almost immediately by say to Niner, "What do you think, Dad, want to give it a try?" As he said this he looked directly at Vlinder, with an, I dare you to say something negative expression on his face.

Niner responded, "Sure why not, it wouldn't hurt a thing to try. And, who knows, it may even work." Vlinder looked directly at Mosaic and shook her head, as if she were saying, you just won't listen will you, even worse you won't even ask if anyone else has an idea as to what might work. Mosaic ignored her, and thought, so much for a total vote of confidence that they could escape, but for Niner to have said. 'Let's try it,' meant a lot. They discussed the plan a few moments more, and it was decided that the birds in the loft would pick those that would try to slip out when the distraction occurred. Not what Mosaic wanted to hear because, he was doing it so that Niner and Koffee could escape not just any bird in the loft. Once all had been decided Mosaic and Trapper flew back up to the top of the wall on the inner side of the courtyard and waited until the evening feeding time was to commence. Darkness came and the humans had left, totally forgetting about the evening meals for all the birds and animals housed in the courtyard cages. So much for the plan Mosaic thought.

With the one night light on to illuminate the area, he flew down to the loft and briefly talked with Niner, with his mom and Vlinder in attendance. Over Vlinder's objections to the plan, to her it would not work, the space was too small for it to work, they decided to try the plan in the morning anyway, because no other viable alternate plan had been offered.

Mosaic flew back to the top of the wall where Trapper was waiting shaking his head. "What's wrong?" Trapper asked his friend once he had landed.

"That Vlinder bird, what a negative bird she is. Just can't believe her, no faith. Can you believe she once again belittled the plan and said it wouldn't work, and even worse, saying I am crazy for even wanting to try it! Well when we get out of here, I'll just say, see miss smarty pants … now that you're free let's hear an apology." Mosaic finished in a huff.

Trapper looked at Mosaic and said tongue in cheek, "Never seen you get in such a huff before, just because someone disagreed with you."

Mosaic smiled, "Okay, it's not that she disagrees, but how she said it, that's what gets me. Who does she think she is, anyway? She did not offer an alternative to what we want to try."

"Just another bird with an opinion." Trapper said, "Just because, you like here… Let us not overreact. Let's get some sleep, we'll need it to be ready first thing in the morning", he finished, not caring if Mosaic liked what he had said or not.

"You're right. No, I don't like, her, if I did that would have nothing to do with it." Mosaic stated, but inside he was still saying to himself, 'who does she think she is anyway.' He then stopped himself, 'what did it matter,' he thought. 'Why did the opinion of a little hen he barely knew, that he had just met, mean so much anyway?' Looking at the loft and the bird he thought was her. He directed his thoughts towards her; 'you do not know me,' and with that said, his mind was at peace and he went to sleep.

While down in the loft, the bird named Vlinder was having the same thoughts and reactions towards Mosaic. Who did he think he was anyway, she thought. Looking over at the spot on the wall's edge where she thought he was sleeping, you do not know me. With that said, clearing her mind of the negative thoughts, she went to sleep.

The sunshine shone through the space between the canvas cover and the wire mesh at the top of the wall. The night had gone by without incident and much too quickly for Mosaic's liking. He got up with the sun and felt tired and not rested at all. Trapper, who had gotten up with the sun as well, looked at him and said, "You really look tired. Didn't you sleep well?"

"I'm Okay, I suppose." Mosaic answered, "Just tossed and turned, restless I guess. Today was on my mind when I went to sleep and I guess I'm more concerned than I thought." He did not tell Trapper that he had several dreams where the bird Vlinder was laughing at him because his rescue attempts had failed and he too was now confined to the loft.

The humans showed up one hour after the sun had fully risen into the early morning sky. They came and started their morning routine of making coffee and cleaning out the small cages and it was at least another hour after they had arrived before they started to taking care of the birds retained in the small loft. The human female of the day before came out into the courtyard area once again as she had done a minimum of twelve times this morning, carrying a bottle of water and a tin can containing pigeon feed. This time when they saw her emerge through the door Mosaic and Trapper knew she was coming out to take care of the birds in the small loft. They both got up and prepared themselves for the aerial maneuvers and dive-bombing attack they had planned to perform as soon as she started to open the door, once she was halfway in and half way out of the door, they would start the maneuver. They had decided that would be the best time to pull their stunt, which should distract her and allow some of the birds in the loft to escape. They had hoped that as she went about trying to recapture those that had escaped this would allow others to escape in the confusion. While all this was going on Mosaic and Trapper would be able to get Niner and Koffee out through the hole in the mesh and to freedom.

The only part of the plan that worked to perfection was their dive-bombing attack on the woman; nothing else worked as planned because, the door had a return spring on it. The minute the woman stepped out of the loft doorway to pursue them it closed. They barely escaped with their own lives.

The idea, the plan had seemed perfect. Mosaic had dove from one direction, while Trapper had dove from the other direction and as they crisscrossed over the woman's head, she had ducked and moved away from the loft. She then had grabbed a large butterfly type net from the wall and chased Trapper first, who barely escaped through the hole in the mesh at the top of the wall. She then went swiftly after Mosaic who was in the wrong position to use the same escape route that Trapper had used. Instead, he flew to the gate and landed on the floor near the intersection of the post and the gate, out of breath. Just as the woman was going to drop the net onto him, a pair of wings grabbed him and roughly pulled him through the space between the post and the gate.

"There! Got you!" Trapper said, "Boy that was close, so now what do we do?" As they, both flew up to the telephone pole adjacent to the building. Both landed there and panting heavily, Mosaic said to Trapper between breaths, "Don't know, and I haven't got a clue."

They sat there for several hours not able to think of another plan that they could use. Everything they thought of made no sense, or their train of thought about it went nowhere, all seemed to lead to dead ends. Mosaic decided to fly down to the wall and tell his parents not to worry, they were still there and that they would think of another plan, in the meantime they would go get a drink of water and not to worry they would be right back.

Mosaic and Trapper flew over to the cultivated field and landed in a small birdbath placed within a patch of sunflower plants, containing water. They got a drink of lukewarm water from the birdbath and then they flew back over to the pet and feed stores cinder block wall. They had discussed what to do, but nothing they had thought to discuss seemed practical. As they were, trying to figure out a plan of action an old fifty-seven Chevrolet pick-up truck pulled into the parking lot and parked next to the pet and feed store.

Two Chinese men climbed out of the bed of the old truck, as three others got out of the cab. All walked into the pet and feed. The next thing Mosaic and Trapper saw was the five men come out into the courtyard and stopped in front of the small loft. Accompanying them was the woman and they told her that they would buy the lot of them. They discussed a few things inaudibly from where Mosaic and Trapper were sitting, and then two of the men left, and the woman went over, unlocked, and opened the gate. There sitting at the gate sat the idling pick-up truck, the other men went over to the pick-up and took out three empty pigeon carrying crates and brought them over to the loft. To their dismay and disbelief all, the birds from the loft were transferred and placed into crates. Once the crates were full, they were carried over to the truck and placed into its bed. They removed several birds from one of the overstuffed crates they had just brought over to the bed, into one of the lesser full crates in the bed. The men secured these crates with several bungee cords. The men then said their goodbyes to the woman and then got either into the cab or climbed into the bed and then the truck took off, out of the parking lot and down the road. All of this had happened quickly and without any wasted motion.

Mosaic and Trapper could only fly after it and hope they would not lose sight of it. So the events at the pet and feed were repeated from stop after stop, as they followed the pickup truck all the rest of that day. Until all the crates were, full. They then traveled along freeways and roads until they ended up at several large ranch type buildings out in the country.

They arrived there at dusk and watched as the men in the pickup truck transferred the birds from the crates into several larger cages that looked like pigeon lofts. Mosaic and Trapper could only watch anxiously from their roosting place atop a light pole sitting in the yard next to one of the many lofts. Once all the birds had been transferred the lights went out, and they found themselves in darkness because dusk turned into night and all they had been able to do was watch. They had followed the truck and now they would have to wait until sunrise before they could do anything. Some rescuers we turned out to be Trapper thought. Mosaic was having the same thoughts, what a boondoggle he thought, we sure made a mess out of this, was anything going to go right on this rescue mission? He only said to Trapper, "I know, we'll see what the morning brings. Good night." With that said, he bristled up his feathers, let them smooth out again and closed his eyes, but his mind would not follow his command to relax, it was plagued by the thought, of what to do? Well I guess it is going to be a long night he thought. Trapper had watched all this and had also decided he did not want to talk about their day of failures either.

———————————   ———————————

The truck left the rail yard with the captured pigeons from the K-bridge and started down the road to its many stops where it would be picking up several hundred more birds on its trip to the game ranch located out in the country. The two Chinese men who had climbed into the bed of the pickup truck had not said much, but by their actions and the smiles on their faces, they were definitely in good humor. One stated to the other that their ancestors were smiling down on them and were bringing them much good fortune and luck. Last week they had been short fifty birds and now they were going to have that quantity and many, many more; thanks to Luo's abilities to know where the wild birds lived. Once again, Luo had saved them. Soon after the phone calls had come, saying several pet stores had birds available which was great, additional calls had come saying many private clubs whose members had birds for sale as well.

Yes, they were happy and their providence had changed for the better. All was right with their world, they had full bellies of their favorite meat and now they were off and would get all the birds they needed to make their pigeon derby a success for the up and coming weekend event.

Kimber had watched all the days activities without as much as a blink. At noon, the humans had provided water and he had not even taken a drink. No need he thought if I die so what. I don't need water, for only birds with a purpose need water. His flock mate Trouble had tried to get him to drink or to even take notice of what was happening, but she was only rewarded for her efforts with a blank stare of bird in shock.

Kimber did not come around until several birds were unceremoniously dumped into the crate at the one of the earlier stops. The thing that brought him temporarily out of his far away daze was a smile given to him by a coffee colored hen as she was pushed into him as she was shoved into the crate. "Sorry." She said, with an apologetic smile. The smile had reminded him of Smelt. However, sadly Smelt was gone. Nevertheless, that smile, it had somehow touched him and a small part of him said; you are not dead. However, almost as quickly as the smile had drawn that reaction, he shut down as if he had betrayed an important memory. Once again, he stared blankly into space.

Koffee looked at Kimber, recognized his blank stare, and felt his pain. She asked what had happened to him and when she was told, she knew she had to try to do something. She talked to Niner and he said that if anyone could relate to Kimber's pain she could. Seeing as how she had lost her first mate and understood the pain of such a loss better than anyone could understand. However, by the time she had found out what had happened and had talked to Niner, they had reached their final destination and had been transferred to their new quarters. During that transfer, she had lost track of Kimber, but had made a mental note to find him in the morning and offer her help if he needed it. She wondered what had happened to Mosaic and his friend, she had seen them following them and she knew they were all right and that gave her some peace of mind. With that on her brain, she had settled in for the night. Niner had watched her carefully and he knew she was okay and that gave him tranquility of being and with that, he made sure she did not need anything before he retired for the night. Then he settled in for the evening. His mind was thinking about all the activities of the day, of what tomorrow might bring. He definitely had to come up with a plan of escape, for the place they were in now had the smell of death about it. Why he knew this he could not have told you. Nevertheless, he knew it to be true and he knew if those feeling were accurate, then they all had very little time.

The hen named Vlinder watched as the multicolored cock named Mosaic and his friend Trapper dive-bombed the human in an attempt to try to cause a distraction so that some of the birds in the small loft could escape. Of course, the plan had failed just as she thought it would, but she was still impressed with his actions. Mosaic what a child he is in his beliefs. How naïve, she thought, of him to think that such a simple plan would even succeed. She still could not help being impressed by his flying, even as she was incredulous in her belief of his lack of maturity. The problem was that it had not been thought through and then she had watched, with her heart in her throat, as he had almost been caught and wound up in the loft with them. She kept asking herself why had she felt so concerned about what would happen with him, it was puzzling and in fact, it was beyond her.

Then, before anyone could do anything, discuss why they had failed in their plan or how it could have succeeded, the Chinese humans had come along and bought the entire stock of pigeons in the small loft. Within minutes everything had changed, they had been divided up, placed into crates that in turn were placed into the bed of an old rickety pickup truck. Then, before they knew it, they were off. She had wound up being transferred and was placed in the same crate with his parents. Then, she had watched the two would be rescuers following them. They had followed them all the way to the final destination, but by then it was dark and there was no chance to talk or plan another rescue attempt. She had seen them both land on the light pole next to the lofts, and somehow, them being there had given her a sense of security. Yes, they were young, naive and overly enthusiastic, but somehow that is what made them endearing to her. 'You are being silly,' she thought, 'you're trapped and they will not free you,' said her cynical side.

What could they do now? She shook her head. It was hopeless. The two would be rescuers, heroes, had failed and now they were in an even larger loft with no chance of escaping. 'Oh well!' she thought, 'no use in worrying, the fates would dictate what would happen now,' she thought. Once again, a part of her felt disappointed. Mosaic was young, naïve and immature, so why was she so saddened by the fact that he had failed and more importantly why had that hurt look on his face affected her so? Caused her to feel such strong empathy for him.

The more she thought about it, she found herself feeling sorry for him and his failure. It was not because they had not escaped, but rather it had saddened her that he had failed. It saddened her that he had felt the kind of pain his face had shown. Why should I care, she asked herself, he is nothing to me. Just another young immature cock trying to impress his parents, and with that thought on her mind she decided enough and she took one last look around her new surroundings before closing her eyes to try and go to sleep.

Instead, Vlinder had watched his parents, a part of her knew that they were special and in knowing that she also knew, he was special as well. Enough she told herself, and she hugged herself, ruffed her feathers and relaxed them, closed her eyes, took several deep cleansing breaths and went to sleep. Not a peaceful sleep; but sleep never the less.

Niner looked at Koffee who he realized was not asleep, "I love you, you know?" He said to her.

"I know." She said in reply, "Promise me something." "What?" he said.

"If we get separated or if one of us doesn't make it, then the other will not give up on life. That the one that survives will go on." She looked at him, "Promise!"

He said in response, "Sure I will. However, nothing is going to happen to us. We'll be fine, you will see." Even to his own ears, the words sounded empty, like he knew, as she knew, that not all would make it from this adventure. So with that not having been said, they fell asleep in each other's wings, content and at peace within each other's embrace and strength.

Interesting Pigeon Fact

They have easy temperaments and are adaptable and hardy, which no doubt accounts for their ability to maintain numbers.

http://www.animalaid.org.uk/h/n/CAMPAIGNS/wildlife/ALL/346/

For Crafco the day had started out just fine and he was in a great mood, even though his reaction to the news of what had happened at K-bridge would have left most with a different impression. Whenever he was in the public's view he looked long faced and upset, whenever anyone told him of what had happened, and asked for his opinion he would react with shock and disbelief, he would say respectively, "Unbelievable, what a tragedy!"

Inside, at his very core, he was exuberant and ecstatic that his plan had worked so well. Nothing had gone wrong, which he had overjoyed greatly, but his greatest joy had been duping them all. The hardest part had been keeping up appearances, but even that had become fun after a while, the acting job he was doing would have made Tom Hanks envious he thought. Most of those that had told him about the unbelievable events at the bridge had believed his reactions to the news, all except Oonal and of course Shamus. They had caught him, or so he thought, in one of his truer moments after having heard the news. However, neither had grilled him nor pursued their first comments concerning why he was so happy. He had told them he was greatly saddened, but what was a bird to do? He had explained life goes on and everything he had heard was only speculation on what had happened.

They explained what they had been told by Donkey, who had been caught out late and had landed in the trees not far from the K-bridge, and wound up spending the night. In doing so, he had been in a good spot to see what had happened. That humans' had again come to the bridge and performed a late night raid taking all the birds that were at the bridge. With that information, Shamus had further explained to him how he had sent out flyers to the other parts of the rail yard to warn them that humans were on the prowl again and to be on the alert. Especially to be on the watch for any unusual, strange, or abnormal activities they might be engaged in. There would be a formal meeting later that day to discuss it further plans they could take and hopefully they would have more information by then. The two of them had then left him so they could tell all the other council members at the Northeast section about the meeting, and explain what they knew and what the action they had ordered to be taken so far, nothing anyone could do would stop what was about to happen.

Of course, Crafco had already been informed of all that had happened by Reaper, who had come to him at first light with the news of the raid. Yes, he thought, let the fools take any action they liked, the plan had been laid and the first step to its completion had occurred. K-bridge was vacant, and his for the taking. The only thing that had stunned Crafco, and somewhat surprised him, was how perfectly it all had gone.

He had been working toward this end for over a year now. For the past months it seemed every time he had set an action into motion, without exception to whatever it was, it had not gone as planned. Maybe Oos was right without mature leadership and their influences the good side becomes weak and scattered and with that going on than the dark side could prevail. Even though he had thrown his lot in with Oos, Crafco did not see himself as evil, he was definitely an opportunist. If he had been honest with himself, he would have realized he was a manipulator, a control freak and only interested in his own ambitions. However, he had disillusioned himself by believing he was doing right, doing this for the greater good, for all those poor souls in the rail yard. Because, he knew what was wrong and how to fix it, he believed this and all he did was for the greater good of all those who lived in and around the rail yard. Ever since he had been hatched, he had witnessed the weak being promoted, accepted and coddled. While he, the strong, had been shunned, rejected, and pushed into the background. Well, that would soon change he thought, for all his well thought out and executed strategies were finally coming to fruition. Soon now, he would control the K-bridge and with his control over the K-Bridge and its future lock, and his puppet master control over the Southwest flock, he would have all the pieces in place to get rid of Shamus and weaken Oonal. He would weaken Oonal's control over the Seers and then he could place whom he wanted as Northwest flock leader, and then he could become Grand flock leader over the entire rail yard and all the areas adjacent to the rail yard. Oh, how glorious that would be, to be known as "Crafco the Grand Overseer" of all that the sun shines on within his vision.

Yes, he thought we are almost there my friends. Then, we'll let you out of your pit and we will rule all that I can see, and more. Oh yes, he would release "Oother" and put him back in power, at least sort of. Oh, how he would rule, with "Oother" under his control he would eventually be ruler of all the pigeons of the region, the section, the nation and eventually the world.

Slow down Crafco, he told himself. Do not get ahead of yourself. Crafco had to go and still meet with Oos and determine what the next step would need to be, or at least be in unison and coordinate and have the same understanding of what needed to be accomplished next. He had been a little anxious about this earlier this morning, but that had all melted away based on the news Reaper had brought him of the events at the bridge last night, with the success there and now he felt relaxed as he left his nesting area to go to the stream and meet with Oos.

As he walked down the corridor to the outside, he found he was humming to himself, "It's a wonderful Day". Stop that he told himself, all you need is for one of Shamus's goody two feet supporters seeing you like this and every bird in the whole flock will suspect you as having been the perpetrator of what has happened. He knew that many already felt that somehow he had been involved just by their accusatory stares and quiet whispers as he had passed them earlier this morning.

As he exited the corridor, and stepped into the sunshine he felt the tension melt away as he took off into the air and headed for the stream. As he flew towards the stream, he felt less tense. The act of flying, of getting away from the stoic accusatory looks and stares, of leaving them behind, allowed him to loosen up. It allowed him to be himself and to mull over the great news that K-bridge had been abandoned. All that had lived there had been taken and the greatest thing of all was that a man, Lou had done it and he was not ever considered a suspect. Yet, he was still worried, would he be allowed to claim the K-bridge as his own? Of course, he would, he told himself and once that was done, he would have the base of operations to launch his takeover of the entire rail yard. His mind ran one scenario after the next and in each he was successful, which pleased him to no end.

However, first things first he thought, go visit with Oos. Let him know that he, Crafco, had pulled it off. He had orchestrated the whole affair; his careful preparation had gotten rid of Kimber, the biggest inhibitor to his ability to keep Trent in line. The fates had been smiling down on him as well, because the raid had gotten rid of Oom and Oon, Seers of the Northeast and Southwest flocks, two of Oonal's biggest allies and two of Oos's biggest opponents. Yes, he thought, thank you Oonal for that added bit of information this morning.

He flew along at an easy pace, rehashing in his mind all the news of the morning and relishing it all. He definitely was happier than he had been in a long time about all that had happened the previous night. The sun was shining, and the early morning air smelled fresh and clean. Then, the stream came into view and there at the water's edge stood Oos, Windsor, Blackjack and several other Northern Border flock members.

He hated to meet with Oos with all these extra witnesses around, but everything had been executed to perfection, and the results had been well beyond his expectations. So, at this point in time, he did not care who was present from the border flocks, yet he should have been. In addition, as time would show it was another thing outside of his control that would benefit his ultimate desires to become the leader of it all. To become the greatest pigeon leader of all time. He figured that their presence here was of little significance to the events already set in motion and them being here made them as culpable as he was for the actions that had already occurred and would occur. As he landed, Oos came up to him and nodded slightly, "Nicely done, nice job, my hats off to you. I'm not sure how you pulled it off, or if it was just dumb luck, but you have my admiration and apologies for doubting you the last time we met. You have demonstrated an ability I would not have suspected."

Crafco bowed slightly in return, be gracious he thought as he replied, "Thank you, and your apology accepted." Was his guarded response to Oos's congratulatory comments.

Oos just gave him a slight devious smile, "Well, my boy." Oos hesitated, expecting a response and then continued, "Ready for the next phase?"

Crafco had stiffened slightly to Oos's last remarks, and responded a little more harshly than he had intended, for he knew Oos was trying to get a reaction and show who was the boss, "I'm not a boy; nor am I your boy. Please address me by my name." By the time Crafco had, his last sentence out it was spoken very pleasantly and the words rolled of this tongue naturally and calmly.

"Of course my B…" Oos caught himself. He smiled a devilish smile at Crafco, "of course Crafco, forgive me; it's just an old bird's idiosyncrasy."

Crafco knew better, but he decided to drop it and be gracious, "Of course no offense taken. I understand how old habits are hard to break." He said this in his sweetest of voices, hoping that the sarcasm he felt would just seep through. Your purpose old coot, he thought, was to let me know the pecking order; you knew exactly what you were doing. Yet, we both know that based on this accomplishment, Vile will grant me what I want. My success in this little endeavor will allow me to become the "Great Flock Leader" of the rail yard, while you my friend will remain a lowly Seer. They looked at each other each understanding that they were leery of the each other, and both knew what was really motivating them to do what they were doing. Both had said it was for the betterment of all involved, but both knew it was for their own ambitions and egos that were really driving the events. At every meeting with these two, there were these little word games that were played. Crafco decided to cut them short, for at this meeting, there were more important things to attend to as he saw it. They both had to go and meet with Vile, and Crafco admitted to himself he really did not like those meetings, with Vile, but they were unavoidable to get to his desires.

Ignoble Vile was a genuinely a very bad spirit of a former bird, or maybe he was a former bird that had been kept alive by magic and incantations that made him so undesirable to be around. It did not matter which, it only mattered that Crafco was using Vile to get ahead and once that had been achieved, his heart's desires to be the "Great Flock Leader"; he would rid himself of Oos and sever his relationship with Vile. Vile was just another tool to Crafco, another tool that would help him realize his heart's desires and then to be disposed of. During their exchange, all the other birds in attendance said nothing, but by their actions were uncomfortable with the tension these two exuded.

"Well!" Oos said interrupting Crafco's daydreaming fantasy, "Vile is waiting. We had better go. You know how he hates to be kept waiting." With that, comment Oos headed off towards a set of rocks at the edge of the pebble strewn waterless riverbed. As they approached the rocks, they could see an opening, which from a distance looked like a shadow cast between boulders. As they got closer, it looked more like a crack between the two biggest rocks. However, once they got closer only inches away, the crack became a space. They stepped into it and then moved immediately to their right into a little breezeway. The small group of pigeons steps down the breezeway and there was another opening to their left, which led into a passageway. The passageway was totally hidden from the outside world and if you did not know it was there you would have walked by it all day long; never knowing it was the entranceway to pure evil.

Oos led the way with Crafco next and then Windsor, Tack and several other birds he did not know, were bringing up the rear, with the rest of the birds not following them into the crack, but staying behind, they were rather a rear guard. Blackjack was the leader of those left behind and his responsibility was to be sure they were not followed or disturbed during their meeting. Usually it was Crafco, Windsor and Oos that had gone and made the short walk down the damp and dank poorly lighted passageway to where Vile lived. Oos seemed to know what Crafco was thinking and responded to his unanswered question.

"Tack is going to be my messenger to Vile, now that my duties on the outside will increase. I will need a way to get information to and from him at any time." Crafco thought, 'yea sure, and how trustworthy is he. Yet, another spoke in the wheel that can get broken, another means to get things wrong.'

Again, Oos seemed to have heard Crafco's unasked question, and told Crafco, "Do not worry, he is a part of me and will not betray me." Oos said this with an ominous tone in his voice, and then he continued, in an eerie whisper, "He and I are of the same blood, we are closer than twins. We are as one."

Crafco did not respond, but pondered the words Oos had spoken and as he mulled them over in his mind, the passageway angled slowly downward. The coolness of the passage gave Crafco chills even though he was not afraid. They traveled along, down the wet and damp underground little tunnel for thirty minutes; the darkness enveloped them all except for where they were presently walking. By some unknown means, a mysterious light was provided and it illuminated the path several feet in front of them, as if it were guiding them towards their final destination. A true guiding light, he thought to himself. Not a word had been spoken by any during the journey; the only sound was the echoing of their breathing and their feet as they shuffled along, each caught up in their own thoughts. The tunnel, which had been relatively straight, then took several turns and after the last corner, the tunnel spilled out into a shaded little brown grassy knoll like burrow, which was totally hidden from the outer world.

The change in the quality of the air caused all of them, even Crafco, to take a deep breath and let it out slowly, making it sound as if all had gasped at seeing the scene that unfolded in front of them. The knoll had a terraced effect, as different plants and other brown earth toned fauna seemed to grow at different levels and heights giving the whole area the look of a circular room. There were also several large trees encircling the space and their roots in places came up out of the ground, providing seating and roosting places, and they all seemed to be facing a specific spot at the far end of the opening giving the whole place the appearance of a receiving chamber. The whole area was shrouded in a veil of mist or smoke, which added to its mystical appearance. As you entered the area, the place had a moist, fugue smell about it. The air definitely was not clear, clean and crisp; it was unmistakably saturated with the smell of decaying leaves and plant matter. The mist that hung over the area seemed to clear, as they entered the clearing. The wisps of smoke, or mist, or whatever it was that clouded the air, moved apart as a curtain does when they entered. Maybe it was Crafco's imagination, but it all seemed to be traveling toward the far side of the clearing where it looked like silvery curtains hiding a stage.

The further they entered the more they were drawn in, or directed to the curtained looking area. Then, the mist parted, as a drapery being drawn back to reveal an old, decrepitated white gray pigeon sitting on an old root three tiers above ground. Even though Crafco had seen this numerous times, before the effect was still impressive, even to his cynical nature. A part of him thought okay, in a sarcastic tone, enough with the mumbo jumbo, I am impressed, but a part of him also was slightly fearful and apprehensive about what he saw and how Vile realistically could control the elements in this situation was inspiring and a little ominous and scary.

The old bird was looking in their direction with unseeing eyes. He seemed to be in a trance because he did not acknowledge them at all. The small group had entered in a less than the normal fashion for his kind; they had stooped and quietly and softly they had entered not wanting to disturb the bird sitting before them. They stood there several minutes before the seated bird acknowledged their existence.

Not looking at any one of them in particular, he spoke in a crackly, whispering, hoarse voice, "Welcome to my nest. All went well?" it coughed and hacked for several minutes as if it hadn't spoken out loud for a long time, as if speaking had been a chore, which had caused it to go into a state of confusion. It took several deep breaths through its mouth, as if it were drinking in air as a liquid, before it spoke again. By its behavior, it did not expect an answer; actually, it answered its own question, "Yes! All went well! We now only have a few left to obstruct us, and they will fall with ease. Yes!" He stopped to once again, took a deep breath of the air, and then had another coughing fit before it continued again. "My Friends, we will be in power soon. Oh, what a glorious day it will be when 'Oother' once again can walk amongst us." Vile then stopped and looked directly at Crafco, as if he was expecting and waiting on an answer from him.

'We!' Crafco thought, 'you really mean me.' However, he replied differently instead of thinking about what he had just been thinking, and he said what he believed all present wanted to hear. "Yes, Vile, we will soon be in total control of the rail yard. Thank you for your help, I will always be indebted to you. Anything you want I will grant, once I am rail yard flock leader." Crafco hoped that what he said did not sound as shallow and empty as it sounded to his own ears.

"Yes, Crafco, I know you will not let me down in my hours of need." Vile said in a very soft and weak, but never the less menacing, voice. "You are welcome, and as always I'm your humble servant and helper in your ambitions. Is there anything else you need help with at this time?" He finished in an even lower, quiet whisper of a voice. Again, the sounds that reached Crafco's ears besides the words sent a cold chill down his spine, a warning chill that said be careful, you are not indispensable! Vile then looked at the rest, as he waited for Crafco to find his voice. He did not speak, but they, his followers, all seemed to have been communicating in a silent unspoken language.

Crafco did not know why, but he bowed slightly and said, "No, I believe all our plans have borne fruit. All has gone better than expected. Give it another week or two at the most and all will be completed." Crafco finished. Yes, he thought, I will be rail yard leader. Once he had the power Vile would come out of hiding and live in the open spaces of the rail yard where Talon would have easy access to him, and wallah! Yet, another troublesome loose end would be disposed of. "You then will be able to come out and live at the rail yard, out in the open once again, free to feel the sun and wind in your face."

"Good, good, excellent," was Vile's response. Between more coughing, and still his facial expression betrayed his words. He was not glad to have to come out of his little hidden perfect world.

However, his words once again said he was looking forward to again being able to go out in the open, but his body language said, apprehension. On the other hand, was Crafco just imaging what he saw as mistrust in what he was being told? Vile continued, "Then I'll expect to hear from you in two weeks. Until then may the wind be your friend and may the sun shine on your nest. Until then," and paused, and then finished with a curt, "Goodbye!" As soon as those words escaped his beak, the nest filled with mist and smoke, hiding Vile from their view once again, as a veil covers the face of a beautiful woman; the mist took Vile and removed him from their preview, they were free to leave.

All turned to leave without another word having been spoken, all knew the audience was over and they had no energy left to talk. Just being in the place and presence of Vile had zapped them of their energies. On the return trip back none spoke.

Once outside of the passageway, and back into the sun, and standing on the riverbed seemed to bring back the energy they had lost. There in the open, in the full sun light, Oos spoke, "We'll keep in touch, and in two weeks we'll come and visit Vile again and let him know all is ready, and safe for him to once again enter the world of the living and stop living his self-imposed exile."

Crafco looked at Oos and smiled. 'Who's side are you on anyway he thought,' but instead of saying what he thought he said, "We will meet in two days after tomorrow and at that time we will get rid of Oonal as head of the Seers. We will also discuss how to get rid of Shamus as flock leader, by then all our plans should have had time to fully develop."

"Yes." said Oos "Until then my bo…, until then, take care. We need you or all will be lost." With that having been said, and not waiting for a response, he and his companions climbed into the air leaving Crafco standing alone in the streambed.

Crafco watched them leave and smiled to himself in great satisfaction. He had done it; he had faced Vile and not felt threatened. Well, not much anyway, he had been in control and Vile had not had the upper hand, had not questioned or challenged neither his timeline, nor what he had said. Yes, he was pleased with himself, for usually Vile would ask questions, down to the minutest detail and Vile would have suggested improvements. He was glad it had not taken much time with Vile. He hated going to see him; the place Vile called his nest was always dank and musty smelling. It was always wet and it had an unnatural feel about it. It always seemed to cause him dread, and always depressed him and made him feel inferior. However, this time it had been different, it had been better and he had not felt as a subordinate. He felt as an equal, sort of, it is because you have succeeded and you have ascended to a higher level, to his level, is what he told himself. Vile, like all creatures of the world, could not argue with success, and let us face it he told himself, you have definitely achieved something with this. He told himself, 'you are in charge now…'

  With that wonderful thought trailing off in his mind, Crafco ascended into the air in a good humor and headed for the K-bridge to claim his prize.

Interesting Pigeon Fact

Pigeons are highly intelligent animals. They are able to recognize themselves in the mirror, to find same people on two different pictures and to recognize all letters of the English alphabet.

Pigeons have exceptional eyesight and ability to identify objects on a distance of 26 miles

http://www.animalaid.org.uk/h/n/CAMPAIGNS/wildlife/ALL/346/

Mosaic and Trapper awoke to a gray overcast sky. The sun was having trouble getting its rays out between the clouds that filled the heavens. It was creating an awesome effect Mosaic thought, it was a spectacular scene, the sun's golden rays were trying to break through between the cloud layers and in doing so only small rays seemed to escape, only to be recaptured by other clouds illuminating their edges. He now understood where the term, "Every cloud has a silver lining" came from. Through all the gray and gloom of the depression he felt, of all the bad things that had happened, the heavens looked truly glorious with the way the light played and glowed on the edges of the clouds. 'It gave you hope,' he thought, 'as the light broke out of the murkiness and its rays brightened the early morning skies, things were going to get better.'

Mosaic yawned and as he stretched, he looked around and was surprised at all the lofts he saw. There were four rows of ten lofts each. Each loft was stocked to the rafters with pigeons, except for the last two rows, which contained white squab pigeons. Six of the lofts contained the breeders and the rest contained the birds that would be butchered and served as squabs. They weren't flyers, but only walking pigeons, never expected to fly, only expected to get fat and when they got to the right weight they were slaughtered, packaged and frozen to be sent to restaurants of the highest caliber. Day after tomorrow several dozen would be killed and prepared for the hunters to take home after the two days of hunting had commenced and been completed.

"Let's go see what this place is, and look at the landscape," he said to Trapper, who was just getting up.

"Sure…" Trapper replied between yawns and stretches of his wings, "And maybe we can find something to eat and drink as we look around."

Before they went on their excursion to examine their surroundings and find food and drink, they flew down to the loft where they had watched the humans place the pigeons from the pickup truck the night before. To their surprise, they found their friends in the loft as well, the ones that they had left at the K-bridge weeks before. They exchanged greetings, as was customary and then were updated by what had transpired since they had left the bridge, and about the raid that had eventually lead to their current predicament. Rambler finished his narrative, "The Bridge is now totally abandoned and up for grabs. I'm sorry Mosaic, we all are." Rambler finished with a tear in his throat.

Mosaic shrugged his shoulder as he said, "You did all you could have done, looking at them all, you all did!" he finished as he looked at the grim and depressed faces of his fellow flock members. We will deal with that once we get you out of here. First, one thing at a time, we need to get you out of here, we'll have to face that dilemma of the Bridge later" he finished with more confidence in his voice than he felt in his heart. What else could go wrong he thought? However, before he could entertain that idea of self-indulgence much longer, Niner asked, "So what are you two planning on doing?"

Mosaic looked at Trapper, who gave a shrug and then responded, "We're going to look at the lay of the land and maybe find something to eat and drink. Then we'll come back here and report what we see and find."

"Good idea!" said Rambler, "maybe we can figure out what type of place this is. Hopefully we can see what routine these humans have so we can formulate a plan of escape."

"My thoughts exactly." Niner said in concurrence with Rambler's comments. Koffee who had joined them while they had been having their discussion, had just stood by as they talked, with a pleasant smile on her face, nodding every so often in concurrence to what they were saying. The other bird that had joined them as well, much to Mosaic's amazement, was the hen Vlinder. She had flown over at Koffee's gesturing. Because Koffee felt she knew humans and lofts better than anyone else in this particular loft. It was because of that reason that she had flown over and Koffee felt she was smart and maybe she could contribute something to the conversation. Koffee saw Mosaic's response, it wasn't anything he said but she knew her son, and his body language was quite plain to her. It was saying, ever so slightly, that no one else noticed, what's she doing here?

Koffee said in a very motherly, insistent, authoritarian gentle voice that Vlinder had some good and important information to tell them about humans and lofts that they should pay attention to what she had to say. This last remark was directed at Mosaic, and he knew it and responded a little impatiently, as sons often do, but with respect, "Okay Mom! We'll listen to what's she has got to say?"

Vlinder, who figured she would say her piece, knew she would not be listened too, but felt she had to make the effort; she could then watch whatever happened with a clear conscience because she had tried. With that thought on her mind, she explained what she knew of humans and their habits when it came to pigeons. How they worked on schedules of when to feed, when to water, when to let them fly, and give medicine.

Mosaic snorted, and stopped himself from laughing. "What?" she asked not liking to be made a fool of, or to be laughed at.

"Nothing!" he said. She gave him an angry, hurt look and again asked, "What?" He knew he would need to respond, she had made a point of it, and he now wished he had not stifled the laugh, no had not laughed at all, "I don't think they're going to let us go flying any time soon," he said lamely.

"Well. I never…" However, before she went on Koffee spoke up, and as she did so she gave him a look of reproach, of that's enough. "Go on dear. Tell them about what the finches said."

Vlinder hesitated, giving Mosaic a look of, you twit, and then continued. She told them of how she had overheard a pair of wild finches that morning, saying that they were at a game ranch and that the pigeons were the prey that would be released for the big shoot tomorrow. She explained she had then asked what the finches had meant. The finches had then described to her how it would happen; they would be transferred to smaller crates, like the ones they came in yesterday and taken to the hedgerows. The hedgerows were at the ends of the green fields and that there they would be released. They would fly out across the fields, where they would be shot at and killed. In addition that they would eventually end up on the human's food plates and to then be eaten with nonchalant arrogance.

"No!" Mosaic said, "You are kidding aren't you. That's simply barbaric!"

"No, I don't think the finches were kidding." Vlinder said in response to his disbelief. How naive he is she thought, did he believe the humans had brought them out here for a relaxing vacation. "Look," she continued, "humans who spend this kind of money only do it so they can get more money." She stopped again seeing he had a puzzled look on his face. "Money, you know what money is right?" He shook his head no.

She took a deep breath, and let it out slowly. What a dunce, she then corrected herself almost immediately for her unkind thoughts. He is wild, what would a wild pigeon know about humans and their money envy. "We can discuss that later," she said if there was a later, and then continued with what she had overheard "They were quite serious and I believe them. They did say that if we make it and fly south to the pond and the old dilapidated church located there, we would be safe. That there are birds there that can give aid to the wounded."

Mosaic realized that what she had told them she truly believed, but he also knew from experience that finches loved to embellish things and at times even made up parts of their stories just for their own flights of fancy. He also knew that every now and again they would tell things that were not one hundred percent true. Therefore, it was hard to believe what they said, without collaborating it. At least for now he would believe what they said, at least for now until he found out differently. Once he and Trapper had departed and while they flew around and determined the lay of the land, he would ask others they would hopefully meet and ask them to try to validate the information. He thought all this as

Vlinder spoke about human's habits and their fascination with guns.

Vlinder who had expected a rebuttal was surprised when it did not come. Instead, Mosaic had been very attentive to all that she had said and he had said in response, "This is really serious and we have very little time to do anything." What he had not said was what he had thought, provided it is true.

Trapper, who was getting impatient because he was hungry, was shifting from one foot to the other and finally said, "Look, let's go and investigate. There has to be others that can confirm this. Maybe if we are lucky they can tell us more and maybe give us more information so we can come-up with a plan that could work and get you all out of here." He said this because he had read Mosaic's subtle body language and he wanted to get him out of there just in case someone else did as well and asked the question, do you believe her.

All agreed that for now that sounded like the best course of action to take. With that having been decided, Mosaic and Trapper said their goodbyes, and with the reassuring comment, "we'll be back" as he took into the air.

The first thing they confirmed was that there were four rows of ten lofts and all were full of pigeons. Two of the rows contained nothing but white birds. The balance contained birds of all types of colored morphs. The interesting thing was, that in the balance of these lofts were all types of wild pigeons, funny looking birds, called show birds and racing homers.

As they flew their circular pattern, they went over a large barn like structure, a large garage type building and several single-family structures where humans resided. There were also a dozen smaller cabins set up in two rows and a large building that stood at one end of the rows of cabins. All of this was set in a neatly laid out and manicured lawns, which reminded Mosaic of a small park. Traversing the lawns and buildings were many gravel paths that connected each building to the next and to the gardens. On the front side of the large building, which they were told later was called a lodge there was a gravel parking area.

Further out from this serene setting were green lawns all around that led eventually out into the wilderness. Off to the left about a hundred yards there was a raised area that had a long wooden plank structure that extended along the length of the all the fields' adjacent to it. Along its front, there was a four-foot high railing, and the entire platform was covered halfway with a green canvas tarp to protect the occupants from the elements. Approximately every hundred yards along the platform there were stairs leading down to the grounds extending from the platform. This area less the structure to everyone at the game ranch and all the guests that came was called the gallery.

The platform overlooked the gallery; a large expanse of green lawn that was four hundred yards deep and six hundred yards wide, it looked beautiful. The emerald green of the fields was broken up every hundred yards by a row of hedges, and on the left side of each row, there was a concrete moat, deep and wide enough for a man to walk down so he could not be seen or see over the top of the hedgerows. Evenly spaced, approximately every hundred and fifty feet apart were small concrete slabs. These were the crates retaining plates and they started one hundred and fifty feet away from the platform and ran evenly spaced along the length of the hedgerows. On the platform is where the hunters stood and looked down over the Gallery lawns and had an easy time of seeing and shooting any unfortunate bird flying across the green expanse below.

As Mosaic and Trapper were flying and looking at the magnificent sight of lawn and air space a group of Sparrows saw them, flew over to them, and said, "Quite a sight isn't it? Beautiful to look at, takes your breath away does it not? However, don't be fooled by its beauty, for it is a killing field. The reason they keep it so pristine is so that the shooters, who stand on the rise can easily see those flying across it and have an easier time making the kill."

"No!" Trapper exclaimed in disbelief, "Something so lovely and immaculate is used for that? What a shame." He finished shaking his head in amazement.

"Yes, very sad." Said the Sparrow that had been talking to them, "The first shoot starts tomorrow, at around three hours after the sun comes up. It will go on like that for two days. They let out birds in small groups, of usually eight birds per group and they time release them, so there are always birds available to fly across the open spaces and get shot."

As the Sparrow had been explaining what would happen over the next two days Mosaic and Trapper felt shivers running down their spines. "Leave it to the humans to build something this beautiful and use it to kill and destroy another species lives." Mosaic said with anger in his voice.

"Yes." The Sparrow replied, "Leave it to humans to do just that. But, it is even worse for the white ones. They don't even get a fair chance; they are killed without being given a chance to escape. At least those flying across the fields have a slight chance of making it. No matter how slim it may seem it's at least a chance." The Sparrow finished with sadness in its voice when he said the white ones.

"Really," Mosaic responded with interest, "How's that? I mean the fact that you believe that the ones flying across the fields have a slim chance? It looks pretty hopeless to me based on what you have told us."

"Well, it's possible if they fly close to the hedgerows and don't fly across the clearing. You know the open expanse between the hedgerows, then they could make it to the wild fields and once there they have a good chance of surviving. That is, so long as they fly directly to the church we told you about." The Sparrow finished with a triumphant smile on its face.

"Why is that?" Trapper asked, looking just a little puzzled, "Because really, once in the wild area they should be harder to see and so therefore should be safe."

"No! Because there are all kinds of dangers in the wild fields and because, mister smarty." The Sparrow said, feeling threatened because he did not feel believed. "Several hunters with dogs roam the areas along the back hedge-row looking for stray and wounded birds. When they find the escaped and wounded birds, they dispatch them. Of course all in the name of being humane." The Sparrow stopped to see if he would be challenged and when he wasn't, he continued, "So if I were you two, I'd head for the church now. You don't want to be anywhere near here in the morning. It's not safe!" and with that the Sparrows said good-bye, and left them, flying over the fields and wishing them well and retreated for the safety of the south.

After the flock of Sparrows had left, they continued their scouting of area and discovered, as they flew away from the emerald fields, numerous large tented areas, covered with cloth mesh netting. They stopped at several of these and tried to determine what they were, for there appeared to be no way in or out. How strange they had thought this to be, for what could possibly be the purpose of these structures, what possible purpose could they have? At the third tented structure they landed, where they discovered in ward facing traps, similar to those used at most racing pigeon lofts that Trapper had been told about by April. Trapper was quite familiar how they worked and stopped Mosaic from going through one. He explained their function to Mosaic. "It only goes one way." he said, "inward, and once you are in, you can't get out without a human's help." He explained this by pushing against one of the bars. It moved inward with ease and when Trapper tried to pull on it, it only came back so far and then it stopped. No matter how hard he pulled it wouldn't move beyond a certain point. "See!" he said, "Only works one way."

"Thanks!" Mosaic said as he stepped through cleanly between the bars and then he was inside looking out at Trapper. He then laughed and stepped back through to where Trapper was standing with a dumbfounded look on his face. Mosaic laughed again, "I'm sure it works as you demonstrated, but this is for a much larger bird or animal than us." Laughing again, "Come on in and let's see who lives in here?" he said as he stepped between the bars from the outside to the inside again, "I'm curious about this strange structure and I want to know who lives here."

Trapper replied, "Okay! However, I'm not really comfortable doing this, you know. We should stay close by and see who accesses this one way door." he finished as he moved a few feet away from the opening and settled in for a long watch.

Mosaic replied, "You stay here then, while I go and see what this place is about." Without waiting for a reply he lifted himself into the air and left Trapper standing there with his mouth agape. Trapper smiled to himself, you go and investigate all you want, Mr. Curiosity he thought. I'll just stay here, safe and sound, and close to the only way out just in case something goes awry.

Mosaic was gone for about an hour and when he returned and landed next to the place where he had left Trapper, Trapper wasn't there. He looked around to find Trapper sitting in the lower branch of a small maple tree, with a Cheshire cat like smile on his face. "Find anything?" he asked, "Like food, water, or any occupants?"

"No!" Mosaic responded, "Okay, why the unrelenting smile on your face, what's up? What have you discovered? Food, water, what?"

Trapper still sporting a huge grin on his face replied, "Well, I've found both, and a lot more."

"Okay!" Mosaic said, "Give, tell me what you found and have learned." Mosaic then waited until Trapper decided to speak.

"This place is a free range cage and it is wild turkeys that live here. They say humans that own this land provide natural foods all over the cage and then twice a year they release them for a big wild turkey game hunt. The humans call it a turkey hunt and the turkeys call it the hide and seek event. Those that are smart enough make it back here and are safe until the next turkey hide and seek event. Those that aren't smart enough wind up on the human's dinner tables. Oh yeah, do you want something to eat? The turkey that I met showed me where they have a grain feeder that travels on a wire and spreads food every time a bird goes through the one way traps we were looking at."

"Yes! I'm starved" was Mosaic's response to Trapper's question. With that said Trapper flew down to the trap door of the tented structure and stepped through to the outside and then back through again. Then into the air he flew and motioned for Mosaic to follow, "Come on, and follow me!" he yelled. Mosaic followed Trapper to an open area not far from the traps and there strewn on the ground lay all types of seeds.

They flew to the ground and Trapper watched as Mosaic ate, every now and again Trapper who was already full, would eat a seed to his particular liking. When Mosaic was done, he asked, "That turkey, did tell you where to get a good drink, didn't he? Because these seeds sure hit the spot and now I am quite thirsty."

"Yes, Follow me," And with that Trapper flew into the air and directed Mosaic over to a small narrow man-made stream hidden behind a small rise to the east of the Feeding Field, as the turkey had called the place they had just been sustenance.

Once they had both gotten a drink of the refreshing stream water, they decided to stay and bathe and while doing so Trapper explained all he had learned from the turkey. He was a good old body, as he had called himself, and had survived three years of the turkey hunting seasons.

"Wow! To have done and survived all of that he really must be smart." Mosaic said. "Or lucky!" Mosaic interjected to the end of his thought to emphasize his awe at what Trapper had said.

"Yes, crafty is what I think." Trapper said with a little admiration in his voice as he continued, "he told me that the humans that own this place came in the first year of his life and that they had set traps and captured all the game birds they could find. They placed them in these large covered areas and made them safe places to live. All the birds that lived in these places became complacent. He said he tried to tell them that they would have to pay for their prosperity someday; of course, they did not listen. Then, sure enough at the end of the second year they were transported to the open wild places and let go, thinking they were free. Instead, it was where they were hunted relentlessly for four weeks. He told me he saw many die. He told me he was lucky that first season. Somehow, by dumb luck, he made it back to this cage and found a way in and once inside he was safe. He learned that once inside the cage the humans took care of you, but outside the cage all bets are off. Once outside you are not free, but game, and it becomes a real struggle to live."

"Wow!" Mosaic exclaimed, "So this is a game hunter's ranch! April told me these types of places existed. I just didn't believe her, it seemed so morose to capture and raise animals just to hunt them for sport."

"Well if the sparrows and turkey are correct," Trapper interjected, "than we don't want to be anywhere near here tomorrow, nor the day after. So, we had better think of something quick. Don't you think?"

Mosaic continued with verbalizing his thoughts, "Yes, of course we should act. But what should we do? It seems pretty hopeless in a way, don't you think?" he paused with a desperate look of concern and a what should we do expression on his face. Trapper didn't offer an answer, and so Mosaic continued, "I guess the first thing is to tell the caged ones what we have learned. But before we do that, let's fly over the fields once more so we can describe it to them accurately and then maybe an idea or answer will present itself." Mosaic finished lamely.

Trapper nodded his head in agreement and they both took to the air flew over to the fields. They sure were beautiful, Mosaic thought, as he looked at the emerald green sea of grass. It was hard to believe that such a peaceful, serene site would be used as a shooting gallery, with live pigeons being the targets. The Sparrow's words came back to him, "don't be fooled by the beauty of the place, it's not what it appears to be, they say that salvation resides along the hedges and death on the platform". What exactly had he meant by in the hedges being the salvation, was on Mosaic's mind? He looked with curiosity at the lay of the land, at how the hedgerows ran. They flew over the fields and platform where the hunters would be standing and back again and then on the third pass Mosaic got an idea. The more he looked at the lay of the fields and the hedgerows the stronger the inkling of an idea crystallized itself. "Follow me!" he yelled at Trapper, who was looking really disinterested in what they were doing and was about to voice his objection if they would have flown the field, platform route again. He watched Mosaic dive for the deck.

Mosaic dove down until he was flying two feet above the ground. Then, he headed for the hedgerow. He flew along the parallel to the platform until he got to the hedgerow where he turned and now he was flying parallel to the hedgerow and perpendicular to the platform. He flew the entire length of the hedgerow three feet from it. Once he got to the back hedge that intersected the one he was flying next to, he had to quickly climb two feet to clear it. He shot just a foot over its top and then just as quickly dropped back down, so that he was once again flying two feet above the ground behind it. Trapper had followed him through the whole maneuver and flight path and when they were done, said, "Okay! So now what? We flew the field and jumped the back hedge. So!"

"Don't you see?" Mosaic asked, as he pointed back to the hedgerows they had just followed and jumped.

"So what?" Trapper asked looking perplexed and wondering if Mosaic had lost his mind as he followed where Mosaic was pointing. "So, we flew down along the field and parallel to the bushes, so what does that prove?"

Mosaic had thought it appeared obvious and now that he'd done it and Trapper obviously didn't understand, he doubted what he had been thinking and what he thought he had proven. He thought that what he had done had been self-explanatory and the fact Trapper hadn't seen it right away made him wonder if he had been right. He flew over to the branch of a nearby tree, landed and waited as Trapper to followed and landed next to him.

"Well?" Trapper asked again, "Are you going to tell me what that was all about? I'm not a mind reader you know."

"Don't you see it?" Mosaic asked with amazement in his voice, "If we fly close to the bushes, the humans will have a harder time at seeing us. If they fire at us when we are close to the bushes, they will ruin their landscaping and you know how fastidious humans can get about their landscaping."

"Yes, of course, they really do get persnickety over their plants and trees. It just might work. If nothing else, it's worth a try. It will make us harder to see and I believe April once said, or maybe it was Eric… doesn't matter, it is harder shooting downhill rather than uphill." Trapper agreed.

And so, they flew it again and again practicing along each row and it seemed to work, except on the second row in, there the terrain was different. Coming out and away from every bush, at a forty-five degree angle there were nets set sporadically along the bush line. The nets were attached at the top of the bushes and then stacked down to the ground about six feet out from the bottom of the bushes. Being that far-out would make it impossible for any released birds to fly along the base of the bushes. Birds released at this section of the fields would really have to be lucky. They would have to try to fly low in a zigzagging motion, in and out from the release spots at the base of the bushes and then out again to clear the netting. Once out at the farthest end of the netting they would be easy targets for the shooters.

Mosaic looked at Trapper after they had flown the field twice, "This one is really going to be tough. I pity any bird that has to fly these release points." Trapper agreed with Mosaic's assessment of the situation and couldn't offer any solution to the dilemma that the birds released from this area would have to face. "You know." he offered as a thought and as an answer to Mosaics comments, "If they landed in an area between the nets and laid low they would be safe." Trapper stopped looked at the Fields, "because the hunters can't really see them, I'm thinking." he finished.

Mosaic thought about Trapper's comments and then said, "Look you fly to where the hunters are going to be positioned on the raised area, and I'll fly the course and you can then tell me if what we are thinking will work."

"Which position?" Trapper asked, "Between each hedge row there are at least six positions marked."

"The furthest!" Mosaic responded and with that decided, each took their position, Trapper watched, as Mosaic flew as close to the hedgerows as he could and then out again. He then flew back to where Trapper was sitting. "Well?" he asked.

Trapper looked apprehensive and discouraged, "It seemed like a good idea." he said, "But from here it doesn't look as good. Most birds will be exposed to at least one hunter down the line at any one time. You know how we are all built the same way; loud noises and the like scare us. We are born to fly. Hiding and flying low isn't an easy thing for a pigeon to do, especially when just being released from confinement. It goes against our nature, our psyche. Many will die." He said in a low voice, feeling defeated and shaking his head.

"I know, but it's all we have. We are either overcome by our fears, or we overcome them. However, in this case if we fail, it's almost certain death." Mosaic finished grimly. They both agreed they had done all they could and decided to return to the loft with all the information they had obtained and would then present it to the captured birds. They could offer some hope, but that was it. Mosaic had wanted to present them with a course of action that would have unequivocally been foolproof, which would have saved them if they followed it, but he had none. As he flew he thought, 'how can I break this to them, so that they believe what we say and so they can survive?' The more he mulled it over in his mind, the more he came to the realization, tell them the truth, don't sugarcoat it and then leave it in the hands of fate. Apparently Trapper had been thinking about the same thing because when Mosaic told him what he thought they should say Trapper responded, "My thoughts exactly. We'll each take a row of lofts and tell them what we discovered and what we think will work to save them and then we go and wait to see who makes it."

Mosaic didn't like hearing it said that way, but he knew Trapper was right. Lay the seeds out on the ground and then let each bird decide what they would do and try. "I'll take the loft that my parents are in and that row, if that's okay with you." Trapper didn't have a problem with Mosaic telling his parents, but he thought, that's a hard thing to do, but leave it to Mosaic not to take the easy path. They reached the row of lofts, "See you at the other end."

Trapper said. He started from the opposite end from where Mosaic's parents were being kept.

The reaction ranged from hostile denial from the birds that breed squab pigeons, to astonished amazement from the bought and captured birds from all the various sources. Mosaic had worked his way up the row of lofts and now was standing before his parents and his fellow flock mates. "So you see, you have to fly as low and as close to the hedgerows as you can. If at all possible, hide until dusk, and then make for the wild fields at the back hedgerow.

"Why don't we just fly back over the top of the bushes and head in the opposite direction?" Vlinder asked who had been listening in the background. "Yes!" several others chimed in, "That makes perfect sense, we just fly in the opposite direction."

Mosaic shook his head; "Because, at the first row of bushes there are large nets that hang from telephone poles and to clear them you'd have to fly really high making you even easier targets for the hunters."

Many said as in one voice, "It sounds really bad. How good are our chances? What are the odds?" they asked Mosaic. He hesitated before he answered and in doing so many knew it wasn't good, maybe even worse odds than they had thought. Mosaic replied by saying, "Fifty-fifty or even less that any one individual will make it, all depends on where you are released from. At least that's what the Sparrow had said," Mosaic explained. He didn't tell them what the turkey had said that the odds were more like ten to one. Why tell them that, when fifty-fifty was bad enough odds already on them surviving.

Niner had seen the look on his sons face and knew the odds weren't even as good as he had stated. He looked at all those gathered around and saw anguish and despair on their faces, and said, "Look, whatever the odds and they don't seem good to me based on what I've heard, we can't give up. Those that make it from our flock and this group must go to the church and meet Mosaic there. You then need to go home and reclaim the bridge and go on with life, which is the best way those that don't make it can be honored. At least that's what I want to have done in my name if I don't survive tomorrow."

Niner looked at his youngest son through the chicken wire wall of the loft and told him, "No heroics, do you hear me? I don't want you trying to fly any diversionary tactics or anything else. You stay away, you stay safe. You are their future. I see that look in your eyes, promise me, no heroics." He finished in a strong yet weary voice.

"But Dad! I could maybe think of something…" with a look of surprise on his face, "… how did you know I was thinking of doing something to distract the hunters?" he asked.

"Because that's what I would have done at your age." Niner responded with a little hint of pride in his voice, "But now that I'm older and wiser. I know it's too dangerous, in this particular situation and shouldn't be attempted. So, promise me on your mother's name, you will not try it, or anything else either. No heroics, promise." Niner waited for a response as he looked sternly and knowingly at Mosaic.

Mosaic looked at his father and then, his mother, and realized that if he didn't, his father and especially his mother, who had been listening silently, would not sleep this night because of worry. He also realized if that happened they'd be tired in the morning and not at their best shape to really have a chance to escape. "Okay! I promise. I'll not put myself in danger." he finished.

"Good!" His Mother said with a sigh of relief, "Good, that will allow me peace of mind. Thank you. Now go, before the humans show up and capture you as well." She finished with a smile of concern on her face.

He looked from her to his dad, who nodded in concurrence with his mate's statement, "We love you, son." He said, "Take care and we'll see you tomorrow."

With that having been said, Mosaic took off and flew up to the light pole. Trapper was sitting there waiting on him. "You were there a long time. What's up?" he asked Mosaic as he landed next to him.

"They made me promise, I wouldn't do anything to put myself in danger. That we wouldn't try to free them."

"You did what! I thought we weren't going to tell them about your idea to create a diversion until we talked about it some more." Trapper said a little upset with Mosaic.

"Well, I had to, didn't I?" Mosaic said in his own defense, "I had to see if they could do it, if we tried what we had talked about, if they could, if they escape. Well they don't even think we should try anything and so, well, they made me promise that I'd stay safe." He finished quietly in an awkward juvenile voice.

"Good!" Said Trapper with sigh of relief, "I agree with your folks on this. They are smarter than you, at least on this, they are right, you know?" With that having been said neither had anything else to say. They sat silently each was lost in his own thoughts, as they were sitting there reflecting on all they had learned. It wasn't long until the humans showed up and fed all the birds in all the lofts. As the day progressed from noon to late afternoon the parking lot and lodge filled up with cars, and the hunters that brought them.

Mosaic watched the activities as more and more hunters showed up, the more depressed he became with each arrival. 'Here I sit', he thought, 'watching the very creatures that are planning on killing my family and friends, and here I sit doing nothing'. He shifted his weight from his left foot and then to his right foot and back again; back and forth he rocked with a nervous energy. Trapper looked at his friend, "Do you mind? I'm anxious and nervous enough, without you doing that."

"Doing what?" Mosaic asked not realizing he had been rocking and shifting, being fidgety. "Oh! Sorry, I guess I'm really nervous and full of energy."

"Full of energy! You mean you are mad and don't know what to do about it. Let's go and do something." Trapper said, "Let's take our minds off of this stuff. Nothing we can do anyway and staying here isn't my idea of fun. Especially seeing that, we can't do a thing about what is going to happen."

"I can't," said Mosaic, "You go and find yourself something you can eat, and then come get me once you find the place."

"No! I'll stay. What you said doesn't make sense, anyway." Trapper said in response to Mosaic's suggestion.

But before Mosaic could respond their attention was diverted by the noise of a small tractor's engine. There below them, putting down the road came a small toy like green tractor with a yellow dear painted on its engine cover. It was towing a trailer behind it, and stacked on the trailer's bed were four rows of neatly stacked, eight high pigeon carrying crates.

The tractor and trailer combination stopped next to the door of the loft that contained his parents and friends. The two humans stepped down off of the tractor, and each went to the trailer and they removed all the carrying crates and stacked them next to the loft's door. Once they had placed all the crates by the door of the loft, they each picked up one crate and entered the loft with it.

Once inside the loft, they herded all the birds to the back end of the loft and then placed a net over the opening to the flyway, cutting off access to three fourths of the loft normal living area. They had placed the crates into the smaller area, and they then started catching birds and placing them into the two crates. When they had eight birds in each they took the crates out of the loft and placed them onto the bed of the trailer. They repeated this process until they had several crates stacked on top of one another.

Mosaic watched with great interest and carefully counted and looked closely at the birds being caught and placed in the crates. By the time they caught Niner and Koffee four crates full of birds had been placed rather haphazardly onto the trailer, compared to the way they had been stacked when empty. The humans took two more empty crates, after having placed the crate holding his parents on top of those already on the trailer, they then went back inside the loft. Mosaic said as he prepared to fly down, "Come on, you keep watch. I have an idea… glide, don't fly." And with that he jumped off of the wire and glided down to the trailer and landed on the crate that confined his parents.

"You keep watch, while I try to move the clasp." Mosaic instructed Trapper, who had followed him down and landed next to him, "okay, do it will you." Trapper said in a hurried concerned and worried response, "Before they see us," Trapper finished as he moved to the end of the farthest crate and settled in as the watcher.

Mosaic worked hurriedly and somewhat unsure that what he was doing was correct. Nevertheless, he pecked at the clasp with his beak; it seemed like the right thing to do, based on what he had seen the humans doing earlier. They had moved the clasp in their routine as they were preparing the crates for their occupants, so he knew it was way into the crates. At first it did not move. How hard can this be he thought, it was starting to get frustrated, but with persistence and after the seventh peck the clasp moved slightly. With the twelfth peck it was almost loose and with the fifteenth it was all the way out, undone and yet the door stayed closed.

His parents had told him to leave before he was caught as well. Instead, he smiled at them, shook his head, no, and ignored then and kept working at the clasp. "It's undone, but the door is still closed." he said, "Get ready to fly out when the door opens." He instructed with impatience and frustration in his voice. He grabbed the clasp with his beak and jumped over the side of the crate: just then a third human was coming around the far side of the loft to see how the crating of the birds was going.

The following happened all within seconds of the door opening. The door fell open, well more ajar and Niner, Koffee and Rambler darted out and were free. Mosaic had been caught under the door as he had pulled open and was now trapped under it. The human threw his jacket, which he was carrying, over the crate opening created when the door opening, which stopped anymore from escaping and trapped Mosaic all at the same time. Trapper heard the noise of the door falling open and out of his peripheral vision saw the shadow of jacket being thrown over Mosaic and the opening, and took off. He thought the jacket was a screech hunter landing where Mosaic was, and in an instinctive, panic induced act, took off instantly in a flurry of motion. Flying for his life from the shadow that the jacket had created.

As he flew up and away from the commotion, the three escapees joined him. All watched in stunned disbelieve as the human captured and removed Mosaic from under the jacket, closed the fallen door to the crate, and then place Mosaic into the crate. He then went to the loft door and talked to those inside with an excited animated voice telling them to be more careful. They laughed at his concern, saying they had plenty of birds and gave him two pigeons that he placed into the same crate he had just placed Mosaic.

"Blood Tics!" Trapper thought and said, "now what to do." However, before he could do anything, Niner had seen the look of desperation on Trappers face and had flown over next to him and had said, "No son! We can't do anything right now. Let's go to the light pole and see what we can see."

They flew to the light pole where he and Mosaic had sat only minutes before, free. There waiting for them was Mosaic's Mother and Rambler. No one looked very happy. "Hello!" he said to them both in a discouraged and depressed voice, "Well that turned out to be a really bad move on our part, didn't it?" Trapper said in disgust, and then he saw the look of sadness on their faces and added, "It's okay, it's what he wanted to do, and he'd rather have you all safe then worry about his own safety." He finished lamely, yet knowing it to be true.

As he was placed into the crate, Mosaic had once again regaining control of himself after being shoved by the human through the small opening at the top of the crate. To Mosaic dismay and surprise he was looking straight into the face of Vlinder. He could not define the look she was giving him. Was it satisfaction, pity, shock, I told you so, or a combination of them all. He responded to her I told you so look he thought she was giving him, "Yes, I know. But at least my Mom and Dad got away, didn't they?" was what he asked as a rhetorical question. Then, he said, "What's it to you?"

She wasn't trying to be egotistical however, she couldn't help herself, as a small smile crept onto her face, "Yes, hero, they got away. But, you paid the ultimate price. You got caught." As the smile he had seen on her face turned into a look of pity and then to a sterner look of, how stupid was that. As she looked at him standing there, she did feel pity for him, he had done what was really a brave thing and his reward had been to get caught and now face the same dismal fate he saved his parents from. 'Life just isn't fair,' she thought especially, 'if you look out for others before you look out for yourself.' A part of her knew what she had just thought wasn't charitable, but somehow it always seemed to be correct.

"Good! That's what was supposed to happen." He said more forcefully than he had intended as he brushed the sawdust from his wings and body, and then took, a I challenge you to dispute that stance.

"You were supposed to leave." She reminded him sternly, "Your Mom and Dad made you promise and instead you pull a stupid stunt and wound up in here and for…" she stopped. She knew why he had done it, for love, for family, just as her older brother would have done. Nevertheless, she finished her thoughts anyway, because stupid was still stupid she reminded herself and someone had to say it, "And for what? So you could, be a hero?" Vlinder thought he should have listened to Niner. He should have found a safe place, stayed there and then seen how providence would play this whole situation out. No, instead, he had played hero and now here he was in the same mess as she was. 'Why did it matter anyway,' she thought, 'he's just another dead pigeon anyway. Maybe she should apologize and tell him,' but before she could say another word, he responded to her negativism.

He shook his head slightly, "Thanks, for your concern." He said sarcastically and acted as if, what would a hen know about these types of things attitude. "But I have a plan, thank you very much! And, I'll be just fine."

"You always seem to have a plan! And, from what I've witnessed, so far, they haven't been very successful either." She said back in a huff. How dare you speak to me in that tone of voice, she thought, you little dweeb. With that she turned away from him, and as she did, "You booby!" she exclaimed and moved to the opposite side of the crate.

Mosaic wanted a chance to explain his response because he realized he had been a little short and abrupt with her. Still, at the same time he kept telling himself she deserved it, especially with her last derogatory comment. Yet, another part of him wished he had not been so abrupt and he wanted to say he was sorry, too late now he thought, for her holier than thou attitude and her walking away had prevented that.

Vlinder couldn't help herself as she watched him out of the corner of her eye, maybe she shouldn't have cut him off like that by walking away, so abruptly. She was mad, yes, she was mad at him for treating her like a stupid hen. 'He had,' she thought still in a huff, 'dismissed my opinion, and me as if he were a king and I was just one of his lowly subjects. How dare he! Next time I'm really going to give him a piece of my mind.' But a part of her really wanted to go over and say I'm sorry, but then she looked at him and changed her mind, dismissing her thoughts of going over, and thinking, 'what a the little twit!'

So the rest of the afternoon went, her fuming and him being macho each one staying away from the other, which was not an easy thing to do in the small confines of a fourteen by thirty-six inch crate. Still somehow they had were doing it, each stewing over the few words that had been exchanged, each feeling the other had really been insulting and derogatory to the other. The tension in the small crate, which was already palpable to begin with, became even more unbearable, with the added tension between two of the crate's occupants, making it stifling to the other eight birds also confined in the same space. Which became even more crowded, after some reshuffling by the humans, there wound up ten birds per crate.

Kimber who had been listening and watching the exchange could not believe it. 'How could two young birds that apparently cared about each other acting so childish and immature? Especially seeing that it may be their last days of being able to see one another, to be able to talk, to be alive… what a waste,' he thought. He had told himself, 'it's none of your business, and to keep his mouth shut, but a part of him that Smelt had touched so long ago,' said he should do something. It told him you should go tell him to apologize, that life's too short to hold grudges, especially with someone you care about.' "Excuse me, I'm not trying to butt in," he said to Mosaic, "but you and your young girlfriend should really make up. Life's too short, you know, especially with all we are going to be facing, and tomorrow will be here sooner than you think."

Mosaic was taken aback. His girlfriend? As he was denying it to Kimber, his mind and a large part of who he was said, 'yes, that's what it is. That's what makes me feel so uncomfortable around her. It's because I like her and don't know how to tell her, how to talk to her, especially seeing as how we seem to communicate so well', he thought sarcastically to himself. "I will!" he said to Kimber, "Thanks!" As he was about to go over to do what he had just said, the top of the carte was opened, a hand reached in and took her and the other dark check from the crate and replaced them with two red checks. Mosaic stood there in shock, just as he had figured it out, bam, fate had dealt him another blow, and she was gone.

"There!" said one human to another, "That should satisfy old man Jasper and his superstitions." Just like that everything was turned upside down and right way wrong in Mosaic's world by those callus-uncaring humans. He looked at Kimber, who shrugged his shoulders as if he were saying, such is life, and I tried to warn you, always giving you the unexpected to deal with. Mosaic gave a small faint smile back, and resigned himself to the turn of events that had unfolded to date. We will just have to wait and see what happens he thought, and he said a silent prayer, "Great Creator, I put myself in your hands. Take care of those I love, especially Vlinder, which he thought with a slight hesitation, of really! Sure why not he thought, she'll never know, and it makes me feel good." He then took several cleansing breaths, and with the great creators help he forced his body to relax and closed his eyes, as a blissful peace overcame his tired body and mind and he fell asleep, knowing what would happen tomorrow was out of this hand, out of his control.

Interesting Pigeon Fact

Pigeons are our most common urban bird.

http://www.animalaid.org.uk/h/n/CAMPAIGNS/wildlife/ALL/346/

Chapter 12

Vlinder found herself in another crate with birds she thought she recognized as being from Mosaic's flock. She was almost sure that the grizzle looking at her, as being from that flock. The hen named Colors was looking at her and gave her a smile, "Hello!" she said, "Too bad you and Mosaic couldn't have met on different circumstances, maybe you two would have had the time to really get to know one another."

"Why would you say that?" Vlinder asked with a puzzled what do you mean look on her face.

"Because, personally I think you two, are a natural pair..." She hesitated and then, as if not sure, whether to continue because of the puzzled look of denial on Vlinder's face; shrugged her shoulders and then finished her thought, "Or at least I am thinking, you could have been." she finished and then once again smiled. She then continued expressing her thoughts from where she had left off, "He's really smarter than his actions over the last two days have indicated. He is sweetly sensitive and very loyal and nice. Not a bad choice for a friend, flock leader and even a mate." She finished lamely and gave Vlinder, a you know what I mean look. Before Vlinder could respond she added, "And he's really good looking, too!"

"It sounds as if you are sweet on him yourself." Vlinder replied in her own defense, because she was taken aback by Colors directness. She thought to herself, 'very bold of you my dear to talk to someone you barely know on a subject that I think is very personal and private, and really none of anyone else's business.' Of course, in a loft pigeon's world that was truer than in a wild pigeon's world, where knowing each other's business often times meant survival or death.

Colors realized by Vlinder's expression and comments that she was taken aback by her comments, nor that Vlinder was a true flock bird, offered her an apology, "Sorry dear, but us wild pigeons run our lives a little bit differently than loft pigeons. I forgot that you all are a little bit more private about your feelings. Please forgive my abruptness. I am truly sorry if I offend you, it was not my intent." with that having been said, she turned to walk away.

However, before Colors could fully turn to leave Vlinder stopped her, "Don't go. Stay and let's talk some, please." She did not know exactly why, but a part of her wanted to hear more about how the wild pigeons lived. She wanted to know more about their life style and their social structure. She really wanted someone to talk to, she really wanted to know more about Mosaic and his flock, but if you had confronted her with that bit of news, she would have denied it vehemently. She had liked his parents and as Colors talked more about the K-Bridge, and her flock members and Mosaic, she realized how much she missed her family and brothers. So the two of them talked about every subject imaginable, about siblings, friends, food, likes and dislikes well into the night.

Finally Colors said, "It's getting really late and we should get some rest, tomorrow will be a busy and dangerous day. I hope and pray we make it." She finished in a soft whispery voice, not wanting to offend anyone with her concerns, or disturb those sleeping.

"You will… we will!" Vlinder said with more bravado in her voice than she really felt. "We're racing pigeons and we'll out fly their stupid guns and we'll beat them." she finished, smiling at Colors.

Colors hugged her, "Thanks Dear!" She said, as she looked her in the eyes and said, "Good luck, and say a little prayer for us all." She smiled her cheeriest smile, but her eyes betrayed her smile, for they showed her true concern. Vlinder could see she was scared and apprehensive and hugged her back, held her tightly and felt her tremble. "I know!" Vlinder said, "I know, be brave and do as Mosaic suggested. Whatever you do, do not panic and fly out into the open. Stay close to the hedgerow. I know if we do, we'll make it." She finished with reassurance and encouragement in her voice.

"I wouldn't." Colors assured Vlinder, "I'll remember! Take care and get a good nights sleep." She said with a warm a motherly smile, "See you in the morning." With that having been whispered between them they let each other go and each settled in for a good nights rest. Each lost in their own thoughts and saying a silent prayer for everyone. Each wondering who would make it and who would not make it through the following days hunt.

Vlinder; however, found herself not thinking about herself or the others, but instead about Mosaic. He is sort of cute, and handsome in his own special way she thought. If I get out of this, I am going to find him and tell him how I feel, she promised herself. Then her mind did a somersault; what if I make it and then it somersaulted again, what if he doesn't? What if he makes it and I don't? She admonished herself stop! Look, if I make it and he does not, I will know. Her thoughts continued, if he makes it and I don't, only I will have known, and for him to know would only be cruel. So you see, she finished, you know, if he doesn't all is right with the world, well almost… it was better that way…or was it? Go to sleep. With those two issues resolved, summersaulting around in her head with the pleasant thoughts of how he would react running through her mind, she fell asleep.

Notwithstanding the circumstances, it was a calm and peaceful sleep, as if she hadn't a care in the world. She had made up her mind about two things; the first was how she would fly the event tomorrow, and the second was, what she would tell Mosaic next time she saw him, and both decisions had brought peace to her troubled mind. She knew she loved him, and with that one truth having been thought, and accepted by her, she had fallen asleep. It had made her feel better about herself, and her life, better and then she had felt, ever since her brother's death. Now she felt she had found a fantastic new reason to go on living and to do her best, to survive.

———————   ———————

The morning's light crept into the darkness of the last remnants of night and caused nature to stir to the promise of a new and wonderful day. The roosters were crowing with voices raised high at the arrival of the golden rays of sunlight that would illuminate the new beginning. Of course every-one knew that roosters were not very bright about true social events as they heralded every new day as if nothing could or would go wrong. They did not linger on past discretions, but treated every new day as a new adventure and opportunity to explore their world and to be reborn. To her that seemed like both a good and a bad thing.

Vlinder heard the crowing and wished they would shut-up. That they had nothing to be so excited about, that this day was not going to be a good day, because she knew hundreds would die. One of those hundreds could be her. No, she told herself, one of those would not be her. Like every bird in every crate the thoughts were all the same, the ones that would die that day would not be them. Yet, all knew that it could be them and all hoped it would be someone else. Each bird that wished it would be someone else did it with provisions, anyone else, but not my mate, or my children, my parents, my siblings, my friends… and so it went a million little prayers, all going to the Great Creator asking for this one or that one to be spared.

Vlinder wondered if the Creator could receive so many messages at one time and if not would those that he did not hear be the ones that would not make it through the day? It only seemed logical that with that many prayers coming at one time that a few would be missed. On the other hand, maybe the means by which they were carried to him would be what overloaded his receiving system or that portion of the system would go down and none would reach him, she thought grimly. She felt like, she was being morbid and that she was defeating her desire to have her prayer be heard. Therefore, she opted to be positive and she told herself if she did, all will work in your favor.

Before the roosters had finished their announcements that the new day was coming, it had actually arrived. The humans had come and started the tractors. Then, with little ceremony, they were all off on their short, bumpy, traumatic journey to their individual release points.

They started the short journey down an asphalt road and then veered off down the dirt path that led to the fields. At the end of the dirt path where the fields started, they did not stop, but rather drove out onto the grass until they reached the first hedgerow. Once they reached the first hedgerow, they turned and traveled parallel along the hedge and at every release point concrete pad they stopped and unloaded one crate from the bed of the trailer, the doors were wired for automatic release, with their back up manual release also wired, they traveled down the hedgerow. Once they reached the end of the first hedgerow, they just continue their journey to the next hedgerow by heading out across the grassy plain. They did this until all the crates had been placed at every release point at every hedgerow.

There were thirty-six crates set along the hedgerows with enough birds to go through shoot one, with five birds each for all seventy-two hunters. Each crate contained ten birds, a divider would split the crates occupants in half and they would be released in flights of five birds; the birds would be released in a sequence that would allow every other crate to be opened for shoot one, flight "A" through "C" as required. Three hundred and sixty birds would fly the gauntlet of single-minded hunters that were determined to end their lives. There would be six teams of three hunters per release sequence. With that sequence happening that way, two teams would be shooting against one another at any one time. The best two teams from each group of six teams would advance to the next shooting round. All six hunters would shoot at one time each one occupying a lane between the hedgerows and with the opportunity to kill five birds; all the birds for the six lanes would be released at one time. This simultaneous release allowed each hunter to feel like he was in a real competition, and this brought an excitement and difficulty to the shoot as well, it created a pandemonium that would force the hunters to concentrate and added drama.

The best two teams from each group of six teams would advance to the next round, or shoot as it was called. In shoot two, each team would be reshuffled and a new three man teams would be formed. Then, from shoot two, the best four teams would advance and again be reshuffled into two man teams that would compete against one another in shoot three. Then, the two best teams would advance to the final round, where the teams were broken up and each hunter competed against the other, some being their former teammates, until there was only one hunter left. All these shoots were based on number of kills, the team or individual with the most kills after each shoot would advance until only one supreme hunter was left standing.

The hunters had paid good money to be entertained, be provided with food and service fit for a king and to be in competition with the best. They had paid $ 8,500.00 each for the honor of participating in the two-day annual derby. For the short time, the derby had been in existence it had become one of the major game hunting competitions in the country, both for how it was run and for having the best gourmet food served anywhere.

The money seemed like a lot of money for only two nights and two days of hunting, but the fee included lodging, food that was fantastic, for they served all types of gamebirds at the three dinners. It started with the Friday afternoon social and that great big delicious first evening meal, which would include venison, and wild turkey. After Dinner, they would be served after dinner drinks, they would socialize and the names would be drawn and the hunters were introduced to their first team members that would compete with them in the first shoot and more importantly who they would be competing against and eventually be going head-to-head against. After which a slideshow was given about the previous derbies, the past winners were presented that were present, and they would all clap and cheer and hope to be this year's winner.

There was no prize money or gigantic trophies to win, only your name on a pair of plaques. One that was an individual memento and was presented to the hunter. The other plaque stayed at the Lodge and was displayed prominently in the sitting lounge for all future hunters to admire and aspire having their names added. The first night was really a great social event for all the participants as well as the host. Luo loved to hear the stories about his quests exploits on the hunting fields, it allowed him to get to know his quests and make sure they knew they were welcome. It pleased Luo to no end that over half of this year's quests had been participants in last year's derby. Those that had participated in previous Derbies raved about the event and the fabulous food, drink and meals that had been served in the past. They congratulated Lou on how this first meal outdid any they had ever eaten. May were already contemplating what the final nights feast would consist of? In the past "The Grand Finally", the big last day awards banquet was the best, for at that great meal; they would all be served squab and the birds they had killed during the competition would be presented, dressed and packed in dry ice for them to take home with them, to be consumed later. All the competitors bragged about the past derbies, and what they had read about it and to Luo's surprise and pride, his "Passenger Pigeon Derby" had become one of the premier game hunting competitions in the entire country.

Of course for all those that bragged about the derby, and similar hunts held around the country, there were those that thought it was cruel, to just stand there and shoot innocent birds that were caged and then released out into an open field, unknown to them, in a panic to be shot at and killed. However, the hunters would argue that it was sport, and that it fills a basic need within them to hunt. Besides, they really liked to eat what they shot, and that seemed to be their main justifications for hunting. However, Luo had given several interviews where he explained that; "The truth is, that they served to the hunters a portion of their kills at both the Saturday night squab feast and at the Sunday final awards banquet' and every bird was accounted for and each hunter took home their kills fully dressed and cleaned." The articles had been very well written and even with it having been stated that no birds were just killed to be stuffed, or to take trophy photographs for the hunters, they had gotten hate mail, mail that called them butchers and cruel killers of the innocent. This type of mail had upset Luo tremendously the first years, but now into their third year, he had come to the resolution that there were all kinds out there and that some just did not understand what life was really all about. That these bleeding hearts would not understand, nor attempt to understand, they would go to the grocery store buy their cellophane wrapped chickens and believe that they came that way. He had shrugged them off as being stupid and were ignorant to the true facts of survival and to the whole story about life.

_____   _____

In the crate that contained Vlinder and Colors and the eight other birds there was tension so intense that, you could have cut it with a dull butter knife. The crate had been split in half by a divider and in the section that contained Vlinder there stood Colors and three loft pigeons. Before the humans left, they caught every bird in the crate and placed a blue plastic band with the same number on it around one of the legs of each bird. The three loft pigeons were full of anxiety waiting on the release, that they knew would come, but oddly enough they were more worried about where they would wind up in the flight order, rather than the fact they were about to be released into a shooting gallery of hunters. Colors looked at Vlinder with concern and an unasked question on her face, which she put to words, "What will happen to us?"

Vlinder responded truthfully, and it felt like she had done this before. Hadn't she said this before? "When they open the crate they will expect us to fly out into the field, which is exactly the opposite of what we really need to do. We need to do what Mosaic said, and that is stay low and fly along the hedgerow, as close to the bushes as possible."

The other three pigeons in the compartment shook their heads in disagreement with what Vlinder had just said. The blue bar spoke up, "You've got to be kidding! Are you actually going to do what that young whippersnapper suggested? You will be doomed for sure," He said with authority and continued, "you'll have no room to maneuver, and all good flyers know you need room to maneuver or you're dead before you even get started."

"You are right! Our instincts and our rules of flying dictate it and it's just because of that... that I think we shouldn't do it." Vlinder stopped, hesitated as if she were giving it some thought, and then continued. "Humans are smart. They are predators, would know this about us and that is why we need to do it. It would be out of the norm and maybe it will give us a chance that extra split second we need to escape, to survive this. If you follow the training you were given to become a good racer you will put yourselves in the ideal position for the hunters to knock you out of the sky; and you'll be doomed to failure."

"You are free to do as you wish," The blue bar countered, "But I'm not putting my faith in the hands of an unproven approach. Given by a farel pigeon at that." He said with a slight hint of repugnance in his voice.

"Yea!" said the dark check white flight standing next to him, "How do we know what that young whippersnapper reported is true?" looking hopeful, and that someone else would agree with his train of thought that maybe what he had been told was wrong.

The blue bar shook his head in disbelief, "Look, maybe it's true." He said to the dark check white flight in response to his comments. "Never-the-less; I'm staying with the tried and true method that has worked on every release I've ever participated in. That will give me a better chance at surviving this." he exclaimed and in a defiant voice he finished, "I'm sure of it!" He looked at the others for support and when they agreed with him by shaking their heads he said, "You go and be stupid if you like, after all it's your life." He finished with an arrogance that was palatable.

At first Vlinder took offence to what the blue bar had said, the words he had used and his tone of voice; but then she realized that each bird had a right to their own opinion and would have to follow their own conscience and beliefs. She wished them good luck, for there was no point in debating or getting upset, that took energy she would need, and she needed all she had to make it through the difficult morning ahead. She was not going to change her mind and by the expression on their faces neither where they going to change theirs. She looked at Colors who had not said a word; she just appeared worried and anxious. "I'll follow you." Colors had said in a soft and neutral unassuming voice, wanting also to state her thoughts, but not wanting to see the debate restart.

Before Vlinder or any of the others could respond the wire attached to the front release door, was being pulled, it became taught and then it moved through the pulley. They watched it slowly moving as if they were watching a caterpillar slowly inching its way across a leaf; it seemed to move maddeningly slow. They heard the door sliding on its guides as it was opened, they heard the first section of birds contained in their crate start their run, and then they heard the rustling of the leaves as the birds ran down the little opening underneath the hedgerow as they made their way to the daylight.

They listened in angst as they heard the loud clapping of wings, as the birds from the first half of the split crate's compartment were released into the air, and to their dread, they heard the distant disturbing popping sounds of guns being discharged in rapid succession. They then heard the disturbingly horrible thuds, sounds of plopping, which they knew, was the sound of bodies hitting the ground, and then there was silence. The silence was eerie because all four of the birds in her compartment, including herself, had held their collective breaths. They then let out there breaths in a low even hissing sound, as the air was slowly expelled from their lungs, it did not seem to reduce the tension she felt all around her. She looked at each one of them and they all had a look of distress and fright on their faces. Each face reflecting the others expression of dismay and hopelessness, knowing that she was looking at a reflection of her own appearance. No! She thought I will not give up hope! I can make it, the Great Creator willing and with a little luck, I will survive this madness.

Then it happened again and again, four more times and by the fifth time they seemed immune to the sounds of guns going off and the dull thuds of bodies hitting the ground. At least so they thought, and then they heard what sounded like a rock hitting the ground very close by. However, they knew better, for rocks do not moan and they definitely heard a soft moaning, "Oh, Great Creator, help me through this…" The moaning became inaudible, but continued for several more minutes; without doubt, it was coming from someone who was severely hurt. Then, they heard footsteps, and the sound of something being snapped, and then the moaning mercifully stopped. Once again, they were faced with the eerie uncomfortable silence of their own breathing. It was not just any silence, but a very unnatural silence, not a sound could be heard from any living thing; and even the air was still. Then, a slight breeze came through the crate, not a cool breeze, but a warm breeze that carried on it the stench of death. It was the smell of coppery blood, mingled with it was the smell of half-digested food, of vomit, of excrement. It was awful and it made the waiting even worse.

They waited for what seemed like hours, and then it happened their wait was over. The divider was removed and the wire that would open the crate's door was moving through the pulley. It was now their crates turn to open its mouth and spill its life out into the death. It was their turn to tempt fate, to see if they were the chosen ones to cheat waiting death for their lives.

They all moved as a group towards the opening of the crate and out beneath the bushes towards the daylight. Vlinder was last, and then came Colors, and the blue bar was in the lead. They were no longer walking, but running as the blue bar yelled back, "Good luck!" as he cleared the area underneath the bushes and took to the air. He took off, headed upward, and banked to his right, as did his two companions, just as they said they would. Vlinder and Colors stayed low, took off to their left, and made an arc that brought them back to the base of the hedgerow.

Vlinder looked up and just as the three were straightening out their flight pattern to make the straight-line departure for freedom the guns went off. Two of the three, the blue bar and one of his companions looked like they had hit an invisible wall, and then feathers flew in all directions as they tumbled uncontrollably to the ground. The blue bar's second companion, the dark check white flight made an awkward unpigeon like maneuver and dropped several feet in the blink of an eye and then was flying at breakneck speed towards them. He was flying about ten feet above the ground when three shots in rapid succession went off; one shot behind him, one in front and the third one that caught him, was the middle shot which sent him unceremoniously to the ground.

Vlinder had witnessed enough, as she had been flying she had seen several crumpled up bodies of other dead pigeons, a sight she would not soon forget. The strangest thing was that she was not thinking about her safety, but instead was thinking; she hoped Mosaic was all right. That brought her to the thought that she hoped he had been right about flying low and next to the hedgerows. So far, they had not been spotted or so they thought because no shots had been aimed in their direction so far.

As they passed release station three, Vlinder heard the beating of wing looked over her shoulder, a group of birds was in the air behind them and as they took to the air, they were shot from the sky. 'Like shooting ducks in a pond,' Vlinder thought, 'and they call this sport?' 'How can anyone in his or her right mind call this sport,' she thought. 'Take a bunch of birds, place them in an unnatural environment, and then call it sport when they are shot out of the sky in a totally exposed open field.' A part of her was really angry at the world, at the Great Creator, at life, at herself for having allowed herself to be placed in this disgusting predicament. 'What have I done to deserve this,' she thought.

She had been a good racing pigeon that had obeyed the laws and the rules. She had even won. Been one of the best, and now because of a few incidents that she could not have controlled she was flying for her life. It was not fair she told herself, and then she screamed it, "This isn't fair!" Nevertheless, she kept flying as fast and as low as she could because her anger did not matter, did not change a thing, she was here and she was flying for her life.

Colors yelled back at her, "Are you all right? Are you shot?"

"No! I am fine! Keep flying, keep up with me." She shouted back at Colors, as she looked back to find colors right on her tail.

Then they passed the next release point along the hedgerow and five birds shot out perpendicular to their flight line. All five of the birds took off across the field and then started skyward. They were like silver blue dots accentuated by the green growth backdrop of the field, making them easy targets for the hunters. Three shots went off in rapid succession and the three fastest of the five birds went into strange, but somehow beautiful free fall flight as they tumbled and twisted this way and that, and then hit the ground. The other two took evasive action and circled back towards the hedgerow. Both had dropped down to ground level as they headed back to where they had been released from, in hopes of finding safety.

Two shots rang out, but both of them missed, as the birds were no longer flying in a straight line, but had started a weaving back and forth motion, making themselves harder targets to hit. As they wove back and forth another shot was heard and again no results. The two were still in the air; they changed direction again and now were heading on an intersecting diagonal course towards the hedgerow and to the very spot where Vlinder and Colors would be within thirty seconds. More shots rang out and the bird in the lead was hit, it was as if it had hit a brick wall, by the abruptness of how it had stopped flying and the way it had fallen brusquely to the ground. From the corner of her eye, she had seen its chest get blown away. The word sickening, screamed across her mind, along with a few expletives… just keep flying she thought.

The second bird, only seconds behind, did an upward vertical maneuver to miss his partners falling body. Just as it went completely vertical, with one wing tip pointing to the heavens and the other pointed to the ground a shot could be heard. Vlinder saw his skyward wing get taken off, as if cut off by a sharp knife. The severed wing kept flying towards them and the bird cartwheeled into the ground, flopping end over end until it stopped two feet from the bottom of the hedgerow. The wing that had been severed clanked off of Colors and knocked her off of her course and towards the hedgerow, as she compensated to try and steady herself, she over-compensated and flew ten feet out into the field away from their flight path. An obscenity escaped her beak.

Colors heard another shot go off and go by her on the right. It sounded like twelve angry mosquitoes all wanting a piece of her blood. She dropped down to where she was flying three feet above the ground, and as she dropped and swerved back towards the bottom of the hedgerow a second shot was heard and once again, the whizzing sounds of wingless mosquitoes had passed by her right side. She knew several had gone through her wing as she heard the breaking of feathers as they passed by. She looked over quickly and saw broken feathers and bloodstains and thought; Am I hit! I'm hit! However, she felt no pain. She had heard once you have been shot, that you feel no pain. Keep flying, she told herself. Therefore, she did keep flying, scared to stop for fear of what she would see, scared to stop because if she did, she'd be an easier target and be dead for sure.

So long as I can think, and fly and I do not feel weak, or in pain, I am fine, keep going she told herself. Then she thought, I am getting weak from loss of blood, and I feel light headed. Stop this she told herself, as she had regained control of flight, she had flown back behind Vlinder. Once there and the shots coming her way had stopped, I am safe she thought.

"Are you all right?" Vlinder yelled back at her, over her shoulder. While thinking this is insane, this is nuts.

"I'm not sure! I think I got hit. I felt something go through my wing and break feathers," she shouted back. When Vlinder heard that, she started to slow down. What was she doing? Colors thought, this is no time to be slowing down. "What are you doing?" she shouted at Vlinder, as she came up alongside of her, making a very dangerous maneuver because now, one lucky shot could have taken them both out. "Seeing if you are okay and how bad the damage is. Why?" she responded as she passed her.

"What for!" Colors shouted in dismay, "It makes no difference. I can fly and that's all that counts, get going will you, before you get us both killed!"

Vlinder smiled back at her as she continued to drop back, then she came upon Colors other side and said, "Okay!" and started to pull away again, retaking the lead.

"Well what did you see?" Colors shouted back as Vlinder started to pull away.

"You're fine, I couldn't see any bleeding. Just keep flying, stay close. We are almost there." As she looked ahead and saw how close the backfield hedgerow was gaining in size. ' Dung! I hope we make it,' Vlinder thought. From what she had seen, Colors should have been screaming in pain with every stroke of her wings. However, she was not, 'she must be flying on pure adrenaline,' Vlinder thought. 'Once we make it over the back hedgerow, we will stop and I will see what I can do. This is not going to be easy,' she thought, 'especially once we land and she sees how bad it really looks.' She looked over her shoulder once again expecting any second to see Colors taking a nosedive towards the earth, but every time she checked, she was still there. Colors was flying right on her tail and keeping up with Vlinder's unrelenting pace. 'Amazing!' Vlinder thought, 'what amazing internal fortitude, must hurt like hell.'

Colors felt no pain and was becoming concerned over Vlinder's behavior, maybe she was hurt worse than it felt. Maybe that is why Vlinder keeps looking over her shoulder at me, she thought, to see if I am still here, that I have not fallen from the sky.

They did not look back or to their sides, they had seen enough, had heard enough to last a lifetime. They both just wanted to be gone from this place. They both wanted to find shelter, a safe place to land, to find water and take a bath, to cleanse themselves of the smells of death, of extermination, of blood and guts and the acid smoky smell of gunfire that filled their nostrils.

Vlinder was not sure if she could make it. It had been the hardest three hundred and fifty yards she had ever flown in her entire life. This is even harder than having flown home alone after her older brother had been killed. She was mentally and physically exhausted, and she was finding it more and more difficult to breathe, to supply the air her muscles needed to function at peak capacity. Then, just as she thought I'm done, the rear hedgerow was in front of her, she adjusted her wings got a little lift, she then cleared the top by only inches and made it into the wild fields beyond. She then felt a glorious joy come over her entire being: she had made it. She and her wing-bird Colors had made it safely through the gauntlet of death. They were safe and they were free, and now let us look at Colors wing, she thought.

I need to see if Colors is okay, and if not what can I do to help her, would be the question. She knew she would not leave her. They were a team and no matter what she had made up her mind, she would not leave Colors, no matter what. Colors had landed and had tried to see how badly she was hurt. When she first saw all the blood and bone fragments, she moaned, "Oh my, God! I am really hurt badly! Vlinder…" She said in near hysterics, "by the looks of it I'm really hurt! Odd though, it doesn't seem to give me any pain." As she moved her wing, "but it sure looks bad." She finished with a sigh of acceptance.

Vlinder had also landed and walked over to where Colors was standing and had said, "Put your wing out and let me see. Let me take a look, let me assess the damage." It did not look good and her visual assessment would have mimicked Colors concern that she was really hurt badly. "Let me touch it and you tell me how it feels, Okay?" So with Colors approval, which had been a nod of her head, yes. She closed her eyes, Vlinder reached out to touch her, and Colors flinched as Vlinder's wing brushed against Colors wing in the blood stained area, "What are you doing?" Vlinder asked, "I haven't even touched you yet and you're flinching."

"Sorry." Colors said, "I'm just scared, go ahead. I'll stay still."

Vlinder, who had drawn back at Colors previous outbursts, touched Colors wing, "How's this?" Vlinder asked as she ever so carefully touched Colors wing, where the two broken feathers were hanging out oddly from the wing normal structure. There was a slight, "Oh! That tickles!" Colors exclaimed as she moved her wing slightly away from Vlinder's reach.

"That tickles?" Vlinder asked in puzzlement, "You mean you're not feeling any pain, as I do this?" She once again rubbed her wing over Colors wing in the areas where there were lots of bloodstains, and again Colors did not react, other than to say it tickled.

"Nope! Just tickles a little," Colors responded with a little giggle. With that reaction to her touching of what appeared to be a really badly damaged area of Colors wing, Vlinders exploration became more intense. What had appeared to be a severely hurt wing in fact were all superficial wounds. The fragments that seemed to be protruding from Colors wing at all types of odd angles were in fact the remnants of the severed bird's wing. She touched each one and rubbed them to be sure, but there was no reaction from Colors to her prodding and poking. Vlinder applied a little more pressure, as she so she moved away from the broken feathers, causing Colors to once again start to giggle. "You're not shot." She concluded.

"I'm not?" Was Colors shocked, but very relieved response, "But all the blood and stuff?"

"It looks like you got the splattered remains of one of those poor souls that didn't make it. All you need is to get washed up and pull these two broken feathers. You will have to wait to replace them until the yearly molt and you will be as good as new. You can thank the Great Creator; he was definitely listening to your prayers and looking out for you today." With that having been said, they both broke out in a hysterical, tension relieving laughter. They looked at each other with tears in their eyes as they hugged and laughed and jumped up and down with joy and sadness, they were going to be okay, they had made it.

Their celebration was interrupted by the sounds of human voices. Colors looked at Vlinder, as a small child might to their parents' as they were caught with their wing full of grain coming from the grain sack where they had not been given permission to go.

"Let's get out of here, and find some clean water, so we can clean you up and get a good drink. I believe I heard running water. After which, we can go to the rendezvous place Mosaic told us about south east of here," Vlinder said in a low whispering tone of voice.

"Yes, I hear the running water as well, there must be a stream nearby," Colors said in reply.

"Let's get going then," Vlinder said as she jumped up, took to the air flying lower than the top of the back hedgerow, so she could not be seen. Colors followed Vlinders lead as they headed towards the sound of the running water.

Interesting Pigeon Fact

Though many were enamored with the species, one of the greatest pleasure breeders was the 16th-century Mughal ruler, Akbar the Great. His flock of 10,000 pigeons moved with him wherever he went, and he spent many hours in his dovecotes, picking mates for young squabs, and escaping the pressures of ruling an empire.

http://mentalfloss.com/article/54844/history-pigeon

Niner, Koffee and Rambler had not flown to the safe haven of the church as Mosaic and Trapper had suggested and hoped they would. Instead, the three had wanted to stay and see if they could help. They devised this wild plan and idea they could fly interference, in order to create a diversion and allow those being released a chance at escaping. The one thing Niner had forbid his son to attempt; he and the other two were seriously contemplating on doing. However, at the first release and when Koffee saw how fast those poor birds had been shot from the sky and met their demise she told them. "No! We stay here. It would be suicide to do what you two, what we have planned." She had not been in favor of running any type of diversionary actions until they had seen and evaluated what would happen. Before they could protest she continued, "We'll help those that make it. We will help them get to the church, to safety; and we'll render aid to those that can't and comfort them in their last hours. Us dying would only help the dead. But we could help the living and injured more by staying alive."

Niner looked at his mate, with a puzzled look on his face, "Us dying would only help the dead?" he asked.

"You know what I mean." Koffee said in response, but the look on Niner and Rambler's faces said no we don't, not really. So, she tried to explain, "I mean, we would only add to the death count, that may cause the hunters to spare a few, but I don't think so. We need to stay alive and help those that will be disoriented from all the commotion. You know how our kind is about loud noises, and being released from small boxes, we panic and just fly anywhere we see an open space. In addition, in this situation it will mean death for many, I'm afraid. Are you in agreement with what I've said?" she finished.

Both Niner and Rambler were in agreement with what she had said. As painful as it was to watch, they knew she was correct, them dying would be of no value. There living on the other hand could allow them to help those that made it to the wild fields and eventually to the church. They watched in total dismay as every bird in the first release was gunned down. From that first volley of shots they knew that Koffee had been right, it would have been suicide to have tried any type of disruptive tactic. They watched, in horror, as every bird in the first release lay dead or dying on the beautiful emerald green turf.

In the second release, it appeared that eight had made it over the rear perimeter of bushes without an injury until they had reached it. Kimber had been one of those lucky ones, to make it to the wild fields. The two that had made it to just behind Kimber had been shot just as they cleared the top of the hedgerow and those two now were lying in the wild fields, dead.

Niner flew to the last lane, where he thought he had seen three birds clear the top of the back hedge. When he got there, he found Kimber lying on the ground out of breath. The two broken bodies of the other two birds lay several feet away from where Kimber lay panting try to catch his breath.

Niner asked him if he was all right. Kimber responded between breaths, "How... do I ... look?" Niner examined him carefully and informed him that he looked fine, except that several of his tail feathers were missing.

Kimber responded as he lifted his tail upward to look at it, "That's how close I came to being like them." He said as he pointed with a shaking wing, at his two dead companions.

Niner helped steady him as he got up. "We should get out of here, and head back to the vantage tree." Niner instructed. With that said, the two took off flying lower than the top of the rear hedge, so they wouldn't be seen, as they made their way to the vantage tree.

Rambler in the meantime had flown to the three birds that had made it from lanes four and five, among them much to his delight was Millet, a blue check named Page, and Mosaic. Mosaic was covered in blood and he was in physically shaken, as was Millet. They were hugging each other, and were shaking uncontrollably, with tears welling up in their eyes.

"Are you all right?" Rambler asked as he approached them. He had recognized Millet from a distance, but not Mosaic who didn't look like himself. The blood made him look like a red check. They both looked up, and it was then that he recognized Mosaic, and the look of grief in their eyes was heart stopping. "Rambler!" Millet said between sobs, "It was terrible, she's gone!" Millet couldn't go on; he just stopped and hugged Rambler.

"Who's gone?" Rambler asked, looking at Mosaic and thinking I really don't want to know, but at the same time he knew he needed to know.

"Sky!" Mosaic gasped, "One second she was in front of me and the next she was gone, tumbling towards the ground, nothing but a ball of blood and feathers."

Rambler didn't know what to say, tears came to his eyes as well, keep it together he thought, keep it together, as he hugged them both. All Millet could say was "It's a bad day!" over and over again.

Mosaic responded to that with tears in his voice, "Yes, it was a really horrific; this is a really Bad day. Sky was a great bird and I will always remember her smile and her kindness."

Rambler said in a weepy, whisper, low voice as he kept hugging them, "I know this is hard, but we need to get you three out of here." Mosaic angrily pulled away, to remove himself from the stifling hug; He looked directly into Ramblers eyes and saw the pain there; which stopped him from saying anything.

Page stood there looking at all three with a worried and very pained expression, "You know your friend is right, w..e, we really should get out of here."

It was then that Rambler noticed as did Mosaic the bloodstains on his shoulder. "Are you all right?" Rambler asked as he pointed to Page's shoulder. "What's your name? Sorry so much…" Page responded, with a special gentle force of urgency before Rambler finished his comment, "Page! It's blood from your friend and a stray pellet that grazed the leading edge of my wing. Nothing really, I am fine. Sorry about your friend. I can fly, can they?" she finished with a head nod pointing at Mosaic and Millet.

Rambler looked at both Millet and Mosaic, who were both still trembling, from both grief, the extra adrenalin, and with tears in their eyes. She was right he thought; plenty of time to grieve later, first things first, we need to get out of here and to the vantage tree. "Mosaic, Millet, we need to get going, we need to get out of here. Are you two able to fly? We can grieve for Sky later, us dying too wouldn't bring her back" And it seemed once that statement had been made, there was a physical difference in Mosaic that showed in his eyes, a resolve, a determination that hadn't been there seconds before, "Let's go!" he said

"Come on then." Rambler said, "Follow me, fly low, don't fly above the rear hedge, until I tell you it's okay to do so." With that said, he took to the air, followed by the other three. Flying low to the ground they made it to the vantage tree the same time as Niner and Kimber. Within less than a minute Koffee arrived with Flick who looked no worse for wear, Shadow who looked totally distraught, but who wasn't hurt and Crocker, Flicks older brother. Crocker, however was hurt a shotgun pellet had gone cleanly through his crop, leaving a neat clean hole there where air passed, giving him an odd sounding voice, as if the air he was exhaling as he spoke was taking part of his words with it before they were clearly pronounced.

Both Flick and Shadow were genuinely glad to see Mosaic and Millet, and very stunned at hearing that Sky hadn't made it, she will be missed they said in unison.

"A crying shame!" Shadow stated matter of factually and shaking his head, "She was a really good bird. A great Outflyer, one of the bravest I've ever known. I really liked her. I will miss her immensely. May the Great creator have mercy on her soul." he finished. All said amen to that and then Niner continued with Shadows prayer by saying, "For all those that did not make it so far and for all those that won't; we pray that the great creator keep them and bless them. That he watches over those that were lost by the events of this day and help their families, friends and loved ones through all these troubled times and those yet to come." Again, the group said amen, as Niner finished his prayer. It appeared that those few words had brought them comfort and Mosaic as well as the others found a strange sort of piece and strength to go on.

After the prayer had been spoken, there were questions, upon questions that needed asking and answering. The most important was how many had made it and who were the ones that had not made it? Where were the ones that had a made it now? It was mostly a reporting of we don't know, it would depend on when they were released, and so far who they currently saw before them were the only ones that Niner, Koffee and Rambler had seen escape. This was very sobering news and the harsh reality of being a prey bird, a flock bird a food source for others, you always lived on the threshold of disaster, on the verge of ruin.

Mosaic wanted to change the subject and did, by asking, "Where's Trapper? Has he been hurt, or what?"

"No," Niner said and then explained that some humans had come that very morning that Trapper had recognized and that he had left to tell them what was going on, and that he had gone to them for help. His last words to us were that he'd meet us at the church.

"That was it?" Mosaic asked, "Where they old or young humans? What did they look like? Did he say their names, or anything?"

"Not that I recall," was Niner response, "Except, well they were both older and younger humans. The younger ones were a girl and a boy, blonde hair, I would say teenagers, based on what humans call their offspring."

"April, Eric?" Mosaic said under his breath in a suppressed tone, but before he could put it all together, his mother diverted his attention, "You look terrible." she said, misinterpreting his mumbled response to Niner's comments. She had seen what she thought was more sadness in her sons face and she wished to divert his attention to more important issues like getting cleaned up and to safety, "Let's go to the stream. It's not far and you can get cleaned up, which will go a long way to making you feel better."

"I do need a drink." was Mosaic's response, he needed to get himself back in order, he could ask more about April, Eric and Trapper later, "and a bath wouldn't hurt either." Several of the others that had flown down the hedgerows agreed a bath and a drink would go a long way to making them feel normal again.

Rambler looked at the others, "I'm not thirsty." he said, "I'll stay and keep watch, while the rest of you go do those things. Then, come back..." he hesitated, giving thought to his comment before finishing, "Maybe there will be others that made it by then and will need our help."

"Yes," Niner responded, with more encouragement then he had intended based on the situation. "A good idea. You stay and the rest of us will go get these seven cleaned up and on their way to the safety of the church. Then we'll come back and switch with you so you can get a drink and relax a little."

"I'm fine." Rambler responded, even though inside he felt sick and saddened by all their misfortune, he finished with, "I'm not thirsty. You go, take care of them."

With that agreed to, Millet, Kimber, Flick, Shadow, Page, Crocker and Mosaic headed for the stream guided by Niner and Koffee. Once there they all drank except Crocker who had to wait for assistance, for the water he drank came back out the hole in his crop. Koffee, with Mosaics help placed two small leaves one over each hole and then held them in place with a little moss and mud, and some strands of bark that they had stripped from a small tree growing near the stream. Once the makeshift patch was in place, Crocker was able to get a drink and retain some of the precious liquid in his crop. He definitely looked a hundred percent better once he had gotten a good drink, and his body had a chance to absorb it. While Koffee and Mosaic were attending to Crocker, the rest bathed, and cleaned up. Once that had been done Mosaic also bathed, and as he started to preen himself, they heard the shots of distant gunfire. "Apparently they are letting more go." Niner exclaimed in a sad and weary voice. "Let's fly up," pointing to Shadow, "into the top of the trees and see if we can see anything."

Shadow joined Niner in the tree, and with a slight edge of authority in her voice said, "You need to stay safe. No disrespect meant, but you need to get to the church and be safe. You are our leader, and we can't afford to lose you again."

"None taken." Niner replied, "But it's just for that very reason I need to stay here and help. Maybe seeing me here will give hope to a severely injured bird. The rest of you do what needs to be done at the church. I'm needed here!" Shadow looked at Niner and shook his head in the affirmative, to show he understood. "Good!" Niner said, "And we will not speak of it again. Agreed?" Shadow once again shook his head yes. They could not see a thing even from the top most branches of the tree they were in. "Let's go down and get you all on your way." Niner said to Shadow, as he jumped from the branch they were sitting on and floated down to the ground next to the stream where all the rest had gathered and were watching them. Shadow followed Niner to the Ground and as he landed, he heard Millet saying almost the exact same thing he had said to Niner. I guess we are all thinking the same thing he thought, as Niner disarmed their concerns for his safety.

Kimber knew a true leader when he met one and he stood between two of them, as he looked from Niner to Mosaic. "Rambler will need help," he said, "To get those that survive the shooting to safety. I would like to go back and help if that's all right with you?" He finished as he address his request to Niner.

"Yes." Was Niner's response to Kimber. "You and you, what's your name?" he looked and pointing at Page, "You two will go with me to help Rambler. While the rest of you will go to the church and get things prepared for those that we will be sending there for aid." he finished.

Page responded with a slight stutter of apprehension, "Pa...ge S...i... r, I'm scar..ed. I don't think I c...a...n." As page was trying to respond to Niner, Koffee and Mosaic started to protest, but Niner put up his wing, "No arguments or debates on this! You two are needed there, and if anything happens here, they will need your leadership abilities Mosaic. And, your level headiness and council my dear." He said to Koffee, "And Page here will do just fine" he finished. As he hugged his mate, "You are needed to give support to our son, and to use your abilities to organize and to get others to help is invaluable."

Page was amazed; he had been heard, understood, and responded to, even as the others had started their protests. He had found a leader that accepted him, which pleased him greatly

Both Mosaic and Koffee knew it was impossible to argue and win with Niner once he had made up his mind, and they both understood his logic, but did not like it. They group hugged and wished each other well they parted company. Niner, Kimber and Page headed back to the vantage point and joined Rambler. While Mosaic, Koffee, Flick, Crocker, Shadow and Millet headed for the church. They flew low to the ground for about a mile and then climbed higher into the sky as they headed southeast to the church.

Mosaic could not help himself; he was glad to be alive and to feels the wind in his face and under his wings again. As he flew, he thought of a million things, mostly how lucky he was, how he would do things differently with his life from this day forward. He was still saddened every time he thought about Sky and all those other poor souls that had not made it and as he flew he said a silent prayer for them and wished them well. He also prayed for protection for himself from the Great Creator. With that said, he thought of how he was definitely going to tell that hen, Vlinder how he really felt about her when he saw her again. Then, a dark disturbing reflection crept into the sunshine of his thoughts, what if she didn't make it? No, he told himself, life wouldn't be that unfair, the Great Creator wouldn't be that callous.

———————————   ———————————

Niner, Kimber and Page reached Rambler only minutes after the first shots had been fired at the third flight of birds as they were being released. They were once again shocked at what was played out before their eyes, the fields were picked clean, and there wasn't a bird anywhere to be seen. "What happened?" Niner asked Rambler, who looked a little pale, as he landed next to him in the upper dead branches of the tall vantage tree.

"The humans went through the fields and picked up all the bodies of the dead and dying." Rambler stopped, took a deep breath, and as if he were trying to gain some courage and then, he continued, "Those that weren't dead, they picked up, slit their throats and placed them upside down in cone shaped cylinders so they wouldn't flop about as their life's blood drained onto the ground." By the time Rambler was done telling what he had seen he was visibly shaking.

"What!" Niner exclaimed in disbelief, "How barbaric!" with a shocked expression distorting his usually calm face.

"Yep! Yes sir, if the shoots didn't kill them, then the humans that gathered them up did. Slit their throats from ear opening to ear opening." Rambler stated again, and accentuated his statement by drawing his wing across his throat in a slashing motion. All Niner could do was shake his head in disbelief.

"So much for your idea of going out and trying to save the wounded. If they don't clear the back hedgerow they are doomed." Rambler finished with anger in his voice. "Poor Cows don't stand a chance." he finished, and with that having been said, they watched the carnage unfolding below them.

They watched as the humans released shoot 1-3, and two birds made it over the rear hedgerow and then before any of them watching could go and find the two that had cleared the hedge they released another group of birds. From that release, four birds made it over into the wild fields. Then, the humans came out and started the routine of picking up the dead and dying, doing what Rambler had described to those that were still alive. While that was going on the bird at the vantage tree went out and collected those that had made it, took them to the stream and saw them off towards the church.

They repeated this process once more and they were looking at noon by the time the shooting and gathering of the bodies was completed. Out of those additional releases, six more birds made it to the safety of the wild fields, and once again, those from the vantage tree made sure that those that had survived the killing skies made it to the stream for a drink. After which they were off unhampered to the church. The shooting stopped for about an hour and a half, and then around two in the afternoon the humans released another group of birds.

After the humans had eaten their lunch, they retook their positions at the shooting field and they released shoot 3 −1. It was the release that Colors and Vlinder made it through along with three other birds, but before they reached the back hedge the humans had released shoots 3 −2 and 3 −3, and from each one of those shoots eight birds made it to the wild fields. So once again, when the shooting stopped, and they were sure of it, they took off to get the survivors. All agreed they would meet at the stream, with their charges this time. It would allow those that had made it the opportunity to get a drink, relax, and take inventory on how badly they were injured if at all.

Niner and the others had somehow missed Colors and Vlinders escape from the killing fields and their clearance over the end hedgerow. Vlinder and Colors had made it to the stream all on their own without the help of the guides. The two had drunk and cleaned themselves up, and had started to look for something to eat amongst the weeds and grass that were growing along the stream.

Vlinder was sitting by the steam sunbathing and soon after she moved to a small bolder where she stood surveying her surroundings and the distant fields, glad to be alive. Unbeknownst to her she was the target of two separate pairs of hungry eyes.

The eyes to her left belonged to a small bobcat that had been watching both her, and Colors from the instant they had landed at the stream. Carefully and with great stealthy crawling like motion, it had been closing the distance between itself and Vlinder. On her right, another pair of hungry eyes watched her as she moved about the bolder. They belonged to a large serpent slowly moved and slithered its way through the underbrush towards her. Its forked tongue, flicking in and out in a rhythmic, in and out motion, which had smelled and detected her warm blood ever since she had landed at the water's edge.

The snake had been following her every move, as had the bobcat ever since she had arrived at the stream, as it slowly made its way towards the bolder. Her heat trail had been easy to follow because she wasn't trying to do anything to hide it as his previous victims had. Yes, he thought, this will be easy and I am really hungry. The large six-inch in diameter, six foot long pacific rattler slowly slithered along the ground ever so carefully, not to be detected, as it closed in on its unaware prey.

Vlinder was lost in thought, thinking about all that had happened and her mind kept coming back to the multi-colored grizzle cock, named Mosaic. She liked him and yet didn't. She thought he was cute. No, not really, he was more handsome, not pretty boy handsome, not model handsome, but really every day good old down home handsome. The most amazing thing to her was that he wasn't even aware of how really good-looking he was. That's it, she thought, a really handsome, innocent bird, that's why I kind of like him, she thought. Totally immersed in her thoughts, as she was, she was oblivious to the imminent danger that surrounded her that was slowly creeping and slithering to her location.

Niner had brought the last group of survivors to the stream, and had met up with the others, who had picked up their survivors as well. Between all of the survivors, a total of nine birds that had made it through the gauntlet of gunfire and death. Some with minor to no injures, while others had holes in their wings and various other parts of their bodies. They were now all at the stream getting themselves cleaned up and having their thirst quenched. He had flown up to a middle branch of a close by tree to keep vigilance over them as they bathed and preened and basically relaxed a little. When he noticed movement about one hundred and fifty yards down stream, he yelled down that he was going to investigate it and that one of them needed to take his place as lookout. Rambler and Page both responded and flew up to where Niner had been sitting moments before, and as they landed he took off without another word, as they watched him flying up stream.

They looked at each other inquisitively; Page stuttered to Rambler, "I won…d..er wha…t he sa…w?" Rambler didn't answer but instead stared intently up stream to see if he could detect what had caused Niner to leave in such a hurry.

Not sure, of what he had seen Niner landed in a tree near where he thought he had seen the motion. Within seconds of landing, he had assessed that from the right a large cat was stalking a pigeon first sitting and now standing on a boulder. He looked around and also saw that on the left, which was the motion that he'd seen, was a large serpent moving into position to strike. He also realized that the cat was about to pounce as well. He did not think, he reacted to what he was seeing and with the speed of lightning he jumped off of the branch, with two power flaps of his wings he swooped down and knocked the pigeon on the boulder forward. In a flurry of motion the pigeon half flew, half fell head over tail feathers forward, while simultaneously the snake and the cat struck, only to be greeted by each other's fangs and claws. The snake sank it's fangs into the cats chest; as the cat bit and ripped the snake at the nape of the head; while Niner knocked Vlinder from the boulder and the two of them rolled and tumbled into the weeds.

All Niner heard was the death screams and cursing of the cat and the trashing, slapping sound of the snake's body convulsing along the ground. He grabbed Vlinder by the wing, pulled her up and yelled, "Fly!" Which she did instantly. They both flew to the branch that Niner had occupied only moments before with Vlinder looking at him in shock. "What was that all about?" she said as she gasped for breath. Niner pointed to the ground, he too was gasping for breath and hadn't caught his sufficiently enough to be able to talk.

There on the ground, where he was pointing lay a large snake, with its head almost severed from its body, barely moving in the last minutes of its life. Limping and swaying away from the boulder on unsteady feet was a bobcat, blood running from the two puncture wounds in its chest. It was on its last legs, life was flowing from it as well. It could be heard cursing to itself… "Stupid snake, birds are for cats. Look at what you've done to me!" it wailed as it disappeared from their sight.

Niner brought his wing in from where it had been outstretched to where he had been pointing and grimaced in pain. While all this was going on, Colors, who was at the stream getting herself a final drink of water before going to find Vlinder, was startled by the sudden noise of wings flapping, she took instinctively to the air. As she took off from the ground, she saw two birds rising from the field to her left and watched them do a full circular flight and come around and land in the tree that was to her right. She recognized the two birds and maneuvered herself so she could join them. As she landed on the branch behind Niner, she was just in time to hear his grimace of pain and she exclaimed. "You are hurt." She then stopped and looked closer, "There is a long raspberry like wound on your shoulder between your wings."

Niner looked over his shoulder at the mark, "really more a scrape, between his wings," he stated. The feathers were torn away and an ugly looking red welt, approximately one and a half inches long replaced them. The good thing it was not really bleeding very much, and the little speckles of blood had started to coagulate. "Must have scraped myself on the rocks," he concluded, "At least it was not the cat's claw or the snake's fang, that would have been fatal." Yet it didn't feel right, and the flesh around the wound felt numb, but he dismissed it to old age and the fact he was tired.

"We had better get you cleaned up," Vlinder said as she moved and stretched her neck so she could get a better look at what they both were talking about. Colors agreed that they should at least wash it out and put a moss and mud dressing on it, so that the possibility of any bacteria to prevent infection could be drawn out of the wound. Niner tried to talk them out of it, saying it was only a scratch and that they didn't have the time to fuss over nothing, for there were more important things that needed doing. However, both Vlinder and Colors held their ground, causing Niner acquiesce to their demands that they be allowed to treat his wound.

Niner had to admit between the wheezes of air being sucked in by him as they applied the mud and moss bandage that it felt better. The stinging had gone down considerably and it didn't seem to hurt as much as he moved his wing muscles.

Rambler and the others had flown over to where Vlinder and Colors were treating Niner. What happened, he asked as he hugged Colors, as they both exchanged glad tidings of joy at seeing one another alive. They explained what had happened and it was obvious from their reactions, they were all very impressed by Niner's actions and speed. But the blue bar white flight named, Rydell said that Niner needed to stay calm and not do any flying because a wound like that could easily be aggravated by flight, reopen and get seriously infected and then he would be in real trouble.

Niner smiled at Rydell's comments, "I appreciate your concern, but I'm fine." he said, moving his shoulder up and down. "I'll be just fine. It's only a little scratch. It's not even a cut. There is work to be done and we need to get you all to safety. There will be others to save and guide that will have more urgent things to take care of than my little scratch."

With that having been said and Niner's mind made up, he directed that Vlinder and Colors would accompany the thirteen, southeast to the church. Several started to protest, saying they were okay and would like to stay and help, but Niner said no to their requests, explaining "We need to keep the number low and those that will stay already know the routine." He said this with finality in his voice that left no room for argument. He, Rambler, Kimber and Page would return to the watching tree, so they could be in a position to help the next wave of birds that would go through the shooting lunacy the humans called sport. With that having been decided, they parted company, each group wishing the other the best, and a safe journey.

However, the next three releases only saw two birds per release make it through the shooting gallery of hunters. The hunters were either tired or Lady Luck was on the side of the next four releases, a total of thirteen birds made it to the safety of the wild fields. On the last release of the four, they found Cole laying in the field with his right foot shot off. He was bleeding profusely. Working as an efficient team, Niner and Page worked quickly to place a twine and stick around the leg, creating a tourniquet so they could apply pressure and stop the bleeding. With the bleeding stopped and with his help they took him to the stream. Once there, Kimber took over, created a leaf, mud, and moss bandage and let off some of the pressure from the tourniquet. Kimber decided that he would need to accompany Cole to the church, which all agreed, was a good idea.

They also agreed that the three of them could not handle the rescuing and asked for volunteers. All the birds wanted to stay so Niner asked if any had healing experience. Two, Oon, and Oom, stated they did have experience at healing, they stayed and so the five of them headed back to the lookout tree.

Niner wasn't feeling well. He had noticed that his blood pressure had been slowly climbing, he was experiencing head pain, a slight headache and his eyesight, his peripheral vision, seemed to be blurred. I'm just tired he told himself, you'll be fine, just need to rest. He explained it away as being stress-induced symptoms. Yet with each trip out Niner found it harder and harder to make it back to the tree. They had flown down to the stream with the last group of birds he stumbled and fell down. Rambler rushed over to where Niner lay, "Are you alright?" he asked

Niner shook his head yes and then no and then said, "I've got this really bad headache and my shoulder feels like it's on fire. Can you see anything there?" He finished.

Rambler carefully examined the place where the scratch had been, that Niner had obtained when he had saved Vlinder from certain death. It did not look good, where before there had only been a light abrasion, there now was a raised welt, and it was purple-blue at the center and as it worked its way outward it went to a yellow brownish, with a vibrant red at the edges. Rambler carefully touched it and as he did he asked, "Does this hurt?" It felt warm to his touch, and when Niner did not respond to his questions, he said, "It feels warm to me."

"What do you see?" Niner asked, because he couldn't turn his head far enough around to see it for himself, but the swelling wouldn't allow it.

"Well! What I see is an infection." Rambler replied, "A bad infection. You need to go to the church and see if someone there can help you with this. I can't do anything for you because I don't know what to do. But I do know you should get it looked at and treated." Rambler asked Wings and Checkers; the two that had minimal healer experience, for their opinion, and both agreed that Niner should seek a true healer.

Niner started to protest about what Rambler had told him he should do. Without being asked, several of the birds that had been rescued from this last flight came over and amongst them, there were two birds that stepped up and gave their opinions without being asked. The one called Oon that Niner knew and respected, who had been shot through the crop, similar to Crocker's injury, but not as bad, talked with a wheezing voice. "How did that happen?" he asked as he looked over Ramblers shoulder, he continued, "That looks really bad and infected." He stopped to consult with his associate and then continued, "He needs a real healer and the sooner the better. What do you think Oom?" he asked the bird standing next to him.

They conversed in quit whispers for a minute or so and then Oom said, "I would say the sooner the better." He then paused, as if deciding what or how to say what he was thinking, like a healer that was trying to figure out a way to soften the blow of some really bad news he was about to deliver. "You must get this treated right away, I'm afraid that if you don't," he paused looked at Niner, and then finished. "I have seen birds with less die from their infections."

"No one's dying," Niner said, a little irritated that he was being talked about as if he were an imbecile. "Look, I'm fine, just a little tired. I just need something to eat, to drink. A little rest and I'll be as good as new." He finished, "And as flock leader, I'm still the one capable of making good decisions that I expect to have followed."

"No, Niner." Rambler said with kindness and great respect in his voice, "On this you are wrong. You need a healer and I'm taking over as leader of this rescue mission. You are hurt and are in need of medial care. So as acting secondary leader on this, I'm asking you to comply with my wishes, which is that you go with the rest of the wounded, to the old church and get aid."

Niner looked up at Rambler and by the look in Rambler's eyes or the set of his stance, knew not to argue, but to go along with the decision. A part of him knew that Rambler and the rest were right. He wasn't at top form and by not being at his best he was a liability to those that were doing the rescues. "You are right Rambler, I will do as you ask," Niner acquiesced.

"Good! Oom, please accompany them," Rambler said as he helped Niner to his feet. He hugged him and wished him well, and watched as Niner and the rest of the birds that had made it through the hunt headed for the church. I wish I were going with you, he thought, he then turned to Page, Wings, Oon and Checkers, and said, "let's go, we have work to do."

 By the time they reached the church, Niner's headache was a full-blown migraine. The throbbing of pain seemed to run from his shoulders to his brain and then through his entire body. The pain blurred his vision, his eyes were sensitive to the light and he was running a full-blown fever.

  Mosaic and Koffee had been looking after several other wounded birds when Niner escorted by Oom arrived at the church. Koffee helped Niner to a quit place to rest in the straw, while Mosaic went to get the human animal healers. When they arrived Oom had told Koffee of his fears that the snake had in fact poisoned Niner during his heroic rescue of another pigeon earlier that same day. He had also informed Koffee if in fact that were true that Niner would not make it because the wound had gone so long unattended. Koffee was in shock at the news, but quickly regained her composure. She knew that Niners life was in the hands of the Great Creator, all she could do was pray and hope that Oom was wrong in his assessment of what was ailing Niner, of course he wasn't.

  The human animal and pigeon healers and the young girl, who had been assisting them came and examined Niner. They confirmed what Oom had surmised was what was wrong. Niner in fact had been poisoned and that there was little chance that they could save him. However, he took some blood and said he would test it to be sure he was correct. He came back less then a half hour later and confirmed his earlier diagnoses. Niner in fact had been poisoned. The poison had traveled throughout his body and all that could be done for him was to make him as comfortable as possible in his last hours. The doctor apologized about his inability to do anything and then left them to say their good byes.

April, who had followed the doctor around all day, as if she were his shadow, as he treated all those that were brought in, now stayed. Saying she would try and help make Niner as comfortable as possible. The doctor gave her instructions as how to administer the medication he was leaving. With that having been done, he excused himself and went to render treatment to others.

April took the medication the doctor had left and coaxed Niner into taking a spoonful of the amber liquid and then followed it up with a clear sweet tasting liquid. Niner drank both liquids eagerly, "That's good!" he exclaimed.

"Yes, the doctor recommended a little pick me up concoction he came up with to help your immune system fight the infection. Now rest and don't do anything, just relax." April said.
"What did you give my dad?" Mosaic asked

"A pain killer and muscle relaxant." April replied to Mosaics questions, "It will make his last hours more bearable." She finished holding back her tears.

"Thanks." Mosaic said, "Will you stay with us?" he asked.

"Sure." April responded and then sat down. No one said a word they just sat and watched Niner's slow and even breathing.

The word traveled around the hospital wards like wild fire; that Niner had been brought in with a life threatening injury. Niner had in fact been poisoned; and that the healers, both human and pigeon couldn't do anything for him and that he wasn't expected to make it through the night. Many a bird shed a tear and said a prayer for his soul, his family, and his flock. Any bird that could walk came by and gave their respects and condolences. The healers had come by several times as well to see that he was comfortable and to see if there was anything else they could do. Of course they could do nothing more than what was being done and what had been done.

After the healers had made their last visit, Vlinder and Colors had come by to see how he was doing and to tell Koffee and Mosaic what had happened. They told the story of how Niner had saved Vlinder from certain death at the claws and the coils of the bobcat and snake. "It's my fault that he's lying there." Vlinder said, "If I'd been more alert, if I'd been more careful." Koffee reached out and hugged her, "Now, now my dear you are no more to blame than Mosaic here is." Vlinder was now crying as Koffee kept hugging her as she kept assuring her she was no more at fault than the pigeon in the moon was at fault." April watched the scene unfolding around her and she thought if anyone ever admonished her for her beliefs and feeling towards animals, she would not deny it ever again. Animals do have feelings, she thought and what she had witnessed so far that day only reconfirmed her beliefs.

Mosaic had moved closer to where April sat, "I'm so sorry Mosaic." She said as she watched the reactions of the pigeons that had gathered around their leader's nest site. The doctor had come in to see how things were going, and he was amazed at what he saw. He would have never believed it if he had not seen it with his own eyes. Several birds were hugging one another and the hen that was his mate sat down with tears rolling down her face. The young multi-colored cock named Mosaic had tears in his eyes as well. He realized that they all knew by Niner's shallow breathing that he did not have long to live. He looked at April, shook his head and softly said, "I'm sorry, it won't be long." Shook his head and then he left.

April looked at Mosaic and then at Koffee, "I'm sorry Mosaic, Koffee; I really am." with that said, she got up, tears trickling down her cheek and left the birds to say their goodbyes in their fashion and traditions.

———————————   ———————————

Mosaic couldn't believe it, he was in total shock, and yet through it all he had been there to support his Mother. But now he was alone, looking at the sunrise. He couldn't believe that his Dad was dead. Now he was in fact the flock leader of the remnants of the birds that had been the K-bridge flock. He watched the sun come up in all its glory, with its warm rays of bright light. The sun was chasing the darkness away. How could the world look so new and bright, when he felt so cold and dark inside? Why was the Great Creator mocking him and not showing him any sympathy and compassion for his loss and his grief?

He hated it all, he thought. He hated everything about life, at how unfair it was. He had found his parents, his fellow flock mates, only to watch them die at the hands of man. He had rescued his Father and Mother, only to have to watch his Father die at the hands of the Great Creator. Why? He thought, how unfair. He had needed his Dad, he'd made all kinds of plans as to how he could help teach him how to be a good flock leader and now it was all gone, over. His mentor had been taken from him; once again, he would have to learn it on his own, without any help.

Trapper had watched his friend go from a bird with great confidence, to a bird consumed with guilt, by depression, was concerned. He was concerned because instead of stating his anger, his disappointment, Mosaic withdrew into himself and had walked away from them all and had stayed isolated ever since his Father had died late last night.

Trapper realized that it hadn't been easy or that long since Niners death, but he had hoped Mosaic would have stayed and expressed his feeling, yet instead Mosaic had left and stayed to himself. Trapper had left because he couldn't handle watching the suffering. He knew that Mosaic had stayed with his Mom until the bitter end. That the hen name Vlinder had stayed as well, as had April. Vlinder was definitely a special bird. He had asked her why she had stayed and she had told him, it was because of her that Niner was dead. He had told her what Niner would have said, "No, you are not to blame." He hadn't known Niner very long, but in the short time he had, he knew that the Niner he had come to know would have never done that, never blamed her for anything, and of course he had been right. Niner's hen had heard Vlinder and had admonished her for even thinking that. She had said her mate would never have let anyone make a decision for him, that he did what came naturally to very few, that he was a true leader, always concerned about those he led. That she never wanted to hear it again, that Vlinder was responsible for her mate's death, that it was fates doing, not Vlinder's.

She knew Niner had not blamed anyone for what had happened. That Niner had told her this is the way his life was supposed to end, and he had no regrets. That he could not see himself living to a ripe old age, and becoming a dependent, becoming indigent. It was something he had prayed wouldn't happen to him and the great Creator had answered his prayers, Koffee told Vlinder.

Trapper had watched Mosaic ever since and had finally decided to approach his friend, who looked at him with tears in his eyes. They spoke no words as Trapper hugged Mosaic and then finally Trapper said, "I'm sorry, if there is anything I can do, just ask." he finished lamely.

"Just leave me alone for a while, Okay!" This was all Mosaic was able to get out before he choked up and could not say another word. Trapper patted his friend on the back, said, "Sure.", and with reluctance, and great sadness, left Mosaic there looking at the rising sun.

_____   _____

Two days had passed and Mosaic had stayed isolated from the rest of the flock and birds that had survived the Passenger Pigeon Derby as much as possible. Today he knew he couldn't, today they were going to bury Niner. The Humans had made all the arrangements and they were going to lay him to rest in the small pet cemetery adjacent to the churches human memorial park.

While he had been with his Mom, before he had placed himself in a self-imposed isolation, Colors, Vlinder, Eric and April had made all the arrangements. Koffee had given all the instructions and inputs for the burial, right after Niner had died. April and Vlinder with the help of Colors and Eric, and their parents had taken care of all the particulars as per her instructions. The ceremony was quite simple and elegant in its approach and in the words spoken. Oom had given a short speech based on all their inputs and what he had personally known about Niner. He had called Niner a bird in a million, unselfish in his dedication to his family, friends and flock. Niner's death demonstrated what he believed in, a dedication and commitment for the welfare of others.

As the eulogy was being given, Mosaic reflected back on what his father had said to him just before he had died. "You, Mosaic," he had said, "Are now the one that all these poor souls are going to be looking towards for leadership and direction. I know this all seems wrong to you, but all is as it should be. Not any one of us lives forever, we all have our time. Believe in yourself, in the wisdom of the Great creator's judgment, understanding and knowledge of what is best. I love you and believe in you." Mosaic looked at all those that were in attendance and made a silent pledge. I will do my best to follow your advice Father, but I'm not sure I can, that I know how. Especially with what you told me about a great war that was coming and would need to be fought. That I must be a leader because if we fail, I fail, evil will reign. All the good things we believe in, that I believe in will perish. How was that possible, for he was only a pigeon, and a young inexperienced pigeon at that! What could he possibly do to ward off the kind of evil his father had alluded to, in his final heart-to-heart? 'Very little', he thought.

So with these things on his mind, what his father had told him, he accepted the condolences of all those that passed by, as he laid his father, Niner to rest. Once everyone else had left, he asked Niner for guidance and help. He also asked the Great Creator to help him be good, strong and understanding enough to make the right decisions. That he would try to be as good a leader as Niner had been. With all those prayers said, with everyone else gone, he stood there at the gravesite and then knelt down and silently cried. Inwardly the tears flowed, outwardly, he looked stoic, inwardly through choking requests, he asked for his father's strength and support.

It was then he heard the words in his head again, and felt the touch of his father wings on his shoulder, as if Niner was there standing next to him, touching him, talking to him, "I love you and I believe in you, always!"

Interesting Pigeon Fact

Pigeons can find their way home, even if released from a distant location blindfolded. They can navigate by sensing the earth's magnetic fields, and perhaps also by using sound and smell. They can also use cues based on the position of the sun.

http://www.allaboutbirds.org/guide/Rock_Pigeon/lifehistory

Chapter 14

April had gotten up all excited; for she had awoken from a dream where she had figured out what mountain pass Mosaic, Trapper and Moth had taken to go south. She got up, threw on a robe, shuffled into a pair of Tiger slippers and headed straight for the dining room. She was, wide awake with anticipation and wanted to see if the information in the dream was true. As she passed Eric's room, she stop, she knocked on the door, opened it, and woke Eric up, "Eric, Get up! I've figured out the route they are taking. Get up Eric!" When Eric barely responded, she figured enough time wasted and headed out of his room and finished her trip to the dining room.

When Eric arrived five minutes later, still wiping the sleep from his eyes, April was lying on the rug with several maps and a book sprawled out before her. She was tracing her finger along one of the maps drawn out roads and talking to herself. "There it is." she said, "The grain depot." She looked up as Eric came in and sat next to her. "See the grain depot is listed in the farmer's almanac map Dad brought home last night." Showing it to Eric as she had been talking. "Look!" she said as she pointed out what she had just been saying to him. "Here is where the grain silos are and that's where they made it yesterday." She then moved her finger down the map, "And here is the way they would have gone south, see!" as She continued moving her finger down to a lake about half way down the mountain pass, Eric said in an excited voice, "And there's the lake that Trapper and Mosaic told you about!"

"Yep!" April said, shaking her head in agreement, really proud of herself and her discoveries, "That's where they must have flown through from the south to get here, makes sense."

"What makes sense?" asked their Mother as she stopped on her way through the dining room and into the kitchen. "What do you two want for breakfast? Pancakes, sound good to me." She offered them as a suggestion as what to eat.

"Yes!" Eric and April responded in unison, "With chocolate chips. Okay! Mom." April added.

"While I make breakfast, you two go get ready." she said in response to their reply to her question. "I'll make the batter and you can cook the pancakes with anything you want in them." She finished as they got up. Eric asked over his shoulder as they were leaving. "Can we have hot chocolate as well?"

"If you make it yourself, yes," she responded.

It did not take either of them very long to wash up and change from their pajamas into street clothes. As they walked into the kitchen their Mother asked them, "I saw you with the maps again this morning, have you figured out any more about where you think the birds went?"

April had walked over to the batter and the bag of chocolate chips sitting on the counter next to the stove, while Eric had gotten out the hot chocolate mix, he told his Mom, "Yes, Mom. April had a dream and based on the dream she figured out how they went south." in response to her question.

"That's wonderful." their Mother responded.

"What's wonderful?" there Father asked as he entered the kitchen on his way over to the coffee pot for his first cup of coffee of the day.

"We think we know the route the birds took through the mountain pass and which pass they took to go south." April gave in response to his question.

"That's great! How did you figure that out?" Their father said in amazement to the news, seeing how the night before they were not sure, both started to reply, but he stopped them saying, "We'll eat breakfast and then you can show me." Which stopped April from going and getting the maps to show him by saying, "Finish the pancakes first and then you can show me. After we eat, I'm starving." he finished with a smile, as he sat down at the little table in one corner of the kitchen to start drinking his coffee.

After breakfast, they had shown their father, where the silos were and then the pass, before he had gone to work. In between cleaning up dishes and their rooms, they spent the morning trying to determine the route the birds would have taken once they had gotten through the mountain pass. Over lunch they discussed this with their Mother and explained what they had done and explained that they had done all that they could, and was it for sure that their dad would be able to take them the next day along the route they had plotted. April was a little anxious because she had lost Trappers homing devices signal at around eleven o'clock. "I think a half hour before I lost the signal, they were on the move again." April said in a low, soft concerned voice.

"I know, dear." Was all her mother gave as a response, "It will be all right, your Father has tomorrow off and we'll go on a little road trip to see if we can locate them?"

With that having been said, April was extremely quiet over lunch. She was like this because she wasn't pleased with the fact they would have to wait until tomorrow to set out on what she believed would be a wonderful adventure. An adventure where she and her entire family would help Mosaic rescue his entire family and flock mates. She didn't want to be late; she wanted to be there when they were released. She had it all worked out in her mind; of how it should go, of how Mosaic would be so grateful he would want to return with her and live at their loft forever. She had convinced herself that what she had imagined would in fact happen.

Aprils Mother knew Aprils tendency to let what she imagined become her reality and then when it didn't come out the way April had imagined, she would be disappointed, angry and upset with everyone around her. "April!" she said, "Are you okay dear? You seem preoccupied. Do you want to discuss what's on your mind?" She knew it would be healthy for April to discuss what was on her mind. It was the best way, for it allowed April to come to her own conclusions as to what was usually the best solution to the problem.

Aprils response was, "Nothing, and no!" and then she went into a lengthy explanation as to what was bothering her. How she wished they could leave today, because tomorrow may be too late, and what would the birds be able to do? She talked until she voiced all her expectations and her desires. She talked until she was out of breath. When she paused.

"I know, dear," her Mother, said in a very patient and understanding voice, "We will just have to hope we are still able to help tomorrow. Mosaic is a wild pigeon that knows his way around the streets, I'm sure. Your father has taken the day off from work and we will leave at first light. I'm afraid that's the best we can do for now. April, I think it not wise to put your hopes on the fact that Mosaic will want to come back here to live. He's been raised wild and he seems to like that lifestyle."

April looked at her Mom with her last words she had burst April Bubble. "Mom, he liked it here. He said so himself!" she finished somewhat defiantly, "I know he does!"

"I know, dear, but I believe he liked being free better. Remember, how he loved to fly and would stay out all day, especially near the end there. I think he was ready to leave even if his sister hadn't shown up." she finished.

April looked at her Mom's knowing expression and smiled back at her, "You know Mom. You're pretty smart. I just want him to come and visit." Was April final thought on the subject of Mosaic coming back and staying. Even though she had hoped secretly, he'd want to stay forever, she knew the reality was that he wouldn't.

"Let's clean up, and go to the mall," their Mother said as she got up from the table. "You and Eric pick out a movie you want to see. After which we will go to the store and get snacks and drinks for the trip tomorrow. We'll also get things we need for a picnic lunch," she finished with a smile. She then changed the subject, "You and Eric decide on the menu and we'll get what we need and you two can help me make it tonight before dinner."

With all these plans set, the afternoon went by quickly doing all the activities they had planned and they had a great remainder of the day. They went and saw a movie about a pig that thought it was a dog. After which they went to the store and bought snacks and drinks and everything they needed to prepare fried chicken and make potato salad for their trip.

Their father came home from work at his regular time. They ate a simple meal of hot dogs and chili for dinner that night, and as they ate, they discussed the trip and the food and snacks that they had bought and would prepare, for all the activities of the next day. April and Eric had trouble falling asleep, each one's mind churning and twisting as to what might happen tomorrow into a million scenarios of good and bad things. Eventually they finally did fall asleep, each one imagining how they would help Mosaic and the others rescue and free the captured birds.

After they had gone to bed, their Father and Mother discussed their children's expectations and concluded they would need to be patient. They would do what they could to alleviate the disappointment they feared would come. However, neither one held out much hope that they would actually find the birds; even if they did, they would not be able to do much for the birds. Still, they had promised they'd go and it would be a nice outing and they would go to the beach if they couldn't pick up the signal from the homing device that Trapper was wearing. They agreed they would have to deal with their children's disappointment sometime tomorrow. Because they knew, it would be sheer dumb luck if they actually picked up Trappers signal and then found him. With resignation, they went off to bed and they too eventually fell into a restless sleep as well.

The next morning arrived too quickly. The good thing, it came quietly and calmly without ceremony under overcast skies. They were up before first light and were on the road as the sun tried to break its golden rays of light through the mist of the overcast skies. April watched the sun play hide and go seek or peek-a- boo as it tried to break out from behind the mist. Every now and again, the sun's bright light lit her face and would spread its hope of warmth over the landscape only to disappear again behind the clouds; like a small child teasing its older sibling to try to find them in a game of hide and go seek. As they drove, she thought about the birds, about how the birds were doing and where they could be, and hoped that they were all right. She had a bad dream the night before and was concerned that one of them had become very ill and had died from the illness. It did not help that she had a great imagination that could take the smallest morsel of what others thought of as a normal occurrence and turn it into a dramatic incident, worthy of a Shakespearian play.

Having lost Trappers homing devices signal the other day had not helped ease her worried mind and concerns either. Instead, it had only helped play into her anxiety about their well-being and safety. Unlike her brother Eric, who had fallen asleep almost the minute they had left the house, she was wide-awake with anticipation for what would or would not happen.

It had not helped that her dad had tried to forewarn her to be realistic in her expectations and that there was a really good possibility that they may not find the birds at all. A part of her knew this and had dreaded it, so she had told herself that what her Dad had explained was a real possibility she did not want to entertain. In her mind that if she entertained what her Dad had suggested could be a possibility, then it might come true, but if she believed that, they would be traveling down some freeway or highway and the signal would go off, then it would mean she had found them. Positive thinking, she kept telling herself, and then only the good things will come true.

With the radio playing sixties rock-n-roll; her Mom and Eric asleep; her Dad paying close attention to the road, humming along with the music and his driving, her attention shifting between the receiver in her lap and the sun moving in and out behind the cloud cover, they headed south. After two hours of driving in a southerly direction on the main freeway, April's Dad said, "I'm Hungry! How about you?" he said over his shoulder to April. April who had felt her stomach moving back and forth, up and down said, "Yes, me too! Can we get pancakes and hot chocolate?"

"Sure!" he said in response, "We will stop at the Road Side Café I was reading about on the billboards for the last fifty miles. The last one I read says it's coming up, and that they serve the best breakfast in the valley." As they were slowing down to take the off-ramp, Eric, and her Mom woke up and gave their concurrence to the plan, because both stated they were hungry as well.

The Road Side Café wound up being at the last off-ramp before they would leave the freeway they were on and before they would then take the one through the mountain pass that April and Eric had plotted out on the map as the place the birds also would have attempted on their trip south. They ate a good hardy country style breakfast, each getting what they liked best, made their pit stop, freshened up and an hour after they had stopped they were back on the road again going through the mountain pass.

As they drove, they played the license plate game, and then several variations of the original. The first was looking for different states, then to look for specific numbers over a specific time frame, to looking for specific letters in alphabetical order, and so the time passed quickly. Before they knew it, an hour and a half had passed by and they were descending down the road on the backside of the mountains.

When they reached the bottom of the road. Once again, they were traveling on relatively level ground Eric noticed that the light on the receiver was blinking slightly. He thought he had seen it blink, but at first, he thought it was the sunlight, or his imagination, because it took so long between each blink. After what he thought was the fifth blink, he said, "April, I think the receivers light is blinking."

April picked the receiver up from her lap and stared at it for what seemed to her like hours, when she too saw it blink. In an excited voice, she said, "Yes! It is blinking, but why isn't it beeping?" She asked, "Is it broken Dad? Why isn't it beeping?"

"Because that's the way it works, the light first comes on and then the sound follows." He finished by saying, "If the blinking gets quicker, the closer we get to the source. Nevertheless, once you get really close, like within a couple of hundred yards, then the beep will also sound. The closer we get, the closer together the light and the beep will become until they are in unison, and once that happens my dear, we will be within several hundred feet or less of the homing device."

The excitement level in the car from all the occupants had gone up tenfold the minute the device had started to give the signal that they were on the right track. So it had gone all that day, they had been so close on several occasions, based on the light and the sound being almost in unison, but hadn't been able to find the birds. It was an emotional roller coaster ride of exuberances as the signals came together, but then things went to near depression when they once again diverged. They had visited several pet and feed stores with no luck. The owners had sold all their birds earlier that day, but could not remember the name of those that had bought them. However, their luck changed, and in the late afternoon, they had found the pet and feed store that had just that very afternoon sold all their pigeons, except the fantails, to a group of men that were taking them to their ranch. The owner of the store remembered the name that had been on the side of the pickup truck that had taken the birds and had given it to them.

Their Dad looked up the name he had been given by the pet and feed storeowner. They had headed down the road to where the ranch was located. It was getting late and they were tired, so they had stopped for the night and gotten a motel room to spend the evening. Their Dad had promised they would get up early, drive out to the ranch at first light, and see what they could do. In the meantime, he had called the ranch and had talked to a Mr. Luo, who had been very curious and had said they were more than welcome to come out and see if their pigeons were among those he had purchased earlier that day. He had also said that if they were he would be more than happy to allow them to buy them back at what he had paid for them.

At dinner, their Dad told them about his conversation with Mr. Luo, about his offer to allow them to look at all the birds in his lofts and that if in fact one of them was theirs they could buy it back for what he had paid for it. April and Eric went to bed happy, relaxed and content in the belief that tomorrow they would have their beloved pigeons back again. All their worries were over, they had done it, tracked down the birds and tomorrow they would have them in their possession again, safe, sound and unharmed. All was right with and in their world and they feel asleep without a care in the world.

"I hope they are not counting their chickens before they hatch." April's Dad said to his wife as they watched their children sleeping. "I know, dear," his wife said in answer to his concern. "We'll know tomorrow if we got lucky, if not we'll have to face that bridge when we come to it. I didn't think we'd even get this close." She finished and then said, "Goodnight!" as she went to bed, leaving her husband alone to ponder how and what he would say tomorrow if their ride out to the Luo ranch didn't pan out. He would also have to tell April in the morning that this was a game hunter ranch, another prospect that he didn't much like, for he knew his daughters infinity to speak her mind and knew she wasn't much on gaming ranches. Oh well, he thought tomorrow ought to be an interesting day.

They were up early the next morning, and they ate a good hearty breakfast at the little greasy spoon café attached to the motel where they were staying. Once they had eaten and finished cleaning up they headed out to Mr. Luo's game ranch.

As they drove out into the country, they could see many cultivated fields of hay, corn and alfalfa. Amongst the cultivated farmlands, there were large areas of unspoiled wilderness. They followed the directions that Mr. Luo had given their Dad and they turned off the main highway down a two-lane asphalt covered road until they reached an old western style entrance to the game hunter's ranch. The plaque over the roadway read "Emerald Valley Hunting Ranch." They could see a beautiful large lodge as they passed underneath the sign and drove up the large two-lane driveway to the gravel parking lot. As they passed the front of the lodge there was a large welcoming sign hanging over the entrance to the large wooden hunters lodge that read "Welcome to the Third Annual Passenger Pigeon Derby".

April looked anxiously and with apprehension at Eric as they both read the sign. "Dad, this is a gaming ranch, isn't it?" she asked.

"Yes! I believe so." he responded, "Now April; I know how you don't like these places, but remember we are guests. Mr. Luo has kindly and graciously allowed us to look for the birds. He will allow you to buy them back if they are here, so please behave."

"I will Daddy." was April's curt response to his instructions, "All I want is to be able to find the birds and then leave." April knew she'd be sad for all those she could not help by taking them home with her. As did her parents, they too would have liked to help all those birds that they knew were headed to their deaths, but it wasn't practical. Eric just thought it was neat, he had read about these types of ranches and was fascinated by how they ran, more so than alarmed about what they did here. He had read that the hunter who participated in these controlled hunts ate what they hunted and shot, so what was the harm. Eric didn't believe in killing for killing's sake, but he didn't have a problem with hunting something if you liked eating it.

Their Father and Mother were almost equally divided on the issue. His Mother taking Eric position, while his Father leaned more towards April's views; at least on the hunting and sporting side of the issue. He felt kill them humanely and then go and eat them for food, not merely for a stuffed trophy for a display case or a wall plaque. Hunting was such a messy affair and the animals hunted were wounded and suffered until they were tracked and found and killed, and that was the part that he objected to mostly.

They parked the car in the gravel-filled parking lot and as they approached the lodge, they read a sign that welcomed the hunters to the lodge. It was a duplicate of the sign hanging over the lodge entrance; only this sign had several pictures of patches that depicted the previous derbies. April looked at Eric, scrunched up her nose and rolled her eyes in disgust. As they climbed the stairs, they passed several excited groups of hunters talking about what order they were in and when they would be shooting. They then walked through the doors and headed for the main desk, where they passed several small signs standing on easels that directed hunters by group numbers to different conference rooms for checking in of their weapons and to get their shooting order.

They all walked up to the front desk of the lodge, which was decorated, as an authentic hunting lodge would have been expected to be decorated. The walls were all paneled in beautiful dark oak and hanging on the walls were the heads of several large game animals. In addition, there were several plaques showing ducks, quail, and pheasants flying, and several large fish as well. There were also three large glass cases sitting, one at each end of the front desk and one in the center. The one at the left side of the front desk contained several wild turkeys standing in an open field, while the on the right contained a mountain lion standing on a branch that was angled downward overlooking a canyon. The case in the center of the lobby contained a large bear trying to catch a fish out of a stream.

Behind the desk stood a distinguished looking middle-aged Asian gentleman, who introduced himself as Mr. Luo. He shook hands with all four of them and welcomed them to the lodge. He asked if they would like anything to drink, or to eat? They politely said no. April asked impatiently if they could go see the birds. Mr. Luo smiled a knowing smile and said, "Of course! The little one is anxious to see if her birds are here. Please follow me." As he led them from the lobby out of the lodge, they walked through the grounds and to his golf cart sitting at the back of the lodge. They got in and traveled for about ten minutes around a large barn structure and to the area where four rows of pigeon lofts were standing.

"In those two rows," he explained, "are all my squab birds and in those two rows are all the sport birds. You are free to look at them all. If you see the ones you seek, please let me know, and I will get them out for you." He said this in a warm soft caring voice with a cordial smile on his face. "Please, please go," he said at there hesitation, "there is nothing here that will harm you."

April and Eric jumped from the cart the minute Mr. Luo had brought it to a stop. They ran to the first loft, full of anticipation and fully engaged in their search of the birds as they went from loft to loft.

Their Mother stepped off the cart and shouted instructions after them, about being careful and taking their time, and that they not to make a lot of noise and startle the birds, and she then looked apologetically at Mr. Luo. All her instructions were given out of nervousness rather than concern that something would go wrong, but more to the fact, that if they did not find the birds she would have to deal with a monstrous disappointment.

Mr. Luo smiled back at her and assured her they couldn't hurt a thing and that they were quite safe. She said she understood, but that if they didn't find the birds, then they would feel very let down and disappointed.

As April and Eric looked through the lofts, the adults talked about how they had come to believe that the birds were even at the ranch, and Mr. Luo was very impressed with what he heard. They talked about how seven years ago Mr. Luo and his family had bought the ranch. How at first it had been hard to make ends meet, and how they had decided to create and build it into a game-hunting ranch and how it had created and turned it into a thriving business. Even though their Dad didn't agree with it, he realized that the Luo family were trying to do the right thing, and that they were in fact running a business.

It didn't take long for the disappointment to set in, especially as they looked at the last loft of birds and discovered that none of the lofts contained Moth, Trapper, or Mosaic. They both had long faces as they walked back to the golf cart.

"No luck, eh?" Their Dad asked as they approached the cart, "sorry, maybe they are still flying and we just need to track them some more." he finished. April looked at her Dad, "I looked at the monitor and it showed the signal the strongest when we pulled into the ranch." she finished with a sigh of major exasperation and frustration. "Trapper should have been here." April finished with another sigh, "I guess the thing is broken, piece of junk!" She finished with a frown on her face as she got into the cart.

Mr. Luo, who saw the looks disillusionment and disappointment, offered them each the pick of any bird they wanted and that they could take it home with them free of charge. Both April and Eric said, "No, thanks, it wouldn't be the same." With Mr Luo's off being rejected, Eric, April and the three adults got back into the cart and headed back to the lodge.

They wore their disappointment on their faces as a model wears a new gown, on display for all to see, and made everyone wonder what could make two such young children so unhappy on such a beautiful new day. Mr. Luo, who now felt really bad for them, offered once again any bird in his lofts and then also offered them to eat at the lodge as his guests. As a reply to his offer April said she didn't especially feel like eating while Eric on the other hand was disappointed, but not enough to ignore his hunger pains. He looked at his parents and then at April and said, "Let's just have a hot chocolate and a sweet roll, before we go. I'm hungry! Come on April it won't hurt and we know they're not here. We just have to keep looking and us starving ourselves isn't going to make it any easier to find them. We'll just have to keep looking, but let's do it on a full stomach." He then looked at his Mom and Dad for help, his Mom smiled, "Sounds like a good idea to me. I could use something to drink."

"Me too!" their Dad added to the conversation, "You know Eric you are right. We all need a little pick me up. And then we'll recalculate where we are and maybe we can come up with a plan on where to look next."

Mr. Luo was pleased when April acquiesced and said okay to her families persuasive arguments in favor of having a bit to eat. "Great!" he said, "I'm glad you will accept my humble invitation and I may be able to direct you to where you should look next. There is a church, just south of here where strays and wild pigeons sometimes go. I'll write down the directions while you eat. It's only about thirty minutes or so from here."

"Thank you, Mr. Luo," their Dad said.

"Yes, so kind of you," their Mother chimed in, as she gave April and Eric that, what do you have to say look.

"Oh! Thank you Mr. Luo," both April and Eric said almost in unison.

"My pleasure, my pleasure!" he said as they stopped at the front door of the lodge. They got out and he took them to the dining room, talked to one of the waiters, who looked a lot like Mr. Luo and then excused himself. They ate a wonderful brunch type meal and while they were eating Mr. Luo brought the written directions to the church. He and their Dad talked to make sure the directions were clear and the Mr. Luo excused himself, "Lots to do," he said, "Big day today, good luck!" They thanked him for his kindness and he then left them to finish their meal.

They finished their drinks and food and left the lodge full and content, the food had helped curb their disappointment in not finding the birds. After their snack they left the lodge and headed for the parking lot and got into the car, headed back down the asphalt road driving away from the lodge and towards the main highway. As they were traveling down the road, a pigeon flew up alongside of them. April yelled, "Dad! Stop! Stop the car, it's Trapper!"

Their Dad pulled over to the side of the roadway onto the shoulder, and April and Eric were out of the car even before it had come to a complete stop. The pigeon that had been flying alongside the car, circled and landed on the shoulder of the road just behind where they had stopped. April put out her hand and Trapper flew to it and as he landed, he said, "Hi! It is you, what are you all doing here?" He queried and then continued on before he got an answer, "Great to see you! Now you can help me save Mosaic and the others." He finished, a little out of breath due to his excitement at seeing them and his desire to get his story out and solicit their help.

April looked at him a little puzzled, "Save Mosaic and the others? From what? Where are they?" she asked.

"Oh, from back there," Trapper responded as he pointed back down the road to the ranch they had just left.

"We were just there," April said, "and we saw not one bird we knew, no Mosaic, no Moth. They weren't there Trapper. So where are they?" April finished with apprehension and concern in her voice.

Trapper looked puzzled and then said, "Look, maybe I had better start from the beginning." And so, Trapper told his story of their trip south, of what had happened to Moth, their failed attempts at rescuing Mosaics family and flock mates at the pet and feed store. He explained their failed attempts at the ranch as well and then how Mosaic got himself captured. He then described the big pigeon hunt that was suppose to start this morning, and all the other events, until he got to the part where he had seen them and had come after them to tell them they were here.

April explained it all to her Mom and Dad, who looked at her with skepticism, but Eric spoke up and said, "that's what Trapper has told her." Just as she finished, they could all hear the distant sounds of gunshots.

"Well, it's started!" Trapper exclaimed, "their only hope now, is lady luck and that they make it to the church."

"The church?" April asked, "What church?" Trapper explained what the sparrows and the turkey had told them, and how the church was where all the birds that survived the derby would go. That they would go there for medical aid and sanctuary. April explained it all to her parents, how now the obvious course of action was to go to the church and see if they could be of help.

Without any hesitation, it was decided they would head for the church, to render whatever aid they could. Trapper said, he'd follow them there and help as best he could, that he would be the go between for the birds and the humans. They all got back into the car, and off to the church they went, all deep in their own thoughts of what they would find there and hoping it wouldn't be as bad as their imagination had seen it.

Their Mother finally spoke up, "Let's say a little prayer for them and hope we can be of service once we arrive." With that having been said, they each said a silent prayer for the birds and their safety.

They traveled the rest of the way to the church in silence, each still wondering how they could possibly be of any help. From what Trapper had told April and how April had interpreted, what he had said and what she had explained to her parents, to her it seemed pretty hopeless. When they reached the church they discovered it was more than a church, they discovered it was also a country vet's office. The vet's office was next to the church, not a part of the church building, but on the same property as the church. There was also a well-kept human and pet cemetery on the property adjacent to the gravel parking lot next to the Veterinary office. They pulled into the small parking area next to the sign that read, "Sanctuary Veterinarian Hospital and Animal Boarding" As they got out of the car an older gentleman in a white coat came out of the front door and down the porch of the white, neatly painted building to greet them.

"Hello! Good to see you." He said in a warm and personable voice. "I am Doctor John. You have come to help with the care of all those that will be coming in here today, I hope?" he said this with his hand out stretched and a smile on his old and wrinkled face. The smile left his face and was replaced by concern, as he saw the puzzled looks on their faces "You, don't know what I'm talking about, do you?" he said as April's Dad gripped his hand in a warm handshake.

"No, I'm afraid not." April's Dad replied.

April liked Dr. John instantly; he was a friendly, jovial looking man in his late sixties. He was as tall as her dad was, but he had at least forty pounds on him in weight. "Well let me explain myself then." he said with concern on his face. He told them that he was expecting several volunteers to help with the wounded and dying today because the game ranch was having one of its annual derbies. He continued by saying normally there would be several people there to help, but so far today no one had shown up. Not that he could blame them he had said, "You see it's a messy affair, with not only hurt and dying birds to treat, but there was usually all types of other small woodland creatures as well. The hunters were always trying to hit only the pigeons that were released, but the pellets they shot weren't very smart about what they hit, or how they damaged those they did hit." After hearing that, they all said they had come to help.

His pleasure at hearing that was palatable as he said, "Good, good, great, come on in then and help me finish my preparations. I sure can use all the help I can get." He then ushered them into the house and through the front lobby and into clinic area of the building, as he did so he explained what needed to get done and showed them where the treatment rooms were and where the additional boarding areas were. "We need to get everything cleaned, and new bedding laid into each cage, and then we'll need to get all the bedding laid out in the treatment rooms as well. There are all the surgical tools that still need to be sterilized. So much to do, so little time." he finished.

They helped him finish all his preparations by setting out bandages, the needles, the thread and all the other instruments he would need to treat the patients he was expecting soon. When they were all done and none had shown up, he looked at them all and said, "Now we wait. Would you like something to drink or eat? I know it is early, only nine a.m., but we better eat and drink now, because, once the casualties start arriving we may not get another chance to relax for quite some time. And more the likely will not want to eat much of anything once they do, especially if you've never done this before." He exclaimed.

With his encouragement, they sat down, and ate for the third time that morning and talked a little while waiting for the first injured to arrive. "You all are not from these parts, are you? What brings you here to my little piece of the world?" he asked. It was the first time since they had arrived that they were able to just talk. April told their story and why they were there. "I hope your pets aren't anywhere near here today, they sure will be in for a rude awakening if they are." he finished.

April, seeing the look of concern on Doctor John's face, wanted to divert the conversation away from her beloved birds and asked what they might expect. Dr. John explained that they would be treating all types of animals and birds today, with all kinds of wounds.

A short while after he had explained what to expect, it started, a car pulled into the gravel parking lot and a young woman stepped out carrying a shoe-box. She came in through the front door in a flurry of motion and commotion, "Dr. John! I have a small rabbit here that's been shot." And sure enough, the first patient treated for a gunshot wound to the leg was a little wild rabbit. Dr. John had a way with animals, the minute he touched the rabbit it seemed to sense it was in good hands, and would be safe. Dr. John gave it some anesthesia and then proceeded to pull two pellets out of its left leg. He then sewed it up and placed in one of the cages in the boarding area. He gave April's Mom some instruction, as what to look for and do, and just as he finished the first pigeon arrived for treatment. By the time Mosaic and his mother showed up they had treated a dozen or more cases for gunshot wounds.

April, Eric and Trapper were really happy to see Mosaic and even happier that he wasn't hurt. Trapper was physically shaken when he heard the news that Sky was dead. Trapper had liked Sky and had thought her one of the bravest outflyers he had ever met; to think her dead was shocking, sad and well, unbelievably hard to comprehend.

April and Eric talked briefly about it all and then they were all so busy attending to all the additional birds and other animals that were constantly dribbling in with all types of major and minor injuries they didn't give it another thought. It seemed the wounded kept coming in waves, which was a blessing and a curse all at the same time, because if they all had come in at once they would not have been treated effectively and efficiently for the caregivers would have been overwhelmed. However, on the downside, those caring for them never got a chance to really rest and so the fatigue factor started to set in. Then late in the afternoon, they had a break between casualties that lasted more than an hour, which gave them all a chance to drink and eat and get somewhat revived. During that time April got to meet some birds Mosaic had told her about and she really liked Colors and the new one named Vlinder. To April she was one of the most beautiful racers she had ever seen. She was everything a good racer should be, sleek, with great body form, strong wings with powerful shoulder to help propel her through the air, she looks daunting. To April, a perfect thoroughbred of the skies.

Just as things seemed to have calmed down a little, is when all bedlam broke loose. All the K-bridge survivors went into a frantic flurry of action, and all she heard them say was to make ready, that Niner was there, he was hurt, and he needed the doctor's immediate attention. When she saw Niner, April knew instinctively that he wouldn't live. She did not know exactly why, maybe it was in his eyes, or the way he carried himself, but she knew he wasn't going to make it, she knew he was going to die. She said nothing of her beliefs, but Dr. John confirmed her diagnoses that Niner's wounds were fatal based on the test results; he was dying from rattlesnake poisoning. At that moment in time she had never felt so helpless, she couldn't think of anything to say, so she did all she could to make Niner and his family as comfortable as possible, but it all seemed to no avail, for their sadness was palatable.

All she could do she had done, she had watched as Niner suffered and his family grieved and in the end she hadn't been able to help relieve the pain. She had heard how his being poisoned had come about. About his bravery, and how he had saved Vlinder from certain death. She had met with Vlinder and they had talked and talked about how guilty Vlinder felt and how hard it was not to be able to do anything to ease the pain and suffering. She had also talked to Niner, who she had liked instantly. He had told her he had heard how she had helped Mosaic after the falcon attack and he thanked her for her help. He had then told her to stay a friend to Mosaic, for in the days and weeks to come he would need her help and strength. She had promised she would. They then talked briefly about guilt and how we sometimes have to do what's right over what is best. He had then asked to be left alone with his family.

Niner, the flock leader of the K-bridge flock, with his family in attendance, later that night had died. After several days of grieving and various pigeon ceremonies, they had buried him in the pet cemetery next to the church. Their Dad had gone back home, because he had to work, but her Mother and Eric had stayed as Dr. Johns guests and had helped him care for all those recovering from their injuries.

April had kept a watchful eye on Mosaic as she had promised Niner. However, she had not been able to get Mosaic to respond to her council, as one day had turned to the next she became more concerned about his self-imposed isolation. He seemed to be listless, lethargic and showed no interest in daily activities that were going on all around him. She had felt useless, as she watched him. She felt defeated and was not alone in those feelings all the others that had tried to get Mosaic reengaged with the flock, with them his flock mates felt that same way as well. She was worried, she felt frustrated, she felt discouraged and angry, not with herself as much as with him.

She decided to approach Trapper one more time for his assistance. Trapper had exclaimed what was he to do, he had tried everything and so far nothing he had said had gotten Mosaic to come out of himself, out of his grieve, out of the blame game he was playing with himself. Mosaic was in the what if mode, and had blamed himself for not having perpetrated the rescue his father, his mother and the others earlier. Trapper knew as well as all the others Mosaic had done all a bird could have done, everyone understood, everyone but Mosaic that was, and how to get through that guilt is what Trapper was not sure how to achieve. Yet as he and April talked, he promised her he would give it yet another try, even though he held out no hope of being able to really do anything to bring Mosaic around and accept the facts. The most important fact, the hardest one to swallow, they had done all they could have done, that fate just wasn't on their side, when there failed rescue attempts had been made.

He promised April he would try. What to say or how to say it escaped him, and yet he knew he had to try, the flocks' life depended on it. He did not know why, but all the rail yards flocks lives depended on it as well all would be, would be doomed if he didn't. The harsh realization of him failing hit him making it clear, failure was not an option.

Interesting Pigeon Fact

Pigeons have strong muscles used for flying. They can fly
at the altitude of 6000 feet.

Pigeons can move their wings ten times per second and
maintain heartbeats at the rate of 600 times per minute,
during the period of 16 hours.

http://www.animalaid.org.uk/h/n/CAMPAIGNS/wildlife/ALL/346/

Chapter 15

While back at the hidden meeting room, Pieth stood where Crafco had stood only hours before. He was accompanied by the same companions, but unlike Crafco, Pieth did not feel confident nor at ease. In reality, he felt nervous and depressed by his surroundings. The dampness and the unclean smells were aiding in his feelings of uneasiness. Every time he took a new breath, the anxious feelings that were creeping into his every fiber, and they only seemed to be worsening. He told himself to think happy thoughts, of sunshine and cool breezes under his wings. Of cool water on a hot day, and how good it felt, of the freshness of air after it had rained. Yet, every time he took a breath all his efforts at trying to visualize, a clean and good environment seemed to be wiped out with one intake of the foul smelling air. Maintain, he would tell himself, maintain, think of family, of the flock, of all the good things in the world and yet every time he felt he had things back under control he'd have to take a breath and it would all disappear, as if a wisp of smoke. With every new breath, it was harder and harder to keep focused on the positive, bright and cheery things about life.

Pieth kept thinking, why did I agree to do this? Why did I? Was all that ran through his mind as the nauseating smells of decaying vegetation and other dead things kept assailing his nostrils. He had done this at the behest of Yukon, the Southwest flock's leader, who was now dead. He had promised Yukon, he would do this and help those currently in power determine how bad the threat really was, and when it would strike. Yukon had explained many things he had heard as a youth and had always believed to be fairy tales, great imaginative fiction and great story telling. However, as Yukon lay dying, from an incurable illness, he did not know he had, Yukon had shattered any naiveté of youth by telling him stories of Oother and Ignoble Vile that were incredible. That he felt that the events at both the K-bridge and the North West flock's emblems being stolen were signs that the evil that everyone thought was gone forever and was now the verge of returning and in fact had returned.

The disappearance of the blue feather and the stone pin were not a coincidence, nor were they a good thing. Then to top that off, the birds at K-bridge disappearance, been taken by humans, so that the bridge stood vacant, this too was really a bad omen and a sign that evil was ready to reappear. He knew that all good pigeons would need to rally; would need to become united and prepare themselves for the fight of their lives because one of the greatest evils known to pigeondom, Oother, was coming.

Yukon had scared him. Yukon had made him promise to help. If he believed him, he would seek out Oonal. Pieth had said he believed him and that he would not let his uncle down. Of course, he would help, he had promised. With those words barely out of his mouth, his uncle had taken one rasping, torturous last breath and had said, "Good! You will become flock leader of the Southwestern flock. You will be responsible for all their safety. Do not let me down." With those words spoken and Pieth's additional reassurances that he would not let his uncle down and would do as he asked, Yukon had died. Therefore, now he was here based on that promise. He felt his stomach moving towards his throat.

His stomach was doing somersaults brought on by nerves and the unbelievably foul smells. Just as he had felt he was okay a smoky whiff of dank, damp, moldy air came in contact with his nostrils and he would once again start believing the worst. Stay focused he'd tell himself this will be over soon. Even when the fog in the clearing had lifted and exposed the old decrepit bird they call Vile, his inner turmoil hadn't stopped. The pigeon who was sitting there in front of him was very old looking. The waddle around its eyes was very layered and almost totally blocked off his vision. When a portion of his eyes became exposed, they looked somewhat milky and gray, adding to the appearance of being unearthly eerie. The smoke that was there appeared to be rolling out of his body into the air. He looked at the others around him and all were bent over, bowing and saying, "Yes, master Vile, we are all here to do your bidding. Command us and we shall obey." He found himself also bowing and saying what the rest were saying. He was trying to stop himself but could not, he was scared, more scared than he had ever been before in his entire short life. Not scared of Vile, which he should have been, but that he was not in control of his own action and that was a very unsettling feeling.

He once again looked up at Vile, who had not moved. The smoke still looked like it was emanating from his being. The fact that he was a gray with white grizzle that had a few blue checks on his wings and that he had all white fights, which only enhanced the illusion of other-worldliness. His neck feathers looked distorted and he looked and acted very old and frail. The only thing that let you know that the bird sitting there was alive was the slow movement of his chest as he breathed in and out. As he watched, the brightness that came into those gray eyes as they turned a brown red in the little spot that was visible between the layers of waddle. Other than those two things that showed it was alive, looking at him you would have thought he was a stuffed taxidermist dusty old pride and joy.

Vile sat there for several more minutes just watching him before he spoke in a dry, crackly rustling of leaves voice, as he asked it's question, not directed at Pieth, "Oos, why have you come? Twice in one day, I feel honored."

"Master, it is I who must be honored, that you would take the time to see me again. I come to bring you a new subject," Oos said in a low whispering voice, as if afraid that to speak louder would have caused his master harm.

"You bring one that wishes to lead?" was Vile's response, and then he continued not waiting for an answer, as if it already knew the answer, "And how can I help him with this? Maybe he asks me himself so that I can determine the sincerity of his request." As he spoke the words he had turned from Oos and was now looking directly at Pieth, waiting.

Pieth's mind had traveled back once again to his uncle's deathbed as Vile had spoken. He tried to keep his mind on the present and on what was going on in front of him, but he kept being drawn back to his Uncles last words. "Promise me, that you will do whatever is required so that you know I speak the truth, and you will help." And with that having been requested of him, he had agreed, he had agreed to help, to do everything his dying Uncle had requested, which now found him here in this disgusting place, facing this unbelievable creature, that once had been a pigeon called, Vile.

"Well!" Vile said for the third time, having lost all patience in his voice, "I guess we have a slow one here. Are you slow boy?" He asked with a look that said my patience is running out or of boredom with the entire situation.

Pieth finally realized what he had been asked and felt embarrassed, and as if he had been found out, as a child who hasn't spoken for fear that what they said would reveal the truth when he spoke. He spoke with a cool confidence of one who knows that if he failed he would be dead. "I'm sorry!" He said nervously with a slight stammer in his voice, "I'm sorry, I was momentarily overwhelmed by your greatness." As he spoke, he saw a satisfied look creep across Vile's old decrepit face, as he spoke he gained strength from it and continued with more confidence and conviction. "I seek the council of the great Vile." He put emphasis on the word great, and once again saw Vile's chest expand with pride. "I will become flock leader of the South West flocks of the rail yard tomorrow and I wish to do it correctly. I was told that you could help me keep my power for as long as I live. That you need allies that would be loyal to you and I need allies that are strong and that will help me and stabilize my position if I am ever threatened, or have to go to war. I come to ask that you become one of my allies."

"Who told you that I need allies? Who else were you thinking of asking to become your ally?" Vile said with an inquisitive, slightly mocking tone to his voice.

"Well, Oos here sought me out," he said, pointing to Oos who was nodding his head yes, "Master Vile, it seemed like a good idea at the time. We do need allies as …." before Oos could finish, Vile had raised his wing and said "Enough!" which had stopped Oos in his tracks, as if the words were cut off and sucked up by the unpalatable air. Vile, who did not seem to notice that Oos's words had stopped abruptly, motioned for Pieth to continue.

Might as well tell the truth, tell it all Peith thought, "I was going to also go to the new leader of the now abandoned K-bridge and ask for his alliance. I went to the North West flock's leadership and was denied their commitment to grant my request for now. They say there is too much turmoil right now. And that eventually they will help me, but for a true alliance to be forged they would need to go through all the formal pomp and ceremony and that could not happen until... for at least a month." He stopped and by the look on Vile's face, his explanation had been accepted, just as Oonal had said it would. "So you see I am vulnerable until then and with what transpired at K-bridge and at the North West flock, I need an alliance to be safe." Again, he paused to assess if Vile had accepted and believed his story before he went on.

However, Vile raised his wing. "Yes! Yes..."-said Vile, with a vulture's evil sullen smile, of a bird thinking, I cannot wait to eat on his face, knowing that his prey could not move and was there for his consumption. "Yes, of course you need an alliance to be safe, and you've come to the right place for that." He finished with a fake disgusting smile beaming from his face.

"But of course we need to be sure that all is on the up and up, as it were. That you, in fact, want what you say and that you have no ulterior motives?" He finished with a very serious, adult like expression on his old pathetic face, having replaced the fake smile.

"So will you allow one of my little servants to accompany you and report back to me with your intentions?" Vile finished with a slight high-pitched glee in his voice, once again showing his disgusting false smile of friendship.

"How will I explain a servant?" was Pieth's logical response to Vile's question.

"Oh, don't worry." Vile responded with a crafty expression on his haggard face. "No-one will know he is there. Only you and I will know."

"How is that possible?" was Pieth's cautious guarded response. "How can you send someone along with me and not have it be known?" Pieth was not sure he really wanted to hear the answer. Because Vile, just sat there giving him a sinister you can trust me grin as he rocked back and forth on his feet. The silence was deafening, he could hear his heart pounding in his chest.

It seemed to Pieth that Vile was never going to answer him, and then as if Vile had made a decision, after having had a debate with himself, he spoke. "You will be a host to my servant. I see by the puzzled look on your face you do not understand. Don't ask what is already obvious to me." Vile gave a knowing older person's smile as he spoke, "You will carry him where no one can see him. But you will know he's there, observing you, obtaining and taking in all you do and say." Vile let the comment hang in the air as he looked at Pieth's continued puzzled expression. "I know," he continued, "you are wondering, how, could that be possible? Well, let me show you… that's if you are in agreement with what I have just said?" Vile finished still looking down on him as a vulture looking at his next meal to die, and was waiting for an answer.

Pieth was not sure how to respond, it would have to be yes. Whatever it was the old coot wanted to do would be done; the dye was cast and he could not very well back out now. He was sure that if he tried he would be dead before he could even turn around to leave. So he shook his head yes and said, "If that's what it takes: to get you as an ally, then let's do it," he finished with a bravado in his voice that he did not feel.

Brave words he thought, when I do not even know what is about to happen to me or even what he's talking about. He had expected there would be some type of loyalty test or trust test. I have prepared he thought, bring it on and may the Great Creator protect me.

Instead, what happened next no creature, at least no sane creature, would have been prepared for or expected. Vile started slowly rocking back and forth, and as he did, he also started humming, or what seemed like humming but instead was a chant. The chant was spoken very low at first, with a specific rhythm, that started to create a vibration. The vibration was so nerve racking and electrifying that the feathers on the back of Pieth's neck started to stand on end. As his feathers started to prickle and stand on end, portions of Pieth's soul were also being vibrated and squeezed and it was scary to know that Vile's chant had so quickly moved through the fiber of his being and was able to attach itself to his spiritual self.

Pieth felt the ground starting to move slowly up and down with the rhythmic highs and lows of the chant. It seemed that every dead leaf in the filthy space was pulsating up and down with the barely audible words coming from Vile's slightly opened beak. The closer Pieth looked the more convinced he was that the ground was in fact moving, and then a small white maggot appeared from the moving earth. As the chant continued another and then another maggot appeared until there were thousands of him, or her, them swaying upright, in unison to Vile's melodious chanting.

Pieth found that he was swaying in time with the maggots and with Vile's voice. He then found himself slowly bending down and lying down on the ground with his beak wide open. He was scared near to death now because he had lost all control over his being. His body was moving to commands his brain was no longer giving.

As he lay there on the ground with beak agape, one of the farthest maggots started swaying, to and fro, back and forth, in a slow rhythmic dance towards him. The rest of the white creepy crawls parted in its path, creating a gauntlet of swaying bodies that seemed to be moving it along as if it were floating in the air, riding the crest of a wave towards him. He kept telling himself close your beak or that disgusting little white creepy crawly thing will slide and glide right inside. If he does, he thought, I'll gag and lose my lunch. However, the closer it got, the less was his sensation to gag, until finally it was at the threshold of his open beak.

He felt if move right in, crawling along his tongue and along the floor of his mouth. A part of him said close it down and spit it out, while another part said it is not real, it is a test. As it wiggled down his throat and into his crop, he still could not believe he was allowing this to happen without physical protest. Then he felt it, the searing pain, as if thousands of small teeth had clamped down into the rear soft tissue of his crop and had slowly started to burrow into his flesh.

He heard himself yell and then scream in great pain, as if he was hearing an echo from some unknown voice in some large empty tunnel or cavern, and then he fainted. When he awoke, he found himself lying face up in the sunlight in an open grassy area next to the stream.

As he focused in on his surroundings, he thought, wow, what a strange dream, as he ran his tongue around his mouth to discover a strange, bump near the rear of his mouth. It was then that he noticed Oos and his two companions sitting there watching him. Oos smiled at him, "No my friend, it was not a dream. You are now one who is aligned to Vile. You passed the inquiries and scrutiny of Oother's, and he has granted you ally status. He will help you maintain your status as flock leader and you will succeed in that role. Your other allies will be all the flocks of the rail yard, except for the North West flock. But that will soon change." He finished with malice and contempt in his voice, as he said the later.

"Yes, you are starting to regain your wits. I can see it in your eyes. In addition to the rail yard flocks, you also have allies in the southern and eastern border flocks," he said this smiling broader than ever, "And of course." he said with a slightly sadistic smile, "I'm always available to aid you in any matter you need help in, like getting rid of an enemy. Yes, Pieth you are now a member in the army that serves Oother, the greatest leader that ever drew a breath upon this planet, maybe upon this universe."

Pieth had not really thought, hooray or I am so lucky. Instead he kept thinking, 'what in the world have I gotten myself into? What has my uncle gotten me into?' He also realized he had decided to play and not his uncle, and now he had to play the hand he had been dealt. He did not like it very much, but the chips were on the table. He had anted up, and knew he must play his hand, he only hoped it was not the dead bird's hand... He smiled to himself, 'you are now in it to the end.'

What would his Mother and Father think? They had always accused him of not being or really getting involved. Look at me now, Mom and Dad, he thought; 'I am up to my eyes with involved. I am up to the nostril of my beak in it; I hope I have made the right decision? I hope you are proud of me, I hope I'm right in what I'm doing, because there's a war coming and for once in my life I'd like to be on the winning team.' His thoughts were interrupted by Oos's congratulatory comment.

"Welcome brother Pieth." Oos said as he put out his wing to help Pieth up, "Welcome to the Oother alliance." Oos finished, "Are you alright?" Still seeing what he thought was the far away look of a creature that had just passed the trial of truth, Pieth nodded his head, yes.

Pieth shook his head yes, several times, afraid that if he spoke, he'd betray his true feelings and of how he really wasn't all right, that he was having doubts, that he was sick all the way down to his gizzard, over what he had gotten himself into, that he wasn't what they thought. Oos took his silence as an affirmation to the fact he was speechless after having been accepted.

"Good, good!" Oos continued, "We will leave you then." with those words fresh out of his mouth, he gave Pieth a last knowing smile, and then he and his companions took to the air, leaving Pieth there alone to ponder his fate.

Pieth watched them fly away and as they became specks in a clear blue sky, he asked himself, 'what have I gotten myself into?' He had done it because he wanted to help his uncle and to rescue his flock from being led by one of Crafco's cronies. 'He was going to save his flock, but then, who was going to rescue me,' he thought; with that on his mind, with several hard slaps of wings, that took him into the air he headed home.

–––––––––––– ––––––––––––

Mosaic stood at the edge of the pond not far from the Veterinary Hospital, deep in thought and feeling sorry for himself, no not sorry, angry with himself. He was deep in reproaching himself for his failure in having come up with a good rescue plan that would have prevented all that had happened from happening. 'Because of his naiveté, his unworldliness had cost the lives of his fellow flock mates and that of his father." He thought. He bent down, picked up another relatively flat stone and flung it out across the water. As he watched the stone skip along the surface, he pondered, 'what was life all about anyway was it about striving to do good and failing and then those failures costing others their lives?' As he thought that, he admonished himself for being so self-absorbed, of his self-pitying, others were dealing with worse he admonished himself again.

'Look, you twit, you are not the only one hurting, think of what your Mother is going through, or Colors, or any of the others recovering from their wounds both physical and mental. You need to pull yourself together, easier said than done.' he thought. Again, he bent down and picked up another stone, and again threw it and watched it skimming across the surface of the pond, sinking before it got as far as the previously tossed stone.

'Is that what life was all about, you were like a stone tossed out into the sky and depending on how the forces of life, of the wind propelled you, you either went far or sank into darkness and disappeared never to be seen again. What caused some to live longer than others? Was it blind luck, a predetermined course, that no matter what you did or how you did it determined when it would all end and you would sink like that stone into dark black waters of time, into nothingness.' His mind mused.

Again, he bent down and again sent a stone skimming across the pond's surface; this last stone had gone farther than any of the others' he had tossed before it. 'Why?' he thought. 'Alternatively, with his kind was it the shape of your body, the way your mind worked, your genetic make-up, or was it those that you trusted or were exposed to? Was it the wind, or the sun, what was that one deciding factor that made the difference if you lived or died was there an answer? No!' His subconscious screamed there are no answers.

'Look.' the voice of his Father interjected, 'there are no answers that can be found easily, it will all become clear over time, it always does. The reality of it all, it is all fate and the decisions we make or do not make that establishes when we die.' Hearing the words in his father's voice only made the no answer, the not knowing answer even more painful.

Picking up yet another stone, he shut off the voice, threw it and again, he watched it skim across the pond's surface, it came to him. 'It was the decisions that you made, it was your ethics; it was that part of you that takes action when you thinking in control mind can't. In reality, it was in fact, the fight or flight response that determines a lot of what happens to you in your life. Besides that little bit of truth, there has been just plain dumb luck as well. Now that is ironic,' his grieving mind yelled!

'That one factor that you had no control over, that predetermined course… how depressing,' he thought to himself, 'even if I make all the correct, right decisions, it could still all go bad.'

In reality, as he saw it now, humans were the bane of his flocks' survival. They were that strange dichotomy, a contradiction, of both being a benefactor and tormentor. As he saw it now they were more a negative than a positive to the survival of the flock. How can you say that the voice in his head demanded, 'look at the doctor, look at April and Eric's family, look at all the volunteer's, look at what they have done '… it all seemed too much. 'What unpredictability, what inconsistency, in behavior they display; humans are so illogical as a species. How do you reconcile it all?' he thought.

For no matter what else he could have done or not done, what had happened had been beyond his control. The callused reality was it had all been in the hands. Who was responsible was a nagging question; 'this had not been just dumb luck,' he thought. 'It seemed all wrong, all the events that had lead up to now, or had it been the work of an unknown force operating in secret? Even the actions of the humans had been random,' was his conclusion. How insignificant that had made him feel was beyond words. That feeling of worthlessness, of feeling being trivial was palatable and tasted very rancid to his grieving mind.

Before he could go on with his self-incrimination, his attention was diverted. Out of the corner of his eye, in his peripheral vision he thought he saw Pepper… but no, it was Trapper approaching him with a worried look on his face. On seeing that worried look, he thought of his sister, it redirected his thoughts, from his self-pitying thoughts, to one of wondering what was happening with the quest birds. It started him musing on how the five birds on the quest were doing, where were they? Were they okay? Were they safe, would he ever see them again?

Interesting Pigeon Fact

Racing pigeons more accurately described as racing doves are, in fact, one of man's oldest feathered companions.

Pigeons date to antiquity! Far from being a lowly servant, the racing pigeon was the special prerogative of kings, princes, and nobles of all kinds. During these past times, it was contrary to law for a common man to own pigeons.

The great empires of Carthage, Egypt, and Rome made full use of them in many ways including the production of squabs (a great delicacy) as well as high-grade nitrogen (droppings) for their fields. The aforementioned civilizations also used pigeons in a great network of advanced communication. They kept emperors in touch with the most remote areas of their lands during a time when horse and riders or caravans would have taken weeks to deliver the same information. Caesar made formidable use of them during his conquest of Gaul.

It is now extremely difficult to imagine that our feathered companions were at one time the ultimate communication tool used in the greatest of all communication networks! It is further difficult to comprehend that these little warriors of the airways made possible both great empires as well as great fortunes. As already mentioned the Egyptians and Persians trained rock doves to carry messages. They were an exceptionally reliable method of communication hitherto unheard of. As these empires spread across the then known civilized world capturing country after country they discovered that these other countries had also trained rock doves.

These countries included China, Greece, Italy as well as India. Among these many countries, China had in fact organized a postal system based upon the use of messenger pigeons. Knowledge is power, and at one time, the surest and swiftest way to deliver this knowledge was with racing pigeons.

One would, at first glance, believe it difficult to draw a connection between racing pigeons and the Rothschild banking dynasty. However, it seems that they increased enormously their fortune in 1815 with the exceptional help of what was then called a carrier pigeon. When Napoleon was defeated at Waterloo, Count Rothschild knew of his defeat long before any other persons in England. He had received this critical information via carrier pigeon. This advance knowledge allowed him to make critical decisions that made an enormous fortune possible. Here is a prime example of the reality that, knowledge and its timely use, in fact, are the ultimate in power!

In the 19th Century Julius Reuter founded the news service that globally still carries his name 150 years later. The Reuters news service was actually founded as a line of pigeon posts. The Reuters pigeons helped the banks of Aachen make fortunes and avoid bankruptcy.

http://pigeon_racingsc.tripod.com/history.html

About the Artwork

All the artwork in the book is drawn by the author/artist: Lucien F.A. van Oosten.

Selected pieces of the have characters gallery have been reproduced as Limited Edition Geclee prints and are being offered for sale.

The four pieces presented here can be purchased exclusively from the author or from The American Pigeon Museum and Library at the museum or on their on line store on their web site. The APM & L also has copies of the first book, "K-Bridge: A Story About Discovery".

Mosaic and Trapper, two of the main characters in the "K-Bridge: A story about Discovery", are available as signed and numbered Limited Edition prints. Edition size is 1000 Giclee prints. Prints cost $35.00 each.

"Hen with Squabs – Nestlings" and "Courting" are from a body of work from the Authors series, "Daily Activities in a Pigeons life", each print is a signed and numbered Limited Edition print, the edition size is 300 Giclee prints. Print cost $50.00 each.

Artist contact information:

e-mail: mijnimages1artl@gmail.com

The American Pigeon Museum and Library contact information:

web-site: TheAmericanPigeonMuseum@gmail.com

I also have Face book pages:

The books page is: https://www.facebook.com/Lucien-F-A-van-Oosten-812631648784697/timeline/

My artwork page is: https://www.facebook.com/The-Artwork-of-Lucien-van-Oosten-173222972762393/timeline/

"Mosaic"

8 x 10 image size, Geclee print, in color.
From a colored pencil drawing.
Edition size is 1000 Giclee prints. Prints cost $35.00 each.

"Trapper"
8 x 10 image size, Geclee print, in color.
From a colored pencil drawing.
Edition size is 1000 Giclee prints. Prints cost $35.00 each.

"Courting"
5 x 7 image size, Geclee print, in color
of a colored pencil drawing.

"Hen with Squabs – Nestlings"
5 x 7 image size, Geclee print, in color
pen & Ink, a pointillism drawing.

Rear Cover Artwork

April and Eric researching, is a colored pencil drawing.

Shadow and Sky of K-Bridge flock.

Colors of K-Bridge flock.

Moth of K-Bridge Flock.

Vlinder.

Crafco.

Joel.

Talon.

Spline Artwork

Niner.

Koffee.

**From the Second book
the following
pieces of artwork are available
as Limited Edition Geclee prints.**

"**Vlinder**", 8x10 and "**Talon**", 5x7, each print is a signed and numbered Limited Edition print. The edition size of the Vlinder, edition size is 300, and Talon, edition size is 300. Each prints cost $50.00, plus tax and shipping & handling.

The prints can be ordered directly from the author, send inquiries to the e-mail address:

mijnimgaes1artl@gmail.com

Or to:

Lucien van Oosten
421 E Ada Ave.
Glendora, CA. 91741
USA

A personal note from the author, if you enjoyed this book and would like to see what happens to this cast of characters and many more, in "K-Bridge: The Quest" and in "K-Bridge: The Reclaiming", send me a note, would like to hear what you think about the story so far.

By mail:

Lucien F.A. van Oosten,
421 Ada Ave. Glendora, Ca. 91741
USA

By e-mail:
mijnimages1artl@gmail.com